Nothing to See Here

Brendan Walsh

D1568763

Published by Brendan Walsh, 2022.

This is a work of fiction. Similarities to real people, places, or events are entirely coincidental.

NOTHING TO SEE HERE

First edition. May 27, 2022.

Copyright © 2022 Brendan Walsh.

ISBN: 978-1914288548

Written by Brendan Walsh.

I would like to dedicate my first novel, to my sister Rita McGoldrick and my brother Peter who despite being exposed to draft after draft of my book, battled on without even the slightest regard for their own personal safety. Special thanks to the lovely Jackie Walsh and her beautiful daughter Aoife for their unrelenting support and encouragement throughout the entire process. Thanks to Davy Mac and Michael Power for their tough love. A big shout out to Terry Hernon for pointing me in the right direction. Of course, I'd be remiss not to commend my dear friend, Karen Borsotti across the pond, who because of her assiduous attention to detail, I was able to put a spit-shine on this gem. Thanks in advance to all my readers for taking a chance on me.

Chapter 1.

The financial meltdown of 2008 was directly responsible for Maxi Dillon losing the love of his life - his beloved little 'fixer-upper' on Long Island in New York City. When that greedy beast stepped in, it stomped indiscriminately all over the globe with its big heavy boots, trampling financial empires and monetary institutions into the ground while kicking nest eggs, college funds and retirement plans into oblivion. *'For Sale'* signs sprung up like some weird mutant crop in the front gardens of many homes across the land, as plywood became the new décor and padlocks, a scarce commodity. Maxi showered more time and money on that little house than a sugar-daddy did on a bimbo. Unfortunately, after spending all his money and countless hours working on his 'get-rich-*relatively*-quick-plan', his cash-cow fell prey to the acquisitive mechanisms of that ignoble catastrophe, and he found himself – just as he had done twenty-five-years earlier – penniless and sleeping on a friend's couch. But this time round, instead of the promise of adventure in a new land, he had to, somehow, find the will to survive in the cut-throat environment he knew only too well.

When he lost the house, he also lost his live-in girlfriend, Priscilla. It's hard to say whether or not, in the two years he'd known her, they ever had a meaningful conversation. Admittedly, she did call all the shots in the bedroom, but their 'discourse' rarely evolved beyond grunts and moans. No question, they did look well together, both tall and athletic, and when they walked by on the street, people turned their heads to wonder - what supermodel clung to which rock star? Pricilla wallowed in the attention while Maxi, instead of being conceited, felt cursed by his good looks. Judging by his previous relationships with beautiful women and how they usually imploded from the baneful effects of jealousy, he was beginning to doubt whether or not he would ever know what true love really meant. But he wasn't giving up just yet. He thought Pricilla was different from all the rest. He was right. She was only interested in what she could gain financially from the relationship. She was much like his little 'fixer-upper'... always on the take.

Ironically, Maxi worked as a contractor, building and remodelling the high-end homes for those very same Wall Street brokers and hedge-fund managers who caused the financial shit-storm in the first place. When the construction industry practically vaporized after the crash, his income took a decisive hit. The instant Pricilla's cocaine supply was interrupted, she vaporized as well. The only real casualty from their break-up was Maxi's libido.

What pushed the whole kit and caboodle over the edge for Maxi was another life-changing crash, all the way across the pond in Ireland. Nora Dillon, Maxi's mom, was fast approaching eighty years old and without a care in the world until, somehow, she found herself driving down the highway, on the wrong side of the road with the oncoming traffic flashing their lights and waving furtively to alert her of the danger. Of course, she was oblivious and waved back. All that concerned her was... how come so many people knew her, so many miles away from home? She put it down to her celebrity status as a 'scratch' golfer in her day and continued on her way. She may only have suffered a broken wrist in that collision, but her most valuable asset – her independence – was stolen from her that day. With her confidence on the fritz, everyday living became an uphill battle.

Maxi did a quick take on his current circumstance and, with no foreseeable improvements in his immediate future, decided to return home to Ireland to care for his ailing mom. His decision to do so didn't come without its fair share of trepidation. Nora Dillon was a headstrong woman who was set like concrete in her ways. He knew his party animal persona would have to take a sabbatical and his mindset, a major overhaul. He couldn't believe he was contemplating swapping out the city that never sleeps for a sleepy town in Ireland where nine a.m. was time enough for the *early* bird to catch the worm. His mother needed his assistance, and that's all that mattered. He decided he'd dust himself off in Ireland, and after his mother was able to fend for herself, return, invigorated to claim his rightful slice of the American pie.

He was assigned a window seat, 35C, on Aerlingus flight 109E from JFK airport in New York bound for Dublin, Ireland. He would have preferred an aisle seat. That way he could stretch out those long legs of his. He was terrified of flying, or maybe it was crashing that gave him the heebie-jeebies. Besides feeling uncomfortable sitting next to a window, he didn't need to be reminded for six solid hours that his ass dangled in the clouds. To combat his fear, he had already mustered up some Dutch courage in the airport bar. He alternated between Guinness and whiskey for the best part of two hours. His last swallow of whiskey, washed down one hundred mgs of Oxycodone, a prescription pain-killer that he purchased earlier in the week from 'Hairpin' Joe - his bipolar drug dealer - who had an anxiety attack every time he did a deal. If Maxi's calculations were correct, he'd be taking off along with the plane, except he was logged in at a much higher altitude.

As the last of the stragglers struggled to cram their carry-ons into the overcrowded overhead bins, a Roman Catholic priest, in all his regalia, made his presence felt at the top of the aisle. He seemed incognizant of the disgust shared by most of the seated passengers as he went about scanning the illuminated seat numbers on the overhead console in search of a match to the one on his boarding pass. Maxi christened him Fr. Tool on the spot.

'Oh, please God,' he prayed to the heavens above and to any other deity that happened to be tuned in on his frequency, '...don't have Fr. Tool sit next to me.'

And with that unanswered prayer, the priest, who blatantly flaunted his affiliation as a 'man of the cloth', buckled up next to

him in 35B. Thankfully Maxi was an avid reader, and if books were
guns, the speed with which he drew his from the seat pocket in
front would have astonished any gunslinger. He immersed himself
headfirst into *Misery* by Stephan King. As the pilots were doing their
check-list in the cockpit, Maxi was doing his on the sanity of the
crucifix wielding maniac to his left.

*Is this guy so out-of-touch with mainstream, he didn't get the pedo
memo?*

*Does this predator think he can prowl, in pursuit of prey in broad
daylight, uncontested?*

*Maybe it's 'suicide by priest'. Similar to 'suicide by cop' except, the
layman is expected to pull the trigger.*

The numbing effects of the booze and the soothing influence
of the drugs soon began to clash into one another. His mind right
then was not in the proper state to even attempt simple deductions,
let alone conduct the mind-boggling mental deliberations that this
quandary proposed. He had shut the mains to his brains which is
basically what he always did on aeroplanes. The only option available
to him was to remain cocooned within his book for the entire
duration of the flight.

'I'm not a real priest,' 35B whispered.

Maxi barely heard the remark from behind his book. He froze.
'What de fuck?'

'Seriously, I'm not,' 35B qualified.

'Seriously?' Maxi responded, stealing a peep over his book.

'Seriously,' Fr. Tool echoed.

'Well, then what de fuck are ye?'

'Relax, I'm in fancy dress.'

'Fancy dress in May? Here's the news, that party's going south
when you show up.'

'It's not really a party, as such. I'm going to a friend's wedding. He hasn't seen me in a while, so when he gets a load of this get-up, he'll freak.'

'Him and every altar boy within an ass's roar.'

'Why do you say that?'

'Seriously?'

Maxi turned away in disbelief and hid behind his book. Maybe, he thought, the hopeless case beside him might take the time in the future to deliberate more selectively over his choice of costume. Already, a stark reminder that the island of Saints and Scholars - like New York City - had its own contingent of demons lurking in the shadows, and he... still sat on the runway at JFK.

Maxi was well aware that he would have to shed his 'Yankee' skin like a snake if he wanted to assimilate seamlessly back into Irish society. The Paddies, who didn't jump ship when the economy cracked her starboard bow all those years ago, would still bear a grudge. He had to be very careful to discard all American colloquialisms in exchange for the native vernacular. A slip of the tongue, like referring to 'garbage' rather than rubbish, would raise the alarm and he'd be ostracized on the spot. Thank God he didn't acquire an American accent. That would be equivalent to him having a 'bullseye' tattoo on his forehead with the caption; 'Punch me quick, I'm such a dick.'

He arrived in Dublin airport on a miserable Sunday morning in early May. As he savoured that long anticipated cigarette outside Terminal A, the reality of his decision to vacate New York and return home began to take root. The first thing that struck him was the shitty weather. As he took a deep drag of his cigarette, he had to squint his eyes to partake in the memory of a recent barbeque on Long Island - the sun was so bright. He began to well-up with feelings of remorse, knowing that from then on, the sun would only be a distant memory. Out of nowhere, a gust of wind in cahoots with the rain soaked his jeans like the spray from a speeding car hitting a roadside puddle. It even quenched his cigarette. It was as if Mother Nature herself felt obligated to certify his misgivings, up close and personal. An elderly couple waiting with their bags under a bus stop canopy witnessed the dousing. Maxi looked to them for a little sympathy but got none.

'You should know better than to stand there,' he could lip-read the gist of the husband's remark, 'fucking foreigner.'

Maxi grabbed his suitcase and retreated back towards the shelter of the building.

'Too little, too late,' he saw the wife say.

He lit another cigarette and turned his back on the opinionated couple. Next thing ye know, this angry looking Jack Russell came trotting across the car park, through the taxi rank, and right up to Maxi and his bag. He braced himself. He knew there was no way to mask his traitorous scent. It stopped to sniff Maxi's shoes and, after careful deliberation, his suitcase. Once the sniffing concluded, it raised its little hind leg and hosed down his bag with a quantity of piss that far exceeded the amount expected of such a small animal. A Jack Russell with the bladder of a stallion! It looked up at Maxi for, who knows? Approval? Maxi couldn't maintain the stare. He looked away in shame. Since he was already soaked to the skin from the rain, he got a piss-pass from the mutt. Job done, it trotted off back the way it came. That dog was the *'spokesperson'* for all the mutts whose masters abandoned them all those years ago to find work in America. Maxi felt slighted. He never owned a dog.

He took a taxi to Symphony Station and boarded the 11 a.m. train bound for Ballydecuddle. He found himself a window seat and settled in for the two-hour journey with the lashing rain, his traveling companion. The carriage he selected was almost empty, leaving him alone to stew with his thoughts. Once the train broke free from the confines of the city, a verdant panorama with its patchwork quilt of green fields and lush meadows presented itself in the rain-drenched window for his perusal. This was a well-nourished landscape, and it certainly had no qualms strutting its stuff. He had forgotten how green, green could be. For the first time in his life, he could appreciate all the hype over the forty shades of green and how it was no wonder the American tourists - especially the ones from the inner cities - went googly-eyed when faced with such spectacular scenery.

He could feel the rhythmic pulse of the train underfoot as another tidy little town passed across the glass. As his journey progressed, the benefits of living in Ireland began to make themselves known. He saw children playing outside in the rain, with no sign of an adult in the vicinity. A different world to the one he left. Kids playing outside in New York City was a rare occurrence but unchaperoned, an absolute no-no.

He felt strange sitting comfortably on the train. He was used to being jampacked into an already overcrowded subway car among other contorted commuters, as he made his way to and from work in New York City. The Transit Authority even had people on their roster whose only job requirement was to squash commuters - during rush hour - into the already overcrowded subway cars. He recalled, besides his personal space being violated with him being squashed cheek-to-cheek to total strangers, how he was forced to endure the miasma of noxious effusions that pervaded the air from body odours to emissions of ethnic cuisine from every orifice specific to man. Yesterday's burritos or garlic riddled koftas tested the commuter's resolve. One had to 'man up' not to puke when such foul fetor pervaded the subway car. Of course, Maxi could retaliate with his own Celtic pong - the ultimate olfactory grenade - none other than the knee-buckling Guinness fart.

Maxi was whipped from his reverie by the noisy entrance of the ticket inspector, who slammed the carriage door behind him like he just had a row with his missus. *Why are those doors that connect train carriages still being designed by meat locker engineers?* he wondered. The inspector started to work his way slowly down the aisle, using the high-backed seats as leverage to keep as much weight off his arthritic knees as possible.

How did Maxi know the ticket inspector had trouble with his knees? That he was an insomniac? That his missus left him for a younger man? That his son was a heroin addict and his daughter a whore? Because he spent 10 minutes of his life feigning interest, as Eugene - the ticket inspector - rattled off his miserable life's story like the Greek playwright Euripides – a man who encouraged his audience to participate in his works. Once he was done reciting his autobiography, he looked to Maxi to hear his.

With Eugene, there was no, 'I'll show you mine if you show me yours.' He went straight into the inquisition.

'So where are you coming from?' he inquired with a big smile on his face as if they were old friends playing catch-up. He brandished Maxi's ticket in his face to evoke a response. Both men knew the importance of that ticket. Without it, Maxi couldn't pass through the turnstile in Ballydecuddle. He would be forced to pay the fare a second time. His ticket had become a bargaining chip and diplomacy, the dictator of discourse.

'The States,' Maxi replied, refusing to embellish. He figured his mono-syllabic response would be a good indicator that he wasn't taking the bait, and hopefully, the annoying little man would return his ticket and mosey on his way.

'I see,' Eugene retorted. 'That's the way it's going to be.' There was a noticeable pause while he re-evaluated the situation. He looked like he was physically changing gears in order to climb an obstinate hill.

'The States,' he repeated. 'There's a lot of them States,' he stated, 'in them there, United States of America.' He had to pause to catch his breath. 'Which one applies to you?'

'New York,' Maxi responded, staring straight ahead, his imagination setting the scene, as a lone light bulb swayed to-and-fro above his head and with blood dripping from his torn lip onto his ripped shirt as he slumped forward in a chair, his restraints keeping him from falling to the floor.

'If you can make it there, you'll make it anywhere in old New York,' Eugene sang poorly. No surprise there; the man did nothing well, according to his autobiography.

'How long were you there?'

'One week.'

'Wrong answer,' Eugene replied like an agitated game show host. 'Skin don't turn golden brown like that in a week.' He pointed at Maxi's face with the much-coveted ticket. 'No sir-e, it takes years of exposure for skin to tan like that.' He leaned in to get a closer look at Maxi's face. 'So, let me rephrase the question. When did you leave Ireland?'

'Twenty-five years ago,' Maxi relented. It seemed there was no fooling Sherlock.

'What's the purpose of your visit?' he asked, suddenly assuming the tone of a Customs officer. His railroad jacket did have epaulettes and an achievement patch of sorts stitched to the sleeve, right next to his broken heart, so maybe he felt empowered by his uniform. Whatever came over him, he was making Maxi work for that ticket.

'I'm just here for a visit,' Maxi replied. Busybodies like this 'Wehrmacht SS' wannabe reminded him why he left Ireland in the first place. The only thing that functioned correctly in that man's whole anatomy was his curiosity, and like his son's heroin addiction, it craved instant gratification.

'Not with a big bag like that, you're not.' He spun the ticket punching tool that he had hooked in his middle finger, and it spun round and round in his sweaty hand like a mini propeller until he decided he had twirled enough to impress.

'All right already. I'm here to take care of my mother,' Maxi confessed. 'She's not well. Are ye happy now?'

'See, that wasn't so hard, was it?' Himmler clicked his heels and returned Maxi's ticket. He moved on through the carriage like an orangutan swinging from seat to seat in search of his next victim while his autobiography rewound in his empty head.

Chapter 2.

U p to that juncture in time, Maxi never once contemplated the notion of death or indeed any of its arresting ramifications. He was too busy being a party animal to notice. To support that declaration, he had a tattoo of a raging bull charging through an assortment of colourful balloons on his right shoulder, with several of them escaping over his collar bone and onto his upper chest. From the moment he arrived home, Nora Dillon - his mother - being the self-appointed liaison for all things dead and dying, forced him to begin viewing life through her own murky lens. In no time, she knocked the pep out of his step and the gusto out of his day. As he desperately tried to acclimate to her saturnine temperament, he contemplated getting the 'grim reaper' tattooed on his other shoulder, to help counterbalance that awful, morbid mood his mother was always in.

'Good morning, Mother.'

Maxi would cheerfully greet his mom at the breakfast table, and her response every morning would be,

'I'm dying... what's good about it?'

Almost overnight, he began to see life through the eyes of a cadaver. He became preoccupied with the futility of man's existence. When a bus full of school children passed him by on the road, all he saw were dead bodies in their nice, neat uniforms heading straight to the cemetery - via the schoolyard. He saw young lovers on park benches as entangled skeletons, a mishmash of entwined bones, their empty skulls alluding to love with no beat from no heart. He wondered why young corpses in business suits rushed about to catch trains and planes when their only destination was the grave. He was fascinated by dead dogs chasing dead cats. He shivered in the shadow of dead trees, no longer comforted by the warmth of a living sun. He figured, why delay? Press fast forward and be done with it!

11

Once Nora ate breakfast, the monotonous routine of staying alive ensued. Conservation of energy was vital to her, the least amount of exertion for maximum gain. She exploited Maxi's assistance beyond all reason.

'Maxi, get me this...'

'Maxi, get me that...'

He had no idea when he signed on to be her carer how physically and mentally demanding the job would prove to be. He had to basically take charge of the controls that operated his dear old mother's broken carcass and, much like a puppeteer, manipulate her through the day. He had to assist in all bodily functions much as you would a new-born baby, the only difference being, his eighty-year-old mother had a tongue on her like a South Bronx rapper and would lash out obscenities, en masse, with little or no provocation. The only time she was civil was when Father Jim - the parish priest who was her ticket into the Afterlife - or her *la-di-da* golfing friends - came to visit. She would immediately fabricate this alien tone with exaggerated pronunciations and inflections and orchestrate this synthetic language to smoke screen her country origins. Words were elongated and stretched to the breaking point. Precise titters replaced her country guffaws. Feigned interest sprinkled with lashings of insincerity shielded her apathy and disdain. The instant the visitors left, the masquerade concluded, and she returned to being her nasty old self.

Doctors, psychiatrists, mental health nurses, social workers, and the Polish cleaning lady were the new contingent of people besides her friends that Nora interacted with on a daily basis. They got to witness her true colours, vividly. Anyone she deemed below her, she treated with the utmost contempt. 'Where do you think you're going at this hour of the day, missy?' she spat at Helga, the Polish cleaning lady who had to explain why she was leaving fifteen minutes early even though Nora was aware of her arrival, fifteen minutes before the hour. She didn't even have the decency to ever call the young woman by her name. The irony of the situation was that Helga was studying for her master's in physics while Nora didn't even sit her 'Leaving Cert' exam. Maxi was aware of his mother's hypocrisy, but in his twenty-five-year absence, it had acquired a ferocity that made him cringe, forcing him to stomp out the many fires her blazing tongue would ignite, prefacing each episode with an excuse:

'She's old and cranky.'

'She doesn't mean what she says.'

Maxi's social circle was identical by association. He did have a few close friends that he maintained in his absence, whose company provided him with a respite from the drudgery of Nora's bad humour and the sterility of healthcare professionals. Once he got Nora to bed at precisely nine p.m. and after filling her full of pills - one of which put her in a coma for eight blissful hours - only then did he get some semblance of his life back. One good thing about caring for Nora, he didn't have time to think or, more importantly... mope.

With each passing day, Maxi could see a discernible deterioration in his mother's physical condition. It was quite apparent that climbing the stairs, even with his assistance, was becoming more and more precarious. He decided to convert the dining room into a bedroom and fix up the downstairs bathroom so Nora could be self-contained on the ground floor and thus render the stairs redundant. This decision was met initially with some *face-saving* resistance but silently appreciated, once initiated.

Doom and gloom had by now successfully staged a 'coup d'état' throughout the entire ground floor. Anyone in search of '*warm 'n fuzzy*' had better vamoose. Only miserable people with a morbid outlook on life were encouraged to step up to the welcome mat. All this time, Maxi had remained somewhat complacent, allowing that black cloud to reign. He made several feeble attempts to fumigate the macabre atmosphere that pervaded, but like humidity in a Bayou swamp, it seemed like it was there to stay.

'Guess who's dead?' Niamh Conway asked Nora, who was nodding in and out of sleep by the open fire in the living room. She had just celebrated her ninety-fourth birthday, and she loved playing this morose game, especially when she knew all the answers. While the remote control for the T.V. baffled Nora, Niamh was intrigued by technology. She had the latest I-phone and even had her own Facebook account. She downloaded music on her laptop, which she was never without, and she lived on the website for the dead - RIP.ie. She knew who was dead even before the '*stiff*' did.

'Mary O'Shea,' Nora guessed.

'Not yet. Try again.'

'Clair Dowling.'

'Jesus Nora, she's only a young one in her early eighties.'

'Tommy McCarty.'

'He's dead years ago. Ah, you're not concentrating,' Niamh conceded. 'Peggy Maloney, that's who.'

'What happened?' Nora was suddenly 'all-ears.'

'She dropped dead yesterday at three o'clock in the afternoon while she was standing in line at the supermarket - you know the one she goes to over on Dean Street? Anyway, just as she reached into her bag to pay for her groceries, she hit the deck. Lights out. Game over. Hasta la vista, baby.'

'About time that old bitch kicked the bucket,' Nora snarled.

'Why, what did she ever do to you?'

'She wrote me up on my score card for double tapping the ball on the eighteenth hole in Trumpet Valley golf links in 1986. I lost the President's prize, an all-inclusive three night stay in some castle on the west coast, by one shot, because of that bitch.'

'Well Nora, shame the devil, did ye double tap?'

'Of course,' Nora admitted without any hesitation. 'But the bitch could have turned a blind eye and no one would have been any the wiser!'

'Now, now, Mother,' Maxi interrupted. 'It's not right to be talking about the dead like that. Do ye two not know any other games to play besides this one?'

'We could play,' Niamh suggested. 'Guess who's going to die within the next three months!'

'No, no, no, that's it.' Maxi shook his head. 'No more morbid guessing games allowed from here on in. This house is depressing enough. From now on, we are going to have proper discussions and debates about,' he searched for topics, '... the meaning of life, truth, justice and honour. Let's get philosophical. Let's think like Aristotle, Sartre and Heidegger. Let's throw out our preconceived ideas and start all over with a brand-new perspective where knowledge is deduced from a logical sequence of events, where conclusions are iron clad and immune to cross-examination. In other words, we are going to do as Descartes did and doubt our own existence. Let's start with Cogito ergo sum, I think therefore I am.'

'Maxi studied Philosophy in College,' Nora bragged to Niamh.

'Oh really.' Niamh sat upright in her chair. 'It's fascinating stuff, all that thinking.'

'I agree,' Nora replied. 'I think we should start thinking about things. We don't have that much time left.'

'Speak for yourself,' Niamh replied, folding her arms defiantly.

'Well Niamh, how long do you think you're going to be around? You just turned ninety-four for feck sake!' Nora jeered.

'It's only a number, Nora.'

'Fair enough, Niamh, but numbers add up, and one of these days, yours will be up.'

'Right, girls, enough,' Maxi interrupted. 'You seem to turn every conversation deadly. Let's get away from the grave for a spell, shall we? Come to think of it, we can start by discussing the impact numbers have on our everyday lives. Did ye know that the Australian Aborigines never came up with a method of counting? No actual numbers. Do you think,' Maxi inquired, leaning in to stoke the fire with the poker, 'you would be able to manage your day without numbers?'

'It would be very difficult to call up the 'chipper' on the phone and order three sausage suppers without numbers,' Niamh remarked.

'Sure, you wouldn't even be able to dial the phone without the numbers,' Nora said, getting involved. 'You would have to physically go down to the chipper and figure out some way of telling the man behind the counter that you wanted three sausage suppers without using numbers.'

'Yes, Mother, now you're thinking along the right lines.' Maxi smiled to himself as he realised the potential of this thought provoking 'game' he had just improvised.

'You could stick three fingers up in the air at the counter,' Niamh suggested.

'But...' Nora tried to interrupt.

'Hold on,' Niamh reacted. 'I'm not finished. When you have your man's attention,' she continued, 'you shout *sausage suppers* and at the same time, you point with your other hand at your three raised fingers.

'The man can't count,' Nora barked, her competitiveness beginning to egg her on.

Niamh felt the concussion from Nora's remark and it sent her back in her chair. She realised she hadn't given her proposal enough thought. She knew now to dig deep for her next remark.

'Here's how you do it,' Nora said as she sat as far forward on her seat as possible. 'You ask the man for a sausage supper, right?' Niamh and Maxi nodded their agreement. 'Once he gives it to you, you ask him for another one, and when he gives you that one, you ask him one last time for another one. He's bound to be pissed off, but now you have your three sausage suppers.' Nora sat back in her chair, pleased with her analytical approach to the proposed hypothesis.

'That's good, Mother,' Maxi acknowledged, 'but how do you pay for the sausage suppers?'

'You wouldn't have to pay for them because nobody would be able to count the money.' Niamh laughed.

Nora frowned at her. She wasn't happy with Niamh's light-hearted approach to serious questions that required careful deliberation.

'I'm afraid, Niamh,' Maxi butted in. 'As you are well aware, you get nothing for nothing in this world.'

'So how did the Aborigines get by without numbers?' Niamh inquired. 'How did they know how many people were coming to dinner? How many kangaroos to kill? How much moonshine to make?' She threw her arms up in despair.

'Moonshine?' Nora made a face.

'Even the Abo has to have a way to wind down after a hard day in the bush.' Niamh chuckled.

'It's impossible,' Nora exclaimed, 'to imagine a world without numbers.'

'Nothing is impossible,' Maxi countered, 'all we have to do is flex our brains in this mental gymnasium we have just created and let our thoughts and feelings run rampant.'

'I was never a gym babe,' Niamh sniggered as she struck the pose of a bodybuilder by flexing her skinny little arms. 'What do you make of these guns, Nora?'

'I've seen more muscles on a knitting needle,' Nora sneered.

'I suspect,' Maxi continued, oblivious to their little aside. 'The Aborigines must have had some other way to denote quantity. They probably used symbols. For instance, they may have used a stone to represent a person. So, when the cook wanted to know how many

people were coming to dinner, the Abo maître d' would dump a
bag of stones in the sand. Since each stone represented a person, she
knew by looking at the pile to hack up at least two kangaroos to feed
that lot.'

'Stones for adults and pebbles for kids!' Niamh joked.

'Yabadabadoo, Wilma,' Nora mocked.

'Just imagine,' said Nora as she began to appreciate the inherent
humour in their discussion. 'If Gucci or Armani showed up for
dinner and started to discuss their latest spring collections with a
man who wears a koala-bear hide to cover his lizard?'

'Oh my God, Nora, did you just call his thing - a lizard?' Niamh
roared, laughing.

Maxi's phone rang. He excused himself and headed to the
kitchen to take the call. A man introduced himself as Rory
McGregor, the mental health nurse assigned to evaluate Nora's
cognitive awareness. Fair dues to this highlander from Scotland who
fought tooth and nail on the phone to get his message across. His
thick, guttural accent made him sound like he had his head in a
bucket of water while his pitch ricocheted between soprano shrieks
and baritone barks. Maxi had to devote all *his* cognitive capabilities
to decipher the purpose of the call. It turned out Rory McGregor
needed to make an appointment to see Nora the following Friday at
two o'clock. Both men were physically exhausted by the conclusion
of the call.

Maxi returned to the living room and was pleasantly surprised
to see that Nora and her friend were ensconced in a mathematical
debate that had gravitated towards Fibonacci and his 'golden ratio.'
They accumulated their vast wealth of knowledge from the likes
of 'Google' and the 'Discovery channel' and were excited to be
suddenly sharing their 'know-how' with each other. When Maxi
realised how keen they were to continue debating - even in his
absence - he knew he was on to something.

He decided there and then to present a structured philosophical debate with an evocative title and start time for Nora and her friends to partake in the following day. If it was a success, and he couldn't see why not, he figured these debates could continue on a regular basis. He would need to put a notification each day in the front window to drum up interest in these debates. Once the word got around that Plato, Heidegger, Descartes, and even Frank Sinatra and Bing Crosby were all hanging out in Nora Dillon's front living room, he was hopeful for a dramatic mood swing in the house.

He retreated to his back office to draw up the following day's debate. On an A4 sheet of white paper, he wrote with a black marker:

Welcome to the 11 o'clock debate.

Is there such a thing as a Universal Generalisation?

Tea and sandwiches during the break.

Donations kindly accepted.

Chapter 3.

Maxi Dillon's homecoming incited a tongue-wagging frenzy. Nowhere was this more evident than in Gretchen's beauty salon, located on the corner of Bugle and Main in Ballydecuddle. This was the 'go-to' place in the small town where women of all ages congregated - not only to be pampered and bombarded with fallacious compliments on their beauty - but also to catch up on the latest gossip. They were like wildebeest at the watering hole, shaking their bangs and swishing their tails. There were no flies on this lot. Each arrived with what they hoped was a snippet of showstopping hearsay that would afford them an ingot of time to bask in the limelight with their audience agape. The reputations of upstanding members of the community would be celebrated or obliterated, pending solely on the credibility of the gossip at hand. Much as Gretchen's salon professed to be all about beauty and glamour, it was basically a slaughter yard where rumours with dorsal fins gorged on innocent souls.

'Some say Maxi Dillon is on the run from the law after a crime spree in America,' the hairstylist with the half-shaven head remarked. 'Now he's back home, to lay low and go on the... what's the word?' She tapped her client on the shoulder with her curling tongs to solicit the answer.

'The lamb,' the woman in the chair - with thin foil in her hair – replied.

'That's it,' the half-shaven head responded. 'The lamb. He's home to go on the lamb.' She tapped again with the tongs to demonstrate her gratitude for filling in the blank.

'I heard he's planning to rob a load of banks,' the same young lady - soon to be cooked in the chair - followed up. 'Isn't that what got his old man put away?'

'His father didn't rob a load of banks,' Gretchen objected. She was the owner of the salon and never strayed beyond arm's reach of the cash register. 'He embezzled money from the bank he worked at, is all. White-collar crime sounds more eloquent, don't you think?'

'Still sounds like he robbed a bank to me,' the half-shaven head responded, and the salon erupted in laughter.

'Some say he deliberately set himself up to get caught,' Gretchen announced, regaining the podium, 'so he could spend some quality time in prison, away from that bitch of a wife of his.' Her confabulation of events did seem plausible when Nora Dillon's *eccentricities* were taken into consideration.

'What's that they say about the apple and the tree?' the middle-aged woman in the adjacent chair postulated.

'Maxi Dillon is not at all like his father,' the half shaven-head insisted. 'He's one handsome son of a bitch. I'd eat chips out of his y-fronts, that's how hot.'

Ella Hickey, even though she wasn't an active participant in the conversation, let out a soft sigh when Maxi's name was mentioned. Her manicurist heard the sigh and felt the accompanying twitch that was relayed to her through one of Ella's long fingers. That soft sigh, coupled with that particular twitch in that manner, meant only one thing - sexual arousal. The manicurist stole a peek at Ella's chest and got the confirmation she needed. Ella's nipples were like bullet casings poking through her t-shirt. If asked, Ella would have had a hard time pinpointing the last time she had sexual intercourse with her husband. It was certainly over a decade ago, so little things had a tendency to really turn her on. The manicurist, who was a recent blow-in from Ukraine, had no idea who Maxi Dillon was, but she knew by Ella's reaction, a second order of y-front chips would not go astray. Her occupational touch changed momentarily to a caress, and both women coughed together in a show of solidarity.

'I'd say he's a drug dealer,' Gretchen suggested. 'Wasn't he caught smoking marijuana when he was only fifteen years old?'

'He was sixteen,' Ella blurted out in Maxi's defence, 'and no marijuana was found on his person.'

Every head in the place turned to study the freedom fighter by the front window. The manicurist, who held the Bolshevik's hand, was the only one to avert her stare.

Ella took a deep breath. 'If you must know, Maxi Dillon is home to care for his mom. Nothing more, nothing less.'

The whole salon responded in a communal bombinate that resonated their collective disdain with having to pull the plug on that particular vein of gossip... at least, until Maxi Dillon's spoilsport ally left the premises. In the meantime, the half-shaven head was obliged to select some other poor local bastard to act as a temporary target for their defamatory befouling. They waited patiently like hungry hyenas, orbiting the carcass, until, at last, Ella left the salon.

'Wow,' the half-shaven head exclaimed. 'Didn't see that coming.'

'Who's she?' the young woman in the chair, with squares of thin foil ravioli in her hair, inquired.

'That's Ella Hickey,' said the half-shaven head, pointing with her curling tongs at the front door. 'She's married to that drunken bastard, Jasper Hickey. Herself and that hunk Maxi grew up on the same road, but I didn't think they knew each other that well.'

'I think,' the manicurist butted in, seeing an opportunity to be one of the girls, 'da lady like to know da Maxi guy... much, more better.'

'No shit,' the half-shaven head replied, 'Who wouldn't? I'd let that Maxi guy - *much more better me* - anytime.'

Ella drove her minivan to the supermarket to do some grocery shopping. As she was weighing up which head of broccoli to buy, someone behind her deliberately crashed their shopping cart into hers. She turned to berate the offender only to see Maxi Dillon standing there with a big grin on his face.

'So, the rumours are true,' she said, spreading her arms open wide to give him a big hug. 'Welcome home.'

'Thanks Ella,' he said as he held her in his arms. 'That's more of a welcome than I got from my mother.'

'So, how are you settling in?' Ella asked, still cupping a head of broccoli, like the scales of justice in each hand.

'It's early days, but already I know it's going to take some getting used to.'

'Take it day by day,' she advised. 'It'll all work out for the better.' She knew she was lying... Judging by the way her own life was playing out, any advice from her was to be disregarded immediately.

'How's Jasper?' Maxi asked.

'The same annoying, fat bastard he was the last time you were home.'

'You know what,' Maxi said. 'It's time for you two guys to part ways. Ella... you need to get a life.'

'What can I do?' She sighed. 'If we got divorced, who'll take care of him?'

'You quit that Zumba dancing job you loved so much all those years ago so you could be home to care for him,' he said, reaching out with both arms to hold her by the shoulders. 'And does he ever show you any gratitude? No. All you get is abuse from him.'

'The problem is.' She paused for a moment to get her answer straight. 'He's too young to be admitted into a nursing home, and he's not mental enough for the asylum. So, I'm stuck with him.'

'I don't know,' Maxi sighed. 'It's not right.'

'Tell me about it.'

'Looks like I'm in for a taste of *your* medicine with my mother,' he said, attempting to steer the conversation away from her flagrant distress.

'Nora will be a walk in the park in comparison to my Jasper,' she promised. 'So, thank your lucky stars. Oh, by the way, nobody believes you're home to mind your mother,' she blurted. She didn't know where that remark came from, but it was out there now, so she'd deal with it.

'No shock there,' he said as he tossed a bag of potatoes into his cart. 'What are they all saying?'

'They think you're this big international drug smuggler who's going to have every kid in kindergarten pushing drugs for you.' She chuckled.

'Wow, I'm flattered,' he said, smiling back at her.

'Some think you're home to rob a bank like your old man,' she said in a way, more inclined as a question than a remark.

'I'm not surprised.'

'I honestly thought you'd be upset,' she replied, and she kicked the wheel of her cart in frustration. She wanted answers. She wasn't getting them. She, too, had her suspicions.

'I'm not exactly jumping up and down with joy, but because I've always been painted with the same brush as my fucked-up father, I can't say I blame them for thinking that way. However, I am pissed off over that fucking wimp Cillian Mulcahy and the little encounter I had with him in the gym the other day.'

'Cillian Mulcahy?' she said, shrugging her shoulders.

'Yeah... the butcher.'

'Oh yes, Cillian Mulcahy, the butcher's *son*.'

'That's him,' Maxi confirmed. 'Anyway, I was in the steam room the other day after my workout...'

'Wow, you joined a gym already,' she interrupted. 'Good for you.'

'Let me tell you the story,' he pleaded. 'This yahoo, the butcher's son, came slithering along the seat to sit right up next to me. With no hello's or how do-you-dos, he started rattling off a list of facts about my life in America. Shit like... you were a contractor for twenty-five years. You lost your house in the recession. You never got married. You have no kids. I just sat there like... what the fuck? He didn't want any involvement from me. Then, out of the blue, he t-boned me with another fact about my life in New York, something he shouldn't have known anything about. "I'll be in touch," he said, and he slid back into the steam.'

'Uh oh.' Ella sighed and, feeling the tension, declined to pursue.

'Uh oh is right,' he said, nodding in agreement. 'Listen, I can't talk about this shit here. Besides, I have the mother in the car. Can I meet you for a drink in Cassidy's later?'

'Sure, yeah. What time?'

'Once I get Nora to bed. How about nine-thirty?'

'That works.'

While Maxi cooked Nora's dinner, he scolded himself repeatedly for involving Ella in his little steam-room episode with the butcher's son. As he turned the pork chops on the frying pan, he wondered if maybe he could contrive a story to throw Ella off the scent. God knows he could paint any picture he wanted with his father's brush. Then again, he thought, there was no fooling her. Better fess up, he decided. If nothing else, he could do with a shoulder to cry on.

'Maxi, may I have another glass of Port before dinner?' Nora's request was disguised as a plea when both of them were well aware it was an actual command.

'Sure thing, Mom,' Maxi meekly replied. To deny her was the right thing to do to safeguard her health - especially with the consignment of drugs she was taking - but he relented. He had no job, he was homeless, and now this thing with Cillian Mulcahy - he certainly didn't want his mother's scorn tossed into the mix. He dutifully poured Nora her Port and delivered it to her by the log fire. His focus shifted back to Cillian. That was three days ago, and still not a word. Cillian was waging psychological warfare, and by the way Maxi was behaving, he was winning.

With Nora tucked away for another day, Maxi walked to Cassidy's pub, which was about a ten-minute walk down Song Bird Road. When he got there, he sat up by the counter and ordered a pint of Guinness and a vodka and white from a tall, skinny kid in a grubby white shirt. Ella always drank vodka, so he thought, why not have it sitting on the counter when she arrived? He was halfway down his pint when she walked through the door. Two old men, nursing their pints at a table inside the door, looked like they were visually stripping her naked as she made her way to the counter. Maxi, regretfully, found himself doing the same.

She wore a black velvet jacket over a lime green turtleneck sweater, Levi jeans and black combat boots with blood-red laces. A black beret was pulled to one side of her head, and slung over her shoulder, a petite, red leather bag. She leaned over and kissed him on the cheek before mounting the stool next to him. He recognized her scent immediately. He was certain it was 'Joy' by Jean Patou - one of the most expensive perfumes in the world. He should know; he spent almost one thousand dollars on a small bottle as a gift to an ex-girlfriend. He was somewhat taken aback that Ella, who barely eked by, would have such an extravagant indulgence. *She's certainly full of surprises*, he thought, *and who more deserving than her to appreciate some of life's finest pleasures?*

'Cheers,' she said, lifting her glass to clunk his.

'Cheers,' he replied. 'You look very nice.'

'Thanks.' She smiled. 'So, do you. Listen, I'm mad for a cigarette. Want to go out back?'

'Let's go.'

On the way, Maxi caught the barman's attention, and with two fingers held aloft, he repeated his drink order. Maxi and Ella sat opposite each other on one of those wooden tables with the inbuilt benches. Maxi aimed his cigarette at the tongue of flame she presented in her outstretched arm. That same flame, under her own cigarette, illuminated her beautiful face. Her skin seemed as smooth as the desert sands. Her eyes glowed like burning embers from the flame of her Zippo lighter. Smoke began to ooze from her ruby red lips and slowly billow into the air. The whole scene - like a rocket about to launch - assumed an extramundane vibe.

'You didn't tell Jasper you were meeting me, did ye?' Maxi asked.

'Of course not,' she snapped. 'I never tell him my business. Why, what difference would it make if he knew?'

'Ah, I don't want him to get the wrong idea, that's all.'

'Maxi, the drums are already beating on this one,' she said, pointing her finger at him and back at herself. 'Us, sitting here like this, having a drink together, is primo tittle-tattle.'

'How can you live like this?' Maxi said, shaking his head. 'This fucking town is a goldfish bowl.'

'C'este la vie,' she said. 'Right, let's have it. What's all this carry-on with the butcher's son in the steam room?'

'Do you know him?'

'I know his sister, Georgina.'

'Georgina? Sounds Italian.'

'I know,' Ella replied. 'She used to be Maria Mulcahy until she hooked up with some greaseball in New York whose previous girlfriends were all named Maria so, just like that,' she made an explosive gesture with her hands, 'Poof – Maria. Buongiorno – Georgina.'

'Let me get this straight,' he said as he took a long pull from his cigarette. 'This Georgina babe is Cillian's sister, and she's married to some *wop* in New York.'

'Correct.'

'Well, that explains my steam room episode with the butcher boy.'

'What are you talking about?' Ella implored. 'You're not making any sense.'

'The thing is,' he confessed, 'I borrowed a bunch of money from the Banditti family.' He had to stop to catch his breath. Just mentioning the name made him nauseous. 'These people have connections with the mob in New York City. I never paid back the money, so they're not exactly happy campers.'

'That's not good.' Ella sighed, reaching across the table to hold his hand.

'No, it's not,' he agreed. 'Anyway, the plan was to use the money to finish renovating my house, slap a *for sale* sign on it, and with real estate prices going through the roof, I stood to make a sizeable profit on the sale. Once the house was sold, I'd pay back the mob and have enough money left over to start another project. Everything would have been honky dory; only the *perfect* shitstorm came to town.'

'So, how does the butcher boy know all about the money you owe?'

'That Georgina one must be linked somehow to the Banditti family, and she must have told her brother all about me.'

'Why would she do that?' Ella asked, blowing smoke at her glass.

'I don't know,' he sighed. 'This feels like a shakedown, and that's something I need like a hole in the head. 'Fuck!' he exclaimed. 'I could end up getting whacked.'

'Don't be silly,' Ella insisted. 'People don't go around *whacking* each other anymore. What would be the point? If you're dead, then they can't get their money back.'

'Problem solved,' he replied sarcastically. 'Thanks Ella, that's a load off my mind.'

'You're welcome,' she echoed his cynicism.

'I'm sorry,' he said, 'but these people I owe the money to *will* fucking kill me if I don't pay them back.'

'I have some money saved. You're welcome to it.'

'No, no,' he snapped, pounding the table with his clenched fist. 'That's why, right there, I didn't want to tell you any of this.' He took a pull from his cigarette. 'I have my own money,' he confided. 'I sold my pickup truck and all my construction equipment before I left New York, so I'm not stuck for a crust.' He took a sip of his pint. 'I'll tell you one thing... I'm fucked if I'm going to hand it over to the butcher boy.'

'You'll just have to wait and see what he wants.'

'Yeah, you're right.'

Chapter 4.

An inquisitive beam of sunlight broke through a gap in the Venetian blinds striking Jasper Hickey in his good right eye and causing him to jolt like he was the victim of a violent assault. Naked within the confines of the small bathroom, his dull reflexes triggered him to slam his midsection into the corner of the retro pink ceramic sink. Wallop! His gonads suddenly demanded his full attention. Normally, these numb nuts dangled in a wrinkled papoose from his undercarriage and, for all intents and purposes, brought nothing to the table until their collision with the retro pink ceramic sink. It was unfortunate their reinstatement as functioning body parts came with such trauma. Initially, snippets of pain here and there began to peep over the impenetrable blockade that Jasper had built up over the years with his cache of pain-killing drugs. Pain or, indeed, its associates had lost all purchase until then. Alarm bells started going off all over his anatomy. Doors were urgently slammed shut in the pleasure zones of his brain while receptors and neurons in the command tower cleared the tracks for a tsunami of pain.

He bent over in a nut cuddling embrace, and while his slow brain was crunching the numbers and evaluating the input, he peered over his right shoulder but couldn't see anything, except that mound of useless flesh.

'That fucking hump,' he groaned.

He rubbed his good eye with his right knuckle, hoping to regain some semblance of sight while his left hand slashed the air in a big arc above his head, with a full open container of talcum powder. The fine white dust consumed the confines of the small bathroom. Only recently did talcum powder become a part of his regimented daily routine. Overnight - as with all his obsessions - he felt the urgent need to smother his armpits, his feet and his balls with a liberal amount of baby powder. His previous obsession, where he lathered his face with carpet cleaner - believing it to be an anti-aging solution - was non-ceremoniously dropped from his compulsive agenda when the two cats targeted his face as a potty. The scent of the carpet cleaner must have been coequal with that of the kitty-litter tray.

Suddenly, his knees gave out from under him, and as he descended in haste towards the fake tile floor, he clawed furiously with both hands for something to arrest his fall. He clipped the near corner of a framed poster of Georgie Best with one hand and a small shelf adorned with several dwarf cactus plants with the other. Georgie Best, the Manchester United striker, wavered for an instant. The shelf slid to an acute angle and began to jettison miniature pots of cacti-like depth charges from a destroyer. Once Georgie was done levitating, he took off like a 'Stuka' dive bomber and violently crashed into smithereens onto the bathroom floor.

Jasper ended up in the foetal position on the floor. A sizeable number of cactus pods had embedded themselves all down along the right side of his body, so the slightest movement prompted the most excruciating pain. He groaned in agony. He was now a prisoner, mentally bound and gagged. His unscrupulous captor, forcing him to lay still on the floor, amid shards of glass like broken ice and dusted over with a snowy powder in that winter-wonderland scene, the sun, ironically, had just created.

Normally Jasper was a little hallucinogenic from his assortment of prescription drugs and farmyard tranquilizers. His brain, or what was left of it, was punch drunk from the alcohol and its wiring, short-circuited by the drugs. Not only was his brain seriously compromised, his body also took a beating. He had to have a quadruple bypass, numerous stints inserted, chunks of his colon extracted and yards of damaged intestines removed. Some of his body parts were swapped out for pig parts, so, over the years, poor old '*Porky*' was called upon for more and more body parts to keep Jasper 'ticking.' He had pig veins, pig valves and pig bowels. Jasper

Hickey behaved more and more like a pig after each operation. His appearance didn't alter drastically, but his demeanour certainly did.

Ella Hickey - his estranged wife - heard the 'thud' from the upstairs bathroom, paused for an instant and made a mental note to check upstairs later but right then, she had more pressing matters on her mind. She desperately needed to get naked and out into the back garden to soak up each and every ray of precious sunshine before the clouds regained control of the sky. She was like a junkie, prepping for a fix as she set about gathering up all her solar paraphernalia.

'Oh baby, I want you to stroke that thing and get it nice and hard for me,' Ella moaned into the mouthpiece of the cordless phone which was tucked between her shoulder and her jaw. 'I want you to play with yourself first, and then you can play with me.'

'Oh, yeah, baby... playtime.'

She needed both hands free to get at the deckchairs that somehow managed - over the winter months - to work their way to the back of the garage and end up bound together by the garden hose along with the lawnmower and the stepladder.

'How the fuck did you manage to get all tied up like this?' She shook her head in disbelief, momentarily forgetting her client on the line while she busied herself unravelling the knots in the hose with her eager fingers.

'Bondage, baby, I love it.' Her client groaned with delight. 'Now, you're talking.' He gasped excitedly. 'My dick's so hard, I could sink a railroad spike with it.'

Ella paused for an instant to consider 'bondage' in future phone sex conversations. She never considered that genre in her sexual dramatizations before. To her, the whole S&M thing felt a little 'icky.' However, when she saw how excited her client became with the mere mention of restraints, she was inclined to re-evaluate her reservations. Much as she wanted her clients to have fun, she didn't want them peaking too soon either. In her line of work, it was necessary to keep her client on the line as long as possible – her pay was directly related to the duration of the call. She decided she would only incorporate whips and chains in the latter portion of her calls.

'You are completely naked – except for your school tie – and you're all tied up in knots,' she informed her client, mimicking the tone her headmistress employed when she misbehaved in school.

'I've got this big wooden paddle in my hand, and I'm going to spank your bare ass with it,' she threatened her listener. 'You naughty, naughty boy.' She slapped the free end of the garden hose against the lid of the trashcan and her client yelped as if his own ass was being struck with the paddle.

'Oh yeah,' Ella moaned into the phone. 'Stroke that thing for me, baby, oh yeah.'

'Oh momma,' he groaned. 'I've been a bad boy; I need to be punished.'

'It's so fucking hot in here,' Ella gasped as she finally freed one of the recliners from its restraints.

'Oh, yeah, baby, I'm burning up over here too.'

One down, two to go. She left the recliner against the side wall in the back garden, and with the phone still tucked between her shoulder and chin, she headed for the kitchen. Ella knew it was time for the *oral sex simulator*. She reached under the sink to retrieve the modified coffee plunger, which was half-filled with a concoction of mushroom soup, lemon chunks, peeled tomatoes and a few teaspoons of olive oil. She held the mouthpiece of the phone to the rim of her invention and began a slow rhythmic action, up and down with the plunger. The exuding sounds closely replicated those of someone giving a blowjob. Every now and then, she leaned in towards the mouthpiece to offer a moan or a groan. This accompaniment helped to lend a little humanity to her illusion. It never failed to please, plus it made her job easier. No slurping, no gagging, no convulsions. Mission accomplished.

She hung up the phone and checked her watch. She only earned ten minutes of call time, but she shrugged it off. Since the sun had taken precedence over everything else, she called Petra, her phone-sex dispatcher, and cancelled all her calls for the rest of the day. She returned to the garage like an amazon warrior intent on slaughtering anything that got in the way of her sun.

Once Ella had the three recliners and the two oval side tables set up in the small back garden, each one free from intrusive shadows and pointing directly at the sun, she called her two best friends, Debbie and Ida and invited them over for cocktails. Twenty minutes later, the two friends were togged out in their swimsuits, seated in recliners and armed with Pina Coladas in Ella's back garden. These two women were just like Ella - ardent sun worshippers - whose devotion to the sun was right up there with the Aztecs and the Mayans. This triad of inseparable friends took their summer holidays together each year in June, and this year was no exception.

Technically speaking, none of them had a significant other. Ida was divorced. Debbie was a widow. Ella was in a grey area regarding her marital status to Jasper since she murdered him every night in her sleep. Most nights, she blew his brains out with a shotgun. However, if he was particularly mean to her during the day, she might decide to tie him up and sever his limbs with a blunt axe or pummel him to death with a lump hammer. Every night, without fail, was devoted to some heinous scheme to rid her of her spouse. So hypothetically speaking, she was single.

'Isn't this fantastic,' Ida chirped, taking a sip of her cocktail. 'All we're missing here are the sights and sounds of the ocean.'

'Okay, we don't have an ocean,' Debbie agreed, 'but look on the plus side. We don't have to put up with those annoying hawkers, shoving their designer knock-offs in our faces.'

'That's true,' Ida conceded. 'Still, the sun without the sea is like a garter belt without the stockings. It looks and feels – incomplete.'

Ida was an aspiring fashion model in her early twenties until a freak accident took out her right eye. While in Paris, she worked as a barmaid in the evenings so she could chase down photo shoots by day. One night, just before her shift ended, some drunk threw an ice cube across the bar and struck her in the eye. Twenty years later and her bitterness was still bubbling just below the surface. Since then, she was never seen without her eye patch.

'I don't see any connection,' Debbie snarled, 'between garter belts 'n nylons and the sun and the sea.'

Ida had a tendency to mope in the past, and this was one of these occasions where she chose to deploy her beauty-based ideology to express her opinion. Her intent was not to spotlight her own beauty but rather to mock it, instead. Any chance she got, she would put *beauty* on a pedestal... only to knock it down. While Ella was sympathetic to Ida's misfortune, Debbie didn't give a hoot. In fact, she would have gladly gouged out one of her own eyes, or for that matter, hacked off an arm or a leg, to have the bubble-gum ass and perky breasts that Ida had. To say Debbie had body-image issues would be an understatement. She was kept awake at night by eidetic images of glamorous cover girls, leering and jeering at her thin lips and tiny tits. Her chubby body in her swimsuit made her feel all the more demoralised, especially when sunbathing alongside her two beautiful girlfriends. She didn't feel too bad at a crowded beach. There, the odds were stacked in her favour. The majority of specimens on display would be carnivores with flabby bellies 'n butts, with bald heads 'n hairy backs, with bingo wings or humongous thighs, all attributes working in synergy to distract from her own deformities. In her estimation - when viewed through beer goggles - she was a six out of ten.

Debbie misinterpreted Ida's beauty-based analogy as a personal affront, so she countered with a hostile jab of her own.

'So why not ask that whore, who's wearing the garter belt, to take a run and jump into the sea?' Debbie growled. 'That's the only way I can connect the dots.'

'You don't need to be a whore to wear a garter belt,' Ida snidely remarked. She made it clear she didn't care to be paired with a prostitute. 'Don't tell me you don't have a garter belt in your knicker's drawer?'

'Of course, I do," Debbie asserted in that - *how dare you ask* - tone. 'Lingerie is a must have in every girl's closet.' She did have a drawer full of garter belts and even an assortment of fishnet stockings, but with the price tags still intact. In her present physical condition, she wouldn't dare wear anything provocative. That would all change when she had enough money saved.

'When you go into battle,' Ida advised, 'that is - the battle of the sexes - your garter belt is the most lethal weapon in your arsenal.'

'Thanks very much, Ida, for that priceless gem of wisdom,' Debbie jeered. 'I'll be sure to release the safety catch on my garter belt before I woo my next lover. If nothing else, I'll have somewhere to put my cigarettes when I lead the charge on my lover.'

Ella was busy mixing up another batch of Pina Coladas by the outdoor bar and was completely lost in reverie. Her earlier encounter with Maxi in the supermarket sparked the picture show she was enjoying in her head at that moment in time. She recalled it was about fifteen years ago when Jasper decided he wanted to build that outdoor bar in the back garden. Maxi happened to be home *on vacation* from New York around that time, so Jasper invited him over to the house to pick his brain on his little DIY project.

By that stage, Maxi had been back and forth several times from the States, but Ella remembered she hadn't seen him since she was that pimply faced, flat-chested teenager with the big crush. She was a stay-at-home mom who was preoccupied with being a loving wife to Jasper and a caring mother to her two beautiful daughters. When

Jasper told her Maxi Dillion was coming over, her voracious curiosity was amped up to the max. She remembered the instant she clapped eyes on him and how her teenage crush came charging through her veins like top-grade heroin. It overpowered her completely, buckling her knees, drying her lips and sending shivers of delight up and down her spine. Maxi, too, she recalled, had difficulty retaining control. Once the dust settled, it was apparent they were both mutually enamoured by one another, although neither let on. Lucky for them, Jasper was delayed at the lumber yard. After a brief discussion, Ella remembered how delighted she was when Maxi volunteered to build the outdoor bar for free. He told her it would be his belated wedding present to them both.

She replayed the part of Maxi sawing a length of lumber, over and over, in her head. How strong and rugged he looked with his bulging biceps, flexing and straining on each pass of the saw. She wondered what it would feel like to be wrapped up tight in those arms of his. Watching him work over that long weekend – him bare-chested with his broad shoulders bathed in sweat – was pleasurable torture for her in the extreme. She remembered feeling guilty for lusting after another man, and she a happily married mother. Then she smiled as her fingers traced the outline of a heart that was chiselled into the countertop of the bar with the letters *J loves E* entrapped within its confines. She had some difficulty bringing that lovely memory back to life, but she managed somehow, and for a fleeting moment, she could feel that aching love she once reserved for Jasper. Then, bullying their way into her thoughts, the horrible consequences that drink and drugs had on her marriage. When she bumped into Maxi in the supermarket, her salacity was still alive and kicking, but any feelings of guilt were long gone.

'Easy, you two,' Ella advised as she noticed a change in tone in their conversation. 'Let's enjoy the sun. It's too nice a day for bickering.'

'Yeah, you're right,' Ida agreed.

'Truce,' they all said together and clunked each other's glasses.

Ella settled in on the third recliner, and as the day wore on, the three friends began to cook like rotisserie chickens in the hot afternoon sun.

'Did any of ye happen to notice,' Debbie asked. 'The *look* on the weatherman's face when he pointed at the emoji of the sun on his weather chart?'

'Oh, that was so funny,' Ida squealed. 'He looked like a deer in the headlights, poor man.'

'Yeah,' Ella agreed, 'he just stood there, pointing. I'd say he thought he was being pranked.'

'And did you see the way he jumped back from the chart,' Debbie continued, laughing out loud, 'with the coming, three-day forecast? Nothing but wall to wall emojis of the sun.'

'Yeah,' Ida replied. 'Big yellow freckles all over the TV.'

'All joking aside,' Ella cautioned, as she presented her Marlboro box to each of the girls. 'An American weatherman was shot dead because one of his viewers couldn't deal with another snowstorm. Maybe, this poor bastard was terrified that his promise of the sun would surely be broken and a whole world of hurt was coming his way... the minute the clouds were back in the sky.'

'And yet,' Debbie offered, 'here we are reaping the rewards of his forecast.'

'Can you imagine,' Ella proposed. 'If indeed his forecast does pan out and we do have that sun hanging out up there for the next week or so?' She pointed at the sky with her cigarette. 'We might just get to bring a suntan onto the plane with us before we fly to Spain.'

'Imagine when the metal detector goes off in the airport.' Ida lowered her voice to sound like a man. 'Hey lady, what are you trying to smuggle under that skirt of yours? A suntan, BITCH.'

'Wouldn't that be something,' Debbie declared. 'Imagine the natives, peeping out from under their sombreros and the look of shock on their faces as we all head straight to the beach like retired Californians.'

'We don't need no stinking sun umbrellas,' Ella jeered.

What's more,' Ida suggested. 'We won't need any of those expensive creams to soothe the third-degree burns normally associated with our arrival.'

'Maybe, if this global warming keeps up,' Debbie insisted. 'We might end up shaking the sand out of our swimsuits, onto our own living room floor, without the need to ever go abroad.'

'Hold on, now you're really getting carried away,' Ida remarked. 'The sun has only been out for a couple of hours and already you've Ireland pencilled in as a tropical paradise.'

Ella burst out laughing, which set the other two off. A few more Pina Coladas and the laughter got louder and louder. Abba was belting out 'Fernando' on the CD player, and the girls couldn't wish for anything more. Well... maybe. Debbie wouldn't say no to a new body, Ella a 'late' husband and Ida, her own financial independence. Otherwise, their dance cards were full.

Chapter 5.

While Ella was flipping burgers on the grill and tapping with her spatula to the beat of Robert Palmer's *Addicted to Love*, she heard some peculiar groans that she hadn't noticed in the song before. Debbie and Ida were laughing hysterically at some remark or other, and with the sizzling sounds from the barbeque, Ella – being a *groan* connoisseur herself – had to strain to discern what value these particular groans were contributing to the song. It was only when the song faded out and the groans persisted, did she realise they didn't belong to the song. Her gaze travelled up the back of the house to the source of the noise. These groans were emanating from the upstairs bathroom window, which was always kept ajar to defuse the miasma of noxious odours that Jasper was capable of exuding.

'Oh, shit! It's Jasper.'

She beckoned Debbie to take care of the grill while she raced through the kitchen, across the living room and up the stairs to the bathroom. When she turned the doorknob, Jasper screamed at the top of his lungs.

'Stop.'

But it was too late. Her attempt to open the door caused a number of cactus pods that had fallen down between Jasper and the door to be mercilessly rammed into his naked body. Ella was transfixed by Jasper's horrendous shrieks.

'Leave door be,' he squealed. He had a cactus pod embedded in his throat, so even trying to talk was painful. Whatever way his larynx performed to utter the word 'I'... it proved to be insufferable, so he tried 'me'. *Me* still hurt, but not as bad as *I*. He urgently needed to relay a message to Ella, to have her stop pushing at the door. He knew uttering the words would hurt, and for some reason, broad vowels hurt the most, so he was very much restricted in his choice of vocabulary. Jasper had to treat each utterance like an extremely

40

expensive telegram and the only acceptable method of payment...
excruciating pain.

'Me like leave door be,' Jasper relayed his request in agony and
went completely still.

'Why are you talking funny?' Ella spoke through the gap in the
bathroom door. 'If you're drinking whiskey in there, I swear on all
that's sacred, I'll cut your balls off and fling them in a meat grinder.'

He had to hastily compose another sentence to combat that
threat, but as he was still thwarted by the resonating pain of his
last utterance, his response yet again was barely one step up from
babbling.

'Me no drink. Me in pain.'

'I'll tell you one thing... me fuck you up even more, if you don't
open this fucking door right now.' She slammed her fist into the
raised panel of the door to punctuate her command.

'Aaah.'

Jasper roared with the same intensity as if he had his balls flung
in the meat grinder still attached. Ella retracted from the door in awe.
She never heard a human screech like that before. For that matter,
she never heard any living beast even remotely come close.

'Hang in there.' Ella, at last, responded in a reassuring tone
knowing that something was seriously wrong. 'Stay still, I'll get help.'

Ella raced down the stairs and out the back to get her phone.
She explained the situation to her girlfriends. She told them that his
screams were a direct consequence of her attempts to open the door
and that she could hear broken glass being disturbed, but other than
that, she had no idea what was causing all the angst.

They debated for a moment to determine the best course of
action. Whether Jasper was the victim or the culprit, there was never
any panic. Since the emergency services – fire, ambulance and police
– were all no strangers to the house, with Ella making legitimate

calls and Jasper crying wolf... there was no knowing how long their response would be.

'How about we call Jasper's friend... Maxi Dillon?' Ella proposed, trying her best to disguise the excitement in her voice.

'Maxi Dillon,' said Debbie. 'Home from America, is he?'

'I thought I saw him, in the corner of my eye, the other day downtown,' Ida remarked, 'but I couldn't be sure. So, it *was* him then?'

'Yeah, he's home to take care of his mom,' Ella confirmed all matter-of-factly.

Debbie took everything at face value. Skulduggery didn't exist in her black and white world. Ida, on the other hand, wasn't buying into Ella's *'goodie-two-shoes'* act for a second. In the past, when Maxi was home on holidays, they all went out together to party. Ida could see the *looks* between Ella and Maxi on those nights out. Nothing untoward was going on between them, but it was obvious to her they were itching to blast out of the friend zone and into some other strata where everything sizzled, red-hot. How Debbie didn't notice was purely bizarre. How Jasper didn't notice was due to his roaming eye. He was always looking into faraway fields.

'Hi Maxi, it's me... Ella. Ella Hickey.'

'Hi Ella. Ella Hickey,' Maxi teased. 'What's up?'

'Well it's Jasper. He's fallen down in the bathroom, and I can't open the door with him in the way.'

'Is he conscious?'

'Very,' Ella replied.

'So, ask him to move out of the way.'

'Dah! Don't ye think I tried already? He won't budge,' Ella assured.

'Why not?'

'No idea, but I heard broken glass being shuffled about and he sounds like he's in serious pain.'

'All right,' Maxi conceded. 'I'll get over to you as soon as I can.'

Maxi arrived at number six to a symphony of raucous sounds; dogs barking, music blaring, Jasper groaning and the women in the back garden, laughing and shouting over the din. Ella always left the key in the front door so any visitor could let themselves in. Besides, who would dare attempt to rob the house with four big dogs on patrol and a foul-mouthed parakeet named Prudence doing sentry duty on his perch in the kitchen?

'Hello?' Maxi shouted into the living room, using the front door to shield himself from the pack of dogs.

When he caught Ella's attention through the French doors, he took a deep breath and bravely stepped into the room. The four big dogs surrounded him instantly, and his big frame was jostled about by their thrashing bodies and swishing tails. Deploying both hands, he patted each one on the head, showing no favouritism as he tried desperately to disguise his fear. He felt like a Christian in the Colosseum with a pork chop tied round his neck.

'Ella!' he bellowed, the fear in his voice resonating above the din.

The hounds responded with a raucous chorus of high-pitched howls that drowned out his pleas for help. Even though these dogs were used to his comings and goings and would never harm him - ever since he was attacked as a young child by a pair of fluffy French Poodles - he would always remain secretly terrified of dogs.

'Thanks, Maxi, for coming so quick. I don't know what I'm going to do with that eejit upstairs.'

She pointed at the ceiling with one hand and casually dispersed the dogs with a wave of the other. Maxi's relief was palpable. With the dogs out of the picture, he was able to steal a moment to appreciate Ella's well-toned body in her flimsy bikini. She was unaware of his appraisal as she replaced several cushions the dogs had dislodged from the couch. She was tall and slender with all the bumps in all the right places. She had shoulder-length, jet black hair, and a beautiful olive complexion. Since her family originated in Galway, there was little doubt, but she was a direct descendant of some Spanish conquistador who swam ashore after his Armada was shipwrecked off the Galway coast in the 16th Century. She had an hourglass figure, bolstered by a regimented exercise routine that would test the resolve of a Navy Seal. Maxi was in good shape himself, but he did have a bit of a gut. Not having six-pack abs was a fair price to pay for his beloved Guinness.

'Let me see what's going on with Jasper,' Maxi said as he headed for the stairs.

'Good luck with that,' she replied. 'I'll be out the back if you need me. Say hello to the girls when you get a chance.'

'Will do,' he assured.

'Oh, by the way,' Ella spoke softly, as she checked over her shoulder to ensure they were alone. 'Did the butcher boy get in touch?'

'No,' he sighed. 'Nothing yet.'

'What's he up to, I wonder?'

'I wish I knew,' he replied. 'He's been wrecking my head all day, every day since the steam room. And as if that's not enough, my mother is pulling out all the stops to drive me completely insane.'

'You have a lot on your plate, that's for sure, but you'll manage... you'll see,' she said, doubting every word that crossed her lips. *Who am I to be dishing out assurances?* She thought. *With my messed-up life, I'm certainly not qualified.*

'Yeah, it'll all work out,' Maxi replied. His doubt was as blatant as Ella's false prophecy.

'Let me see what's going on with this clown,' he said, climbing the stairs two steps at a time. When he reached the landing, he got down on one knee and focused his attention on the gap between the door and the jamb. He accidentally nudged the door ever so slightly with his knee, and Jasper exploded with a loud shriek. Maxi was startled by the sincerity of his howl. Jasper was literally crying wolf. This was no attention seeking ploy, he reasoned; this was a genuine cry for help.

He spoke through the gap in the door. 'Hey buddy, it's me, Maxi.'

'Eh.' A painful groan from Jasper, who still had to be vigilant in his use of broad vowels to minimise the pain.

'I need to open the door to get you up and out of there. Are you able to move?'

'No,' Jasper growled as he fought back the tears. 'Me want leave door be.'

'I don't understand. Why are ye talking funny? Are ye drunk?' Maxi inquired as he peeked through the gap in the door to discern the situation. All he could see was one cheek of Jasper's bare ass, covered in talcum powder.

'Cactus,' he uttered in an exasperated snort.

Maxi scratched the stubble on his face. 'You can't move because of cactus, is that right?'

'Yeah,' he whispered.

'I have to cut the door off its hinges,' Maxi informed Jasper. 'I've got to get some tools. Don't go anywhere.'

'Ha, ha,' Jasper groaned.

He ran down the stairs and out to the car to retrieve a reciprocating saw along with a few other hand tools that he kept in the trunk. He returned to the landing, set up the saw and cut through the hinges on the door with ease. He lifted it out from the frame and leaned it against the wall in the corridor.

'Right, let's have a look at ye,' he said as he bent down on one knee.

Maxi took a moment to investigate the scene. Jasper was completely motionless on the floor. He was covered from head to toe in Talcum powder, and there were shards of glass and a number of cactus pods littered about the floor. It was only when he bent down for a closer look did, he notice the numerous cactus pods that were embedded in his naked body.

'Hold tight. I'll be back in a minute.'

Maxi went downstairs, across the living room and out through the back door into the garden. He waved at Debbie and Ida and beckoned Ella to him.

'I'm afraid I had to cut the door off its hinges to get at him.'

'That's no biggie,' Ella replied. 'How is he?'

'He'll live.'

'Unfortunately.'

'He's a little cut up from the broken glass, and he's got a shit load of cactus pods stuck in him, but otherwise, he's the same grumpy, fat bastard he always was.'

'That's a relief,' Ella smiled, 'I was afraid the fall might have knocked some manners into him.'

'Some chance.' He laughed. 'Oh yeah, I nearly forgot, he's in the nip. Can you find something for him to wear? I don't need to be staring at his pecker.'

'God be between us and all harm,' Ella moaned. 'What about the cactus? Do we need a doctor?'

'No need,' he confirmed. 'I'll remove the cactus pods myself, but I'll need salad-tongs. Got one?'

Ella went into the kitchen and Maxi followed. She rummaged about in the utensil drawer and found a stainless-steel pair of tongs. She handed them over. He flexed them a few times in his hand to familiarize himself with their action. In the meantime, Ella found a pair of shorts in the laundry basket.

'Do you need a hand up there?' she inquired, half-heartedly, pointing at the ceiling.

Her pleading expression made her intentions quite clear. She wanted so bad to get back out in the sun. Maxi tortured her by stalling his answer. He hummed and hawed while she was forced to maintain that longing look on her face until, at last, he let her off the hook.

'When I'm done with those cactus pods, I'll need a hand to get him up and out of the bathroom. I'll give you a shout when I'm ready.'

Maxi got a pair of work gloves from the car and raced back upstairs. As he went about extracting the cactus pods from Jasper's riddled body, he couldn't help but feel sorry for him. He remembered the first time they met. It was a cold, wet miserable Saturday afternoon, and the team and himself were getting togged out in the dressing room to play a practice game of soccer. The coach arrived in with this new kid and introduced him to the team.

'Everyone, say hello to Jasper Hickey... our new striker.'

Jasper was roughly the same age as Maxi, thirteen or fourteen years old with a similar height and build, but what made him stand out from the rest of the kids were his well-defined, muscular legs. It was like he was created specifically to play soccer. Maxi played full back while Jasper was up by the goal in the centre forward position. That afternoon, Jasper demonstrated his incredible skill for the game and scored three goals... the hard way. He had to tackle several opponents and dribble the ball until he got the opportunity to shoot. He could strike equally well with either foot, and the power he put behind the ball was frightening. It's an awful pity, Maxi thought. If only Jasper could have steered clear of the drink and drugs, he would no doubt have been a 'striker' for some Premier league team in England... just like his idol Georgie Best.

It took him about a half-hour to extract all thirty or so golf-ball-sized pods from Jasper's flesh. If there was anyone outside listening, with the shouts and roars, they'd think someone was being murdered. Unfortunately for Jasper, the ejected spines from the cactus plants remained embedded in his skin, so once again, he could expect a 'curtain call' from pain in his immediate future. Maxi

dressed Jasper in his shorts and not without a struggle or an earful
of profanity - both broad and slender vowels - being indiscriminately
dispensed, now that the cactus pods had been removed. The next
problem was to get Jasper and his 350 pounds of blubber up and out
of the bathroom. Jasper couldn't stand up since the soles of his feet
were riddled like the rest of his body with cactus spines. This was
the only bathroom in the house, and extracting spines there would
take forever. With Pina Coladas flowing freely, it was unanimously
decided to remove him out into the back garden where no one would
be deprived of either the calls of Nature or the rays of the sun.
Once Maxi removed the lockset and laid the door down flat on
the landing, he stepped over Jasper and shouted out the bathroom
window to summon help.

'Let's go, girls. Show time.'

The girls made an awful racket, pulling and dragging at one
another and laughing and joking as they clamoured up the stairs. By
then, Debbie had a beach towel wrapped around herself while the
other two in their skimpy bikinis struggled to contain their tits in
their tops. Maxi didn't know where to look. He had to shout to get
their attention.

The plan was for each one to assist in hauling Jasper's fat ass
onto the bathroom door. Then, the improvised stretcher with him
on board was to be hauled to the stairway and shimmied, step by
step, down the stairs until they reached the ground floor. From there,
they would have to lift the door with its heavy cargo onto several
well-placed towels on the hardwood floor and drag it out to the back
garden. Everything went according to plan until they got midway
down the stairs. One over-eager push from someone and the door
took off like a toboggan with Jasper wailing at the top of his lungs.
When the stretcher hit the bottom step, he was jettisoned halfway
across the living room floor, which delighted the girls since the
hauling part of the plan had been drastically reduced. However,

Jasper's collision with the hardwood floor resulted in the cactus spines being embedded even deeper into his skin, so now the extraction process would prove more tedious.

Eventually, after a lot of pulling and dragging, shouting and swearing, and with shrieks from Jasper, the likes of which were only heard in the dungeons of medieval castles during the inquisition, they managed to lift him back on the door and out into the back garden. He lay stretched out on the door with one arm bent at the elbow supporting his head while the other arm seemed to hover in mid-air, aloof from his body, his fingers twitching in synchronicity to the pulsing pain being dished out by the unscrupulous cacti spines. This was the freehand he attempted to remove the pods with. He looked like an obese Caligula about to indulge in a sex orgy, except the scantily clad women enveloping him were armed with tweezers and hell-bent on doing some serious plucking. Jasper was in store for yet another bout of ass-whipping pain.

Chapter 6.

Maxi volunteered to clean up the mess in the bathroom, thinking that one of the girls would surely object. But there was no protest. Nothing short of a catastrophe would get them girls indoors, so instead of sipping a cold beer by the bar and watching the girls pluck Jasper, he headed upstairs to clean the bathroom. He placed the broken picture frame along with the large shards of glass into a garbage bag and swept up the smaller fragments into a dustpan. Then he wiped down the walls with a damp cloth. He did the same with the sink and the toilet bowl. Next, he had to get down on his hands and knees to wash the bathroom floor. Before he could do that, he had to psych himself up to lower himself down. His knees had taken some serious abuse over two decades in the construction industry, and now he was about to be reminded of the damage he'd done. That bathroom, which only moments ago was a torture chamber for Jasper, was now one for him. He moaned and groaned with every move.

While he was cleaning behind the toilet bowl, he found the partially rolled-up poster of Georgie Best. He spread it out carefully on the bathroom floor to inspect for any damage. Thank God there wasn't any. He knew only too well the importance of that poster to Jasper. Georgie Best was one of the greatest soccer players of that era and Jasper's idol. He must have got some rush, Maxi thought, when he got this autographed poster of Georgie on his tenth birthday. Jasper was living in an orphanage at the time. His mother died giving birth to him and he never knew his dead-beat dad. When he was adopted, four months later, that poster was the only thing besides the clothes on his back that he brought with him to his new home.

As Maxi continued his inspection, he was surprised to find a folded piece of paper taped to the back of the poster. The adhesive qualities of the tape had deteriorated over the years, so it just fell away in his hand. He put the poster aside and carefully unfolded his discovery until it grew to an A4-size sheet of paper. It felt a lot more substantial between finger and thumb than regular stationary. On further scrutiny, it seemed to lean more towards cloth than paper. The cloth was riddled with numbers, co-ordinates, signs and symbols but what stood out from all these markings was the faded red 'x' in the top left-hand corner of the cloth.

'A treasure-map.'

Maxi sprung to his feet, his knees, momentarily bionic, in his excited reaction. He knew he would pay dearly later. He stretched out the map in both clenched fists and began to study the details. It was an attempt by the composer to symbolically replicate a particular area of terrain so that the 'reader' could establish a reference point and, from there, dutifully follow the precise coordinates to arrive at the spot in the ground where the booty was buried. He took a moment to appreciate how that treasure could well be the solution to all his problems. He could pay back the Banditti family and tell Georgina and her scumbag brother to take a hike. He could return to New York City, buy a house for himself and his mother and focus on becoming a wealthy property developer. Since his arrival home, this was the first time the fog lifted is his mind to offer some glimmer of hope for the future.

He raced down the stairs with the fervency of a child on Christmas morning, knowing that what he held in his hand had to be sensational in some form or other. The girls were done plucking Jasper, who was already back in his chair gulping down a flagon of cider. Maxi waved at him as he sped past, but Jasper ghosted him.

'Girls, girls, girls, listen up,' he shouted over the music, frantically waving the map in the air. 'Look what I found.'

He bopped up and down like a drugged-up rave dancer, his enthusiasm once again making more impossible demands on his messed-up knees. Huddling the women together in a tight circle around him, he displayed, with outstretched arms, the taut map between his fists. Unfortunately, his fanaticism was not shared by his baffled audience. The women shrugged in unison and swapped concerned looks before they all clamped eyes on Maxi for an explanation. Once he informed them that the parchment, he was brandishing about was a treasure map and that it could possibly lead to 'untold' riches, he got their undivided attention.

'Oh my God, Maxi,' Ella said excitedly. 'What kind of treasure do you think it is?' She stole a sip from her drink to pre-maturely celebrate her newfound fortune. 'Could it be,' she mused, 'the old gypsy fortune-teller at the carnival last week was right when she predicted good fortune would soon be coming my way?'

'I have no idea,' said Maxi, 'but if someone went through the trouble of drawing up this map and carefully hiding it in the back of that poster, it's bound to have some value.'

Maxi handed the map to Ella and excused himself to go use the bathroom. Ella quickly invited the girls with a wave of her hand to convene by the bar. With a clean cloth, she wiped down the countertop and carefully spread out the map.

'Do me a favour,' Ella pleaded with her two friends. 'Let's all play along with Maxi and his treasure hunt. You saw how excited he was waving this thing about.' She pointed at the map. 'He needs something to hope for.' She fought hard to downplay her own excitement and maintain her stoic facade.

'Don't we all,' Debbie remarked.

'Ye never know,' Ida said. 'This map might just lead us to a treasure.'

'Well then, what are we waiting for?' Ella said. 'Why don't we all just saddle up our unicorns and go for a gallop in them, there candyfloss clouds.'

'Sounds like fun,' Ida yelped.

Ella topped up the girls with a fresh surge of Pina Coladas and presented Maxi with a cold beer upon his return.

'Cheers to our newfound fortune,' Ella shouted over the music. 'Whatever it may be.'

They all clinked glasses and cheered. The more they drank, the more convincing the treasure map became, and with every sip of alcohol, its booty more bountiful. As they became more and more inebriated, make-belief with its fairy-dust and shooting stars began to gain substantial traction over logical deduction... which was renowned for bringing nothing to the party except angst. All four of them, in one way or another, needed some aspiration or dream to cling to. It's not surprising in that particular circumstance, even though none of them would admit it, the treasure was unanimously embraced like the Second Coming. And then, right on cue, Jasper stuck his head out through the back door and yelled at the top of his lungs.

'What's all the fucking shouting about?' he growled. 'I can't hear the TV.'

'We found a treasure map,' Ella shouted back. 'We're all going to be rich.'

'Whoopie,' Jasper jeered. 'You found a fucking treasure map. Well, isn't that just dandy?'

'Ah, go back and watch your TV,' Ella snarled, disappointed with herself once again for allowing Jasper to invade her hopes and dreams.

'And you all think I'm mad,' Jasper said, waving his stick. 'Fuck the lot of ye.'

It didn't take long for him to return to his nasty old self. He wobbled off back into the living room, cursing and swearing as he went. Maxi and the three women refocused their attention on the map.

'I'm looking at that red X, and it's telling me I'm off around the world in my private jet,' Ida tittered excitedly, 'with my personal supply of Columbian cocaine, Belgium chocolate and Russian vodka.'

'Ah, shut up, Ida,' Debbie snapped. 'Give us a break. You're already able to do that shit with that rich, Brit boyfriend of yours... what's his name? Sebastian.'

'Not exactly,' Ida confessed. 'He doesn't own a private jet... yet.' She made a sympathetic face. 'We're still flying about in that tin-can Cessna.'

'Boohoo,' Ella sneered. 'I feel your pain.'

'Enough,' Maxi butted in. 'Let's enjoy the moment. What about you, Debbie? How would you spend the money?'

'I would spend a lot of time and money,' Debbie divulged, 'under the knife.'

'Plastic surgery,' Ella spurted. 'Why?'

'Isn't it obvious?' she said, inviting them to examine her body. 'I'm not happy with the way I look.'

Maxi and the other two women were startled by Debbie's extensive, anatomical, wish-to-do list. A complete overhaul was basically what she had in mind. She was a little chunky, and she did have small breasts, but otherwise, she was an attractive woman. Of course, it didn't help that her two best friends were 'drop dead' gorgeous. They all wondered, if Debbie did manage to achieve the look she was after, would her personality take a hit? If so, would they still be friends?

'I see myself sunbathing on the private section of beach by my villa in Cambodia,' Ella smirked. 'Wearing nothing, only a smile on my face and the birthday suit the good Lord gave me.'

'What about you, Maxi?' Ella inquired, a little flushed after her revelation.

He was a little flushed himself after he imagined himself trying on her birthday suit. A tight fit... skin-tight, to be precise. He found himself probing the pockets. Even though he didn't find any loose change, he continued his search. He abruptly erased that image from his mind and started anew.

'I see my Rolls Royce parked next to my Lamborghini, next to my Bugatti, and I wonder, where's my Bentley? Oh yeah,' he said, touching his temple with his index finger. 'I forgot, I'm driving it.'

They all laughed and cheered like they were a bunch of Bel Air kids at a pool party. Jasper reappeared in the double glass doors, intent on pulling the plug on their impish glee. He was already inebriated and eager to fight. He couldn't bear to see Ella having fun. He was a miserable bastard, and his misery craved company.

'Jasper, don't start. I'm warning you,' Ella commanded as she glared at the glass doors.

Jasper saw four angry faces staring at him through different panes of glass in the French doors and somehow, in his sozzled state, made the correct decision to retreat back to his chair. Maxi had to admit to himself, he got a little rattled by Ella's challenge.

'Okay. Let's get busy.' Maxi stood up and raised his arms above his head to get the girl's attention. 'Ladies, I hate to burst your bubble, but this map is useless unless we find a starting point.' Everybody got really quiet, really quick. He pointed at the map and then at the sky. 'That point could be anywhere.'

'We don't have a scale to go by either,' Debbie declared, allowing a smidgen of reality to step in and slap their fairy-tale across the face.

'Well then,' Ida decided, 'this map may as well be a chicken burrito.'

Ella was the only one totally focused on the map while the others became despondent and began mumbling about *'never catching a break'* and all that *'woe is me'* horseshit.

'Here's our reference point right here.' Ella raised her voice to get everyone's attention. Her finger pointed at the crude drawing of a square with a small circle attached to it.

'Look at the little wheel with the spokes. This has to be an attempt to represent a watermill of sorts, and that meandering line must be a river. Let's find that fucking watermill.'

Her determined glare made it quite apparent that this treasure seeking quartet should remain focused while overtones and innuendos were now suddenly disbarred. *'Don't dare fuck with my dream,'* is what she really wanted to say.

'That watermill could be anywhere.' Ida frowned but immediately regretted doing so.

Everybody frowned at Ida. Their frowns were directed at her to dispel doubt and encourage certainty and positivity in its stead.

'We must make a few assumptions in order to get started. Does everyone agree?' Ella propositioned the group and she was met with a unanimous endorsement.

'Okay. Let's speculate that this map represents some area next to a watermill in Ballydecuddle.' She directed her attention towards Ida. 'Ida, on the top shelf, to the left of the stove in the kitchen, there's a booklet which has a detailed map of Ballydecuddle. Bring it here, please.'

Ida jumped from her stool and raced to the kitchen. All eyes remained focused on the map. Ida returned a moment later with the booklet.

'Open the page for Ballydecuddle,' Ella instructed.

Ida found the page and laid the open booklet next to the treasure map on the countertop. The booklet was one of those pop-up types where the churches, castles and buildings were represented in a two-dimensional format to assist children in their understanding of maps. Once they all accepted the cartoon like quality of the booklet, inquisitive eyes scoured both parchments with impunity.

'Let's find how many watermills are along the river and its tributaries in this vicinity.' She invited the girls to concentrate their focus on a specific area on the Ballydecuddle map rather than the whole location all at once. It was time to eat the elephant, one morsel at a time. Ella pulled away from the treasure map to defuse the dictatorial vibe that would certainly rear its ugly head had she persisted hogging the logistics. She employed that interlude to sip her drink and light a cigarette. She took a deep draw, filling her lungs to the maximum, and relishing a long, slow, satisfying exhale, she rallied her senses to wallow for an instant in the luxurious bliss, her mind perceived, untold riches could evoke.

Debbie and Ida swooped in on the map like seagulls on a ham sandwich at Symphony Beach. After some inaudible exchanges and some to and fro gesticulations between the map and the local booklet, the two girls reached a verdict.

'There is a total of five watermills in Ballydecuddle. However, two of these we can discard immediately since they are lone structures in remote areas,' Debbie confidently relayed the information. Ella smiled to herself. She knew now her best friends were back on track and focused like falcons on the day's prey. After careful study and cross-referencing of both maps, the brain-storming session was beginning to pay off. Through a process of elimination, another conclusion was reached.

'We can also disregard this one,' Ida assured as her forlorn expression was replaced with one of purpose, 'It has only a few buildings nearby, so it can't be this one.'

'So,' Maxi ventured, 'we're left with only two watermills. Cool.' He blew a gust of smoke at the map. 'This one in Trombone,' he placed his finger on the location in the booklet, 'and the other one,' he moved his finger across the map, 'is over here in Fiddle Fern.'

'Does anyone understand these Latin notes?' Ella inquired. 'They may help us pinpoint the correct watermill.'

The two girls shook their heads in consternation. Maxi, however, stood up and took a premature bow as if to infer whatever he was about to disclose would warrant an ovation.

'What gives?' They blurted out in unison, and all three girls immediately burst out laughing at their synchronised retort. Their coincidental, concurrent remark exemplified the bonds of friendship that existed between them for eons.

'My mother Nora will have no problem translating those scribbles,' he assured. 'The nuns beat the crap out of her in school, so she had to learn Latin real fast, just to survive.'

'We all got beaten by the nuns,' Ida retorted, sprinkling a little doubt on Nora's proficiency in Latin.

'Ah yeah, that's right,' Maxi jeered. 'But let me tell ye, while the nuns in your time were a bunch of worn-out, bitter, auld hags who could barely lift a ruler, the ones in Nora's day were young and angry bull-dykes in the prime of their lives.'

He pranced about the garden with both fists clenched and flexing his elbows; he punched the air with one fist while he allowed the other to hover in front of his face like a drunk holding a microphone in a karaoke bar. The girls egged him on with shouts and cheers.

'Every single one of those nuns resorted to some form of violence as a way to vent their frustrations. You see, girls, that's what happens when the hens don't allow any cocks in the chicken coup,' Maxi raised his voice. 'Frustration in the bedroom. Bedlam in the classroom.'

The girls laughed and cheered as they stomped their feet on the ground and banged the countertop with their fists. They were loving the little open-air improv show that Maxi was putting on, and being somewhat inebriated – under a hot sun – only amplified their enjoyment.

'Sister Aquinas was Nora's Latin teacher, and she preferred to use her bare fists to get her point across. One day, Nora arrived home from school with two black eyes and a fractured jaw.' He returned to the countertop to grab his beer. 'That'll show ye how violent those bitches-without-britches were,' he concluded, taking a swig from his bottle.

'No way,' Ida exclaimed, shaking her head in total abandon.

'Yeah, way.' Maxi nodded. 'After five years brawling with this bitch, Nora was not only fluent in Latin but a fierce contender in the ring.'

'So, your mother is bi-lingual at kicking ass,' Ella concluded, and Maxi laughed along with the girls.

'Okay, boys and girls,' Ella said as she brought order to the meeting. 'We'll have to wait until Nora translates these scribbles before we can go any further. Here Maxi, take the map home with you and call me later when Nora does her thing.' Ella folded the map and handed it to Maxi.

He saluted the girls and stepped into the living room where Jasper was planted in his chair, eyes glued to the TV. He had a half-empty flagon of cider next to him on the side table and six empty ones by his feet, at the foot of the chair. He was wasting no time catching up on the 'downtime' he spent on the bathroom floor.

Every time Maxi came face to face with Jasper, he was torn between pity and disgust. More often than not, he had to resist the urge to punch him in the face. Besides Jasper pulling the pin on his 'self-destruct' grenade, he confided in Maxi one night when he was half-loaded that he was having an affair with a married woman. Maxi was disgusted. Here Ella was staying home to mind the kids, and this asshole was out banging other women. Maxi was sure, after listening to his bragging, there was more than one woman. When they were building the outdoor bar together way back in the late nineties, Maxi was tempted to tell Ella but decided against it, hoping that Jasper would mend his ways.

Maxi thought about the broken clock getting it right, twice a day, but that didn't even apply in Jasper's case: The man was never right in the head. Plus, he never knew how good he had it. There was no point in mentioning the treasure map again. Jasper's mind was so out of sync with reality, all he cared about was soccer. He was very upset about the broken Georgie Best frame, but when Maxi assured him, he'd get it repaired... he calmed down.

'Got to go home and feed the mother.' Maxi stood up, slapped Jasper on the shoulder and slipped out the front door.

Chapter 7.

Once Nora Dillon translated the Latin notes that were scribbled on the treasure map, there was no doubt that the salvage yard by Fiddle Fern was the site where the treasure was buried. However, the nature of the booty still remained a mystery. Maxi convened a meeting that day with the girls in Ella's kitchen. He was first to arrive and he greeted Ella with a hug and a kiss. He reserved that American custom specifically for her, and it was his little slice of Heaven whenever they met. Everyone else had to make do with a wave.

'Debbie is running a little late,' she said, taking his leather jacket from him and flinging it on the couch. 'Something about her having to wait for an E.R. nurse to replace her. Some poor man got mugged and he's in and out of consciousness, so he can't be left alone.'

Maxi mumbled, 'Oh, the poor bastard.'

He expressed his concern while his eyes never left his 600 quid leather jacket that was non-ceremoniously discarded on the couch and bound to be ripped to shreds by the pack of hounds that were surely lurking about in the vicinity. With total disregard for his own personal safety, he would willingly pay the ultimate sacrifice to save that jacket.

'Where are the mutts?' he asked, trying not to sound unduly concerned.

'Relax, they're locked up in my bedroom.' Ella smirked. 'I know you love that jacket.'

'Oh,' he sighed, 'that's a relief. *Locked up in Ella's bedroom,*' he thought to himself as he followed her shapely ass into the kitchen, '*I wish.*'

Ella's beige Levi jeans were so tight they may as well have been spray painted on her, as was her matching beige top. If he squinted his eyes, with that particular hue so close to skin tone, he got to see a blurry picture of her naked. He rebuked himself for having such a filthy mind. Sitting at the kitchen table, he poured himself a mug of tea. Ella sat opposite, flicking through the pages of some girly magazine. He waved at Jasper through the double glass doors. Jasper blanked him completely.

'Shoot a load on these titties, bitch,' Prudence squawked from his perch in the far corner of the kitchen.

'Fuck sake, Ella, you shouldn't let Prudence listen in on your sex calls.'

'I don't,' she said. 'Prudence comes up with that shit all on his own-e-o.'

'You're kidding, right?' Maxi waited for confirmation.

'No, I'm not. Prudence makes up all sorts of shit. Admittedly it can be nasty at times.'

'Well, he must have gender issues with them titties.'

'Yeah, he likes to flip between Betty and Bob,' she replied, turning the page in her magazine. 'Same confusion in the animal kingdom as us humans, I guess.'

'I still think it would be more prudent to move Prudence to another room. Preferably out of earshot,' Maxi suggested. 'We don't want him blabbing about the,' he leaned across the table and whispered in Ella's ear, 't-r-e-a-s-u-r-e.'

'Relax, Maxi, nobody believes a word out of that bird's beak,' she vowed. 'Besides, he's half-deaf like you, so he doesn't know what's going on. If I move him into a room on his own, he'll go ballistic.'

'Why can't ye put him in the living room with Jasper?'

'Are you nuts?' Ella snapped. 'Those two hate each other. You want to hear some nasty shit, put them two together. Let's just leave Prudence where he is, okay?'

'If you say so, but he better keep his trap shut about the you-know-what.'

'Yeah, yeah, yeah,' she waved her hand dismissively. 'Oh, by the way, any word from the butcher boy?' Ella asked, staring intently at him.

'Yes, as a matter of fact,' Maxi confirmed, 'Just before I came over here, I found this under the windscreen wiper on the car.' He handed her what looked like a birthday card in a red envelope.

'Fairly brazen way to embezzle somebody,' she said, taking the card from him. 'To each their own, I suppose.'

'*Money* is not the issue,' he informed her.

'Oh, well... that's good... right?' she replied as she began to read the card.

'All depends on which angle you're looking at it from,' he answered cheerfully.

My sister, Georgina, is coming home on vacation from New York in two weeks' time. She wants you to show her a good time!

Ella recoiled from the card with a startled look on her face. She studied Maxi for a moment to measure his reaction but only got a blank stare in return. She returned to the card and continued reading:

If you fail to comply with her wishes, I'll have no option but to make your whereabouts known to the Banditti family. Her ETA is May 30th. I'm deadly serious. Don't fool around. Signed, Cillian Mulcahy.

She looked across the table at Maxi, thinking that the card was a hoax. She expected him to break face any minute and burst out laughing. But he didn't. Instead he said, 'Here was I thinking, I'd have to pay a fortune to shut the butcher boy up and now all I have to do...'

'Stop,' she yelled.

The kitchen fell silent. She sat still, staring down at the card until her eyes began to water. One part of her was outraged, the other... astonished by the gall of this Georgina bitch. The mob and their *clingons,* she thought, muscle in on everything that is good and decent in society. Seems nothing is out of bounds to these creeps. She stole a peek at Maxi, whose sanguine disposition confounded her. What was he waiting for? Her blessing? Well he certainly wasn't getting that. If only he knew how much she craved the exact same outcome as that bitch Georgina but with scented candles... not loaded guns. She turned the card over, willing it still to be a hoax. It was blank. She figured the end of May was only two weeks away. Something had to be done and soon.

Maxi reached across the table to hold her hand, but she jerked back like she'd been stung by a nettle. With her head bowed, she began to inhale a loud, deep breath. Once her lungs were filled to capacity, she let him have it.

'You're not seriously thinking of going through with this... preposterous proposal.' She spat the last two words at him.

'Why is Georgina... ugly?' he asked, wiping her spittle from his face.

'What?'

'Is she ug...'

'I heard you the first time,' she barked. 'It's just... I can't... I don't... What the fuck?' She screamed and threw the card in his face.

'What's the matter?' he pleaded.

'Don't you see?' she cried out. 'These people are treating you like a piece of meat.'

'It's better than the alternative,' Maxi replied, leaning in over the table towards her to pretend he wasn't afraid.

'Oh yeah,' Ella replied. 'And what might that be pray tell?'

'Dead meat,' he groaned as he tried to win her favour.

'You weren't going to tell me about this?' she said, pointing at the card. 'Only for I asked.'

Maxi didn't answer. She knew by his silence, she was right.

'This is insane. Whoever heard of such a thing? These people are animals,' she said, shaking her head. 'No, I take that back. Animals wouldn't behave like this. They are depraved. They're the scum of the earth.'

'Well, it's a better deal,' he gambled, 'than having to come up with the money... don't you think?'

'No, it's not,' she growled. 'Don't you get it? If you dare fuck that bitch Georgina, that's it, she owns you.'

'Woe Nelly, woe,' he blurted. 'Where does it say on this card that I have to fuck her?' He asked, waving the card about.

Ignoring his question, Ella shrieked, 'The only way to deal with this situation is to pay back the fucking mob.' She lit a cigarette and took a long pull. She didn't offer Maxi one. Right then, she couldn't even look him in the face.

'How much do you owe them?' she inquired, softening her tone.

'One hundred thousand dollars,' he meekly replied.

'Jezzus,' she gasped. 'That's a lot of money. Let's hope this fucking treasure map of yours delivers up the goods.'

'So, you think, ignore the card,' Maxi said.

'Here's a question,' Ella asked, once again disregarding his question. 'Would you fuck Cillian?'

'Fuck no,' he snapped.

'Cillian is gay! Did you know that?' she stated matter-of-factly. 'Hello,' she continued. 'So, what if he decides he wants to stand in line for a piece of ass,' she paused, staring him straight in the eye. 'Your ass, that is?' she qualified. She poked him repeatedly in the chest with her ridged index finger to evoke a response. 'What then?'

'Okay, okay... I'm convinced.'

'Keep that card in a safe place,' she relented. 'We might need to use it as a bargaining chip when the time comes. I can't believe the butcher boy signed his name to it,' she said, shaking her head from side to side. 'How do you think Georgina's husband will react when he sees it?'

'How's that going to happen?' Maxi wanted to know. 'I'm certainly not going to hand it to him... and either are you.' He lit his own cigarette. 'That fucking butcher boy knows if that card gets to Vinnie or Pauley or Tony or whatever that grease-ball's name is, I'm a fucking dead man.'

'We'll figure something out,' Ella assured, knowing full well she was lying through her teeth. 'Right, here come the girls,' she said, pointing at the front window. 'Hide that fucking thing and let's keep this *gigolo* bullshit between ourselves?'

Once they were all seated around the kitchen table, they got right down to business.

Maxi announced. 'The treasure is buried in the salvage yard over by Fiddle Fern where the old sawmill used to be.'

They all cheered at the news.

'Don't get too excited,' Maxi butted in. 'We still have to find it... and get it out of there without the Aechmea brothers being any the wiser.'

'Where on earth,' Ida asked, 'did they get the name, Aechmea?'

'Their father, Ramone Aechmea grew up on a cattle ranch in South Africa, so that's where the weirdo name comes from,' Maxi said, and he offered everyone a cigarette. They all accepted. 'Nora remembers when the sawmill was up and running sometime back in the seventies.'

'What brought a South African to Ireland in the first place?' Ella asked as she filled the kettle. 'Wasn't South Africa booming in those days?'

'According to Nora,' Maxi replied, 'Ramone was a bit of a boyo when it came to the women. Seemingly he was caught cheating with his wife's best friend and her husband went looking to kill him. Ramone didn't want to be hacked up with a machete, so he split.'

'I guess he picked Ireland to put as much distance between him and the machete as possible,' Debbie joked. 'Can't say I blame him.'

'He married an Irish woman, and they had two boys together,' Maxi said as he held up his mug to the spout of the teapot. 'It didn't take long before our man Ramone strayed from his Irish nest.'

'The horny bastard,' Ida remarked.

'He had an affair with some other woman, but this time, he was caught in the act,' Maxi said, slapping the table with his open palm. Everybody jumped in their seats. 'The husband, who was a big burly Cavan man, beat Mr. Ramone Aechmea within an inch of his life. He was taken to hospital, but four days later, he died.'

'Wow,' Ella gasped, 'that's a horror show.'

'Like father, like son,' Debbie exclaimed.

'What do you mean?' Ida asked as she tugged at the elastic band on her eyepatch with her hooked finger.

'The Aechmea brothers are just like their father,' Debbie explained. 'They can't keep their dicks in their pants.'

'Biscuit?' Ella offered. She hovered the plate in front of Debbie.

'I know I shouldn't,' Debbie said as she reached for her third chocolate biscuit. 'Where was I?' she asked while her taste buds held her captive momentarily. 'Oh yeah,' she uttered. 'Daniel, the older one,' she continued, 'married one of the Kavanagh girls, and Ritchie married her sister. Neither one of the brothers was happy with just one of the sisters, so each brother banged the other sister.' Debbie paused for a moment to allow the insanity of the situation to sink in. 'Now the brothers are divorced and consequently hate the sight of each other. The two sisters hate one another, and they hate the two brothers. Some setup, huh?'

'That's some carry-on,' Ella remarked. 'A lot of hate being bandied about.'

'Plus, here's the kicker,' Debbie continued. 'They both work together in the one scrapyard.'

'They don't work together,' Maxi corrected. 'The yard is split in two. Most people who go down there don't have a clue there's two separate businesses operating on the one property. Get this,' he said with raised eyebrows. 'They even share the one entranceway. You can't make this shit up.'

'They're not so good at sharing,' Ida joked. 'Look what happened when they shared their wives.'

'The atmosphere,' Ella proposed, 'must be fairly toxic down in that yard with all that hatred buzzing about. It has to spill over onto the customers.'

'I'd say,' Ida jumped in. 'I remember being down there one time looking to buy a headboard for my bed. I was dealing with the older one, Daniel, in his part of the property, when a tractor tyre, engulfed in flames, came careering into the yard. It was deliberately set on fire by Ritchie and aimed at the showroom door.'

'You're kidding,' Ella exclaimed. 'No way!'

'Cross my heart,' Ida assured. 'Only for there was a fire extinguisher close by, I'd say the whole place would have gone up.'

'These people are psychopaths,' Ella concluded.

'Wait until you hear,' Maxi said as he listed off some more maniacal behaviour. 'They've slashed each other's tyres, sabotaged each other's deliveries and even frightened customers away by fighting one another in the yard. And what's more,' he said, reaching across the table for a biscuit. 'The police are up and down to that yard more times than a Ritalin kid on a pogo-stick. The hostility between them is so bad, there's a filing cabinet down in the police station devoted exclusively to the Aechmea brothers.'

Maxi got up from the table and positioned himself next to the whiteboard that he brought with him from his own house. He wrote on the board as he spoke.

'Now that we know who we're dealing with, the first thing we must do is case the joint.'

'We could do a fly-over,' Ida suggested. 'Sebastian could take us all on an aerial reconnaissance mission. I think that would be fun.'

'For fuck sake, Ida, you and your toff boyfriend,' Debbie snarled. 'Don't ye think he'll want to know why we need to fly over a fucking scrapyard? We don't need anyone else knowing about the treasure.'

'Relax Debbie,' Maxi interjected to defuse the tension. 'All ideas are entertained. I'm afraid, Ida,' he returned to the table to place his hand on her shoulder, 'we would only get a vague idea from the sky, so no fly-over.'

Turning his attention to the group. 'What we need are *boots* on the ground.'

'Copy that, LT,' Ella replied, mimicking a manly voice. 'We need to insert Alpha company at eighteen hundred hours for recon.'

'Rodger that, Corporal Hickey.' Maxi saluted.

'How come I only get to be a Corporal?' Ella whined.

'Ella, you can be anything you want,' Maxi insisted as he attempted openly to win back her favour over his callous reaction to Georgina's degenerate demand. 'Pick a rank. Any rank.' Everybody laughed.

'Commander in Chief of the Universe,' Ella replied. She laughed out loud, signalling to Maxi all was forgiven.

'I see.' He smiled back at her. 'You want the very top spot on the totem pole.' He paused for a moment as if to evaluate her credentials. 'You know what, it's about time we had a woman in charge of the cosmos, and who better than... Commander Hickey.'

Everybody clapped and cheered.

'All right, settle down.' Maxi's tone changed. 'It might be no harm to treat this treasure hunt like a military operation with the same regard for discipline and timing as the army. Hopefully, there's a lot of money at stake here so let us use every means at our disposal to make this mission a success. Can I get an Oorah?'

'Oorah.'

'How are we going to get intel on the salvage yard?' Maxi allowed his question to hang in the air for a moment. 'We know we can't just go down there and start pacing out the coordinates of the map without arousing suspicion. Remember, the brother's own the property, so both of them will want their share of what's in the ground. They must be kept in the dark, no matter what. For this mission to be a success, we have to get in there somehow, locate the treasure, dig it up and get it out of there... undetected. Any ideas?'

Maxi stared intently at each of the women not only for answers but to inadvertently check their resolve. Unable to withhold his surprise any longer. 'I have a confession to make,' he divulged. 'Last night, I drove over to Fiddle Fern to get a feel for the place. It seems the two brothers have something in common besides their taste in women. They both share a penchant for pissing off staff. There was a 'help wanted' sign on the front gate of the property, and by the looks of it, it's been there a while. But guess what? It's not there anymore.'

'I don't get it,' Ida inquired, twisting a strand of her bottled blond hair around her manicured index finger. 'What does that sign have to do with us and the treasure?'

'Oh my God, Maxi... you didn't,' Ella shouted. 'You did,' she screamed. 'You got the job!'

'Correct. You are now looking at the new 'go-for' for Daniel Aechmea salvage yard.'

He took one of his customary bows while the girls applauded and gave him a standing ovation. Ella threw in a few 'wolf-whistles' to macho things up a little. After a moment, they settled back into their seats, giggling and mumbling to each other.

Ida asked, 'What if the treasure is buried on Ritchie's section?'

'I brought the map with me,' Maxi told the group. 'When I compared it to the layout of the buildings on the property, it was easy enough to figure out the whereabouts of the red x. There's no doubt in my mind that the treasure is buried on Daniel's portion of the property.'

'Oh, my God,' Ella squealed. 'I'm so excited I could wet myself.'

'Easy Ella,' Maxi cautioned. 'I'll personally hose you down... in Dom Perignon, when we find the treasure.'

'Deal.' She cheered.

Maxi continued. 'I called the number on the sign. A man by the name of John Windsor Junior answered. Anyone know him?'

Head shakes all round.

'Nobody knows much about him,' Debbie answered for the group. 'Seemingly, he went through a nasty divorce a long time ago, and he has kept much to himself ever since.'

'I introduced myself and asked about the job,' he said as he accepted a lit cigarette from Ida. 'This Windsor guy rattled on about the hours, the pay and all that jazz, but it went in one ear and out the other. All I know is, I start Monday. He's even going to pick me up at my house on Monday morning to drive me to work.'

'Brilliant.' Debbie cheered.

'So, we've got boots on the ground already,' Ella said, nodding her approval. 'There's no doubt, Maxi Dillon, but you are a sly one. We're halfway to the treasure already,' she added.

They all clapped their hands and cheered.

'Now that we have a foot in the door, let's plan our next step.' Maxi returned to his chair by the kitchen table and sat next to Ella. He smiled at her and she smiled back. That treasure hunting quartet spent the next the next thirty minutes ruminating. Cigarette smoke filled the void above the kitchen table, the heated exhaust from the brain-storming below. Maxi returned to the whiteboard and wrote: Calamity.

'We need something to draw attention away from the objective. Usually, people step back when there is a calamity to allow the person in charge to dictate the protocol. For instance, in the event of a fire, we follow the instructions of the fire-chief unequivocally. People blindly obey the person who wears the corresponding uniform to whatever calamity occurs.'

'That's all very well,' Ella remarked, 'but which one of us is going to be able to keep it together in that uniform while Daniel is giving us the one-over? I know it's not me.'

'Me neither,' Debbie agreed.

'I think none of us will be able to wear that uniform and be convincing,' Ida affirmed. 'It's a small town. Everybody knows everybody... at least to recognise,' she insisted. 'We need a stranger to wear that uniform.'

'Oh great, here we go again,' Debbie moaned. 'Ida wants to give the treasure to every Tom, Dick and Harry even before we find it.'

'Not at all,' Ida retorted. 'We *hire* a complete stranger, but we say nothing about the treasure.' Ida was obviously a little unnerved by the many liberties she took in that one sentence.

'A stranger certainly eliminates the likelihood of any recognition,' Maxi offered in her defence. God knows Ida's remark needed a champion to give it legs. 'I can't remember the last time I recognized a stranger, do you?' he said sarcastically.

'Ida, do you know any strangers?' Debbie sneered.

'Keep this shit up and you'll be one,' Ida confirmed.

'Easy, you two,' Ella snapped. 'Let's bury the hatchet, at least until we find the treasure. Okay.'

'Okay,' the two women moaned.

'What Ida meant to say is that,' Ella said, winking across the table at Ida, '...we need an actor or maybe two actors to play the part of the uniform!'

'Exactly,' Ida confirmed with a nod, jubilant that her contentious remark had been laid to rest.

'Where do we get one of them, you might ask?' Ella posed the question but immediately supplied the answer. 'At a drama class, that's where.'

'Very good,' Maxi offered. 'However, you do realise these actors of yours must be plucked from some other drama class besides the one over here in Ballydecuddle.'

'Duh... really,' Ella replied, making a funny face.

'Stating the obvious, huh.' Maxi bowed his head in shame.

'I'll take care of the actors,' Ella volunteered. 'The person who runs the drama class over in Moanamora is a good friend of mine. We went to school together. I'd say that's far enough away that whoever I get won't be recognized by Daniel.'

'Sounds good,' Maxi applauded. 'Let's get it done.' He pounded the table to conclude the meeting.

Ella planted a bottle of red wine on the table and signalled to Ida to open it while she went to retrieve the wine glasses from the cabinet. When she returned, she emptied the contents into the four glasses.

'A toast to Maxi.' They all raised their glasses. 'Bravo.'

'Now, while we're at it,' Maxi insisted, 'let us toast to the success of this mission.'

'Oorah.'

He was pleased with the perfect toast. They were already working as a platoon, and he knew if they could maintain that mindset throughout the whole operation, their chance of success would increase considerably. He smiled to himself with his glass raised high.

Chapter 8.

Even though the two o'clock debate was cancelled, several old ladies still showed up to the house in the hope the notification of the cancellation was incorrect, and the two o'clock debate would go ahead as planned. Maxi was chuffed by their enthusiasm, but he needed to scatter them like crows from the front stoop before Rory McGregor - the mental health nurse - came calling. In order to vocally joust with the Highlander again, he decided his best offensive strategy would be to curtail all unnecessary discourse outside the meeting itself.

Nora's focus was elsewhere. She was infuriated by the audacity of this Scottish man to dare impersonate a nurse. As far as she was concerned, women and only women were entitled to occupy that role. Maxi attempted on a number of occasions during the week to enlighten her as to the ways of the modern world.

'It's commonplace, Mother, for a man to be a nurse these days,' he assured.

'That's a load of cod's wallop,' Nora insisted. 'He's a pervert. You know it and I know it. All he's going to want to do is look up my skirt.'

A little after two o'clock, a black, dented Ford Fiesta, with one of its side mirrors clinging from its colourful entrails, pulled into the driveway, and after a number of foiled attempts to park next to Nora's car, it finally came to rest. Maxi studied Rory McGregor's arrival through the living room window, and so far, he wasn't scoring any points. Eventually, a tall, skinny man in a wrinkled grey suit began unravelling himself from the front seat. Secured firmly to his head with a robust leather strap, was one of those furry Trapper hats, likely found on Davey Crocket's hat rack. He carried a worn-out leather briefcase with the corners frayed so much, the metal bracing beneath the fabric was beginning to show. Such excessive wear and tear suggested Rory McGregor was at this *mental* racket for quite some time. Truth be known, that very same briefcase, only six weeks earlier, contained sales dockets for kitty litter trays produced by a company called – *Purring Potties ltd.*

Maxi invited the ex-kitty litter salesman-mental health nurse in and introduced him to Nora. She sized him up like a gazelle in the Serengeti and began to salivate like a hungry lioness about to pounce on her dinner. Rory mistook her spittle to be dementia-driven drool. Once seated comfortably on the couch next to Nora's armchair, he removed the furry beast from atop his bald head. The imprint of the strap that held his hat in place remained embedded in the sides of his face for the duration of the meeting. Inspired by Nora's drool, Rory took off on a rant about dementia, and like a donkey with a thistle up its ass, he kept going on and on. Neither one of them understood a single word the man was saying. His incomprehensible spiel soon became identical to elevator music and quickly dissolved into the background. Nora fell fast asleep with her mouth wide open. Her dentures clacked together, recreating that clickety-clack sound of the castanets when flamenco dancers are let loose on the dance floor.

Since Rory McGregor was a one-way street with his guttural harangue, Maxi was freed up to brood. He found himself deliberating over his future home in New York City... The one he was going to buy with the treasure money. Would he opt for a closed community in Scarsdale? Maybe a brownstone in Manhattan? If he got a place in Montauk, would a six-car garage be sufficient to cater to his lust for automobiles?

'Decisions, decisions... but that's to be expected,' he mused, 'when you have a shitload of moola.'

His phone rang, obliterating his dwam. It was Ella on the caller ID. Maxi looked to be excused, but there was no point. Rory McGregor seemed to be in a trance with his eyes slammed shut, as spittle spat from his mouth, like the bubbles from a boiling pot. Maxi went into the hallway to take the call. Nora continued snoring to the beat of her clacking teeth.

'Hi Ella.'

'Hi Maxi - Great news!'

'Go on.'

'Last night, I sat through a play in the theatre over in Moanamora. Remember I told you about the friend of mine who runs the place? I called her just after our meeting and she invited me over to see a show. Anyway, I got the two actors we need to play the parts of the County Council workers.'

'Well done, Ella. Tell me more.'

'These two beauties were acting in this play... what was it called?' There was a long pause on the phone while Ella experimented with various sounds to trigger her memory.

'The... something... rise of the... something.'

'The... sunrise of... the something.'

'Ah fuck it, it's not worth remembering. I think my mind repressed the name to protect it from any more brain damage. I'd safely say the worst experience since my "hammer-toe" operation last year.'

'That bad, huh?' Maxi sighed.

'And some,' she continued. 'These two beauties were in one scene together where this lad with the big gut was laid out in a hospital bed with an IV in his arm and both legs suspended in that traction thing-a-ma-gig. He had a bloodied bandage about his head and his two eyes were painted black. Now I mean painted black as pitch. The make-up artist must have been a Goth. He looked like a Panda bear in labour. I nearly wet myself. Then the big lad came on stage, in plain clothes, and sauntered over to the bed. We, the audience, had no idea who this guy was supposed to be. This is when I knew we had found our Laurence Olivier.

'Anyway, he takes out a notepad from the inside pocket of his overcoat and sits down on the chair next to the panda bear. The sweat was dripping off him like a hooker in a confessional. There is a long awkward silence while he searches frantically for a pen. The audience begins to shuffle about uncomfortably in their seats. Not a word is exchanged yet. At last, he finds the pen and begins to doodle in his notepad.'

'Tell me, Mr. Rasher, in your own words exactly what happened.'

'It's Rashad,' a mumbled correction from the mummified Panda. 'I was deliberately run over in Dunne's Store car-park, by a racist bastard.'

'The audience did its' best to contain itself, but a few pockets of hysterics broke out here and there, yours truly being one of the culprits.'

'Sorry... Mr. Raison, you say a racist bastard ran over you. Is that correct?'

'My name is Rashad,' an angry mumble from behind the bandage. 'Yes, that's correct, and then the racist bastard reversed over me and ran over me again.'

'Was he driving a car?'

'No - a Sherman tank - you moron.'

'Now, now, Mr. Randal, there's no need for name-calling.'

'I wish you would call me by my name - Rashad.'

'Excuse me sir, but it should be obvious to you at this stage that I don't speak Hindi.'

'Now,' the big fellow continued, 'did ye happen to get the make and model of the car that ran you over?'

'No... because I was under the fucking car, but I can give you a vivid description of the chassis.'

'What makes you think he was a racist bastard?'

'He kept shouting, go back to Pakistan, ye wog prick.'

'Whereabouts in Pakistan are you from?'

'I'm from Sandymount in Dublin, you... racist bastard.'

'These two boys brought the house down with laughter. They were so deadpan with their lines that they pumped up the humour beyond what the paranoid Pakistani playwright - with the big chip on his shoulder - had intended.

'The next two hours and we were right back to root canal. Anyway, I hooked up with the two boys after the show. I think they will prove to be very convincing County Council workers. I told them the story about you and the play you wrote. They were all ears, especially when I mentioned the money.'

'Perfect,' Maxi commended. 'I knew I could rely on you, Ella. What time did you tell these guys to come to the house?'

'Tomorrow morning, between ten and eleven,' Ella chirped excitedly. 'Let me know how you get on.'

Maxi returned to the living room with the rudiments of a plan beginning to hatch in his mind. One look at Rory - who was still rattling away in Arabic or Swahili or whatever - and he decided he'd had enough.

'Right, Mr. McGregor,' Maxi interrupted his soliloquy. 'It's time to pack up and split.'

Rory didn't seem at all perturbed by his eviction. He simply got up, replaced the furry hat on his head, and securing it tightly in the off chance of gale force winds, he headed for the front door. Maxi herded him out onto the stoop and over to his car.

'Delete my mother's name from your playlist,' Maxi instructed. 'You won't *ever* be coming back this way again.'

Rory McGregor made several attempts to reverse his car into the road. Now Maxi got the opportunity to inspect the clinging mirror up close and personal. Since there was no sign of any damage to the mirror's housing, a collision was ruled out as the cause. It could have been the result of a girlfriend's scorn, but he knew it had to have been some misdiagnosed mental patient who was obliged to forfeit an hour of his life listening to this man's gibberish. While he was there, he was tempted to rip off the other mirror, but this time instead of leaving it dangle, he'd yank out the guts as well. After some careful deliberation, he decided not to. He didn't want to deprive the next, more deserving patient the opportunity to vent.

Chapter 9.

While Maxi was juggling his mother's needs along with the concerns of five other geriatrics, pouring tea from a large pewter kettle and serving up thick slices of Black Forest gateau, the doorbell rang. He stole a peek out the front window. A blue pickup truck was parked in the driveway. He couldn't help but notice the sign on the hood of the truck that read 'Happy Jack' in big, black, bold lettering on a transparent, Perspex background. He was pleasantly surprised by what he saw. His brain began immediately to conjure up the jubilant feelings that the state of happiness inspires. By the time he answered the door, he had a big, doozy smile on his face that was a little too excessive - even to greet the Dalai Lama.

Two big men in their late forties crowded the top step of the stoop – the two actors that Ella commandeered from the play. One had an enormous beer belly that he carried about in out-stretched arms like a delivery man about to drop off a washing machine. He wondered how skin could stretch that far. The other was built like a monolithic pillar, muscles wrapped in taut sinews with rebar replacing the bones. This man was all decked out in denim and plaid, and he wore his rope-like veins on the outside of his body. His brow had deep, irregular lines like the scribbles made by some frustrated four-year-old who couldn't quite nail the mountain range he was attempting to draw. The beer belly wore a shabby blue, pin-striped suit and a black, xxx-large t-shirt under the jacket that failed miserably to conceal his navel. It peeped out like a periscope buried in blubber.

Maxi tugged whom he considered to be Happy Jack by the sleeve, and reeling him into the hallway with the other big man in tow, he pointed to a door at the end of the corridor. He brought his index finger to his lips to command silence and gave each a separate nod, like a Sergeant Major directing his men on the battlefield to cautiously move forward under fire. He wanted to instil discipline and stealth from the get-go, plus he didn't want Nora to know he had company. Of course, all she had to do was look out the window and she'd see the pickup truck.

'Right lads,' he whispered, 'off to the back room with ye. I'll be along as soon as I get this lot sorted.' He pointed at the mumblings coming from the living room. 'I'm taking care of my mother,' he muttered. 'And a bunch of other mothers, too, it seems.'

The two men froze for a moment, not really knowing how to react to his remark. Once they got the nod, they did as they were bid and disappeared down the corridor and into the back room. Maxi assumed Happy Jack was the beer belly with the big smile. He was wrong. The one with the angry scowl was *Happy* Jack. He returned to the living room to ensure that Nora and her friends were all set up with full cups of tea and within easy reach of the chocolate biscuits and sugary buns. All he needed to do then was spark the philosophical debate that was scheduled for that time and make a profound statement to capture the attention of the cackling hens that sat around the coffee table.

'There is no such thing as a Universal Generalisation,' he announced, writing in black marker on the white notice board as he spoke. He turned to face the group and gauge their reaction.

'All dogs have four legs! Is this a universal generalisation?'

The coffee table fell completely silent for a moment until slowly but surely, the rusty cogs in the ancient skulls that showed up for the debate began to clang 'n clatter into action, and then the chatter commenced. Niamh Conway was first out of the blocks with her declaration.

'*Tripod* is a Shih Tzu that lost his hind leg in a freak accident. Last time I looked, *Tripod* is still a Shih Tzu even though he only has three legs. So, to be a dog, you don't have to have four legs.'

Maxi knew from the reaction at the table that he had bought a substantial increment of time - at least an hour - with that debate. He quietly retreated from the living room and down the corridor to the back room. That back room was his late father's retreat – a no-go zone for Maxi and his siblings when he was growing up. It's ironic, he thought, how his father swopped out that little room for one just like it in the *Big House*. He remembered talking about strangers to the girls during the week, and it struck him, as he stood by that door, that his father was one to him. Maxi didn't even know the colour of his father's eyes. He was only seven years old when his dad went to jail. Andy, his older brother, was ten years older than him, and his older sister, Joanie, was eight years older. They were basically strangers to him as well. By the time he was ten years old, it was only Nora and himself living in the house, and now twenty-five years later... it's Nora and himself again. As he entered the room, he wondered, did his brother or sister ever think about him and their mom and how the two of them were getting on together.

'Why would they?' he thought. *'They have their own big jobs and their own families to worry about. Let the loser take care of Mom.'*

The two big men sat on an old leather couch that clashed with the previous owner's curtains. Freddy Boom-boom – the man with the big beer belly – stretched his legs out on the green shed door that was supported by two plastic milk crates, but because its doorknob was still intact, it seemed reluctant to accept its new role as a coffee table. He continually caressed his beer belly in big circular motions like he was providing assurance to some strange beast in that enormous womb that his love was unconditional. His navel, which was on permanent display, seemed to wink in delight at the ceiling.

Happy Jack sat bolt upright next to him with a frown on his face that contradicted his moniker. Since this man had all the appearance of a malcontent, Maxi wondered about the origin of the sign on his truck. He guessed the truck in the driveway was over ten years old, so a lot of shit could have hit the fan in the meantime. Was this sign an antonym? In other words, was this miserable bastard trying to be smart with the world, or was he, in fact, happy at some point, and something dismal occurred in the interim to sour his deportment? Of course, there was the remote possibility that this angry Jack bought the truck second-hand from some real *'Happy Jack'* who just happened to share the same first name. Maxi only just met the man, and he already thought it was time for Jack to drop the *Happy*, but he was a little leery about how this six-foot-six monster of a man would react.

'Here's the news,' Maxi announced the moment he entered the office. 'I'm going to turn you two individuals into walking, talking, breathing County Council workers.'

He stood completely still to allow the two men to process his statement. He felt he had injected just enough *'oomph'* into his opening remark to grab their unbridled attention and have them salivating for more. He gripped the chair by the little table, spun it around on one leg and straddled it like he was riding a pony. He studied the men carefully. He didn't quite get the reaction he was expecting. Freddy Boom-boom looked surprised. Happy Jack looked angry.

'The play that you wrote is all about the Ballydecuddle County Council?' Boom-boom announced with a glint in his eye as if he had just solved some impossible equation in Neuro-physics. Then after a slight interval, he shouted, 'Boom, boom.' Then he pounded the green door twice in quick succession with his clenched fist to punctuate each 'boom'. Maxi was a little startled by his antics. No further mystery with regards to Freddy's nickname. This irritating, table banging Boom-Boom sequence accompanied any statement that Freddy Boom-boom deemed remarkable. Happy Jack wasn't animated in the least. He just sat there like a steel column.

Ella convinced them the night before that Maxi had written a play and it would prove to be the ideal podium for both of them to exhibit their true potential to the world stage. They were a little apprehensive at first, but when the sum of five hundred euros each was mentioned, they were sold.

'Well,' Maxi sighed, 'it's not really a play.' He got up and paced the small room with his hands behind his back as he searched for a credible explanation. 'It's more a scripted performance.'

Not a sound from behind the coffee table. These two men needed further clarification. They had been brought there under false pretences, and now they were beginning to feel slighted.

'It's not a play,' Happy Jack barked.

'No, it's not a play,' Maxi acknowledged shaking his head from side to side.

'What's a scripted performance?' Boom-boom inquired sarcastically.

'Okay, let me level with ye guys.'

'I wish you would,' Boom-boom groaned.

Maxi returned to his chair, and plucking a cigarette from the pack, he tapped the tobacco end repeatedly on the coffee table. All eyes focused on the cigarette tip.

'You two guys are going to pretend to be County Council workers. I have a script here already prepared for you.'

He stood up again and went over to the little table and retrieved two identical folders from the side drawer beneath. He waved them in the air above his head, and with a big smile on his face, he presented each confused man with a copy. While they familiarised themselves with the content, he lit his cigarette.

'This will be the greatest performance of your lives,' he announced like a ringmaster in the circus pumping up the audience before the lion act. 'Your job is to convince one man that you have been sent by the County Council to recover a *torpedo* which is a type of hydraulic probe that some idiot engineer from the town hall, misdirected and somehow ended up buried on this man's property.'

Sitting down in the rickety chair and without encouraging a response, he continued his prepared monologue.

'This man in the office will not be easily fooled.' Maxi pointed to the folders. 'You must recite the script verbatim, word for word, line for line, and remain in character for the duration. If you drop your guard even for an instance, it's curtains and the show is over.'

He chose his words carefully. These two men were unaware that they were being played. Maxi was acting out his role - in a one-man show - to persuade them to act out there's in his up-and-coming production. He studied them both carefully to weigh up in his mind whether or not all the 'smoke and mirrors' were having the desired effect. So far, so good, he decided.

'I can assure you this man will not be pleased with the inconvenience of having his property dug up. It is imperative that you guys come across as professionals, with an air of confidence but not cocky, mind you.' Maxi took a pull of his cigarette.

'Contained in this folder you will also find the appropriate...'

Boom-boom suddenly recoiled his legs with the surprising agility of an acrobat and planted them firmly on the floor.

'Hold your horses. Let me get this straight,' he gasped. 'This is not a play.'

He clenched his fist and pounded the table several times with his annoying *Boom-boom* accompaniment. 'We must learn our lines which are in these folders. We have to act like we are County Council workers and convince this bloke that we have to recover a bomb that's buried somewhere on his property.'

'It's not a bomb,' Maxi corrected. 'It's a probe. Torpedo is just a name they call it.'

'Whatever,' Boom-boom snapped, 'This probe thing must be very important if you have to go to all this trouble and expense to get it back. By the way,' he raised his voice, 'we're actors, not manual labourers.'

'Do we have many lines to learn?' Happy Jack blurted out, the frown suddenly morphing into what he himself considered to be representative of a concerned look. Unfortunately, he failed. He looked furious now that he had contorted the frown, and it took a moment for Maxi, who leaned back in terror, to realise that Happy Jack had only a limited number of expressions in his repertoire, anger and fury being the only ones represented thus far. He studied Happy Jack for a moment and saw the furious expression retreat to a frown. He regained his composure. He certainly didn't want that man to leap over the green door and punch him in the head.

'You don't have to learn any lines. You just have to read from the folder. Okay, Jack?'

'It's *Happy* Jack,' he corrected.

'Sorry *Happy* Jack,' Maxi replied. He didn't want to lose his flow of thought but gnawing away in the back of his mind, the origin of *Happy* began to scratch away at his brain like the bent spoon Andy Dufresne used to escape his cell in the '*Shawshank Redemption*.'

'You'll only be required to answer 'yes' or 'no' to the few questions you may be asked.'

'That's a relief,' Happy Jack said, 'my memory is not what it used to be and even now I forget, was it ever any good.'

Maxi concluded with Happy Jack, and refocusing his attention on Boom-boom, he continued his explanation.

'Yes, that probe is an expensive piece of equipment. The top brass in the County Council really needs to get it back. As regards manual labour, I'm sure you're well aware, County Council workers are notorious for breastfeeding the shovel, so fear not on the work front, I'll be doing all the digging. For your part in this little saga, you'll each get two hundred euros now and another instalment of three hundred euros each when the probe is retrieved. Any questions?'

The small room fell silent for several moments. The two big men huddled together on the couch and began to mumble to each other as they considered Maxi's proposition.

Freddy Boom-boom inquired, 'Why doesn't the County Council get the eejit who lost the probe in the first place to recover it for them?' His navel seemed to suck on his middle finger like a baby's pacifier.

'Good question.' Maxi gulped. 'The fact is the County Council is embarrassed over this whole affair. They don't want any more bad press, especially so soon after the botched job they did with the so-called 'non-slip' tiles in the public pool. Besides having to close it down for three months, compensation payments to the injured parties went through the roof. So, you see how they want to keep this little mishap hush hush. The deputy mayor, Harry Houlihan, approached me to see if I might be able to make this little incident go away. He made me an offer. I accepted. Now that's it in a nutshell. So, are you with me?'

'I don't think so?' Boom-boom hissed. 'Everybody is going through an awful lot of trouble to recover this probe thing. The mayor is involved for God's sake! The reputation of the County Council aside, there's something fishy going on here. I can't quite put my finger on it, and I dare say I don't care to, but I know one thing, we're coming in at the shallow end where the money is concerned. I know you're not doing this for the good of your health, so I think five hundred euros now and another thousand euros when the job is done.'

Maxi stole a quick look at Happy Jack, who was busy trying out some other expression, but since it was in its early stages, no one could see any difference except that his eyebrows were raised

considerably. He was a little taken aback by Boom-boom's rebuttal.
He certainly didn't see that coming.

'Easy Tonto,' Maxi blurted in a bid to buy time.

He suddenly found himself in an unexpected dilemma. On the
one hand, he didn't want to be seen to roll over so easily; on the
other, he didn't want to lose these two. He decided to pull a Texas
Hold 'em poker move on them and move *all-in*.

'How about you and Happy Jack go back to Moanamora and
forget all about this little play?' Maxi stood up and pointed to the
door with one hand while he welcomed the folders with the other.

'I thought,' Happy Jack snarled, 'it wasn't a play.'

'It's not a play.' Maxi sighed as he retrieved the folder from
Happy Jack.' Just as he reached for Boom-boom's folder.

'How about three hundred now and five hundred when you
get your stupid probe thing-a-ma-gig?' Boom-boom counteroffered,
retaining his folder which he had placed, hands free, on top of his big
belly.

Another interval elapsed in complete silence while the
compulsory stand-off ran down the clock.

Maxi relented. 'You're on.' He smiled and shook their hands to
clinch the deal.

'Okay,' said Maxi, 'here's the plan. I want you two guys to
familiarize yourselves with the content of these folders. Come back
here tomorrow evening after six and we'll do a dry run. Actually, a
dress rehearsal is the more accurate theatrical term. Ella - the lady
who recruited you - will be along tomorrow evening as well.'

As Maxi handed over the money to each of the men,
Boom-boom inquired, 'How long do we have to rehearse before the
real thing?'

'Another good question.' Maxi pointed at Boom-boom with his
ridged index finger, and with the same finger held upright, he
answered, 'One week from today.'

'It's not enough time,' Happy Jack whined like a puppy dog with its first glimpse at the moon.

'For fuck sake, we're not doing Hamlet,' Maxi shrieked. 'Look, relax,' he changed his tone. 'I'm sorry for shouting, but you're blowing this little performance out of all proportion. All you need to do is read the appropriate response to whatever question is asked. Everything you need to know is in these folders. You don't have to learn anything by heart. You'll have these folders with you on the day of the big performance.' He dared pat Happy Jack on his big back.

'After a week of practice - believe you me - you will both think that you actually do work for the County Council.'

'All right, whatever you say,' Boom-boom replied. 'It's your money.' He herded Happy Jack along the corridor to the front door.

'See you tomorrow at six,' Maxi shouted after them as he stood in the doorway waving 'good bye.'

He returned to a heated debate in the living room with Nora at the helm, demonstrating her philosophical prowess over the fledglings who had only just discovered the *drug*.

'Mary... there is always an exception to the rule, and that's all there is to it,' Nora concluded. She sat back in her recliner after delivering a knock-out punch.

'I disagree,' Mary mumbled with a mouthful of cake in her gob. 'One can categorically state, without reproach, that water always flows downhill. No matter where you are in the world, water obeys the law of gravity. This is one universal generalisation that cannot be contested.'

Mary, too, sat back in her chair. She folded her arms, and with the defiant expression of a champion peeping through her many wrinkled layers of make-up, she began to prematurely revel in the spoils of victory.

'Well done, Mary,' Dolly, her bosom buddy, remarked, clapping her hands together to incite an applause. The other two attendees, who were Nora's allies, didn't budge. One look at Nora, and they knew something was amiss.

Mary's sly smirk made its way across the coffee table to end up on Dolly's wrinkled puss. Both the victor and her ally now stared impatiently at Nora, willing her to wave the white flag.

'Indeed, ladies, water flows downhill.' Nora paused to allow her combatants to sink a little deeper in the mud. 'However, water doesn't *always* flow downhill.'

A collective groan exuded from the coffee table, likened only to frightened animals in an abattoir.

'It is a fact that water is governed by the law of gravity. That said, water is one of the few elements that can either be a solid, a liquid or a gas. Ice, as we are all very well aware, is its solid state. Ice plays by a different set of rules. It defies gravity. Just look at a stalagmite in your freezer. Ice can back-peddle up an incline when it meets an obstruction or when its path of least resistance is curtailed. So, ladies, water doesn't always flow downhill. Your attempt, Mary, at a universal generalisation, if you'll pardon the pun, doesn't hold water.'

Nora stood up and underlined the statement on the board.

'There is no such thing as a Universal Generalisation,' she announced.

'Surely there must be one instance,' Mary pleaded to the Heavens, 'where a Universal Generalisation occurs? Think, Dolly, for feck sake.'

Eventually, Dolly proudly proclaimed. 'The sun always rises in the east.'

'My God Dolly, you found one,' Mary responded excitedly. 'Good girl yourself. The sun certainly always rises in the east.'

She reached across the table in an attempt to high-five Dolly, who unfortunately failed to recognize her intention. Dolly was a spinster, and with no exposure to off-spring, she wasn't privy to the antics of the younger generation. Consequently, Mary almost threw out a disk in her back when she met no resistance in her 'solo' air-slapping venture. She had to reorient herself before continuing. Once the dizzy spell passed, she refocused on Nora.

'Now, Nora Dillon, put that in your pipe and smoke it.'

'Once again,' Nora responded with a mischievous smirk on her face. 'I'm afraid to disappoint you two, but that's not always the case. In the northern hemisphere, the winter sun rises in the southeast, transits the celestial meridian at a low angle in the south, more than forty-three degrees, and then sets in the southwest. By comparison, the winter sun in the southern hemisphere rises in the northeast, peaks out at a low angle in the north, and then sets in the northwest.'

'All men have dicks,' Dolly blurted out in pure desperation.

'All men are dicks,' Mary stated.

'Now, now girls, behave yourselves,' Maxi encouraged as he copped the escalating tension at the coffee table. 'These debates are designed to stimulate your imagination, encourage deductive thought and enrich your lives with a deeper understanding of yourselves and your role in the great order of things. Let's leave a man's anatomy out of it.'

Mary and Dolly, her sidekick, got up out of their seats and approached Nora.

'There's no catching you. Nora Dillon, you were a fierce opponent on the golf course, and now you are proving how equally fierce you are in debate. I look forward to our next encounter.'

They all shook hands, and like military adversaries, they saluted one another, knowing that they would soon face off on the proverbial battlefield in the not too distant future. Maxi was delighted with the success of the debate.

Chapter 10.

The white Ford van that Maxi was expecting pulled up outside his house on Monday morning at exactly seven-thirty a.m. and was swallowed instantly in the pursuing cloud of black smoke. A nanosecond later, there was a loud bang, like the Concord's sonic boom, and he ducked down instinctively, expecting a round to smash through his bedroom window. Twenty-five years in New York City will do that to a man. When he surfaced, the smoke had dissipated and a tall skinny man wearing a Mackintosh overcoat, Wrangler jeans and a bright orange woolly hat cautiously opened the driver's door and got out onto the road. A plume of cigarette smoke escaped with him. Maxi followed the tip of the smoky orange hat along the roof of the van until John Windsor Junior reappeared at the back of the van to reveal his true identity. He was now able to put a face on the phone call but was surprised by how wrong he was with his own preconceived depiction of the man. His first impression elected to label him 'eccentric' until only moments later, he witnessed the brutal manner in which the man extinguished his cigarette. He stomped on it, repeatedly, like he was crushing the skull of an opponent in a life or death altercation. Such excessive force to complete a trivial task promoted him immediately to 'madman' status, instead.

Maxi watched him light another cigarette, and after he scrutinised his immediate surroundings, he leaned against the back doors of the van and slid down until his ass rested on the fender. With all this cloak 'n dagger drama, John Windsor Junior seemed oblivious to the scrutiny he was getting from the second-floor window. He believed his ex-wife hired a hitman to kill him, so he was constantly looking over his shoulder. Fourteen years later and still no hitman, this precautious manoeuvre – unbeknownst to himself – metastasized into an intrinsic component in his body language.

A light rain persisted while the sun jostled with the grey clouds for a spot in the sky. Initially, they toyed with the sun but then decided to shut it down completely. Maxi grabbed his lunch and stuffed it inside his backpack. He threw on his jacket, and as he exited the front door, he waved an exaggerated salute at John Windsor, who stared him down without the slightest acknowledgement.

'Wow, this guy's ice.'

With a meter or two to spare, Maxi slowly raised his right arm with open palm in readiness for a handshake. He noted, since John Windsor's right hand hadn't left his coat pocket since his arrival, there was the possibility it could have been deformed at birth or mangled in an accident, so he prepared his left hand for a handshake... just in case. Feeling a little edgy after the attack on the cigarette stub, he wondered if he should have brought along some trinkets, as the 'paleface' was known to do in the wild-west, to appease this potential savage.

John Windsor stood up and grabbed Maxi's right hand with the ferocity of a conger eel, and pulling him almost into an embrace, he leaned in so that his smoky lips brushed Maxi's deaf ear. Locked together like squabbling moose in that awkward embrace, John Windsor looked left and right and left again to ensure that nobody was listening even though it was quite evident they were alone. Maxi's olfactory glands were bombarded with the eye-watering pungency of stale sweat coupled with the rancid pong of cheap alcohol, cigarettes and strong notes of piss. That foul odour reminded him of the Christian Brothers and their total disregard for bodily hygiene. John Windsor certainly achieved full marks for reincarnating that unforgettable stench. Maxi held his breath while John Windsor leaned once again towards his deaf ear and introduced himself in a deep baritone voice that completely contradicted his feeble deportment.

'I'm John Windsor Junior,' he said. There was a slight pause accompanied by a tightening of his already firm grip. 'You can call me 40%... everybody else does.'

While John Windsor Junior still held Maxi in his grip, he briefed him on the backstory of his moniker. 'I went through a nasty divorce fourteen years ago.'

'Sorry to hear...'

'Don't interrupt,' 40% snapped. 'My ex-wife wants me dead. She hired a hitman to get rid of me. As you may appreciate, I have been unable to devote my entire attention to any particular task or endeavour due to the daunting prospect of a bullet, addressed to me, looming in the background. Therefore 40% of my focus has been repurposed over the past fourteen years to act much like radar and alert me to the presence of the hitman when he, or indeed she, eventually shows up.' He stopped talking and looked over his right shoulder to check for the hitman. 'I'm telling you all this personal stuff so that I can recruit your eyes and ears in my quest for self-preservation.' He released his grip. 'Can I rely on you to finger the hitman, should he show on your watch?' he asked.

'Absolutely 40%... I mean 100%,' Maxi assured, not really sure whether he was being pranked or not. 'Oh, by the way... I'm Maxi Dillon.'

Losing all interest immediately, 40% relinquished his grip and hightailed it to the driver's door of the van - his need for speed overruling his decorum. Maxi seized that opportunity to devour a huge gulp of fresh air like someone who had been submerged in a frozen lake and had just broken through the ice. He felt slighted by being discarded like a spent condom. Short attention span, he pondered, or just pure ignorance as his brain began to recover from oxygen deprivation? He was absolutely flabbergasted. After surprise came anger, then regret and finally sympathy. From what he had seen so far, Maxi decided that 40% must have had some underlying mental issues to account for his peculiar behaviour.

In the meantime, 40% was revving the accelerator like he was at a stop sign next to a muscle car and he wanted to show off what was under the hood. Maxi jumped into the van and buckled up. Black smoke once again enveloped the van, but before it managed to cloak the windscreen; 40% released the clutch and after an agonizing screech of tyres, the van took off down the road like a heat seeking missile. Now the alternative personality of Nicky Lauda sat next to Maxi as the van veered off the main road and onto a narrow country lane with no reduction in speed to navigate the sharp bends and steep declines.

The van's interior was adorned with all sorts of colourful string beads draped haphazardly across the windscreen, over the tops of the doors and across the backs of the seats. Numerous miniature artefacts, with no obvious affiliation to each other, like the position indicators in the game of Monopoly, the top hat, the boot, the ballerina and the double-decker bus, were all indiscriminately secured to the string. This higgledy-piggledy daisy chain of everyday household items initially suggested a harmless childish shrine of sorts but, on closer scrutiny, proposed a more sinister interpretation. Every single item had some sort of minor defect; a teapot without a spout, a ladder with a broken rung, a dog without a tail, etc., so now it seemed that 40% was paying homage to broken stuff like himself.

Maxi was reminded of the interiors of some of the yellow cabs driven by Latinos in NYC, who had everything but a canoe full of coconuts in the cab with them. When you entered the taxi, you felt like you had just wandered in off the street into Carlos Rodrigues's living room. It was a little intimidating to have three generations of the Rodrigues family smiling back at you from photographs pinned to the sun visors. Not to mention the foot-tall statue of the Madonna perched on the dash and the rosary beads swinging from the rear-view mirror. All these Religious impedimenta were inclined to infuse a little doubt in the passenger's mind, whether or not it was himself or his spirit that would complete the journey. Seashells, colourful buttons and shiny stones were glued to every available square inch of the console, while the Hawaiian doll in the grass skirt moved her hips to the rhythm of the salsa music blasting over the quad speakers. And Carlos, without a single word of English, was totally reliant on you to direct him to your destination.

40% found almost every pot-hole in the road which juggled kidneys, paper cups, a pair of binoculars, a microwave oven, a tennis ball, a pair of nylon stockings and an assortment of other knick-knacks.

'I wear them during the winter months,' 40% announced as he furtively snatched at the nylons in mid-air and shoved them behind his seat. Upon reflection, he must have felt the need to qualify his remark. 'Just to keep warm.' He looked over at Maxi, who was glued to the dashboard and oblivious to him and all the items in that tumble dryer. He continued his qualification. 'The soldiers wore them in the trenches in the first world war, that's how I know.'

Maxi held onto the strap above his left shoulder like he was riding 'Halley's Comet' in the rodeo – fifteen hundred pounds of pissed-off bull.

40% kept mumbling, 'Oh dear, oh dear,' over and over to himself.

Maxi kept filling in the blanks in his mind to distract himself from imminent death.

'What could the matter be?' and again, 'What could the matter be?'

He could vividly envisage an MGM horror movie with kids wearing bloodied pyjamas and waving headless dolls about, chanting this very same nursery rhyme. 'Oh dear, what could the matter be?'

This white-knuckled roller coaster ride came to a sudden arrest in front of a pair of old and dilapidated wrought iron gates which were bound together with a bright silver chain. Maxi didn't relinquish his grip on the overhead strap or the handle on the dash. His eyes began to water, not because they didn't blink for the past twenty minutes of utter horror but with joy at the realisation that their 'commute' to work was finally over.

40% shouted, 'Welcome to Eden.'

Just as he was coming to terms with his demise, 40% leaned over, and like a cold war spy, he whispered the numbers 3978 in Maxi's deaf ear. These numbers were relayed in a stealthy manner so no one within earshot might know the combination to the Kingdom... including Maxi. 40% waited for him to jump out of the van and unlock the gates. He didn't budge. 'I'm sorry,' Maxi said excitedly, 'I didn't get that. My hearing is very poor. Would you mind repeating what you just said, but up a notch?'

40% reacted like he'd caught his cock in his zipper. He shook his head violently from side to side and bobbed up and down in his seat. He dislodged the orange woolly hat from his head and ran both hands through his long, grey, greasy hair, mumbling gibberish.

'I am not in the habit of repeating myself, and that's going to change for no man,' 40% retorted, a little louder than necessary. His focus remained on the gates of Eden. 'We have another broken person in our midst... blah, blah, blah.'

While 40% pontificated about all the broken shit in the world, Maxi thanked his lucky stars for getting to work alive. 40% unbuckled his seat belt and jumped from the van. He left the driver's door swinging in his wake. He fumbled with the numbers on the combination lock, and he kept constantly looking over his shoulder for fear of the hit-man. He pried the gates apart and returned to the van with the ousted party twins - solemn and dejected.

The van moved slowly down the steep incline, and as it negotiated the many dips and folds in the unkempt laneway, it assumed the characteristics of a fishing trawler undulating in a choppy sea. Stubbornness between the two feuding Aechmea brothers was the sole cause of such blatant neglect. Neither one would lift a finger to repair the shared entranceway even though they both had the heavy-duty excavating equipment on site to do the job.

Maxi's attention was captivated by the multitude and variety of directional signs that flanked the laneway. The New Jersey Turnpike paled in comparison. In that tug-of-war for clientele, each angry brother tried to overrule the other one's signs with ones of his own. These signs leap-frogged each other all the way to the bottom of the hill. Since each one contradicted the other, instead of being informative, they proved to be nothing more than a display of stupidity.

STAY LEFT
NO LEFT TURN
TURN LEFT NOW
STRAIGHT AHEAD ONLY
PRICES SLASHED – TAKE A LEFT
50% OFF SALE – STRAIGHT AHEAD
BARGAINS TO THE LEFT.
SALE, STRAIGHT AHEAD.

40% stopped the van at another gate and repeated the same actions as before. He got back in the van and drove into the pothole-riddled yard, where he parked behind a garbage container. He pointed at the largest of the few surviving buildings that were peppered haphazardly about the property. 'Meet me over there by that blue door,' he said, and he headed off in haste around the back of the building for a piss. There was no functioning toilet on the premises.

Now that he had a moment alone, Maxi whipped out the map from his backpack and unfolded it on the dashboard. He studied it for a moment and then perused the terrain. He did a quick count on the number of structures and their proximity to each other. His calculations tallied with the symbols on the map. A sly grin crept across his face. He got the confirmation he needed. He was, no doubt, in the vicinity of the red X. He returned the map to its hiding place in the inside pocket of his backpack and then headed for the blue door.

40% fumbled with a huge bunch of keys that only a jailer might carry. Another set of steel doors with a keyed entry lock, then a sprint to a keypad on the far wall where he entered a sequence of numbers to disarm the alarm. Next up, a pair of sliding steel doors that had padlocked latches on both sides. Another frantic search for another key. Finally, two more wrought iron gates, wrapped together with chains and locks to prohibit access to the backyard.

Panting like he'd escaped a lynching, 40% threw himself into his chair in the office and hit the flashing red button on the answering machine to play the messages. Still in the stone age, Maxi mused. There was only one message... some farmer looking for a barn door. 40% took down the details on a slip of paper, and rolling along in his chair on the bare concrete floor, he placed the note on the other identical desk, separated from his by a row of battleship grey filing cabinets. Maxi stood looking out the dirty office window at acres of garden furniture, old lamp posts, ploughs, all sorts of building materials, fountains, pergolas, bar and restaurant fixtures, etc., etc.

He noticed several spots here and there in the small office where the paint was peeling off the walls. Rolling back on itself in tight curls, it afforded the old paint underneath the opportunity to peer into the future. Indelible, square markings on the bare concrete floor gave evidence it was tiled at some stage. It was perfect, Maxi though, for kids with chalk to hop about the floor in a game of hob-scotch. With him being so close to the treasure, he had to resist the urge to hop about himself. A sorry looking electric heater governed by a time-switch dictated the temperature and a lone light bulb suspended from the ceiling, the illumination.

Security cameras scanned the premises and presented a quad-screen visual display of all activity in the yard to a monitor on Daniel Aechmea's desk. This monitor was particularly useful in alerting the office to customers arriving down the hill. 40% had to react instantly when a vehicle appeared on the screen and race out from the office to the bottom of the laneway, flapping his arms as he went, to attract the patron's attention. His job was to lure customers into Daniel's yard, otherwise - regardless of the contradictory signs - that customer would be inclined to drive straight on into the brother's yard instead. Should that ever happen, 40% was guaranteed to be *torn a new asshole* by Daniel.

Speak of the Devil, the instant 40% saw Daniel's grey van at the top of the hill, he jumped up out of his seat and began pacing around the office like some caged animal about to be euthanized. Maxi was a little unnerved by his behaviour. Anxiety built up in the small office, and he could feel his chest compress. He heard the sound of the ignition die, followed by a door slamming. A few seconds later, Dandelion framed himself in the office doorway carrying his laptop under one arm and his lunch box in his hand. He had a copy of the 'Times' newspaper clamped under his other arm and hooked in his middle finger a plastic carrier bag.

Maxi was taken aback by how handsome the man looked. He shouldn't have been surprised, considering the rave reviews Nora gave his father. He had everything going for him – chiselled features, a strong nose and a square jaw. He wore that musketeer-type beard and moustache with the ends curled up. Not many men were able to pull that look off... but he did. His olive complexion took kindly to the sun. He had a slim, athletic-looking body that insinuated a healthy diet and regular exercise. 40% looked like death warmed up beside him. Of the three boxes - tall, dark and handsome - Dandelion could certainly tick the latter two. Unfortunately, he didn't reach the height requirement deemed necessary to tick the tall box. However, he was so conceited, he wore shoes with elevated heels to conquer that box.

Dandelion nodded at 40%, who immediately converted that slight head movement into action. He had to side-step Dandelion in the doorway and make his way across the hall to the small kitchen. 40% filled the kettle with just enough water to approximate three mugs of tea. Any more and he would get a rollicking for squandering electricity. It was startling how frugal this man was! It wasn't like he had to operate under tight margins and costly overheads. He acquired discarded goods from the community for little or next to nothing and in return, crucified his customers with exorbitant fees.

40% was now functioning from the 'neck down'. While he stood like one of the Queen's guards with his full attention devoted to the kettle, Dandelion was focused on Maxi. He stepped into the office and placed his belongings on his desk. The plastic carrier bag, however, fell to the floor with a thud. Maxi nodded back. Both men behaved like wild animals, sniffing and tasting the air in search of weakness and fear. Deductions are drawn from that data and snap decisions will decide their fate.

'You're Maxi Dillon,' Dandelion remarked as he stabbed the air repeatedly with his index finger in the vicinity of Maxi's face. Maxi was just about to respond but was interrupted.

'You were in New York for a long time,' he continued without waiting for an answer, still stabbing the air.

Dandelion turned his back on Maxi and flipped open the screen on his laptop. Once again, Maxi was about to respond but not to a man who hadn't the decency to face him, eyeball to eyeball.

'I'm Daniel Aechmea, as I'm sure you're aware.' He turned his face just enough for his profile to be visible. 'However, most people call me Dan the Lion,' he proudly remarked.

The Aechmea brothers shared their surname with a beautiful South African flower... the *Aechmea* or *Zebra* plant. A previous disgruntled employee, acquainted with this knowledge, christened him 'Dandelion' - obviously leaning towards the weed in the plant world. Daniel Aechmea was delighted with his nickname since his narcissistic personality interpreted Dandelion to mean Dan the Lion, king of the jungle. He took pride in his distinguished pseudonym. The same composer when it came to Richard, his younger brother, opted to remain among the weeds and named him: 'Thistle Dick'.

Dandelion, continuing to hog the limelight, reached down into his carrier bag and retrieved a red building brick. He spun his head around to savour Maxi's reaction as he held the brick in the air.

'What's this?'

Maxi thought, now that the pleasantries are out of the way, quiz time.

'A brick,' he answered without hesitation... deliberately stepping into the trap.

'You're wrong,' Dandelion replied. 'It's a Euro.' He cradled the brick in a loving embrace and then set it down on his desk.

'Would you walk past a Euro if you saw one on the ground? No, you wouldn't. So why would you walk past a brick? Because you don't see what I see. What do I see? I see a night out on the town. I see a holiday in the sun. I see a trip to Vegas, I see...'

Since Maxi's contribution to the conversation was zip, he let Dandelion jabber on while he imagined slapping up four bricks on the counter at his local to pay for his pint of Guinness and the bartender returning from the register with a fistful of pebbles.

'Ah, keep the change.'

Dandelion was now up on his high horse, enforcing Maxi to endure a scrapyard symposium without his consent. He was firing off questions and supplying the answers himself. This was a one-way debate. Pure torture having to endure this asshole massaging his own ego. Thoughts of the treasure persuaded Maxi to grin and bear.

'Enough time wasted,' he concluded, 'We've got work to do. I want you to go with 40%. He'll get you a pick and shovel and show you where to dig.'

All the while he had his back turned to Maxi, and with the slightest motion from the fingers of his right hand, he shooed Maxi away, just like Louis XVI shooed away his own 'piss-boy' once he relieved himself in the piss-bucket, while strolling about the Palace gardens of Versailles.

'Right off ye go,' Dandelion said with the same distain, as if Maxi was gum on his shoe. 'No need to dilly-dally.'

Maxi was being told what to do, for the first time in his life, by the back of a man's head. This took humiliation to a whole new low. He was so mad he had a headache. He wanted to jump on this guy from behind and rip his fucking head off. Besides his hurting head, he also had a bad taste in his mouth. This Dandelion prick churned up the acids in his stomach, and now he was beginning to taste bile in the back of his gullet. He squeezed his fists so hard, his knuckles looked like they might burst out of his skin. He thanked the Heavens above that he was only there for a short spell. As 40% and Maxi headed out the back door and across the muddy trail to the tool shed, neither spoke a word. Of course, yet another padlock on the tool shed door. Suddenly there was a whiff of Auschwitz wafting about in the dank, bitter air over 'Eden.'

'Hey man, what de fuck?' Maxi looked at 40% straight in the eye as he was handed the pick and shovel. 'this Dandelion is a complete prick,' Maxi exclaimed, pointing the handle of the pick at the office door.

'You shouldn't talk like that after the man giving you a job and all,' 40% replied with his head still bowed. 'Just keep your head down and do what you're told. That's how I get through each day.' He lifted his head proudly and announced, 'Daniel is the boss and that's all there is to it.'

It became abundantly clear that 40% was a lost cause, so Maxi changed his tune in order to pacify him. 'Yeah, I suppose you're right.' He took a practice swing with the sledge and buried it into the hard, cold clay, visualising Dandelion's expression as the point of the pick slammed into his skull.

'I'm very grateful to have a job in these hard times,' he assured 40%. 'Oh, by the way, what's the story with the tea break?'

'That's entirely up to Daniel's discretion. When he decides, that's when we may have our tea.'

'I see,' said Maxi. 'What time do we take lunch?'

'That's also entirely up to Daniel's discretion. He will decide when and the duration will depend solely on his mood.'

'Let me ask you, does Daniel's discretion dictate your bowel movements as well?'

'Pardon me?' 40% leaned towards Maxi with his open palm cupping his listening ear, daring him to repeat his remark.

'Ah, nothing.'

40% highlighted the parameters of the required hole in bright orange paint from a spray can that seemed to miraculously appear from one of the many pockets in his trench coat. The result was two parallel lines about a foot apart running along the ground, a distance of approximately two hundred feet. The purpose of this hole was to facilitate an underground electrical cable from the tool shed to another small building, which at that moment, appeared abandoned.

'Dig a channel to a depth of two feet within these confines,' 40% commanded.

'Fair enough,' Maxi responded as he raised the pick above his head, all the while feeling Dandelion's stare on the back of his neck. 40% returned along the same muddy pathway with his head bowed and his hands clamped together like a monk doing penance.

Maxi wasn't afraid of hard work. In fact, he relished it at times. It afforded him the opportunity now and then to skip the gym.

Swinging a pick was a good way to vent, but, on that occasion, it proved to be invaluable. He was dumbfounded by how despicable a human being Dandelion was, while 40% was so pathetic. The polarity between these two individuals could not have been more pronounced. While each scored high at opposite ends of the spectrum, it was quite apparent their mutual existence was heavily reliant on their inter-dependence. They were like two upright planks leaning against each other for support. Take one away and the other falls to the ground.

As Maxi got into the swing of things, the rhythmic thud of the sledge sounded like a metronome in his mind as he hummed along in a catatonic trance to the primitive chant his mind had just composed. The sluice gates to his imagination were suddenly flung open, so he could begin to fantasise about the untold riches that lay buried in the very ground he was pulverising. He found himself negotiating his way down along a very long line of blow with his right thumb pressed hard against his useless nostril. He didn't think he'd make it all the way to the end. It was hot and humid -no amount of money could eradicate humidity from his dream. He began to waver. Only for the naked quartet of busty 'escorts' egging him on, it's doubtful he would have crossed the finish line. He gasped a sigh of relief and withdrew from the cloudy mirror. He threw his head back to surrender his naked body to the recliner, which was deliberately positioned in the path of the AC's exhaust. Consequently, his nipples were erect as was his coke-fuelled cock. He savoured the waves of pleasure washing over his entire anatomy while all his countless nerve endings twitched with delight. He was fondled all over by oodles of hands and licked and kissed by a procession of sultry lips. Both chemical and tactile arousal engaged in tandem to surpass the boundaries of pleasure and drive the apex of rapture into a distant wonderland that could never be realised by a mere mortal... until then.

One of the naked girls presented him with a golden goblet filled with a vintage Brandy, circa 1800. Another, the ice blue blonde with the perky breasts, fired up the end of a Cuban cigar with a blow-torch lighter and circling her moist, red lips around the tip, she oozed out an erotic parade of candy-floss smoke rings that lingered momentarily in mid-air, before being chopped up in the blades of the AC. Just as he was about to savour this red tipped delight, a sudden loud noise made him spring up from his recliner like a pissed-off Cobra driven to the edge by the snake-charmer and his fucking bugle. The golden goblet fell from his hand and the naked quartet vanished along with what he estimated to be a year's supply of Columbia's finest. His last thought before his trance vaporised:

'Did I forget to put the Bentley in park?'

Then abruptly, back to the pick and shovel.

'You, you. Hey you. Pick Man,' he heard Dandelion's voice coming over a bullhorn. 'It's lunch time.'

'What the fuck?' Maxi scowled.

'The prick forgot my name,' he hissed. *'Now I'm Pick Man.'* He dropped the pick and forced himself to take a few deep breaths.

'A bullhorn! Fuck,' he growled, and he spat at the ground. It's all he could do to counter the unrelenting barrage of dehumanising tactics that seemed to be stock-piled in Dandelion's arsenal.

'This guy is one demeaning motherfucker. Fuck the treasure, I'm going to end up killing this piece of shit.'

As he made his way back along the muddy trail to the office, between biting his tongue and spewing obscenities he happened to notice a very slight movement in the corner of his eye as he looked to the Heavens for divine inspiration. He stopped dead in his tracks and focused his full attention on the roof of the main building. He could just about discern the shape of a look-out tower amidst the grey clouds. It was like something you'd expect to see in a war zone. A circular turret with row upon row of interlocking sandbags to beyond shoulder height. Wooden beams supported a galvanised roof, which seemed to hover about a foot or so above the last row of sandbags. This void afforded the observer a 360-degree surveillance of the whole property. A military-like camouflaged netting cloaked this structure to further disguise its footprint on the horizon.

'Holy shit!' Maxi exclaimed.

Every part of the yard, including Thistle Dick's portion of the property could be viewed from that vantage point. It was evident that Dandelion had just vacated the lookout a moment ago. The bullhorn still swayed on the leather strap that clung to a nail on one of the supporting beams. Hanging from another nail on the same beam, a pair of binoculars. Maxi felt violated. Not only was he being scrutinised, he was being magnified in the process, which only intensified his disdain that much more. On top of all that, his identity was trashed. He was now being addressed as '*Pick-man*' and bossed about by a bullhorn. Just as he was about to enter the office, his peripheral vision caught a glint from the sun ricocheting off some other reflective object. It was just a tiny needle of light, but it was enough to pin-point Thistle Dick's location in an open window in his house, high on a hill overlooking the property. It seemed he, too, was busy scoping the property with his own pair of binoculars. He was paying particular attention to the van that was being loaded by 40% out front. Maxi knew he had been carefully studied not only by Dandelion's binoculars but by Thistle Dick's as well. He remembered seeing another pair of binoculars on the ride to work that morning in 40%'s van.

'*Better get myself a pair of binoculars,*' he said to himself, '*so I can keep up with the rest of these fuckers. This place is worse than the 38 parallel! These two brothers are watching each other like hawks, and that other fucker is watching them. With all these gates, security cameras, the look-out tower and now all these magnified eyes,*' he wondered, '*how in God's name am I going to find this treasure?*'

Dandelion had just finished his lunch when Maxi walked into the office. 40% sat at his desk with a half-eaten chicken sandwich on a sheet of tin foil in front of him. He was preoccupied writing down a list of instructions that Dandelion was dictating to him. Even the lunch-break wasn't a lunch-break. Maxi planted himself on a chair next to Dandelion's desk to eat his lunch.

'No, no, no, not here,' Dandelion pointed to a spackle bucket in the corner of the room. 'Over there. These desks are *antiques*.'

Maxi wanted to knock this guy's block off. How much more could he endure? He was being bombarded left, right and centre since he arrived that morning. Even thoughts of the treasure were beginning to wane. He sat on the spackle bucket in the corner of the room. He felt so dejected, he wouldn't have been at all surprised if Dandelion planted a dunce's hat on his head.

'I see your brother is paying particular attention to the load you have in that van out front,' Maxi said, desperately looking to stir some shit. 'He's got a pair of binoculars just like you.'

Dandelion hesitated for an instant as if not fully comprehending what he was hearing. A man not used to rebuttal might have to wonder where did *Pick man* grow those balls?

'Oh!' An unlikely effusion from a bewildered knight after losing his forearm to a broad sword. 'Is that so?'

'Curiosity must run rampant in your family,' Maxi jabbed.

Dandelion was on the ropes. Maxi felt revitalised. The silence in the office was interrupted only by the chomping sounds he made, biting into his sandwich.

'I'm taking those items of interest down to Chorus Lane,' Dandelion retorted, gritting his teeth while he choked the back of his leather chair with both hands. His eyes darted frantically about the office, from one piece of trash to the next, in a desperate bid to discover some *smart-aleck* remark that would put a lid on the banter, but he came up empty-handed.

'You know what to do,' he pointed at 40% and switching his attention to Maxi, 'and so do you.' There was another awkward silence before Dandelion left the office in haste. Maxi relished his little victory. At least it stopped the haemorrhaging for the time being.

'You shouldn't rile him up like that,' 40% chirped, unable to disguise his delight with Dandelion gone for the day. 'He can make life exceedingly difficult for you. It's best to just go with the flow.' His cheerful beratement sounded comical.

'You can't let that man walk all over you,' Maxi retaliated. 'In every aspect of life, there are boundaries, expectations and requirements. This guy has total disregard for everything that is civil in human interaction. Honey gets the fucking bee.' He jumped up off the spackle bucket and plonked himself in Dandelion's imported Italian leather chair to finish his lunch by the *antique* desk.

'Let's just agree to disagree.' 40% waved the sheet of paper with his list of chores. 'I've got work to do. By the way,' he suggested in a sombre tone, 'don't let Daniel catch you sitting in that chair. He doesn't like to share his shit.'

Once 40% was all the way down the back of the yard, Maxi retrieved the map from his backpack. He placed it on the desk so that the boxes on it were correctly aligned with the surrounding buildings. One look and immediately he knew the whereabouts of the red x. A shiver of delight ran the full length of his spine. He couldn't believe his luck when he realised that the treasure had to be buried somewhere close to the spot where he had been digging all morning. He remembered, while on his walk to the tool shed, being surprised by the presence of a huge boulder, the entire surface of which was adorned with megalithic type carvings, inferring an ancient monument of sorts. Now there was no question this boulder was the starting point of the hunt for the treasure. Only then did all the little squiggles in the oblong on the map make sense. They were there for no other reason other than to replicate those carvings. Maxi tingled with anticipation. He wolfed down the rest of his lunch and raced back to his hole.

Once he got his bearings, he stood with his back to the boulder and stepped out the ten yards as instructed by the coordinates on the map. Next, he had to position himself at a forty-five-degree angle to the line he had just taken and step out another twenty yards. Just as he had completed this manoeuvre, he saw 40%' s orange woolly hat bobbing up and down as it made its way along the top of the brick wall that encircled one of the crumbled buildings nearby. He marked his position with a rock and quickly returned to the trench where he loaded his shovel just in time for 40%'s arrival.

'Well, how are you getting on?'

'Fine,' Maxi replied, straining to remain civil. 'There's a few stubborn spots here and there but nothing I can't handle,' he added to showcase the relationship he was having with the hole. 40% accepted Maxi's tap-out and a truce between the two was initiated. Maxi realised the importance of him feigning to be a numb-skull with both lunatics if he was to have any hope of retrieving the treasure. He needed to play the part of a 'broken' person in front of 40% and a soulless masseuse with the other egomaniac. Only then all would be quiet on the Western Front.

Chapter 11.

Ever since 40%'s rocket-launch on that fateful Monday morning, Maxi was obliged - having had a brush with death - to borrow his mother's car to get to work. 40% was incensed by this and gave him the cold shoulder all week. Maxi didn't care. In fact, it suited him down to the ground. Now he could go about his business as a 'brain dead' employee, digging his trench while secretly stepping out the coordinates of the map, unnoticed... or so he thought.

Since another of Maxi's job requirements was to open the yard in the mornings, he decided to go to work early on *T-Day* - the day they chose to dig up the treasure - and retrace his steps according to the dictates on the treasure map. After pacing around the property for about 30 minutes, he arrived at the exact same spot he had done the day before. This confirmation sent a bolt of excitement through his body. At last, the treasure was literally within arm's reach. He stood over the spot and stared intently at it like he was attempting to x-ray the ground and telepathically exhume the treasure.

At precisely 8 a.m., 40%'s white, tin-can van with its smoky black cape careered unimpeded through the gates of Eden, down the hill and into the yard. The woolly hat made its way above the cloud of black smoke to the office. Maxi was already pounding away with his pick. Once again, no salutations were exchanged between the two men.

Still got a bug up your ass, Maxi mused. Oh well, once today is done, you and your asshole boss are history.

The previous day, he had instructed his two budding actors, Boom-boom and Happy Jack to come to the yard around eleven o'clock in the rental van with the magnetic County Council logos adorning the sides. No matter how hard he tried, he couldn't concentrate, not that he needed to be firing on all cylinders to dig a hole. He positioned himself in *his* trench in such a way that his peripheral vision would alert him to the slightest twitch on that hilltop even though he had hours to wait.

At last Dandelion's van arrived down the hill. 40% was obliged to run out from the office to greet the van and commence his daily grovelling regime. Dandelion slid the side door open and loaded up his personal pack-ass with whatever junk he found along the road on his way to work. 40% led the way back to the office, weighed down with an assortment of discarded items that would proudly shake the trash stigma and re-enter the marketplace, revitalised with a whole new purpose in life. All it took was a yellow can of spray paint to repurpose a buckled bicycle wheel into a work of art entitled; *'Turn up the volume.'*

Maxi witnessed the longest hour in his time on earth... eventually concede to its successor. At last, the rental van's arrival was only minutes away. Dandelion was in the office, on the phone chasing leads. There were several customers roaming about the yard and 40% was dealing with one individual who was very eager to buy a Belfast sink. They stood about ten feet away so Maxi was privy to their conversation. As soon as the deal concluded and the customer was away to his car with his purchase, Dandelion suddenly appeared out of nowhere and tore into 40%.

'Are you fucking illiterate when it comes to body language? Did you not see how eager that man was to buy that sink?'

'Why are you so upset? I got sticker price for it, didn't I?' 40% brandished the fifty euros in his hand as proof.

'You don't get it, do you?' Dandelion growled. 'People give off clues. You must be able to read those clues in order to know how far you can fuck with them. Forget the sticker price. You failed to see how eager that customer was to buy that item. You should have wangled at least another tenner out of him. You know what?' Dandelion decided. 'That ten quid's coming out of your pay this week. You'll never be a salesman because you don't relish the taste of blood like me.' He stormed off mumbling to himself about how great he was and how the world should rejoice having a man of his calibre operating in it.

'*Wow*,' Maxi thought, '*how does 40% put up with this man's shit?*'

The timing of Dandelion's tantrum couldn't have been more accommodating. Maxi knew from witnessing his many previous outbursts during the week, his whole focus would be devoted exclusively to 40%'s ineptitude and that ten quid deficit. The man grieved over losing money like a bereaved parent, the death of a child. Believing this *angry* window in time would afford their mission a pass on rigid scrutiny, Maxi got the booster jab he needed to take their plan over the line.

Just then, the red rental materialised on the crest of the hill. Maxi celebrated its arrival by burying the point of the pick into the cold, hard earth... one last time. He wiped his brow with the sleeve of his jacket and raced towards the entrance to the salvage yard. His sudden interest in the arrival of the red van wouldn't arouse suspicion, since directing traffic was also an integral part of his job description. He flapped his arms vigorously up and down, rendering a convincing impersonation of Icarus - the kid who got too close to the sun. The two men in the van were flummoxed by Maxi's antics. Who would blame them? Was that a sign to abort the mission? Maxi was now sprinting with outstretched, flapping arms towards the van like he wanted to soar into the clouds. As he got closer, he could appreciate the concern in the bulging eyes of his fellow henchmen. Only then did he realise he failed to alert them, as to that one hoop of many he was compelled to jump through, to appease the Almighty.

Dandelion insisted he and his staff replicate this furtive, arm flapping manoeuvre, to direct traffic into his yard. He forced the two men to suffer one of his asinine lectures, which could have resulted in permanent brain damage if either one paid attention. Maxi had to maintain his composure while he witnessed this grown man flapping his arms and jumping about the place like he had hornets in his underpants. Dandelion gave the impression that he had conducted a battery of tests in this arena, resulting in the Icarus impersonation rising to the top, as the crème de la crème of attention-grabbing manoeuvres. He was certainly right about that. The sole purpose for such antics was to ensure that no traffic made it into Thistle Dick's yard.

Dandelion concluded his circus act with an inspirational remark:

'If scare-crows could move their arms in this manner, farmers about the globe would have much higher yielding crops.'

Maxi stood in the van's way, forcing it to stop. He couldn't renege on those crazy antics. He was on camera and quite possibly being viewed through one, two, or indeed three pairs of binoculars. He had to treat this van as if it were just another customer and deliver a flawless rendition of Dandelion's proven, attention-grabbing technique.

'Sorry about that, lads,' Maxi informed the two men as he leaned into the open window of the van. 'More shit dished out from on high.'

'This man has turned you into a dancing bear.' Happy Jack chuckled, the hint of a smile peeping out from under his angry blockade.

'Ah ha hah,' Maxi conceded, '...very funny.' He couldn't help but visualize Happy Jack's dancing bear with its flapping paws and wonder what the fuck?

'Well lads,' Maxi inquired. 'Are you all set to pull this off?'

'We're both a little nervous,' Boom-boom admitted, striking the dashboard several times with his clenched fist.

'Happy Jack threw up, back there on the road.' He gestured with his thumb pointing over his right shoulder. 'He always does that before a play. 'It's stage fright, that's all.'

Maxi asked Happy Jack. 'Will you be able to go through with this?' He stared intently at him in the passenger seat for clues that might jeopardise the mission. Of course, he didn't find any. Happy Jack didn't do emotions.

'I'll be fine,' he replied.

'Right lads, remember, ye don't know me. I'm going into the office to set the stage, like we practiced in rehearsal. Just follow the script and everything will be fine. I'm right here with you, so relax as best ye can. Go in there and break a leg.'

He slapped the hood of the van with the palm of his hand and pointed to a spot in the yard where they should park the van. Every move was being carefully monitored, so it was imperative to act like this was just another customer. He disappeared into the office.

'Excuse me, Daniel,' Maxi interrupted. 'The County Council are here to see you.'

'What the fuck do they want with me?' Dandelion spat, still in the throes of anger with 40%'s lack of judgement concerning the sale of the Belfast sink.

'I'm not sure what they want,' he replied. 'They said something about a piece of equipment that's gone missing. It's somewhere under the ground on these premises.' Maxi pointed at the concrete floor to somehow clarify his remark, and he deliberately wore his best, baffled face to display his total ignorance of the whole affair.

'A piece of their equipment has gone missing, under my ground?'

'That's the way it seems.'

'Show these mutts in,' he ordered.

Boom-boom just about squeezed his beloved 'washing machine' gut through the office door, forcing Dandelion to retreat in his lavish office chair to the far end of his 'antique' desk. This was the first time he had to put his Italian import in reverse. He was pleasantly surprised by how smoothly the casters propelled his luxurious leather chair along the concrete floor. He felt like he was sitting in a cloud that hovered by his desk. He reminded himself how lucky he was to have secured that chair at a liquidation sale for little or next to nothing.

Next Happy Jack ducked his big angry skull under the header of the door and stood, at full height, next to Boom-boom. He carried the modified metal detector in his right hand. Dandelion's astonished expression would only ever be matched if aliens from outer space were standing there instead. The two men before him were togged out in matching, luminous, bright green overalls with the County Council logo festooned across the chest and down along the legs. They wore immaculate, white hard hats on top of their big heads with, yet again, the County Council logo emblazoned above the peak. They were walking, talking billboards, broadcasting their participation as vital cogs in the County Council mechanism. Around their necks, they wore false I.D. badges, mimicking the police shields of American detectives, to further validate their County Council credentials. Even the shoes they wore on their feet were standard County Council issue.

The constant bombardment of brilliant bursts of bright light from the neon overalls blinded Dandelion, who behaved as if he was in the presence of an apparition. He assumed a submissive posture in his tricked-out chair with his hands shielding his eyes. Normally he would sit, bolt upright with the temperature set high to warm his kidneys while the inbuilt massage unit did its thing on his lower back. However, having slid down along the chair to seek shelter from this sensory blitz, his head was now where his kidneys should be. His beloved chair gave him a good pounding. While he was down there, he managed somehow to pull the plug and struggling to regain his posture; he eventually regained command of the chair.

'Well gentlemen, how may I be of assistance?' he inquired with a ruddy face identical to a Paddy on vacation after his first day in the blistering sun. Thank God he was still a little punch-drunk from his tantrum to notice that the two boys weren't wearing safety harnesses, as was the mandate of the County Council worker.

Boom-boom stepped forward, bringing attention to the clipboard he held in his meaty hand. He flicked over to the first page and began to rattle off the content with the authority of a Town Crier.

'We are here on a recovery mission to retrieve an important piece of excavating equipment that was misdirected by some inept contractor, and as a result, it has ended up here, buried under your property.'

'What exactly is the thing you're looking for?' Dandelion asked, already bored with the intrusion.

Boom-boom searched for the appropriate answer on the printed pages on his clip board and promptly read his reply.

'It's a pneumatic probe which is used primarily to drag electrical cables under the ground in areas that are difficult or impossible to reach from above. For instance, if we want to run wires underground, from one bank of a river to the other, then this probe, which we call a 'torpedo,' is tailor-made for this specific task. The operator uses a joystick to send commands to the probe and its progress is monitored on this screen.'

Happy Jack stepped forward with the laptop/metal detector combo and pointed at the screen. Freddy resumed speaking and Happy Jack stood back.

'Unfortunately, the probe never surfaced. We have traced its path to this location. As you may appreciate, this 'torpedo' is a very expensive piece of equipment and we must do everything we can to ensure its recovery.'

So far, so good. Boom-boom supplied Maxi's anticipated answers to these obvious questions in a confident and professional manner. Maxi was impressed.

'How can you be so sure this probe thing is buried here?' Dandelion asked as he chewed on the end of his pencil. He did that when he was annoyed. Judging by the number of two-B pencils already chewed to bits on his *antique* desk... he was pissed.

'We've traced its' movements with this device which has brought us to this location.' Happy Jack presented Boom-boom with the homemade sonar detector, which was basically a metal detector connected to a lap-top with an abundance of colourful, electrical cables all tangled up in a very busy display of purpose and intent. Not a single wire, in this mass of connections, performed any function. An assortment of large batteries with more useless wires and colourful connections were duct taped to the under belly of the laptop to allude to a device with powerful capabilities. The monitor displayed the looped recording of a hospital patient's heartbeat, courtesy of Debbie, who worked in ER. Freddy Boom-boom encouraged Dandelion to examine the device. He pointed at the bright orange dot that darted across the screen, leaving a residue of tiny L.E.D sparks in its wake.

'This is the hi-tech blood-hound that will find the missing probe for us.' Freddy Boom-boom pledged with the adroit conviction of a second-hand car salesman.

'It actually works just like an ordinary metal detector, except that this baby is on steroids. Not only can it detect metal fragments to a depth of ten feet, it can recognize the identity of that metal, whether it be gold, silver or copper, etc.'

Dandelion studied the contraption for a moment and eventually registered his approval. In that instant, he demonstrated his ignorance of technology and corroborated - to the relief of all present - Maxi's earlier prediction:

'This clown hasn't a clue when it comes to mechanics or technology. He'll make-off. He knows all about everything and anything, but I assure you... he's an idiot.'

Now that their collective anxiety bubble had burst, coupled with the fact that Dandelion was still zoned out over 40%'s ten quid deficit, an air of confidence spilled into the office.

'Well, what are we waiting for?' Dandelion said. 'Let's go find that buried treasure. He laughed out loud and clapped his hands in excited anticipation.

Freddy Boom-boom looked perplexed. This wasn't part of the script. Even Happy Jack softened to almost achieve a puzzled look. Maxi, however, had to retrieve his jaw that had just careened onto the concrete floor.

Happy Jack weighed in after a very awkward silence. 'We wish,' is all he said.

His innocent little two-word ad-lib saved the day.

'Okay, gentlemen, you need to find that thing. This man here,' Dandelion pointed to Maxi, 'will assist you in your endeavour. Now if you don't mind, I have work to do.'

Maxi gambled that he would be assigned to work with the County Council in their recovery effort, and his gamble paid off. He suspected Dandelion would never allow 'outsiders' to dig on his property without some sort of supervision. Now the three of them could go about their business without any interference from above.

'Hi Maxi, I'm Happy Jack.'

Just as Maxi reached out to shake his hand, Dandelion held up his own hand to halt proceedings.

'Wait a minute,' he said. 'You two know each other?'

Dandelion's stupor had suddenly vanished. He swapped his intense stare, back and forth, between the two men. Maxi's temples pounded to the beat of the second-hand on the wall mounted clock, which sounded surprisingly like a blacksmith's hammer striking an anvil.

'It's over,' he surmised.

In Happy Jack's case, this was one occasion where a deficiency in emotional expression proved to be invaluable. He didn't flinch - only because he couldn't. He didn't bat an eyelid - he didn't know how.

'I never met this man before,' *Happy* Jack confirmed. 'I heard you mention his name just as we came into your office, that's all.'

Dandelion looked away for a moment to reflect on their initial meeting. He couldn't be sure whether he addressed Maxi by name. If he did, it was indeed a rare occurrence. He wasn't inclined to be so condescending. He resumed his inquisitive glare, but after a moment, he relented and gave all three of them the *'piss-boy'* shoo.

What a relief, Maxi mused, to survive that grilling and be out of that office and into the pouring rain where it was a joy to get soaked.

'Good recovery, Happy Jack,' Maxi whispered. 'I thought for sure we were done and dusted. 'That man has never called me by my name,' he vowed. 'I don't think he even knows it.'

'Sorry,' Happy Jack confessed. 'I slipped up.'

'It's all good,' Maxi assured. 'Let's head up this way,' he said, pointing at a small incline that would put them out of ear shot of the office and a lot closer to the treasure.

The three men huddled together to minimise the soaking they were getting from the torrential rain. Happy Jack hovered the plate of the metal detector about three inches above the ground, making big, wide arcs in front of them as the three men slowly moved forward. Boom-boom carried the modified laptop and gave hand signals while professing to be directed by the screen. About ninety-minutes later, after plodding around the property like three lost drunks, they arrived at the predetermined spot where Maxi had figured from the coordinates on the map, the location of the treasure to be.

'This is the spot, right here,' Maxi announced, straining to mask his excitement. He had to draw upon the reserves in his will power to present a calm exterior while his insides ran amuck.

'Take it easy, man,' Freddy teased. 'You'd swear you just discovered the crown jewels.'

Maxi got defensive. 'Who said anything about a treasure?'

'Nobody,' the two big men replied.

'Well then, let's get the tent set up.'

'Here?' Happy Jack pointed to the ground beneath his feet.

'No, over there,' Maxi sarcastically replied, pointing back at the office. 'Of course, here. Right fucking here, okay.'

'Take it easy, man,' Happy Jack implored. 'Who put the tack in your top-hat?'

Maxi almost burst out laughing. First the dancing bear, he thought, and now the masculine equivalent of the *'bee in the bonnet'* adage. He decided, Happy Jack was either bent as an 's hook' or the politest serial killer in the universe. Either way, he was terrified.

'I'm sorry,' Maxi confessed. 'I'm a little excited now that we're right on top of this thing. What do you say, guys? Let's get the tent set up so we can get out of this fucking monsoon.'

The tent was a crucial component for the plan to succeed and it served a dual purpose. Not only did it provide shelter from the rain, its canopy ensured that they could work away in secret, despite the magnified eyes behind all the inquisitive binoculars. While the two men headed back towards the van to retrieve the tent, Maxi ran to the cover of the nearest tree and called Ella on his cell phone.

'So far, so good. Everything is going according to plan. Your two actors were very convincing. Dandelion bought the whole act, hook, line and sinker. The two boys are heading off to get the tent as we speak. Oh, and get this,' he giggled, 'Dandelion has ordered me to help the County Council dig up the probe. Can you believe it?'

'Wow, that's fantastic,' Ella cheered, 'and it's raining.'

'Yeah, I know,' he said. 'I'm soaked to the skin, but I'm loving this rain. Nobody, not even those hard-core Paddies who wear t-shirts in the middle of winter would dare mock a tent in this fucking cyclone. It's nearly working out too well.'

'Feels like you're looking for something to go wrong.'

'You're right, Ella, I've got to shake the negative vibe.'

'It's all good.'

'Yeah, I know. Are you and the girls ready to move?'

'Just say the word,' Ella chirped. She did that when she got excited.

'That's what I like to hear,' he commended as he took a few deep breaths to control his own excitement. 'I don't expect the treasure to be buried that deep in the ground and judging by my progress with that trench over the past few days, I figure we should be on it in no time. Imagine, Ella, we're going to be filthy rich, very soon.'

'Oh my God, it's so exciting I can hardly breathe.'

'You've got some sexy gear to wear, I'm sure.'

'I think I can turn a head or two with this little number I'm wearing,' Ella confided.

'I bet you can,' Maxi stammered as his imagination flickered a provocative slideshow of her across the frontal lobes of his brain. 'Stay on your toes, we're nearly there.'

'Rodger that.'

Chapter 12.

They all worked surprisingly well together, erecting the tent. It proved to be an effortless endeavour, each one of them having done *time* in the boy-scouts. Once completed, the three men sprawled out on the wet grass inside the tent. Maxi offered each of them a cigarette from his Marlboro box. Happy Jack accepted. Freddy Boom-boom declined.

'You two did well,' he commended. 'I must applaud you both.'

He lit the cigarettes and took a long pull of his own. 'Now, I want you two to go back to the van and have your lunch. It's almost that time, anyway. I'll have mine when Ghaddafi decides. In the meantime, I'll start digging. Remember County Council workers take the full hour for lunch, so, to be on the safe side, meet me back here in an hour and a half. Sound good?'

Both men agreed. *Boom-boom* was already up off his ass and out through the flap in the tent before it registered with Happy Jack what was going on. He needed urgently to feed that beast of a belly. Now with the two big men out of the way, Maxi had time to gather his thoughts. He took a few deep breaths and then attacked the ground with the pick like an eager dog on some other dog's bone. After forty-five minutes, he had dug a hole about two-foot-square to a depth of three feet. He gambled that he would come across the treasure at around the four-foot mark. He was confident that pirates, scoundrels and ne'er-do-wells didn't care too much for digging holes! Another fifteen minutes and he was in the treasure zone. He was sweating profusely, so much so the interior of the tent began to steam up. He had to stick his head out into the rain in order to see his phone. Treasure or no treasure, it was time to give Ella the signal. She answered on the first ring. '*Go*' is all he said, and he resumed digging. It was imperative that a series of events occur in a precise chronological order, and within that ninety-minute timeframe or this mission was doomed to fail. He was obliged to borrow an actual 'torpedo' from an acquaintance who worked for an electrical contractor. After *Jimmy-fixing* the metal detector, he knew he couldn't chance doing the same with the probe. The two big men were suspicious enough already so, having something credible in the hole was vital to throw them off the scent. He smuggled that probe into the tent in his backpack.

The three girls were parked in two separate cars on top of the hill about two-hundred yards away from the gates of Eden. Debbie and Ida were in the front car. When Ella got the 'green light' from Maxi, she flashed her lights to signal the girls. Debbie drove down the hill flushing out 40% who was already furiously flapping his arms like a hummingbird in a heavy hover. Debbie ignored him completely and drove straight on into Thistle Dick's yard. 40% continued flapping away with a disconcerted look on his face. Obviously, he had never experienced failure when it came to Dandelion's tried and tested, *attention grabbing technique.* He began to gear-up mentally for Dandelion's inevitable hissy-fit over the escapees and yet he had the foresight not to step foot into Thistle Dick's yard. If he did, he might easily find himself in a court of law, contesting a trespassing violation.

Thistle Dick spent most of his time by his desk in his bedroom, composing affidavits or depositions to present to the court. His house was positioned high on a hill overlooking the valley below, where both salvage yards could easily be surveyed. His bedroom window was always open so he could hear any sounds coming from his own section of the property. His binoculars stood at the ready next to his camcorder on that windowsill.

On this occasion, he spotted Debbie's car entering his yard. He instinctively activated his camcorder and placed it in his pocket. It was better to have five-minutes of useless pocket footage than risk losing valuable input because he didn't get to hit the play button in time. Nothing like a motion picture, as evidence in a court of law. He had hundreds of hours of film in his judicial archive, next to stacks of legal documents pertaining to offences and defences regarding himself and his brother.

'Stay put,' Thistle Dick shouted in a gruff manner from the bedroom window. 'I'll be there in a jiffy.'

The two women waved their acknowledgement and began to browse around his yard. As he drove down the hill, he aimed his camcorder at 40% who was still flapping his arms in a futile attempt to lure the women into Dandelion's yard. Unfortunately, 40% didn't encroach on his property. With no infractions to record, he shut the camcorder off and placed it on the dash. He parked his van next to Debbie's car and was onto the two women like freckles on a traveller. The girls had been briefed by Maxi to inquire about metal stools which would take them to the back of the warehouse and out of sight. 'Thistle Dick' was then removed from the equation and consequently posed no threat to the operation.

Once Ella saw Thistle Dick's van pass through the gates, she followed him down the hill. She was greeted, as Maxi predicted, by the flapping wings of Dandelion, who pointed with both outstretched arms at a spot in his own yard where he wanted her to park. Ella followed his directive and parked her minivan.

The driver's door sprung open and a lone stiletto heel, attached to a long stockinged leg, was the first limb to find purchase on the pot-holed riddled yard. Ella allowed her leg to linger while she leaned back across the passenger seat to retrieve her raincoat. Dandelion had a bird's-eye view and was enjoying the peep-show. Ella knew she had him captivated. Once she remained in that compromising position, she knew there wouldn't be a stir out of Dandelion and she was correct. At last, with her raincoat in her grasp, she sat upright and stepped out from the minivan. Dandelion stored those images for later and raced over to her, struggling as he went to open the golf umbrella. Normally he would hand it to the customer but in this instance, with Ella in such a tight-fitting short skirt and exhibiting such ample cleavage, he was inclined to snuggle in as close as possible and steal as many cheap thrills as he could, without breaching the boundaries of depravity. He escorted her over to the showroom like they were contestants in a three-legged race. Another 'player' distracted.

Now that the three women had the attention of the three men, it was up to Maxi to dig up the treasure, plant the 'torpedo' in the hole and hide the treasure in his backpack. His only concern was to ensure that his two County Council thespians got to witness the probe in the hole... and not the treasure. He pounded the ground and shovelled dirt ceaselessly for another five minutes. At a little over 4 feet deep, he felt some stiff resistance from the shovel. Besides the steam in the tent, the sweat in his eyes curtailed his vision. Initially, he suspected a large rock and got down on his hands and knees for a closer look. He clawed away at the dirt with his bare hands to get a better feel for the obstruction. When he realised, he was touching a smooth, flat surface, his heart skipped a beat. He clawed vigorously at the dirt until he could feel the contours of a box materialise in his hands. He picked gingerly around the sides and frantically shovelled away the loose clay. At last, he was able to slip his fingers under the box and yank it free from the ground.

He studied it carefully, but with the misty contaminates of steam, sweat and smoke, all he got was a blurry image of the box. He was forced to rely on his tactile sensitivity for further input. The metal box was about ten by ten inches square and eight inches deep. He was disappointed by its small size and relatively light weight, but relieved it would easily fit in his backpack. He shook it with both hands and listened intently but the contents didn't offer any clues. Regardless of his initial impression, he was extremely excited. He felt around for a lid but couldn't find one. It had no hinges and no form of locking mechanism that he could discern. It was still caked in dirt, so he couldn't really tell. A thorough investigation would have to wait until later. His priority right then was to complete the switch before the County Council boys returned. He barely managed to hide the metal box in his backpack and slip the probe into the hole, when 40% stuck his orange woolly head into the tent.

'Well, well, well.'

That's all Maxi heard as 40% crouched down to enter the tent. Once inside, he sprung to his full height. He took a few steps to get a closer look into the hole and as he went, he rubbed his woolly head along the roof of the tent, oblivious to the significant leakage he was causing in his wake. He may as well have slit the tents canvass with a razor blade. Obviously 40% knew 0% about tents.

'I've been watching you all week,' he said.

'Is that so?' Maxi replied as he grappled with the 'torpedo' in the hole, pretending it was a discovery and not a plant. 'While you're here, give me a hand lifting this thing.'

'Don't you want to leave that there for the County Council boys?' 40% insisted.

Maxi was speechless.

'What triggered my interest in you, you may ask?'

'I don't ask and I don't, fucking care.'

'Come now... don't be like that,' 40% wagged his index finger like he was reprimanding a mischievous child. 'Don't you want to know what piqued my interest in you?'

Suddenly 40% dropped to his knees so he could be on the same plane as Maxi, who was sitting on his hunkers in a pile of dirt.

'When you called about the job on the phone,' 40% sounded like a preacher and a sermon was coming Maxi's way. 'Once you knew you got it, you didn't ask any follow-up questions about health insurance or vacation pay, none of that. Plus, Daniel has a bit of a reputation for being, let's say - a rather cantankerous individual - so what sane person would want to work for a man like that?' He took a fistful of dirt in his hand and let it spill through his fingers. 'An employee with an ulterior motive, that's who. So, I decided to keep a close eye on you, and just like Daniel, I also happen to own a pair of binoculars.'

'Yeah, I noticed them flying about the van along with your sexy nylons on that supersonic ride to work last Monday,' Maxi growled.

'You just can't seem to get your head around my substitute for thermal underwear,' 40% replied.

'Yeah, yeah, the check is in the mail. Anyway, what are you doing here? Can't you see I'm busy?'

'I see that. I just dropped in to check on *our* treasure.' 40% smiled for the first time since they met.

'What the fuck are you talking about? I'm helping the County Council...'

'Give it a rest,' 40% urged. 'I've been watching you all week. I've seen you consult that map of yours and you taking those long strides that only treasure hunters take. I was up on that hill by the main gate every morning before you came to work. So, *partner,* let's work together to get whatever you have in your backpack, out of here without Dandelion or indeed, those two County Council workers, being any the wiser.'

'Don't call me partner... you prick,' Maxi barked. 'Now listen up. Here's how this is going down. You think you know what's going on? Well, let me tell you...'

'Hold on a minute,' 40% interrupted, 'I know what's going on. Let's be very clear about that. When you offered to open the yard in the mornings, I was certain you were up to no good. Who in their right fucking mind would want to unlock the gazillion gates and doors that lock this motherfucker down? Certainly not a man like you. You are broken just like me, except you don't know it yet. You're just waiting in line to sell your soul like everybody else.'

'Like you did.'

'I never had a soul to sell,' 40% confided. 'All I sold Daniel was a bag of dust shaped like a soul.'

'Could we fast forward here with your horseshit,' Maxi blurted, realizing how precarious his predicament was. 'The County Council boys will be back from lunch any minute now.'

'I know all about you in America, working in construction and losing everything. My own situation is not all that different from yours. I know you don't like me and that's okay. I have no friends, nor do I want any. But what I do want is a share in that treasure.' 40% pointed at the backpack.

'I already have three partners. I don't need another,' Maxi replied, still reluctant to admit defeat.

'I'm not inferring that you don't have a choice in this matter,' 40% rallied. 'Of course, you do.'

Maxi, not trusting what he was hearing, encouraged 40%. 'Go on, I'm listening.'

'Unfortunately, that decision would result in Daniel and Daniel alone reaping the rewards of all your hard work. That's his property in that backpack of yours. You know it and I know it. I'd prefer he not benefit from our little joint venture. So, what do you say, *partner*?'

'Stop with the partner already,' Maxi groaned. 'Hobson's choice is all you've given me.'

'How astute,' 40% jeered. 'Now, here's how this is going down. I'm taking your backpack with me.'

'No fucking way,' Maxi shrieked as both of them grappled with the backpack. Neither one would relinquish their grip.

'This plan of yours,' 40% suggested. 'I don't think you've thought it through.'

'Oh yeah,' Maxi groaned. 'How's that?'

'Well for instance,' 40% remarked. 'How did you think you were going to get this backpack out of here without Daniel finding the treasure?' He tugged at it and Maxi tugged back. 'He doesn't like people stealing shit from his yard. That's why he searched your car during the week and correct me if I'm wrong, but didn't he search this very backpack of yours on one particular occasion?' He tugged once more and Maxi resisted. 'I'm the only person he trusts,' 40% proudly announced.

'You think you know it all,' Maxi exclaimed. Even though he was sick to his stomach, his pride needed to show this clown that his plan was indeed thought through.

Maxi got up and pulled the backpack with 40% in tow, along with him to the front of the tent. He peeled open the flap and pointed at Daniel, who was still glued to Ella, under the golf umbrella.

'See that beautiful woman over there by Daniel? She's my accomplice,' he confirmed. 'The *plan* was for me to sneak this backpack into her minivan while Dandelion was distracted. So, the *plan* was fool proof,' Maxi bragged. 'Until you fucking showed up.'

Both men stared at one another as their little tug of war with the backpack continued. Just then, they heard the big men returning after lunch. Both looked at the backpack... and Maxi released his grip.

'Okay, okay, you fucking scumbag.' Maxi snarled through clenched teeth. 'Take the fucking thing but you better bring it to my house after work or I'll, I'll fucking...'

40% peeped into Maxi's backpack. 'Interesting.'

'I swear if you're not there, I'll...'

The County Council men crowded the entrance way as 40% was obliged to squeeze his way out of the tent. Maxi could hear him whistling as he went on his *merry* way. Maxi sat back down in the dirt. He was in a daze. Lucky the optics inside the tent were poor, otherwise the two big men might have suspected something was off. As Maxi struggled to comprehend what had just happened, he had to put on a face in front of the County Council to keep the ball in play.

'Oh wow,' Happy Jack exclaimed. 'That's what all the fuss is about.' He leaned down into the hole to get a closer look at the probe.

'Yes, that's the missing 'torpedo',' Maxi confirmed.

'Right then, that means we're done here,' Boom-boom remarked, frustrated he couldn't find any surface to strike. He was forced to forego his 'boom, boom' bullshit.

'Yes, you're right,' Maxi replied, feigning a smile. He was too distraught to add any pep to his response. 'Take the probe and put it in the van. Better bring that metal detector with you as well.' He paused to allow a wave of nausea to pass over him. 'Drop the van back to my house and leave the probe in it. I'll see you both later with your money. Thanks lads,' he said, and the fake smile hurt his face. 'You both did a great job.'

'What about the tent?' Boom-boom asked.

'Don't worry about it,' Maxi said. 'I'll take care of it.'

They all shook hands, and both men carried the equipment out from the tent and headed off towards the office. Maxi peeped out through the flap to see Dandelion still glued to Ella under the golf umbrella. There was no let up from the rain. As soon as Dandelion saw the County Council men, he excused himself and raced over to inspect their find. They exchanged a little chit-chat, and he nodded his approval. Ella escaped in the meantime. Dandelion headed back to the office. Maxi was satisfied at least with that result. He retreated to the middle of the tent and wilted like a spent prairie dog after caring for all his prairie bitches.

Instead of revelling in triumph he was shaking in shock. He began to piece together in his mind everything that had happened in the last few days. He assumed 40% and his *cold shoulder* would have been overwhelmed with office work and in his quest to appease his master, devote his sole attention to administrative duties. Just then Maxi realised how foolish his assumption was.

'40% never does anything 100%. Fuck.'

Once he back-filled the hole, he set about dismantling the tent. He placed all the various components into their respective satchels and made several trips to load his mother's car. Dandelion ambushed him by the trunk of the car on his final trip. It was still milling rain, but he made no effort to share the golf umbrella with Maxi.

'What are you doing with the County Council's tent?' he asked.

'That's not their...' Maxi checked himself. 'I mean they left it with me so I wouldn't get drenched. The tall one is coming over to my house later to pick it up.'

'I see you're after getting all palsy-walsy with the Council boys.'

'Oh, I don't know about that,' Maxi said. 'I just think it was a nice gesture on their behalf to leave it with me.'

'Answer me this,' Dandelion inquired. 'How big of a fool are you?'

'What are you on about?' Maxi retorted.

'These lazy Council pricks had their lunch while you dug the hole,' Dandelion informed Maxi. 'They didn't lift a finger to help. Work is a dirty word in their idle world. Don't think for one minute that they were doing you a favour by leaving the tent with you. They couldn't be bothered taking it down. Why would they, when they had a dummy like you to...'

Maxi couldn't bear to look at the man in the face so he opted to dip his head in *shame*. He allowed Dandelion to waffle on while he wondered what his next move should be. After finding the treasure, he should have been jumping about the place shouting *hoedown heehaw's* but instead he found himself being sucked, head-first into a pit of despair. As he began to wallow in self-pity, his ears pricked up when he heard Dandelion remark:

'Don't worry. They'll get some shock when they get the bill.'

Maxi never paid any attention to Dandelion since he started work in the yard, but at that instant, he had his undivided attention.

'A bill?' Maxi repeated. 'What for?' he inquired as he desperately attempted to shield his alarm.

'The County Council's got to pay for all the hard work *we* did recovering that fucking yoke for them,' Dandelion said, pointing at the hole. 'Don't you think?'

'Absolutely!' Maxi spluttered as he tried to swallow that hairball of terror, unnoticed.

'Forget it,' Dandelion grunted. 'I'm not going to send them a bill.'

Whew,' Maxi thought, *thank God!*

'I'll blackmail them instead,' he smirked. 'That way I'll get way more money.'

Maxi couldn't believe what he was hearing. 40%'s partnership would have to shuffle over on the bench in the back of his mind to make room for this latest catastrophe. He thought, only an hour ago he was ecstatic, but since then his legs had been whipped out from under him... *twice already.*

'I'm sure you're aware of the County Council's fuck up with the non-slip tiles in the public swimming pool.' Dandelion was off pontificating again but this time, Maxi was on his every word. 'It was all over the papers. I think they're still cleaning the shit outa that fan.' Dandelion moved closer behind the car to shield himself from the wind. His umbrella now spilled its contents onto Maxi's shoulder... but he was detached from his surroundings. 'They certainly won't want their reputation for fuck ups,' Dandelion continued, 'bandied about in the same papers, so soon. Everything comes with a price tag. Look around you, every item here, including you and 40%, all have price tags. The only thing that doesn't have one yet,' he turned his attention to the spot where the treasure was buried and pointed, 'is that hole you dug.'

'So, what do you think that hole is worth?' Maxi calmly inquired as he braced himself against the ropes like a battered prize fighter, praying for the bell.

'I have a good feeling in my gut that the County Council will step up and take care of that Caribbean Cruise my girlfriend has been nagging me about forever.' He slapped Maxi on his wet shoulder. 'I'd call that a good day's work, wouldn't you?'

Dandelion walked away, leaving Maxi to calculate the cost of a Caribbean Cruise.

Chapter 13.

Dandelion left the yard early that Saturday evening. The heavy rain dissuaded customers, so there was little or no money floating about the yard. However, Maxi figured a more plausible explanation would be Dandelion's eagerness to practice his first *baby steps* into the land of extortion. Maxi felt even more demoralised since he need not have given up the treasure. His car would not have been searched. Every ounce of his being was addled by these latest developments. There was no doubt he underestimated 40%, but Dandelion putting a price tag on the hole should not have come as a surprise. However, he couldn't be blamed for not considering *blackmail*. Nobody, in a million years, would have predicted such an outcome. He kept asking himself, could 40% be trusted to show up at the house? The answer to that nagging question would only be answered when he got home. Dandelion's intention to blackmail the County Council was a whole other boatload of stinking fish. He was sure to be on the steps of the Town Hall first thing Monday morning. Maxi had to find a way to intercept him before he got to speak with any one of the 'suits' in the County Council. Above all else, he could not allow that to happen.

At six o'clock on the dot, 40% raced his van up the hill. Maxi couldn't be seen to interact with him in any way, shape or form. It would be all caught on tape! Dandelion spent his down time each evening at home, reviewing those tapes. They were like blockbuster movies to him. He got excited taking money from customers during the day and he felt that very same excitement at night when he viewed those customers on tape. Besides searching for anomalies, he paid particular attention to his brother's wheeling's and dealing's. Something caught on tape that could be used in court and he got his *happy ending.* Lucky for Maxi, those tapes were on a twelve-hour cycle from eight a.m. to eight p.m. Otherwise, he would have been the main star in one of Dandelion's evening movies, with all the pacing about he did in the early mornings, in his search of the treasure.

40% whizzed along the narrow road on his way home from work at warp speed. His windscreen wipers were *flat out* trying to dislodge the torrential rain. He had his favourite Country & Western CD belting out a dreadful song from the dashboard speakers. The lyrics whined about a scornful woman from Cincinnati whose ex-husband was one shot of Jack Daniels away from emptying his shotgun into the roof of his mouth. He patted Maxi's backpack, which was next to him on the passenger seat for the umpteenth time since leaving the yard. It was his way of reassuring himself that, at last, he was a rich man. That evening he hummed along with the music as he always did, but a lot louder than usual. Also, there was an undeniable hint of ridicule in his accompaniment. His newfound fortune had callously relegated his love for that CD to almost disdain.

He swerved onto a side road or laneway to be more precise, throwing up muck and dirt as he navigated the turn. This portion of his *joyride* was basically a dirt road traversed only by farmers in their tractors to interconnect with neighbouring farms. He would challenge his motor skills on this stretch of road when he was excited, but always when it rained. He was enjoying the feel of the wheels grabbing and skidding along the slick surface. He had to wrestle constantly with the steering wheel, pulling it left and right and left again to constrain the wobbles that would, if unchecked, whip the van off the road. He felt invigorated by the physical demands made on him by the speeding van and the unpredictable, slick surface of the dirt road. Now, he was the one in charge. Only he could dictate the speed, and the faster he drove, the more he raised the stakes. Mentally, he broke free from the restraints of his financial woes. He checked his rear-view mirror. No hitman! He was in a good place for the first time since his nasty divorce, fourteen years ago.

As he reached for the skip-track button on the console, in search of a happy tune more aligned with his chirpy mood, he felt a massive blow to the passenger side of the van. He failed to notice a parked trailer jutting out from a laneway. It was difficult to see anything through that curtain of rain. The driver's side window imploded and a blast of glass filled the cab. The rear wheels lifted off the road and the back of the van whipped forward, causing it to flip over on its side and tumble repeatedly along the dirt road. It spun up over the crest of the mound that flanked the road and careened down a steep embankment. After kicking up big clumps of sod and ploughing through brambles and bushes, it finally came to rest in a cluster of pine trees. 40% was violently ejected through the opening where the windscreen used to be. He lay twisted and bloodied in the tall wet grass, about a skip, hop and a jump from the van. The sole surviving headlight seemed to search the dark, empty sky for answers. The music, for want of a better word, played on, indifferent to the distress its sound source had just endured. The miserable song, although capturing the current mood, was barely audible from the road above.

• • • •

LARRY 'LUNGS' WAS THE driver of Brannigan's recovery truck that was first at the scene of the crash that evening. He learned about the crash and its location from his stolen police radio, which he monitored closely every evening. He was a scavenger by birth. To say he resembled a buzzard was an understatement. When the Lord Almighty was assembling that man's DNA, He must have had the blue prints of a vulture on His worktop at that moment in time. Plus, He threw a faulty larynx into the mix to make him even more annoying. The volume control button was stuck on max. He didn't speak. He bellowed, thus the nickname, 'Lungs'.

'Smoky' Joe Baxter was his right-hand-man and equally deficient in moral fibre. This man gladly donated all his teeth in his quest for the ultimate 'smack' high. He was a chain smoker and with his head forever engulfed in smoke, no eyewitness could ever pick him out in a line-up. His smokescreen also made it difficult to pinpoint his age. Somewhere between 40 and 70 was a safe bet which further insulated him from ever 'doing time.' As a safety precaution, since he was a walking chimney, any illicit syphoning of fuel was performed exclusively by Larry.

Accompanying these two reprobates on all their nocturnal missions was 'Ironman' Mandy, Larry's transsexual younger sister. She was a tall, intimidating individual, especially when laminated from head to toe in matt-black spandex where her contradictory sexual organs were on constant, explicit display. She wore a matt black helmet moulded to the shape of her aerodynamic brain and gloves and runners of a matching hue. Her tinted glass goggles completed the ensemble. For someone who agonised over gender identity, such an outfit didn't seem at all appropriate. However, that stream-lined body suit with its complement of accessories made perfect sense when paired with the multi-geared, high speed, titanium racing bicycle that Mandy rode to compete in triathlon events all over the country. In competition, she was a sight to behold.

However, this same garb served another purpose besides winning races. It made Mandy almost invisible at night, which is a big plus for a burglar. Sam Brannigan (aka Buka, since he was so fond of Sambuca) – the owner of the recovery operation – was not only unaware of her participation in looting crash sites, he didn't even know she existed. Mandy may not have been on the payroll, but her involvement in the recovery operation proved to be financially lucrative for herself and the crew.

Larry spent his evenings glued to his police radio. His diligent monitoring and immediate response to reported collisions ensured that he and his cohorts would arrive at any given crash site well before the emergency services, affording them ample time to pillage and plunder. The trio would speed to the location in 'Brannigan's Recovery' truck with Mandy's bicycle strapped to the flatbed of the truck. About a mile or so out from the crash site, Larry would stop the truck, unload the bicycle, and Mandy would covertly ride the rest of the way to the crash site. This premature drop of man and machine was designed to sever any possible ties to the recovery crew. If and when the victim's looting indictments came to the fore, it would be some dyke on a bike, not the recovery crew, that would receive all the attention.

Upon arrival at the crash scene, Larry would seek out the person who alerted the authorities. Meanwhile, Mandy hid her bike in the bushes and waited eagerly for the signal. The good Samaritan who made the call would normally be found consoling the victim/victims. That person was usually relieved to hand over the reins to someone *in the know* and instantly disconnect from any further involvement. Once the site was clear of busy bodies, Mandy got the signal to proceed. She would bolt into action and steal the victim's valuables, along with any other worthwhile items strewn about the crash site. She was immune to the victim's injuries or fatalities - she once stole a necklace from a severed head. It took about three minutes on average to pick a site clean. Mandy's saddlebags would be full with booty and she'd be well on her way by the time the emergency services arrived.

The team of bandits relied on the shock factor and the trauma of the crash to cloak their piracy. Only when the injured parties recovered from their ordeal did they notice that their valuables were missing. Some might recall a shadowy like figure with reptilian features, an aerodynamic brain with goggle eyes and, of course, the substantial genitalia of both sexes rummaging about in the dark. Some might even dare a description. Most victims, realizing how incredible their recollection of events proved to be, didn't even bother to file a report. The emergency services always renounced any knowledge of a tall, reptilian-like species crawling about the site.

Should insinuations of foul play persist, an empty bottle of 'Wild Turkey' was usually considered by the police to be the author of such fiction.

While Mandy's saddlebags contained the victim's valuables, the crew always made sure to fill a box with crash site items of little or no value, to present to the police. Once the police were done picking through those items, junk is all that was left in the box. That night, the saddlebags contained a pair of binoculars, a gold cross and chain, a wrist watch, a wallet, a white envelope with 480 euros stuffed inside – 40%'s wages – and one pair of nylons, which surely Mandy had first dibs on. In the policeman's box, an orange woolly hat, a tennis ball, a selection of Country & Western CDs, a pair of old work boots and a small microwave oven with its door clinging to a hinge.

Just as she was about to mount the titanium bike that faithful evening, she happened to notice a backpack lying in the tall grass by the side of the dirt road. It was so far away from the van's final resting place that it lost any association with the crash. She bent down on her hands and knees and flipped on her head light. She was intrigued not only by the superb craftmanship of the product but with the quality of the material. The star-spangled banner was embroidered on the flap of the main compartment with 'Made in the U.S.A.' stitched directly below. It had oodles of storage chambers and strong durable straps, but what threw it over the edge was the strategic positioning of the water bottle holder. It was smack dab in the middle of the bag rather than the conventional placement, to the side. She appreciated how that ergo dynamic *leg up* would shave milliseconds off her time in her next big race. What a monumental discovery!

She quickly transferred her possessions from her own backpack to the new one. She noticed the metal box in the main compartment of the new bag, but paid no heed. Mandy's ignorance of the origins of that metal box stripped it of its mantle. It no longer generated the heart pounding excitement of its pursuers nor did it stimulate any flights of fancy. The treasure was now demoted to nothing more than a grubby metal box. She jammed her old backpack under a bush and threw the new one over her broad shoulders. Ecstatic with the night's haul, she pedalled off into the darkness.

A few minutes elapsed before the ambulance arrived, followed closely by the police. The medics got busy taking care of 40%. They strapped him to a gurney and humped him up the incline and into the back of the ambulance. It sped off down the dirt road with its flashing lights and sirens wailing. 40% would have been delighted with the speed they were going - high speed being the only way he ever travelled that road - except he was unconscious with an I.V. in his arm and an oxygen mask over his face. There was a strong indication he was pounding on death's door.

Larry operated the steel cable that dragged the crashed van up from the ditch and onto the flatbed of the recovery truck. While the van was being cared for, Joe gathered up all the bits of broken glass and debris that were strewn about the road. They always ensured that they left the crash site impeccable. Pride was certainly not the motivator. They always did a thorough job, to win the boss's favour so they could continue as land pirates behind the legitimate *front* of the haulage company.

• • • •

MEANWHILE, BACK AT the salvage yard, Maxi brought the gates of Eden together and snaked the heavy chain several times around the ornate bars of each. Twenty-five minutes later, he was at his house. The red rental van was parked in the driveway. He nodded his approval. However, his elation was short lived. There was no sign of 40%'s white van. His heart sank, and his stomach churned. Reluctant to accept the evidence before him, he drove bug-eyed up and down the street in search of 40%'s van. He returned to the house, deflated.

'40% wants 100%,' Maxi growled, repeatedly beating the steering wheel with his clenched fists. 'Over my dead body,' he shouted at the dashboard.

When he pulled into his driveway, he could see Nora through the living room window from the car. She was chatting away to some woman who had her back turned so he couldn't tell whether she was a friend or a healthcare worker. He figured, with the car still running and Nora in company, he'd drive over to Ella's house and personally fill her in on the gory details. He reversed the car into the road and drove the short distance. He parked the car, ran to the door, and let himself in. The dogs went ballistic. They had to, that was their job. Ella was on the phone, getting some guy off on one of her sex calls. She nodded to Maxi, pointed to the kitchen and herded the dogs up the stairs before ducking into the bathroom to finish her call in private.

Maxi greeted Jasper, who had his head wrapped around a flagon of cider. He emitted a scarcely audible grunt. Then he lifted one cheek of his fat ass and expelled a loud, thunderous fart into the living room. The encore to these stupendous emissions was a rich baritone belch that rattled the parade of empty flagons littering the foot of his chair. There was nothing he could add to be more indecorous.

'Suck my nipples,' Prudence squawked from his perch by the kitchen window as soon as Maxi entered.

'I'd be glad to oblige,' Maxi replied, substituting Ella for Prudence in his imagination.

He made himself a mug of tea and sat down by the kitchen table. Drumming the table-top with his fingers, he agonised over how his day unfolded. Ella came in a few minutes later and sat opposite him at the table. Her raven hair spilled down over her short, silky, floral dress that clung by little more than a thread to her tanned shoulders. Undoubtedly, a well-aimed sneeze would rid her of that dress. Her silver pendant was lost, deep down, happily tucked away within her ample cleavage. He had no idea what was on the end of that chain; a cross, a half moon, a heart? Whatever it was, he wished he could trade places!

'What's up?' She knew by his body language he was agitated.

'We have a problem, Ella,' he said, deflecting his focus. 'Actually, make that two.'

She paid close attention as Maxi brought her up to speed on the day's developments.

'Bottom line, right now, we have no treasure and Dandelion must be stopped before he talks to anyone in the Town Hall. It was all going so well and now it's all gone to shit.' In a desperate bid to ease his frustration, he added, 'The treasure is probably worthless anyway.'

'Then again,' Ella encouraged. 'It could be priceless.'

'Yeah,' he sighed. 'You might be right.'

'Do you know where 40% lives?' Ella asked.

'He's somewhere over by Mandolin Brook, but I don't know his address. Come to think of it, it should be easy enough to spot that piece of shit van of his. It's too high to park in the garage,' Maxi ventured. 'If he's home, it'll be parked in the driveway or on the road.'

'Well then, what are we waiting for?' Ella said. 'Let's go.'

They drove over to Mandolin Brook, which was on the outskirts of Ballydecuddle, no more than a fifteen-minute drive, with no traffic. It was a nice, neat housing estate with whitewashed terraced houses, all in rows and with their little manicured gardens, dotted with plants and bushes. It was in stark contrast to where Maxi had envisioned 40% might live. They patrolled up and down the streets, checking every driveway in search of the white van. Nothing.

'Maybe one of the residents knows where he lives,' Maxi suggested. 'Let's knock on a few doors.'

'It's worth a shot,' Ella agreed.

By now, the rain had softened to a drizzle. The road glistened like polished silver while the street lights carelessly splashed yellow hues all over the sidewalk. Ella went to one side of the road and Maxi the other. Some people didn't answer the door even though it was apparent by the lights and the TV's that someone was home. People got a little anxious after dark. The few that answered were abrupt in their denials.

'Sorry to bother you, sir,' Maxi inquired of this older gentleman who was already dressed for bed in his pyjamas and slippers. 'Would you happen to know which house John Windsor Junior lives in?'

'That noisy bastard lives two doors up,' the angry man pointed up the road. 'That fucking tuba of his, first thing in the morning, up and down the scale and last thing at night, up and down the same fucking scale. He's been in that house for fourteen years...'

The old man kept ranting on and on while he shuffled his feet on the parquet floor like he was trying to start a fire. His antics reminded Maxi of shell-shocked veterans. The 'airstrikes' from the tuba had taken their toll. Maxi wondered how many others did 40% take out on the estate... with his gift. The angry man slammed the door shut in his face. Maxi thanked the door and raced across the street to grab Ella.

'Seems 40% has made his presence felt around here.' He pointed to the house, two doors up.

No lights, no van, nobody home. Maxi stood by the front door, shaking his head in disbelief. Ella came up behind him and rubbed circles into his broad back.

'What now?' he asked, not expecting a reply.

'Leave a note with your phone number. You never know, maybe he was delayed or got side-tracked somehow,' Ella encouraged. 'Don't give up just yet.'

'What's the point?' Maxi replied. 'He doesn't like to use the phone.'

'Leave your number anyway.'

Maxi got his note pad from the car and wrote his phone number on a slip of paper. He trapped the piece of paper between the door knocker and striker plate on the front door.

He checked his watch. 'I've got to get home and take care of Nora.'

They drove in silence to Ella's house. 'I'll meet you later when I get Nora to bed. Tell the girls what's going on and have them come over to my house after nine.'

Nora was asleep by the fire. Juanita Hernandez, her caretaker, was cleaning up after dinner. Maxi was pleasantly surprised to see that she was still there, and even more so when she presented him with a plate of food from the oven.

'Wow, Juanita, this looks lovely. Thank you very much.'

'Jew well cum,' she said.

'Nora must have enjoyed her dinner?' Maxi pointed with his fork at the empty plate on the coffee table in front of Nora.

'She like very much de fish.'

'I have to agree with her,' Maxi said. 'This is delicious.'

'Good, I glad you like.' Juanita replied as she put on her overcoat to get ready to leave.

'Thanks for taking care of Nora all week. She likes you. Believe me, that's unusual for her.' Maxi slipped an envelope across the table with 500 euros inside and a 50-euro bill on top.

'A little extra for you.'

'Machos gracias senor.' She took the money, put it in her pocketbook and left.

Maxi sat on the couch next to Nora by the dwindling fire. He threw a few logs on it to keep it alive until the girls got there. His phone rang. Nora woke up. It was Freddy 'Boom-Boom.' He postponed his appointment for that evening until the next day - noon on Sunday. Maxi thanked him for returning the van and assured him he would have his money in the morning. He hung up.

'A woman called to the house earlier,' Nora informed Maxi. 'She was upset.'

He remembered the woman with her back to the window. 'What did she want?'

'She wanted to know if I knew where her brother was?'

'Who's her brother?' he asked.

'John Windsor Junior,' Nora replied.

Instantly, Maxi was on the edge of his seat.

'She said he works with you and Daniel down at the yard,' Nora continued.

'Yeah, yeah, that's right he does,' Maxi agreed, eagerly urged her to continue. 'Go on.'

A tiny speck of light began to twinkle at the back of that deep, dark tunnel in Maxi's mind's eye.

'She said he was supposed to be home around six-thirty. She waited for about an hour. He didn't call her or leave a message or give any indication that he was going to be late. That's not like him, she said. Her brother doesn't like to use the phone, but he would if it was an emergency. She comes down from the north every other weekend and stays over at her brother's house on Saturday nights. She went on about preparing the popcorn the way he liked it, with plenty of butter and such. They were supposed to watch black and white movies together. That's what they did every other Saturday night for as long as he has lived in that house.'

The fact his sister didn't know where he was, was disconcerting, to say the least. Maxi had to ask himself, 'Was 40% that callous that he would drop everything, including his own flesh and blood to satisfy his greed?'

'How did she know to come here?'

'She was at Daniel's house before she came here. He must have given her our address.'

'That makes sense.' Maxi nodded.

'She got hysterical when you weren't here and started to wail. I tried to comfort her but you know me - that's not my forte - let's say. She said she was going to the police station next.'

'Did she leave a contact number?

'No.' Nora frowned. 'I guess she forgot, and I didn't think to ask.'

'I see. Anyway,' Maxi sighed, 'it's past your bedtime. You get your nightgown on and I'll get your tablets.'

At exactly nine on the dot, Nora was fast asleep in her bed. Maxi poured himself a double vodka on the rocks and sat on the couch to search the flames in the blazing log fire for the remedy to his plight. The realisation that he had been played by 40% from the get-go finally began to sink in. His sister's concern for his disappearance was proof that the bastard skipped town with the treasure.

The three women arrived over at Maxi's house in two separate cars and within minutes of each other. They sat around the coffee table listening attentively to Maxi's synopsis of the day's events. It wasn't pretty.

'40% bragged to me earlier about not having a soul,' Maxi announced to the group. 'I'd safely say he's got no heart either.'

'He's got *some* pair of balls,' Ella exclaimed, 'that's for sure, but I'm not sold on his missing heart.'

'Ella,' said Maxi, '...the man stole our treasure out from under us and fucked off with it. He lied to my face. He obviously lied to his sister. Take it from me, he's gone. Never to be seen again.'

'I don't see it that way,' Ella countered. 'That man's sister is the only family he's got. Nora said his sister was hysterical when she came to the house looking for him. Think about it,' she insisted. 'Every other weekend, his sister comes down from the North to be with him. I suspect he probably goes up North on alternate weekends to see her. Who knows? They seem to enjoy each other's company, so why would 40% forfeit all that for thirty pieces of silver?'

'Good point,' Debbie replied, nodding her head in agreement. 'If that's the case, maybe we should follow 40%'s sister up North? He might be waiting for her there with the treasure.'

'There's no point in doing that,' said Maxi. 'She's the one going around saying her brother has disappeared. Either she's genuinely upset her brother has gone missing, or like our two County Council boys, she's giving us the performance of a lifetime.'

'You said yourself that you underestimated 40%,' Debbie remarked. 'His sister shares the same genetic code, so who's to say she's not as conniving as her brother?'

'There's been so much subterfuge going on lately,' Ida remarked. 'I don't know which side is up anymore. I need to come up for air.'

'Yeah, you do that, Ida,' Debbie snarled. 'While the rest of us stay down here trying to *come up* with a solution.'

'A little air,' Ida retorted, 'wouldn't go astray on you either.'

'All right, settle down, you two,' Maxi pleaded. 'We're all a little antsy right now.'

After a considerable silent interlude, Ida blurted out, 'All roads lead to Damascus.'

'I thought it was, all roads lead to Rome?' Ella corrected.

'Who gives a fuck?' Maxi hollered, his frustration getting the better of him. 'What has that got to do with our present predicament?'

'We're getting nowhere at the moment,' Ida smugly replied. 'I thought I'd throw in a destination.'

'Yeah, ye know what,' Maxi conceded. 'You're right. Let's call it a night.'

Just then, his phone rang.

Chapter 14.

The rookie policeman Trevor Ward - still wet behind the ears from the Academy - had just started the night shift and was standing behind the complaints counter in the Ballydecuddle police station when he came face-to-face with an irate middle-aged woman whose brother had gone missing. She was dressed in a snug-fitting tweed trouser suit, over a café au lait coloured silk blouse. Her cashmere scarf was deliberately left loose around her neck to showcase her faux-pearl-necklace. By displaying her *junk* in such a brazen manner, the authenticity of those pearls never came into question. In the event a *doubting Thomas* happened by, she would recite the story of how Chunga, her make-belief Bajaus diver, drowned while procuring those oysters from the bottom of the ocean. To add validity to her story, she would pinch one of the faux pearls between finger and thumb and recant how Chunga's fingers had to be broken to release that very pearl. She was the avatar of those filthy rich Anglo-Saxon dames, who sip champagne before noon at polo matches in the Hamptons or at high-roller gaming tables in Vegas. However, the orange woolly hat atop her beleaguered looking head contested such claims, insinuating instead, she might have a crack pipe in her purse next to a notebook full of *Johns*.

'Where the fuck is my brother?' she wailed.

'There, there now, take it easy, Missus.' Trevor reached across the counter to comfort her but quickly recoiled when she snapped at him like a pit bull from the hood.

'Do you see a fucking ring?' Lucy Windsor held up her left hand and stuck it in Trevor's face. 'It's Miss... you fucking flat foot.'

'Now, now, now,' Trevor responded, echoing another useless preposition in his futile attempt to placate this deranged woman. Concurrently, he was trying desperately to contain memories of his

150

fucked-up childhood from escaping the cage in the back of his mind. Already he wanted to slam this woman's head into the wall.

'Now, now, now,' Miss Lucy Windsor mimicked his attempt to console her. 'Why don't you get in your police car right now and go find my brother?'

She cried out, her tears fused with mascara spilling down her cheeks and onto her silken blouse, like blobs of black blood. She wouldn't have looked at all out of place at a Marylin Manson gig.

'I need you to calm down,' Trevor insisted. 'I can't help you otherwise.'

Totally spent, she threw herself on the counter and sobbed. Trevor, without losing eye contact, reached for the missing person's form. After a few minutes, the sobs became less frequent until finally she composed herself and proudly lifted her head.

'What's your brother's name?' Trevor inquired, as if nothing had happened.

'John Windsor Junior,' she replied, also as if nothing had happened.

'Good, now we're getting places.'

'So, what makes you believe that your brother is missing, Missus... Miss... Miss Windsor.' Trevor stuttered as he tripped all over his words like John Akii-Bua, having a bad day with the hurdles.

'He was supposed to be home from work at six-thirty, but he didn't show.' She took a hankie out of her bag and blew her nose. She was about to start crying, but corrected herself. 'He didn't call me to tell me he would be late. He didn't leave a message. Nothing. It's not like him. Something is very wrong.'

'It's only eight-thirty. Do you think, that maybe,' Trevor inquired, as he consulted the form to get the name right. '*John* might have gone out for a few drinks with his friends?'

'No,' she insisted, stamping her foot on the floor. 'He has no friends and never goes out.'

'I see.' Trevor twiddled his pen before scratching a line through the 'friends and associates' box on the missing person's form. 'Where does he work?'

'The Aechmea scrapyard.'

'Oh yes, I've been down there a few times. Come to think of it, I did meet your brother. Quiet man.'

Trevor remembered meeting him on a few occasions when he had to drive to the yard to document some infraction or other between the two Aechmea brothers. It was strange how this woman's woolly hat subliminally triggered a search into the dark recesses of his mind to solve that niggling sensation he had as to why that orange woolly hat seemed so familiar. Eureka! Her missing brother - John Windsor Junior - wore one just like it.

'I'm going to put out an APB on your brother with a description of his van,' Trevor informed her. He had no intention of doing anything of the sort. To warrant such action from the police department, a person would have to be missing for at least 24 hours. In Trevor's case, nothing short of a severed limb or a *bloody* crime scene would get his attention.

'Every police officer in the country will be on the lookout for your brother,' he assured her. 'We will find him, I promise you. Now give me your phone number and the details of your brother's van.'

Miss Lucy Windsor complied.

'The best thing you can do right now is to go home and wait for our call. You never know, he might be there already, waiting for you.'

Miss Lucy Windsor weighed up Trevor's advice and reluctantly agreed to leave. As soon as she was out through the double doors, Trevor retrieved his night stick from under the counter, and after a few fancy twirls above his head, he pounded the seat of the closest chair with reckless abandon. 'Boy does that feel good!' he puffed.

When Lucy Windsor got back to John's house, she noticed the slip of paper trapped in the knocker on the front door. There was still no sign of her brother, so she called the number.

'Who's this?' she inquired.

'Who's this?' Maxi echoed.

'I'm Lucy Windsor... John's sister. I got your number from the front door at John's house.'

It took Maxi a moment to see the link between John's sister and 40%. 'Yes, of course, Lucy Windsor, *John Windsor's sister*,' Maxi replied as he gestured to the girls to get their attention. He set his phone on speaker and continued. 'I'm Maxi Dillon. You spoke with my mother earlier.'

'Yes. I'm afraid she must think I'm a basket case.'

'No, not at all.' Maxi rolled his eyes to the heavens, and he made circles with his free hand to hurry her along with the call.

'I don't suppose you heard from John.'

'I'm afraid not.'

'I reported him missing to the police,' she imparted in a formal manner. 'They put out an APB on him.' She couldn't hold it together any longer and she started to sob.

'Now, now, Lucy, don't cry,' he said, trying to sound like he cared. 'I have no doubt the police will find him.'

'I think something awful has happened to John,' she wailed.

'I know you must be very upset, but try to think positively,' Maxi said as he flipped his middle finger at the phone. The three women listening to the call nearly burst out laughing.

'Yes, you're right,' she relented. Her sniffling made her sound like a bomb disposal dog in a van full of Centex.

'It's late. You should get some sleep,' Maxi proposed, making faces at the girls who were now crowded around his phone like teenage fans at a boy-band concert. 'Lucy... let the police do their job.'

'I am tired,' she confessed. 'I'm going to bed. Please call me if you hear anything, anything at all.'

'Will do,' Maxi replied. 'Fuck you,' he mimed with his lips.

There's no chance of hearing anything, he thought. He didn't feel it was the right time to tell Lucy Windsor that her piece-of-shit brother had split with the treasure and would never be seen again.

'Right, you all heard the woman,' Maxi addressed the girls. 'I think she's genuine, do you?'

'She sounded fairly convincing to me,' Ida admitted.

'Me too.' Ella nodded.

Debbie agreed, 'Yeah, I don't think that's an act.'

'Look it's nearly midnight. There's not a lot we can do right now, so let's call it a day.'

• • • •

THE REST OF THE NIGHT at Ballydecuddle police station passed without incident. Trevor Ward occupied his down time, twirling and spinning his 'virgin' baton. It was important for him to demonstrate dexterity when the time came to wield his weapon. He wanted the perpetrator - whose head he was bashing in - to appreciate that each blow was being delivered by a competent and highly trained professional.

Just before dawn, Trevor answered a 911 call. A man reported a car crash with a possible fatality on a dirt road just east of Cello Falls. Trevor dispatched the location of the crash, via police radio, to the ambulance service and to the station's own police car, which was out there somewhere, patrolling the locality. It never occurred to him that this might be John Windsor Junior. It was only when Miss Lucy Windsor returned at around six in the morning - a little more dishevelled and a lot more distraught - that it occurred to him the crash victim might be her brother. He decided to supress that suspicion until he had further proof. There was no knowing how this man's tormented sister would react to news of her brother's demise.

'Good morning, Miss Windsor, I'm afraid I have no news for you,' Trevor volunteered right off the bat.

'Well I'm not leaving,' she sobbed, '...until my brother's whereabouts are known.' She sobbed some more, and it was quickly becoming apparent her sob-tank would soon be empty.

'Very well. Make yourself comfortable on one of those seats over there.' Trevor pointed to the furthest away chair in the waiting room. 'The station's patrol car has finished its shift and should be back here within the hour. They might have some information about your brother.'

Trevor got no response. Plus, she disobeyed his seat assignment and sat by the counter within striking range of Trevor's baton, which was concealed on a shelf directly below the counter. He gripped the handle and squeezed as hard as he could. He visualised himself delivering a barrage of blows to that woolly hat of hers, with her head still in it. He knew from experience that this mini flight of fancy would get him over the hump until his shift ended in less than thirty minutes. All he had to do was keep his childhood horrors behind bars until then.

As he imagined himself pummelling that orange woolly hat with his repertoire of show-stopping blows, the double doors to the entrance of the police station swung open and the night patrol entered, side by side. The taller of the two police men, carried a cardboard box which he placed on the countertop. The contents were the personal property of the victim who crashed his van at Cello Falls. It was Trevor's job to document each item in the 'Book of Crashes' and then store the box away in the back, to await collection.

Once Miss Lucy Windsor spotted the orange woolly hat peeping over the rim of the box, she jumped up, dove in, and snatched it to her bosom.

She screamed, 'Where did you get my Johnny's hat?'

'You recognize this...' The tall one stopped short, realising how redundant his remark was when he brushed up against its identical twin on top of that woman's sobbing head.

'Where is he?' Miss Lucy Windsor screamed, holding the woolly hat in her clenched fist at arm's length like an executioner displaying the severed head of the condemned party to the awe-stricken crowd. Some say, even though the head is severed from the torso, the brain is still active - for up to twenty seconds - which affords the head one last perplexed look at its accusers.

No one dared look at the hat... either hat, for that matter.

'I'm afraid your Johnny has been in a car crash,' the tall one informed.

'Oh my God,' she wailed, '...is he hurt?'

'He's in intensive care in Ballydecuddle hospital. I don't know how bad his injuries are...'

Miss Lucy Windsor grabbed the box, flung the orange woolly hat inside and was out through the double doors into her car and off down the road to the hospital while the tall one continued his explanation. He had his eyes slammed shut - it was easier to convey horror stories to the victim's kin when he didn't have to look them directly in the eye. He kept talking. He got so embroiled in his explanation, the other two police officers didn't have the heart to interrupt. When he opened his eyes, the woolly orange twins were well gone.

Miss Lucy Windsor barged her way through another set of double doors, this time the entrance to the E.R. in Ballydecuddle hospital. She challenged the nurse at the reception desk and demanded to see her brother. She was denied entry and had to be restrained by a security guard who evicted her to the waiting room where she was forced to seethe for the next hour or so. Once she calmed down, Doctor Mulcahy, who was the surgeon entrusted to care for her brother, approached her in the waiting room and introduced himself. He informed her as to the extent of her brother's injuries and how precarious his recovery prospects were. He told her they were obliged to place John in an induced coma to circumvent the pain. It would be some time before they could tell whether or not he would make it out of the woods.

Chapter 15.

A big, black jackdaw that was a frequent visitor to Nora's house smashed into the living room window with a loud thud. It slid, spread-eagled down along the glass and came to rest in a dishevelled heap on the windowsill. Juanita Hernandez, the temporary carer, who was a clean freak, took it upon herself to wash that window the day before - something that hadn't been done in that house in over fifty years. The glass was so clean, it didn't exist in this jackdaw's eyes.

Maxi was awakened by the noise. He spent the night on the couch after doing a *'number'* on the vodka. He struggled to sit upright on the seat and had to cradle his pounding head in his hands. Still fully dressed from the night before, he stood up slowly, using the backrest of the couch as a prop. His mouth was so dry that if he were offered a million euros to spit, he'd lose. Picking his way carefully towards the kitchen, like a rock climber scaling a cliff face, he engaged the furniture and the walls to assist him on his way. He filled a tall glass with water from the kitchen faucet and drained it in one go.

He checked the time on his phone. It was only seven fifteen a.m. It was still early enough for him to catch up on a little sleep in his own bed before Nora woke up, but he decided against it. It was then he noticed a missed call at five past seven. He immediately returned the call. Lucy was exhausted by then, having spent the whole night darting around Ballydecuddle in search of her missing brother. When she got back to her brother's house, she called Maxi again to let him know that she found John but got no answer. She had just laid her head down on the pillow when her phone rang.

'Hello,' *Lucy* Windsor answered, sounding exhausted.

'Hello Lucy, it's Maxi, what's up?'

'John was in an accident,' she sobbed. 'He crashed his van and now he's in a coma in the hospital.' She said, sobbing some more.

'Oh my God,' Maxi exclaimed. 'That's great news Lucy, and here I was thinking...'

'What the fuck?' she snarled at Maxi. 'You think this is great news. My brother - is in hospital - in a fucking coma - and you think this is great news!'

'Oh no, of course not,' he remarked, realising his blunder. 'I'm sorry,' he apologised. 'I didn't mean it like that, it's just, I'm so happy he's alive.' Maxi tried desperately to back-peddle but couldn't disguise his elation. In fact, he didn't care to. He was over the moon with this news.

'Oh my God,' she howled. 'You're a fucking monster.'

Before he got a chance to reply, she hung up.

His hangover was obliterated by the gush of excitement he was feeling at that moment. Every part of him, his kidneys, his liver, even his spleen all wanted to partake in his celebration. If anyone, he thought, walks in on me now and sees the state of me, they'll run for the hills and never look back. He felt a fleeting pang of remorse for 40% amid all those sparks, but the way he drove, Maxi felt he had it coming. With a clear head and a stupid grin on his face, he called Ella on his cell. His phone rang and rang and rang.

'Oh my God, look at the time,' Ella snarled, 'it's so early,' she moaned. 'It's Sunday, the only morning in the whole week I get to sleep on,' she growled. 'This better be good.'

'Lucy Windsor called me again,' he teased.

'And...'

'She found him,' Maxi asserted.

'Oh my God,' Ella chirped. 'She found 40%... where?'

'He crashed his van,' Maxi cheerfully announced. 'He's in intensive care in Ballydecuddle hospital. Can you believe it?'

'Oh wow! That's great news,' Ella cheered. 'We're back in business.'

'Yeah, my sentiments exactly but...'

'But what?' Ella pleaded, confused by his hesitancy.

'Ah,' he sighed. 'It's just that I upset Lucy Windsor on the phone with... let's say, my overzealous reaction to the news that she found her brother.'

'So what? She'll get over it,' Ella assured.

'Ella,' he cautioned. 'Her brother is in a coma, for fuck sake and here's me jumping up and down like I won the lotto.'

'Well, hello... you did win the lotto,' she confirmed. 'Listen, I know where you're coming from and I can't blame you for reacting the way you did,' she confided. 'Look at me just now, I did the same. So, don't sweat it.' She said as she yawned out loud. She was still half asleep. 'I do feel bad for 40% though.'

'Me too,' Maxi concurred. 'We should say a prayer,' he suggested. 'We'll ask God to give him a speedy recovery.' He tried desperately to disguise the giddiness in his voice.

'I totally agree,' Ella replied, trying hard to sound solemn herself.

The phone went silent for a moment as they both devoted that sacred moment to prayer. Of course, neither one prayed. Instead, they saw their trampled dreams come back to life, and to celebrate they each took off on a mini shopping spree.

'Did you ask God to pin-point the treasure?' Ella joked, to nip the sombre mood in the bud.

'Did you?' Maxi retorted.

'No.' She said. 'I have Him busy doing other shit for me... like making Jasper disappear.'

'All right,' said Maxi. 'Let's jump down from the clouds for a minute and see if we can figure out where that treasure is right now.'

'Obviously, 40% never made it home from work,' Ella qualified as she lit a cigarette. 'Which means your backpack was in the van with him when he crashed.'

'Correct,' Maxi agreed. 'So, the question is... who has it now? That's what we need to find out.'

'I don't know,' Ella pondered. 'What's the procedure when it comes to traffic accidents, but I'm almost sure the police gather up the personal belongings of the victims at the crash site.'

'That makes sense,' Maxi nodded. 'I'll check out the Ballydecuddle police station this morning.'

'Would you prefer if I went instead?' Ella offered. 'I know the way you get with the cops.'

'No, it's no problem,' he assured her, 'I need to practice becoming an upstanding pillar of the community.'

'That you do,' she agreed.

'Do me a favour and call Debbie.' He said which surprised her with his abrupt shift in focus. 'Find out when she's working in the ER and have her keep an eye on 40%. We need to know when he's due to come out of that coma.'

'No problem,' Ella replied. 'Anything else I can help you with?'

'Yeah, ye know what,' Maxi retorted. 'I'm meeting Boom-boom here at twelve o'clock. I have to pay him and Happy Jack the balance. Maybe we use him one more time,' he suggested.

'For what?' Ella exclaimed.

'You know we can't just let Dandelion storm into the Town Hall and blackmail the first big-shot he sees. Whoever he runs into with his *torpedo* story will look at him like he's a mental patient who just took a dump on the floor.'

'Yes,' Ella agreed. 'I'd say that's a fair depiction, albeit a little too vivid at this hour of the morning,' Ella raised her voice: 'I didn't have my coffee yet.'

'That makes two of us,' Maxi countered. 'Anyway, we can't let that happen. We have to find some way to intercept Dandelion in the Town Hall before he has a chance to speak to anyone in authority.'

'I take it you want to use Boom-boom to cut him off at the pass,' Ella reasoned.

'Exactly,' Maxi concurred. 'I was thinking we could use him one more time to show up at the Town Hall tomorrow morning and engage with Dandelion right inside the reception area. Boom-boom can hang around in his green overalls with a roll of blueprints under his arm as if he is waiting for a town surveyor to examine his drawings and jump on Dandelion when he comes through the door.'

'But he won't be behind the counter where Dandelion expects him to be,' Ella sighed. 'Don't you think he'll find that a little odd?'

'I know, but what can we do? He retorted. 'He'll just have to give the impression to Dandelion that he's on his way out to a job in the field. I'm sure if you're in the extortion business, you're not going to want some peasant from the town; who needs a street bulb swapped out or a pothole filled in, listening in on your demands. He already met Boom-boom so - the devil you know, yada, yada - but I'm a little concerned how they'll interact with one another, this time round.'

'Why?' Ella asked.

'Dandelion made no bones about the fact that he hates the County Council and anyone associated with it,' Maxi said recanting Dandelion's remarks. 'They're all nothing but a bunch of lazy bastards who wouldn't work to warm themselves.'

'Well, he's right about that,' Ella agreed. 'Dandelion would put up with snakes in his pants as long as he was getting paid.

'*Snakes* in his pants?' Maxi hissed jokingly.

'I know, I know,' she conceded. 'I need my coffee... bad.'

'Okay so, in my opinion,' Maxi remarked. 'All that's needed, is for the two of them to cross paths in the Town Hall. I really don't think it matters which side of the counter Boom-boom is at.'

'I hate to burst your bubble, but your plan stinks.' Ella groaned as she got out of bed. 'I know I only spent fifteen minutes with the man down in the yard on Saturday, but I got to see what a shrewd dude he is. There's no way he's going to buy our man, on *this* side of the counter,' she declared. 'If we do this your way, Boom-boom is going to have to hang out, fiddling his thumbs, on this side of the counter, until Dandelion arrives. I know you think Dandelion's going to be there first thing. What if he doesn't show until noon? Then what? Boom-boom can't hang out indefinitely.'

'Well what do you suggest we do?' Maxi probed.

'Somehow,' Ella suggested. 'We need to get Freddy Boom-boom behind that counter.'

The phone went silent for a moment.

'Here's an idea.' Ella was first to speak. 'How about he goes into the Town Hall as an IT specialist, sent by head office to upgrade the phone lines and the internet? These IT guys come and go all the time and nobody pays them any soot.' She took a long pull of her cigarette. 'This way he can hang out on the other side of the counter in the customer service area, looking busy pumping up their computers with the promise of faster internet connection and better-quality resolution and all that hi-tech horseshit. Nobody is going to interfere with this man's work. Everyone will be expecting their porno movies to stream seamlessly once he's done.'

'Jezzus Ella,' Maxi gasped. 'You think everyone who own's a computer watches porn?'.

'Every man for sure,' she stated categorically, '...and some women.'

'Wow,' he gasped. 'Women too. That's so fucking hot.'

'Anyway, when Dandelion shows up,' she continued, 'Boom-boom can stop what he's at and greet him from *behind* the counter. A lot more convincing, don't you think?'

'Absolutely,' Maxi agreed.

'We get a second wear out of those custom overalls and he'll have his I.D. badge around his neck... only this time to fool the Town Hall,' she said, but she couldn't stave off another loud yawn. 'It's a no-brainer,' she stated.

'Brilliant.' Maxi commended. 'That works.'

'Maxi... make me a cup of tea.' Nora shouted from her bedroom.

'You hear that?' Maxi asked, aiming his phone at the noise.

'Yeah,' Ella replied. 'I guess your day has already started.'

'And an action packed one it promises to be,' he sighed.

'I got to go,' Maxi divulged. 'In the meantime, will you write some sort of a script for Boom-boom? You know he won't do anything without a script. It doesn't have to be anything fancy,' he promised. 'Some computer geek jargon is all... you know what I mean.'

'Don't worry, I'll put something together.' Ella assured. 'Once-I-have-my-coffee.'

'Okay good. Meet me here at noon and the three of us will go over the plan. That gives you a few hours to type up some bullshit. Oh, what do you think for this gig? A hundred euros?'

'Yeah, I suppose,' Ella concurred. 'We better find this treasure and it better be good or we'll all be in the Poor House.'

'Maxi... where's my cup of tea?' Nora shouted.

'I better go,' Maxi decided. 'Coming right up mum,' he shouted back.

'Okay,' Ella vowed. 'I'll have a script ready by then. See you later. Oorah.'

'Oorah.' Maxi smiled and hung up.

He made breakfast for Nora and they ate together at the kitchen table. He lit a fire and Nora snuggled in next to it with some romance novel. About an hour later, a group of elderly women began to congregate by the front stoop. Maxi peeped out through the living room window to get an impression of the small gathering. He noticed an old man casually orbiting about the cluster of women, seemingly oblivious to his exclusion.

'Hands up, who's pussy whipped?' Maxi pondered. 'Shoot me with both barrels if I end up like that.'

This assembly was there for the ten o'clock debate: *Morality vs. Religion.* Maxi greeted each one at the front door, and while he ushered them into the living room, he made subtle hints to draw their attention to the donation's bowl that was strategically placed in the hallway. Several old women in various stages of decay and one old broken man contributed almost 60 euros to the kitty. Now that they were all seated in two rows of four, Maxi was able to study the old vampire responsible for sucking the life out of this lily-livered excuse of a man. He was forced to do a double-take. This woman, presumably his wife, was not at all what he expected. She was very refined looking and impeccably dressed in a saffron maxi skirt with a cream linen blouse and matching scarf. Her sheep skin jacket was draped over the back of the chair and her Versace bag was next to her seat on the floor. She was tall, slim and shapely. Her fair complexion and full head of wavy hair made it impossible to gauge her age. She was one of those women like Raquel Welch who defied the ageing process and remained a blooming flower among her cohort of weeds.

'*She must have been the one,*' Maxi figured, '*...who put the twenty in the bowl.*' He looked at the husband. '*Lucky bastard. Hold your fire, after all.*'

Nora sat in her own chair next to the log fire. The whiteboard was placed on an easel stand, over to her right. Maxi stood by the board and introduced himself.

'Welcome everybody. My name is Maxi Dillon and I am the instigator, the initiator, the agent provocateur of these little debates. My job is to get the ball rolling! Today's debate,' he pointed at the whiteboard. 'Morality vs. Religion.' He stood for a moment in silence.

'Is our conscience governed by morality?' As he posed the question, he wrote it on the whiteboard.

'We have two types of conscience, lax and informed. Is our appreciation of morality altered, pending on which type of conscience we have?'

'Of course, it is.' One of the newcomers piped up from the second row. 'If you do something wrong and you are aware that it is the wrong thing to do, you feel guilty. On the other hand, if you have a lax conscience, you feel no shame, no guilt, nothing.'

'Very good,' Maxi encouraged.

'It's that little voice in your head telling you what's right and wrong,' Nancy Fleming - Nora's arch nemesis – announced, arriving out of the blocks early to put her mark on the proceedings. She sat in her usual spot in the front row and looked across at Nora to incite a response. Nora shifted in her seat. She wanted to reply but had nothing, yet. She had to grin and bear in the meantime.

'Dat little vice is synonymous wit intuition.' The saffron skirt got involved. Her thick Slavic accent turned every head in the room. 'Jew must listen to vat your gut haz to say.'

'Wow, brains as well,' Maxi thought.

'I disagree,' Niamh Conway, the ninety-four-year-old techie, challenged. 'The little voice in your head can tell you one thing while your intuition - your gut - can tell you the exact opposite. They are not synonymous; they are in juxtaposition. This little voice in your head is often represented by a little angel on one shoulder and a little devil on the other. Your gut has your best interests at heart; not so with the little voice, it can lead you astray.'

'Very interesting,' Maxi said as he directed his next question to the whole group. 'Would you agree with Niamh's interpretation of conscience?'

He retreated away from the white board, knowing that he had dumped enough 'chum' in the waters to incite a thinking frenzy. He nodded his farewell to Nora and slipped out of the living room. He was a little flustered as he drove to the police station. He felt the same nausea en route to the dentist. This would be his first voluntary visit. Any prior involvement Maxi had with the police was usually the aftermath of a bar brawl, where he'd end up cuffed to a bench in a holding cell. When he arrived at the station, he took a few deep breaths in the carpark, and once acclimated to his new role as a concerned citizen, he entered the building.

A middle-aged policeman with a redhead and a bad case of acne stood transfixed at the counter. It was quite apparent that he was caught off guard, having just crammed a fistful of potato-chips into his mouth. He appeared uncertain as to what to do next. He broke eye contact with Maxi and attempted to gulp them down in one go. Mistake. He spluttered crisps all over himself and the countertop. Now he had to contend with the embarrassing mess. Maxi was fortunate to have arrested his approach to the counter... just out of range of the crispy spew.

'How may I be of asss... sssi... sss... tance?' The redhead spat his inquiry all over Maxi.

Crispy bits that survived the purge were non-ceremoniously sprayed all over Maxi, propelled by the abundance of s's. He made it through the artillery only to be cut down by small arms fire. Without missing a beat, Maxi wiped his face and skipped over the little mishap like it never happened.

'I'm curious to know,' Maxi replied. 'In the event of a crash, what happens to the victim's belongings?'

'Oh, the police... that's us,' he said, pointing to himself, obviously still grappling with the idea that he was one of them. 'We collect up all the valuables and whatever odds and ends are strewn about the crash site and bring them here. We label each item and store them away in the back room until someone comes to claim the property. Each box is identified by the types of vehicles involved in the crash.'

'So,' Maxi responded as he searched for confirmation. 'You label the victim's property in accordance with the model of car or truck involved in the crash?'

'Correct,' the redhead police officer proudly announced.

'Would you have anything on a white Ford van that crashed yesterday evening over by Cello Falls?'

'Let me check the *Book of Crashes.*' The redhead besieged.

He ran a greasy finger along the inside collar of his oversized shirt. He was nervous. Admittedly, Maxi's 'antique' leather jacket, his torn Levi's jeans - the tears and rips attained the hard way by physical labour - his leather boots and dark sunglasses had a tendency to unnerve... the long arm of the law. The redhead dipped down and fumbled about under the counter. He resurfaced a moment later with the *Book of Crashes.* He handled the book so reverently, Maxi felt almost obliged to genuflect or maybe carve the sign of the cross in the air. The redhead pried open the thick book and flicked through the pages until he arrived on Saturday, the crash day in question.

'A box of belongings was recovered from the White Ford Van's crash site,' he confirmed, '...but it seems, Miss Lucy Windsor, the victim's sister, took it with her.'

'Would you happen to have a list of the items in that box?' Maxi inquired.

'Afraid not sir. That box never made it across this counter.' The redhead pointed down at the knotty pine slab of wood with both index fingers, each one corroborating the other, to make damn sure that there was no misunderstanding as to which countertop he was referring - regardless of it being, the only one of its kind in the Northern Hemisphere.

'I see,' Maxi replied feeling obliged to give the counter the once over. 'Thank you for your help. Oh, by the way, do you happen to know which tow truck company recovered the van?'

'One minute.' The redhead turned to retrieve a notebook that was stored in a cubby hole next to the one his peak cap called home. After flicking through several pages, he found the information he was looking for.

He read from the pad. 'Sam Brannigan's Recovery, 257 Beat Street.'

The redhead smiled, knowing that their meeting was concluding, but by doing so unveiled his buck teeth for the big finale. They still had some crisp particles clinging to them like bats from the belfry. Maxi committed the tow truck's name and address to memory. Once again, he thanked the police officer for all his help and headed towards the double doors, half expecting at any moment to be jumped on from behind, shackled, and thrown in a cell. It was only when he was back in the car and heading towards home that his breathing returned to normal.

When he got home, he paused by the living room door, to listen. The debate was clipping along at a brisk pace and everyone seemed to be engrossed. They were about halfway through the two-hour session and it was time for a tea break. He already had a buffet table set up by the front window. Several of Nora's best *China* platters were laid out on the table with an assortment of biscuits and buns. Another Oriental platter offered up a selection of sandwiches - devoid of their crusts - to entice those who might have travelled, without their '*eating teeth.*' Maxi got to work, pouring freshly brewed tea into cups with matching saucers. His mother Nora - the reincarnation of Marie Antoinette - wouldn't have it any other way.

After a short respite, the debate resumed with renewed vigour.

'I think Morality and the ten commandments run in parallel,' Maxi postulated to the group. 'Thou shalt not kill. It's immoral to kill someone.'

'But what about a situation where a person kills another in self-defence?' Dolly contested. 'The law of the land is clear that murder in this instance is not a crime. Religion, on the other hand, encourages the victim to turn the other cheek.'

'Every religion, no matter what,' Nora announced, 'has some sort of deity at the helm. Morality only has human conscience as its counsellor. Society's values change over time and our conscience adapts to these changes. Religion, on the other hand, is rigid, steadfast, and true, all the time. So, you see, it's impossible for them to run in parallel when only one is changing and adjusting while the other remains the same.'

The intensity of the discussion began to fizzle out around eleven-fifty. It was obvious by how the *'troupe of geriatrics'* were dragging ass that Maxi's mental gymnasium had taken its toll. All in all, the essence of the subject matter had been probed. He liked to think that each participant in these debates got to savour a little delight from the *food for thought* menu that he posted in the front window every day.

Just as he began to tidy up, his phone rang. It was Dandelion. Maxi sheepishly answered his phone. 'Yes Daniel, what's up?'

'40% crashed his van,' he stated like he was in the witness protection program. 'He's in a coma in the hospital.' He divulged this information to Maxi like a cocky intergalactic space-spy, returning from the arsehole of the galaxy, convinced his information would save the universe from extinction.

'I know,' Maxi replied, irreverently. The silence on the other end of the line, a testimonial to Dandelion's disgust at being the bearer of second-hand, worn-out, old-news, already.

'Who told you?' His curt retort.

'His sister... Lucy Windsor.' Maxi snapped back his rebuttal.

'Yeah, me too,' Dandelion conceded. 'Anyway, the reason I called is to let you know, I'm not going to open the yard tomorrow. I have a busy day with the Town Hall so business as usual on Tuesday. See you then.'

'Very well,' Maxi concluded. 'See ye on Tuesday.' The line was already dead.

Maxi couldn't believe his luck. Somebody out there had the treasure and until he found out who, he had to keep working in the scrapyard, if nothing else, only to monitor Dandelion's moves. Having Monday off gave him a whole day to locate the treasure, and if he found it, he wouldn't ever have to go back to that yard again. He checked the clock. It was almost noon. He was expecting Boom-boom and Ella to show at any minute. He raced upstairs to change his shirt, brush his teeth and comb his hair.

'What are you getting all dolled up for?' Nora teased him when he came back down. 'You're fond of that girl, aren't ye?'

'She's a married woman,' Maxi contested.

'So what?' Nora groaned. 'Look what she married.'

Maxi stood in front of Nora, who was seated on the couch and with his hands on his hips he indicated to her that the conversation was over.

'There are still a few stragglers on the stoop. I better go out there to lend a hand.' He didn't want her to see him blush.

Chapter 16.

Maxi assisted the last of the old ladies, in her descent, down the steps of the front stoop. He placed one arm around her waist and with his other arm gripping her by the elbow; they moved in unison, with him taking every precaution to land her safely on the bottom step. He set her free onto the gravel driveway, sharing the same anxiety as a young kid, placing his toy sailboat into the murky waters of the park pond, praying she wouldn't tip over. The telepathic frequency that Maxi was on to keep the old lady on course was scrambled when Boom-boom pulled into the driveway in a 1992 navy blue Subaru. The driver's door swung open and the small sedan rocked violently on its struts. The old lady, feeling the vibrations, stopped dead in her tracks and braced herself, as if she were standing on the San Andreas fault line, expecting to be swallowed up by the very ground she stood upon.

'Bring it on,' she yelled.

Suddenly, a fat foot poked out from the driver's door and began searching for traction on the gravel. Next, two fat hands grabbed the edge of the door frame and the car dipped dramatically on the driver's side. Another foot emerged. With both feet prodding the ground and both arms pulling on the driver's door, a big belly began to emerge like the dawning of some new age, slowly defining itself, inch by inch, metastasizing into a new globe with its very own sunrise, oblivious to the local time, at high noon on planet Earth. At last, his extraction from that metallic womb was complete.

'Fuck it,' Maxi mumbled. 'This man needs to get himself an SUV.'

Boom-boom had to stand still for a minute, bent over at the waist and with his legs spread wide apart to prevent his big belly from constricting his air intake. He was panting like a mad dog and an Englishman in the midday sun. The earthquake averted, the old lady began to mosey on her way. Maxi went to his assistance and helped him up the steps of the stoop. Fortunately, his breathing returned to normal and he was able to enter the house solo. He directed him, once again, down the corridor to the back room. Ella arrived a few minutes later.

Boom-boom sat beside Ella on the couch next to the green door/ coffee table. Maxi didn't think he'd ever be jealous of this man's exposed navel, but he was. From its vantage point, that navel could give Ella a thorough physical examination, from head to toe like a 'peeping Tom' but without the need to hide.

'Once again, thank you and Happy Jack for a job well done.' Maxi smiled as he handed Boom-boom two white envelopes, each containing 500 euros.

'Thanks,' Boom-boom replied, wasting no time breaking into one of the envelopes to make a Japanese fan with all the fifty-euro notes.

'Good job,' Ella praised. 'You were both very convincing.'

'Now we have another proposition for you,' Maxi offered with a sly smirk on his face to evoke a little intrigue.

Ella reached over the gut and presented Boom-boom with a clip board that had a typed sheet of paper in the teeth of the stainless-steel clamp. She gave another one to Maxi. They both studied the content for a few minutes. Boom-boom was first to resurface.

'I'm confused; who do you want us to impersonate this time?'

'Only one actor is needed for this performance and I'm looking at him, I hope,' Maxi answered, offering them both a cigarette from his Marlboro box. They both accepted.

'Go on, I'm listening.' Boom-boom replied.

Maxi lit all three cigarettes, and focusing his full attention on Boom-boom, he began to impart his intentions.

'The role is the same. You will continue to act as a County Council worker and once again, you will be dealing with Dandelion. The only real difference this time is the location. You will be performing in the belly of the beast... The Town Hall.'

Ella scrunched her face at Maxi's insensitive choice of words, to which he responded with a regretful wince. Boom-boom seemed not to notice and if he did, he didn't let on. He continued caressing his big belly with both hands, rubbing circles over its entire expanse.

'I see, the plot thickens,' Boom-boom acknowledged, as he sprung upright on the couch to whack the green door a few times with his clenched fist. He accompanied each blow with a *'boom.'* Ella was dislodged in the wake of his kinetic energy and forced to rearrange herself on the couch. This was her first encounter with his pounding regimen and it startled her a little. She threw a concerned look in Maxi's direction, but because of his insouciance, she knew not to panic.

'Dandelion intends to extort money from the County Council. He is convinced with all the bad press recently that they will pay dearly not to have their reputation for fuck ups hit the headlines again. The reason we hired you in the first place was to ensure that this mistake by the County Council would never see the light of day. Your performance tomorrow morning will be an extension of the role you played on Saturday. Since Dandelion has already made your acquaintance, we think he will be pleased to be blackmailing a familiar face.'

'Thanks very much,' Boom-boom snapped. 'You think I'm a push-over.'

'Not at all,' Maxi assured. 'Right now, you are the only person I can think of who can pull this off.'

'What exactly am I pulling off and how much do I get for doing the pulling?'

'Tomorrow morning,' Ella instructed. 'We need you will go to the Town Hall and convince the Chief engineer, a man called Tim Summers that you are there as an IT specialist, sent down from Head Office by Mr. Mark Madden, to upgrade the phone lines and speed up their internet access.'

She highlighted the names on the clipboard with her yellow marker.

'Who's Mark Madden?' Maxi exhaled his smoky enquiry.

'I Googled the County Council earlier and this guy, Mark Madden, popped up all over the place. He's the head honcho, by all accounts. Mention his name and the sea parts.'

'I see,' said Maxi, 'you've been a busy bee this morning. Well done, Ella.'

'Part one is only a ruse to get you behind the counter,' Ella explained. 'You will introduce yourself as Fredrick Eschenmoser, the I.T. specialist.'

Both men reacted to Ella like she let one go.

'I know this name is difficult to pronounce,' she acknowledged. 'That's deliberate. When people can't pronounce a name, it's very unlikely they'll remember it either. It's also unlikely that this guy, Tim Summers, will call head office to confirm your status, especially if he can't say the name he wants to vet. So, Mr. Eschenmoser, please say your name for me.'

'Inch en mozer, Ash in muzor, Ehin mooser.' Boom-boom made a number of foiled attempts to say the name. 'I see what you mean. I'll nail it with a little practice, don't worry.'

'No doubt you will,' Maxi picked up where Ella left off.

'Part two is your real purpose. While you pretend to play with the phone lines, you must keep your eyes glued to the door and when Dandelion shows up, drop everything and intercept him before he gets acquainted with any legitimate 'suit' in the office. Once you have his attention, we want you to negotiate a deal with him.'

'In other words,' Ella butted in, 'whatever number Dandelion comes up with, chop that shit in half.'

Maxi felt himself getting a little aroused by her aggressiveness. Once again, he had to call on the reserves in his willpower to stave off an erection.

'You'll only have to work for an hour or so,' he managed as he squirmed in his seat. 'We'll pay you 100 euros for your time. What do you say to that?'

They both looked expectantly at Freddy 'Boom-boom.'

'Not enough.' Each word was punctuated by his annoying slap/boom duo on the green door.

'For fuck sake,' Maxi groaned. 'It's an hour's work.' He violently stubbed out his cigarette end in the ashtray which reminded him of his first encounter with 40% and *his* aggressive extinguish.

'What I do is not work. It's Drama, and Drama's not cheap.'

'Where did we hear this shit before?' Maxi inquired, tapping his pen impatiently on the spring-loaded clasp of his clip board.

'How much?' Ella asked.

'Three-hundred euro.'

'Let's meet in the middle,' Maxi countered. 'One-hundred and fifty.'

'Two-fifty.' Boom-boom snapped

'You drive a hard bargain,' Maxi said, looking over at Ella, who nodded. 'Deal.'

'I know. I also drive a Subaru,' Boom-boom joked.

'Oh yeah, that reminds me.' Maxi diverted his attention to Ella. 'Will you be able to drive our IT specialist,' already sowing the IT seed in the man's brain, 'to the Town Hall tomorrow morning?'

'I suppose I can,' she said, with a curious expression on her face. 'Why?'

'I don't want him to croak on the steps of the Town Hall,' Maxi replied.

'How is my driving him going to save his life?' she asked, still maintaining that curious look.

'That Micky Mouse Subaru may as well be a loaded gun.'

'I don't get it,' Ella replied.

'Neither do I,' said Boom-boom as he placed his clip board on the coffee table. He resumed caressing his big belly with both hands.

Maxi noticed he had been using only the one hand up to that. He wondered, if both Boom-booms hands were occupied doing something or holding something, how long could his big belly go without a caress?

'I'll explain later,' Maxi promised. His focus shifted back to Freddy Boom-boom. 'You've got your script,' he said. 'All you need to know are these three names, Tim Summers, Mark Madden, and of course your own – impossible to pronounce – name.' He pointed at the highlighted names on the clipboard with his pen. 'The rest of this is some I.T. jargon that Ella thought you might need in case you get some smart-ass wanting to face-off with you over codes and platforms. It's doubtful, but nonetheless, it's no harm to be prepared. The County Council hires only wasters, so I'm sure no one will go near you, especially a man intent on doing some work. Any questions?'

'Do I need a toolbox?' Boom-boom inquired.

'No,' Ella replied. 'But you will need a laptop. Remember this?' She showed him the laptop they used on Saturday, stripped of all its pretentious capabilities. 'This bitch looks like she's kicked some ass in cyberspace,' Ella testified. 'Nobody, and I mean nobody, are going to dare question your IT credentials with this baby under your wing. I'll put it in my car for you.' She placed the laptop on the coffee table and handed Boom-boom a pen. 'Write down your address and I'll pick you up at eight-thirty in the morning. Oh yeah, wear the green overalls and don't forget your ID badge.'

Freddy Boom-boom wrote down the location where he wanted to be picked up on a slip of paper and handed it to Ella.

'Good,' Ella remarked as she studied the cross streets. 'You're on this side of the bridge. We're all set then.' Ella made a move to get up.

'Hold on,' Boom-boom whined. He picked up his clipboard. 'There's nothing here telling me how to deal with the blackmail situation.'

'You just proved a minute ago how good you are at haggling,' Maxi remarked. 'We want you to listen to Dandelion's proposition and counter with one of your own. Haggle with the motherfucker. As Ella so eloquently put it earlier... chop that shit in half. Do you think you can do that?'

'I don't think that'll be a problem.' Freddy Boom-boom smirked. 'I'm a Bedouin at heart.'

'I wouldn't argue that,' Maxi replied. 'I could see you sell a Persian rug to an Eskimo!' He followed Boom-boom along the dark corridor with what little light from the doorway being vanquished by his girth.

'Now that's Dandelion sorted,' Maxi shouted back down the corridor as he quickly closed the front door on Freddy 'Boom-boom.' He refused to witness another bout between the big man and the Subaru. He returned to the office and sat down next to Ella in Boom-boom's spot. He accepted a cigarette from her and she lit 'em up. It just so happened that they exhaled their smoky emissions concurrently, which inspired their respective plumes to swirl loosely about one another in a tantalizing display of weightless motion. They were both aroused by the *kinky* smoke as their gaze followed its ascent. Similar to the dance of the seven veils, their plumes of smoke embraced like lovers and soared effortlessly towards the ceiling. Maxi broke the spell with a sweeping wave of his open palm. He coughed into his clenched fist to clear his throat. Ella repositioned herself on the couch.

'Now, let's concentrate on the treasure,' Maxi insisted. 'I've decided to stay working in the yard until we find it.'

'That's a good idea,' Ella agreed. 'After this blackmail bullshit, we do need *eyes* on the guy.' She made a V sign with her two fingers and pointed with them at her own eyes before pointing at Maxi's.

'Dandelion is not opening the yard tomorrow,' he informed her. 'He's got his big gig in the Town Hall so I'm off until Tuesday.'

'That gives us the rest of the day and all day tomorrow. Surely we can find your backpack before then.'

'I hope so, but it's not going to be as easy as you think,' he cautioned. '*My* backpack was in 40%'s van when he crashed. As far as everyone else is concerned, that backpack is *his* property. If we go snooping around asking questions about it, everyone's going to think we want to *steal* something from a man who's in a coma. See how that looks.'

'I see what you mean,' she agreed. 'Not pretty.'

'Remember, we've got to keep Boom-boom and Dandelion in the dark at all times. We're lucky 40%'s in a coma or we'd have another ball to keep in the air.' He sighed. 'And then there's Georgina. She'll be home any day. What am I supposed to do about her?'

'Relax, Maxi,' Ella said, placing her hand over his. 'You're starting to get flustered.'

He was surprised how warm and soft her hand felt on the back of his. How small hers was in comparison to his big spade. That innocent contact between them made him feel like he was plugged directly into her soul.

'Okay,' he said, clapping his hands together as if to frighten away all his misgivings. 'Let's compartmentalize... shit, I need to a nap after that word.'

Ella laughed. 'Com-part-men-tal-ize,' she repeated, as she stomped her foot to the rhythm of her voice.

Maxi burst out laughing. *'This woman is something else,'* he thought. *'Nothing seems to faze her. She deals with Jasper's crap, day in day out, yet she's always upbeat.'*

'Let's get serious,' he pleaded.

'You're the comedian,' she said, pointing at him. 'Not me.'

'Right,' he said, 'Let's figure out the most likely path that backpack took after the crash. We know the police gave Lucy Windsor a box full of items from the crash site. The first thing we need to do is check and see if my backpack is among those items in that box.'

'I agree, 100%,' she said.

'I wish you'd refrain from using percentages. It reminds me of that moron in the coma.'

'Are you going to check out... Lucy Windsor's box?' Ella asked, biting provocatively on the nail of her middle finger, causing Maxi to lick his lips... involuntarily.

'I have no problem taking care of her... box,' Maxi stammered, excited by her smutty ambiguity.

'Oh, I have no doubt,' Ella declared, pouting her moist lips.

The small office suddenly heaved with sexual static. Up to that point, they were never alone. Maxi felt a little peculiar, yet charged with excitement. He wondered, was Ella flirting with him or did she just seamlessly slip back into her role as a phone sex operator - unbeknownst to herself? He searched in his replay for cryptic clues, but his examination proved inconclusive. He was content with that result. He had no intention of ever releasing those fluttering butterflies that hijacked his stomach the moment they met, fifteen years ago.

'What's the plan, Maxi? Are we going over to meet Lucy Windsor or what?'

'I don't think so.' He shook his head.

'Why not?'

'Well, because let's say my over-zealous reaction to her news about finding 40% in a coma didn't exactly match, the one she was expecting... a few fair notches below ecstasy, I'd say. She was disgusted with me, and rightly so. However,' Maxi shifted his tone from regret to blame. 'If she knew how I was bushwhacked by that brother of hers, she might have been a bit more understanding. Anyway, she called me a fucking monster.'

'When you told me the same news, I was overjoyed too,' she argued. 'Where's my monster badge? Tell you what,' she said as she looked him in the eye. 'I'll be your wingman if you'd like. Lucy might be more cooperative if there's a woman by your side.' She nudged him with her elbow.

'Thanks, Ella, but I don't think you understand. That woman spat venom down the line at me. She won't have anything to do with me ever again after that call. Even by some miracle, if she did agree to see me and you came along to ease the tension, she'd lose the head the minute we asked about the box from the crash.'

Ella broke into a gangster rap-type rhythm on the couch, crossing her arms in front of her and shaping both hands with only her index and little fingers protruding from each, she gyrated to the improvised 'beat-box' blabber she spluttered from those lovely moist lips.

You be trying to mess with that bitch's head. A pack a lies, is all I said.

Say one thing, you mean another. Trying to fool her and her brother,

To get that treasure and be on your way. Gotta rob the bitch... it's da only way.

Gotta rob da bitch, do ye hear what I say... gotta do it now, gotta do it today.

'Yoh, Yoh - word on the street.' Maxi copied her pose. This was a playful side to Ella that he hadn't seen before, and he enjoyed it immensely. The more time he spent alone with her, the more fascinated he became. 'Yes,' he proudly announced. 'I would love you to be my wingman.'

'That's the bomb,' she chirped.

'*Tupac* Hickey.' He pointed at Ella. 'You hit the nail on the head with that little rap song. The only way we are going to know whether Lucy has the treasure or not is to break into the house and search for it. If it's not in the house, we break into her car.'

'Home invasion is a serious crime,' she stated. 'You know that, right?'

'Only if we get caught.'

'What's with the *we*? I never stole anything in my life.'

'I thought you were my wingman.' Maxi frowned.

'Yeah but...'

'Relax, nobody is stealing anything,' he promised. 'I'll do the *retrieving* of our property. You'll be the lookout.'

'Fair enough,' Ella agreed.

'Is Debbie working this weekend?' Maxi asked.

'Yeah, she is,' Ella replied, a little unsettled by his shift in focus. 'I spoke to her earlier; she's on Dog-Watch tomorrow morning.'

'Dog-Watch?'

'The graveyard shift, from midnight to four in the morning,' Ella informed him. She was surprised he didn't know the term and him with all his military jargon.

'Perfect,' he cheered. 'We need the cover of darkness,' he qualified.

'Why?'

'We don't want Lucy Windsor at the house when we break-in. I was thinking if we get Debbie to call her from the hospital phone tomorrow after midnight, with some bullshit story about her brother coming out of his coma, she'd drop everything and race over to the hospital to be by his side.'

'Brilliant,' she responded excitedly. 'She'll see the hospital's number on her called ID and won't think twice.' Ella popped two cigarettes into her mouth and lit both. He took one from her and both of them were extra careful this time round to stagger their exhaust.

'Will you give Debbie a call and fill her in on the plan?' He handed Ella a slip of paper with Lucy's phone number. 'I'll pick you up around twelve-thirty and we'll drive over to Mandolin Brook. When Lucy leaves for the hospital, I'll break into the house and you'll be the lookout. Sound like a plan?'

'Sounds good to me,' Ella replied. She stole a peek at her watch. 'Listen, I've got to go. I'm booked in for a training session at three.'

Chapter 17.

A very full moon seemed to dart in and out between the clouds of its own volition. It gave Maxi the impression that it was in a hurry to get somewhere fast, but its progress was questionable. With time on his hands and the moon right there in front of him, he decided to study it carefully through the windscreen of Nora's car. He aligned the right side of the moon with the lower branch of the tree shaped air freshener that swung from the rear-view mirror, and noting the *start* time, he began his research. Not a stir, at least not within the last 15 minutes since their arrival at Mandolin Brook. Ella sat next to him in the passenger seat with her eyes glued to Lucy Windsor's front door, oblivious to Maxi's crash course in astronomy. With these startling deductions, Maxi began to doubt the credibility of ancient stargazers like Galileo and Copernicus. All this mumbo jumbo about the planets revolving around the sun and the moon around the earth was clearly unsubstantiated according to his findings. Maybe Rocco, the plumber he used to use in New York, wasn't that far off the mark after all, with his conspectus of the cosmos. 'All the planets remained put while it is the sun that's doing all the moving and shaking.'

While Maxi was flicking through the history pages in his mind in search of other inevitable falsehoods, he was suddenly winded by an elbow in the ribs from Ella. She reacted instinctively when the light came on in the upstairs bedroom in the house of interest across the street. That was their cue that Debbie had made the call from the hospital, and by all accounts, Lucy Windsor had taken the bait. Three minutes later that light was swapped out for the one downstairs in the hallway - the frosted glass in the front door's porthole bathing the porch-landing in a bright amber sheen.

Lucy Windsor's silhouette appeared in the half-open door, struggling to get her other arm into the sleeve of her overcoat. She pulled the door closed behind her and momentarily vanished into the darkness, only to reappear once again in the light of the open car door. She got in, started the car and reversed out into the road. They watched, both huddled below the dash, as Lucy drove off to be with her brother in the hospital.

Maxi was decked out from head to toe in a matte black tracksuit with black runners, black gloves and a black balaclava. He had a LED headlight strapped to his forehead. It was all the rage among thieves. The coalminer who brought this product to the marketplace never considered that demographic in his business plan. He checked his phone to ensure it was fully charged. He was unaware he had done so three times already within the last ten minutes. He was all amped up and ready to go.

'Keep your eyes peeled,' he instructed Ella. 'And if you see anyone looking any way suspicious at all, call me immediately.'

'Seriously,' Ella replied, giving him the 'once over.' She tried desperately not to laugh.

He closed the car door softly behind him and instinctively crouched down to become amalgamated into the ethos of the underworld. Any delinquent about to commit a crime anywhere in the world would invariably strike that very same pose. He made his way, in leaps and bounds, to the back of the house. As he turned the corner, he accidentally tripped over a trashcan which threw the aluminium lid violently at the concrete path. He was obliged to chase after the noisy lid. He blindly stomped his right foot in the dark, hoping to crush the lid and silence the commotion. After a series of clangs and clatters, it rolled along for a spell until eventually fell on its face and lay still and silent in the darkness. He froze to gauge the reaction, if any. Instinctively, he emitted a loud '*meow*' to throw a cat under the bus.

'*Ah, now it makes sense,*' he reasoned. '*Cat burglar.*'

He knew people needed an excuse, any excuse to explain away the unusual, especially in the dark. It worked. No lights. No sounds. No reaction. He checked the two back windows to see if one was open. Both were secure. He then focused his full attention on the back door. Switching on his head light he got busy picking the lock. Two minutes later, he heard that unmistakable *clink* and he was in. He froze once again, this time in anticipation of an alarm. Nothing. He drew a deep breath. Following the small cone of light that splayed from his headlamp, he made his way through the kitchen and into the living room. Fairly standard stuff; couch, chairs, coffee table, wall mounted TV above the fireplace and twin display cabinets filled with glassware, travel souvenirs and other useless knick-knacks accumulated over a lifetime. The sole purpose of these exhibits in every household is to act as evidence to visitors that the inhabitants really know how to live.

Apart from a woman's magazine spread open on the coffee table, there were no other signs of life. As he panned the room in search of the backpack, his light reflected off a shiny surface to the right of an old worn and tattered recliner. It looked like it should have been in a skip when compared with the rest of the relatively new but ignored seating. He directed the beam to examine that corner of the room. Of course, the infamous tuba stood proudly on its stand, - the Iron Maiden herself - to so many in that housing estate.

He picked his way carefully up the stairs, with some creaky steps causing him to stop and cringe. He quietly cursed the carpenter who built those stairs. He searched one bedroom and moved on to the next. The dishevelled bed told him he was in Lucy's room. He poked his headlight into the closet and under the bed. Nothing. Just as he made his way to the third bedroom, his phone began to vibrate. He quickly retrieved it from his back pocket and pressed it to his ear.

'Quick. There's someone coming,' Ella whispered. 'I can see that flash light of yours bouncing all over the place. Do something.'

'Shit!' Maxi gasped.

He switched off his headlight and ran down the stairs into the living room. He blindly frisked the wall with his eager hands, each finger and thumb searching independently to find the light switch. Suddenly the room exploded in bright light.

Ella was gobsmacked when she saw the room light up. She was disappointed not only with Maxi's abrupt surrender but with her own evaluation of him and how far off the mark she was. She believed him to be a fighter, not a quitter. As she began to mull over the serious consequences of a home invasion, she heard a succession of strange sounds emanating from the house. Maxi had resorted to blowing into the tuba. Rather than a sequence of musical notes, a succession of fart sounds was all he could manage. Ella watched in amazement as the inquisitive neighbour stopped dead in his tracks, paused for a moment and then, shaking his head from side to side, he spun on his heels to retreat back to his own house. He was noticeably relieved not to have had to confront an intruder, yet vexed with John Windsor Junior for rehearsing at such an ungodly hour.

'Wow,' Ella exclaimed. Not only had her estimation of Maxi being reinstated, it had grown wings!

Maxi resumed his search, careful not to wash any of the windows with his beam of light. He was very thorough not to overlook any possible hiding place. He even checked the freezer. No backpack. Tired and dejected, he turned off his headlight and left by the back door, this time paying particular attention to avoid the trashcan. He crossed the street and slinked back into the car.

'No luck,' Ella stated the obvious.

'Close one, huh?'

'I didn't know you played the tuba,' she teased. 'I started to sing along - *puff the magic dragon.*'

'Give me a break. It took me forever to get any sound out of that fucking yoke.' He gasped. 'I blew and blew, I don't know, belly-full after belly-full of air into the mouthpiece before I got anything. My head is splitting after all the huffing and puffing.'

'Now ye know how the neighbours feel,' she said as she reached up with both hands and began to massage his temples with her fingers.

'Wow. You've got such strong fingers,' he stammered, completely caught off-guard by her tranquilizing touch. She had taken the liberty to trespass the bounds of his personal space and needless to say, her breach went uncontested. They shared that moment gazing into each other's eyes. It may not have been the perfect venue for a kiss, but all the other components were in place. However, neither took the initiative.

'We have to check her car next,' Maxi said, sounding all staccato. His failure to cease the moment had the neurons in his brain scrambling around like peas in a boiling pot.

'Did you leave the back door unlocked?' Ella sighed, also frustrated by the missed opportunity.

'Duh,' he groaned. 'How could I lock it? I don't have a key.' What a dumb question, he thought. In hindsight, he realised he did have the option to lock the door by releasing the button holding the catch. He had to admit, not such a dumb question after all.

'Don't get all huffy puffy with me,' she snapped. 'Save it for your fucking tuba.'

'I'm sorry, I didn't ...'

'I'm only asking you,' she interrupted. 'Because when Lucy gets back, I'll be able to sneak into the house and snatch her car keys.'

'Who says *you* are going to sneak back into the house?' Maxi inquired, all high and mighty.

'I say, that's who,' she insisted. 'After the racket you made... I think it's best.'

'I don't know,' he challenged her. 'Do you have the head for this kind of thing?'

'I know I'm not all decked-out for the part like Ali Baba and the Forty Thieves here, but I think I'm up to the task,' she assured, interlocking her fingers and pressing her palms against the dash.

'*Snatch* her car keys,' Maxi jeered.

'Isn't that the lingo we burglars use?' Ella replied in search of confirmation. 'We snatch shit, right?'

'Not exactly. We're not pick pockets,' he announced. 'They snatch shit. We - since you've included yourself in my world of debauchery – are more than that,' Maxi confided. 'We selectively remove items that concern us from a premises.'

'You're telling me there's a difference between snatching shit and removing shit?' she argued. 'All you're doing is dressing up the act of stealing in a tuxedo. It's the same result, no matter what you call it.'

Maxi giggled, and Ella chuckled. Their initial titters blossomed into full blown belly laughs, fuelled by the lunacy of their joint venture. Who else in the world was breaking into houses and cars and debating the proper vernacular to accurately describe their deeds?

Just then, Lucy's car pulled into the driveway. Maxi and Ella clunked heads as they dipped down below the dash, still chuckling away like two idle chainsaws. Lucy Windsor had only been gone a little over an hour. She exited the car and slammed the door. She was obviously distraught by her brother's invariant condition. The stowaways across the street quickly regained their composure.

After affording Lucy enough time to get to bed and fall asleep, Ella signalled to Maxi that it was time. She slipped out of the car and trotted across the road on her tippy-toes to the side of the house. She had her own take on this burglary business. She pressed her back to the wall and with her arms spread out, she shuffled her way towards the backyard like she was on a narrow ledge of a tall building. Relieved to find the back door unlocked, she snuck inside.

There was the remote possibility that Lucy might have locked it before she went to bed.

The porthole in the front door lit-up the hallway like a search light. She was thankful to the full moon for illuminating her way. Both of them had acknowledged the presence of the moon that evening even though they were light-years apart in their respective perceptions. With outstretched arms, she slowly made her way through the kitchen and into the hallway. The light seemed to sizzle like hot desert heat on the hallway mirror. She gambled that the car keys would be found on the hallstand directly below that mirror and she was right. She snatched the keys and retreated back the way she came. Maxi was on the edge of his seat, inadvertently making every move she made as he watched her shadow creep towards Lucy's car. Every few seconds, he checked for spectators.

Ella regretted not borrowing Maxi's head lamp. She had to stab several times at the trunk lock before she successfully inserted the key. When it popped, it lit her up like an escapee in a prison breakout. Maxi dare not chance a breath. She had a quick rummage about. Nothing. The blackness resumed when she closed the trunk. He stole a breath. She clawed her way along the side of the car, the tips of her fingers busy doing the work of her eyes until she came to the driver's door. Another light but quickly quenched when she sat in and closed the door. She searched inside the car. Nothing. She made her way back into the house and returned the keys to the hallway stand. Creeping along on her hands and knees, she exited through the back door. She shuffled her way along the gable end and cautiously crossed the road. At last, to Maxi's great relief, she flumped back into the car with the aplomb of a seasoned criminal.

'Well done,' he congratulated her as he started the engine. 'You're quite the little vixen.'

'Well that's a first,' she replied. 'I've never been called a vixen before. But you know what?' she said, turning in her seat to face him. 'I like it.'

'You do?'

'*I do*.' Ella took a breath. 'Wow, I never thought I'd hear myself say those two words ever again. Two little words, side by side, imagine only three fucking letters and I was sentenced to a whole world of pain... without the possibility of parole.'

'Jasper?' Maxi whispered.

'Oh well.' She sighed. 'At least we know for sure it's not here. Better get home. We both have a busy day tomorrow.'

'Yes, it's late,' Maxi agreed. 'You have to drop Boom-boom at the Town Hall and after that, Buca Brannigan's depot. Are you sure you're up to it?'

'No problem,' she confirmed. 'Anyway, don't you have to bring Nora to the doctor, the podiatrist and the hairdressers? That's your day shot to shit right there.'

'Yeah, you're right, an action-packed day for sure,' he joked.

The atmosphere in the car on the ride home was subdued. Both of them were disappointed with the outcome as they silently battled with their own bouts of despondency. Sharing their plight, however, did strengthen their resolve.

'Let me know how you get on,' he said as he stopped the car by her house. 'As soon as you have any news, call me.'

She saluted him by the car door and waved as he drove away. He kept viewing her in his rear-view mirror until she turned and walked towards the house. It was almost two o'clock in the morning, yet he wasn't tired. He was still amped up with all the covert interplay between Ella and himself. As he headed for the stairs to go to bed, he happened to look in the hallway mirror and spot the goofy grin that was plastered on his face. That *lovesick puppy* expression was instantly swapped out for a look of horror.

'Oh, my God,' he gasped. 'Ella must think I'm a complete jackass.' He shook his head in disbelief and headed up the stairs to bed. As he slid under the covers, he was unaware that same goofy grin had crept back across his face and would remain there, intact until further notice.

Chapter 18.

As Boom-boom wrestled his way onto the front seat in Ella's minivan, he inadvertently caused her to spill her coffee... all over herself. She was furious. Had she been forewarned about what amounted to nothing short of a full-blown rhino attack to the passenger side of her minivan, she would have reneged on her latte supreme from Starbucks and her favourite beige pants would have been saved from extinction. Deprived of her caffeine fix and squashed against the driver's door by the imposing mass of her passenger, she struggled all the way to the Town Hall to change gears with a gearstick that was out of sight and enveloped in blubber. Every time she had to change gear, she was forced to rub up against Boom-boom's big sweaty belly to get at the gear stick. She had to conjure up all sorts of pleasant imagery to stave off her impulse to puke all over the dash.

Upon her arrival, she was panting and sweating profusely, on par with one of her kettlebell workouts. Instead of venting on Boom-boom and risk jeopardizing the mission, she opted to brutally torment Maxi in one of those horrific daydreams she normally reserved for Jasper. Once again, the minivan rocked violently as she deposited Boom-boom by the steps of the Town Hall.

'Good luck,' she managed to offer instead of what she really meant... *Fuck off.*

She drove to a spot in the carpark where she had a good view of the main entrance. She watched Boom-boom in his green overalls with the illuminous stripes, shooting javelins of bright light in all directions as he waddled towards the main entrance with the laptop barely visible under his flabby arm. Others, some wearing similar garb, gravitated towards the main entrance, each of them pledging to themselves as they went to do even less work than the little work, they reluctantly did the day before. He joined the trickle of people

193

at the entrance and disappeared through the glass doors into the building. Ella had his cell number primed and ready to go on her phone. He would get a text from her as soon as Dandelion appeared on the scene.

Waiting in the carpark for Boom-boom afforded her the time to produce and direct the payback daydream that would take the sting out of losing her favourite beige pants. She had already decided since Maxi was terrified of dogs to use them in some way in her production. Setting the scene in her head, she imagined Maxi naked with his arms and legs tied to stakes in the ground... that erotic image made her pause for a moment so she could catch her breath. She cued one lone bark from a dog in the distance and watched his reaction. He grimaced and pulled against his restraints. She imagined more barking from more dogs and as the sounds intensified, so did the pulling and dragging against his restraints. She chuckled as she released the hounds. Maxi's screams of terror only lasted a moment. When he realised, he was being attacked by *Cuddles, Tinkles* and *Bubbles* - her aunt Susie's Chihuahuas - he started to laugh uncontrollably. Ella could never imagine hurting Maxi, even in a daydream; however, there was still Hell to pay for her favourite beige pants.

After locating the Customer Service dept. on the notice board, Boom-boom took the elevator to the third floor. He introduced himself to the receptionist, who sat in a glass pillbox in the foyer, with a look of stoic resignation on her chubby face.

'Hi, my name is Fredrick Eschenmoser and I'm here to see Mr. Timothy Summers.'

The woman was in her early 60s and had been held captive for over 40 years in that confined space. She'd seen and heard it all. She considered herself the last bastion of defence. Nothing was getting by her without a grilling, which she would personally dish-out in her own sweet time.

Freddy Boom-boom got no acknowledgement. He was left hanging while this battle-axe wielded her authority over her three-by-three square foot empire in total silence. She was a big woman which boosted his confidence considerably. Fat people are presumed to be a confederation whose members normally delight in mingling and munching with fellow associates. He waved at the glass with a big smile on his face. No reaction. He faked a cough. Still no acknowledgement from behind the glass. He searched frantically for an '*ice-breaker*' within the small transparent cube, but all he could find was a photograph of a shapely young woman in a skimpy bikini, laying on a beach towel, under a hot sun. He knew instantly, the young woman in the photo was the battle-axe herself, albeit some forty years ago. On closer scrutiny, he realised that photo was bad news. It could not be used as leverage for both of them to bond in the '*love-a-tubby*' federation. The sole purpose of the photo was to refute any notions of obesity. This woman was in denial. She honestly believed her present condition was temporary, and with a little restraint from her savouring fistful after fistful of colourful M&M's from the big bowl next to the photo, she would one day reincarnate that image. Boom-boom could empathize with her. He also had a slim version of himself pinned to his refrigerator door, in the hope that it would one day miraculously shame him back into shape.

'Wow! What a beautiful picture of you?'

Bullseye! Instant acknowledgement from the fluttering eyes of the twenty-two-year-old that somehow got trapped in that fat carcass, forty years later. She nodded her head in agreement and her whole face lit up in a big, bright smile. There was no need for words. The picture spoke volumes. She buzzed him in and immediately rewarded herself with a fistful of M&M's.

'Psychology 101,' Boom-boom mused as he entered the open plan office to stand next to the other two 'civilians' by the counter – the other side of which was his first objective.

One clerk was dealing with a young woman who was renewing her dog's licence.

'What's the dog's name?'

'It's on the collar, Einstein.' She presented the dog's collar to the clerk.

'No need to be smart, Miss,' the clerk retaliated.

'Einstein *is* the dog's name... Sherlock.'

The other clerk was trying to reason with an old man who was griping about having to pay a parking ticket. He provided the clerk with a financial breakdown of his monthly expenditure and he drew a bar chart on the clerk's notepad to demonstrate the impact the cost of that ticket would have on his life expectancy. He equated his expiration date with his bank roll. He kept repeating, 'You're affecting my bottom line. Can't you see you're moving my date with death forward?'

Freddy Boom-boom flashed his I.D. badge to another clerk, who immediately got up and raised the flap in the counter to welcome 'one of their own' into the nerve centre of operations.

'Tim Summers?' Boom-boom inquired, spending his words like a miser.

'This way.' The same clerk - a frugal wordsmith himself - began to weave his way through the maze of desks, effortlessly alternating between forward and backward motion to ensure his follower was still in tow. Unfortunately, Boom-boom got wedged between the first two desks. The clerk, visibly distraught over being denied a chance to beat his own record in that obstacle course of desks, was obliged to backtrack to the start and walk this lard-arsed, spoilsport the long way around to the office of Timothy Summers, Chief Engineer of Ballydecuddle County Council. Once there, his escort defiantly made the return trip through the maze of desks, showing off his fancy footwork with some minor acrobatic feats here and there to jazz up his retreat. The way he stood bolt upright with his arms in the air at the end of his little show was reminiscent of Nadia Comaneci, the young Romanian gymnast who nailed the perfect dismount in the 1976 Olympics. He looked for approval. Boom-boom wasn't really all that impressed. He found the whole thing rather 'lame'.

He knocked on the frosted glass of the office door. On the third knock, his phone hummed. It was a text from Ella. 'He's here.'

'Yes, how may I help you?' A tall, anaemic looking man with rimless glasses above a ruddy nose inquired as he welcomed the big man into his small office. Boom-boom declined, preferring to remain by the door, to keep an eye on the counter and Dandelion's inevitable arrival.

'Hi, my name is Fredrick Eschenmoser and I am an I.T. specialist sent by Mark Madden from Head Office to upgrade your internet connections, speed up your search engines and increase storage capacity. As we say in the I.T. world, we've all got our heads in the cloud.'

'I see, Mr. Fredrick Es-hat-mut-ter,' Tim Summers replied as he stumbled all over the name. 'That's strange. I had a meeting with Mark on Friday and he never mentioned anything about an upgrade.'

'That's Mark for ye, full of surprises.' Boom-boom stole a peek at the counter. Still no sign of Dandelion. The battle-axe in the pillbox must have had him restrained in a figurative full Nelson. A man not usually inclined to grovel would have to grovel now if he wanted to proceed. He knew Dandelion's pride would buy him some time.

'He's normally on top of things,' Tim Summers deduced as he contrived an alibi to explain away Mark Madden's rudeness. 'He is a busy man, what with that new industrial complex and shopping centre. I suppose it just skipped his mind to tell me. I must admit, he did look a little stressed out on Friday.'

'I agree with you, Mr. Summers. He looks like he could do with a vacation,' Boom-boom suggested.

'Don't we all,' Tim Summers replied.

'Right, if you don't mind, I need to get started. I have a lot of work to do.'

'By all means. Oh, there is one little matter,' Tim Summers exclaimed as he pinched the green overalls with his finger and thumb to restrain Freddy Boom-boom while he leaned in closer to be very explicit with his next remark. 'Do you think you might need to mount a stepladder during the course of your day?'

Freddy Boom-boom got confirmation from Mr. Summers's breath that his earlier prognosis for the ruddy nose was indeed correct - excessive consumption of malt whiskey. Coincidently, that was his own *weapon of choice* and since his own nose was beginning to show early signs of tissue damage from alcohol abuse, his eyes were riveted on that man's snout. Such close proximity to Mr. Summers's nose afforded him the opportunity, much like he had been presented with his own crystal ball, to examine up close and personal the damage that this man's schnozzle had sustained over the years. From that split-second encounter, he could paint a picture - not a pretty one - of his own snout in the not too distant future. Of course, that outcome would depend on him maintaining his present relationship with Mr. Johnny Walker.

'No, I won't need to use a stepladder,' Boom-boom confirmed, eager to get back over to the counter.

'If per chance you do need to use a stepladder,' Tim Summers persisted. 'Company policy and all that jazz. You are required to wear a safety harness.'

'Of course! That goes without saying,' Boom-boom decreed with conviction which seemed to satisfy the - by the book - pain in the ass - County Council lifer!

His hasty return to the counter just happened to coincide with the approach of a disgruntled old lady who engaged with him immediately, over some lewd graffiti that was spray painted on the front wall of her Council house. He was trapped.

'It's disgusting,' she shouted. 'I want that big cock and balls gone by sundown.'

The clerks were amused, not only by the old lady's antics but by the determination of the *new kid on the block* to resolve her problem.

'Calm down, Missus, just give me your name and address and I'll make sure someone gets over there to take care of that... offensive graffiti sometime today.'

That old lady was in and out of the Town Hall on a regular basis and her complaint was always the same, lude graffiti. Besides some mental issues, the old lady craved company so badly, the cock and balls were her own compositions. No one let on they knew she was the artist. The individuals assigned to paint over her 'lewd graffiti' often joked how her compositions had improved over the years with sensitive shading and highlights being introduced of late. Local graffiti artists were so impressed, they hailed her as one of their own. They even gave her, her own tag name - *teabag*.

Freddy Boom-boom grabbed a County Council notepad and began to transcribe the old lady's details, his time *'on the boards'* enabling him to slip seamlessly into the role of the *'lewd graffiti guru'*. In the midst of ironing out the wrinkles in the old lady's cock and balls, Dandelion entered the large office and, recognising Boom-boom, immediately approached the counter. A clerk stood up from his desk to assist but was quickly waved away, once again, by the *new kid on the block*. There was no sign of protest from the clerk.

He was pleased to have dodged two irate parties in a row. He would willingly stand down all day if he could.

Freddy Boom-boom was now delighted by his accidental pairing with the old lady. He knew he looked very convincing in Dandelion's eyes. Not only was he on the other side of the counter, he was actively involved as a civil servant, resolving an issue with a member of the public. He raised his ridged index finger at Dandelion, not only to indicate a one-minute wait period but more importantly to demonstrate his authority. He was sending out a message loud and clear that this was his domain.

'*Go ahead*,' he imagined himself as a tiger in the jungle. '*Take a good sniff at this bush over here or that tree trunk over there. Yeah, that's right, that's the scent of tiger piss... my tiger piss baby, so keep your hind leg down and your cock in your pelt. You're in my space now, motherfucker.*'

Dandelion seemed happy to wait. A moment later, the old lady was on her way, satisfied that she would have company later that day. He approached the counter for the second time.

'We meet again. How can I help you?' Boom-boom inquired, crossing the T's and dotting the I's on his pad to demonstrate that not only could he multi-task, but that his workload was immense.

'The matter I need to discuss with you,' Dandelion whispered, 'is of a rather delicate nature. Maybe we could retreat to your office.'

'I'm afraid not,' Boom-boom replied. 'It's getting painted at this very moment.' He tapped his pen on the counter to distract Dandelion's attention from the offices in the back. 'That's why I'm up here manning the trenches, so to speak. Tell ye what, let's go to the canteen.' He checked his watch and made a calculated guess. 'It's normally quiet at this time of the morning.'

Freddy Boom-boom offered the same ridged index finger to each of the three disappointed looking clerks who were just getting used to the new kid doing all the work. He shoved his laptop under his arm and lifted the flap on the counter. He squeezed his way through the tight space and opened the door for Dandelion. They took the elevator to the ground floor and Boom-boom allowed his olfactory glands to show him the way. The brightly lit canteen was almost empty except for an old man reading his paper and a teenage couple, who sat convulsed in laughter at a small table to the rear of the canteen. The exact cause of their outburst was not known, but a gambling man might place a bet at 10 to 1 that Boom-boom's humongous gut was the *fomenter*. The old man lifted his gaze from his newspaper to ascertain the intentions of the new arrivals. He was alarmed by the big man with the suntan, who, as far as he was concerned, had to be a terrorist from the Middle East. His companion, who concealed the largest suicide vest imaginable, qualified his misgivings.

'Wow, that bomb could take out the whole fucking street,' the old man reasoned.

He evaluated the demeanour of the two men and since the canteen was basically empty, he figured, they posed no imminent threat. If that man was a suicide bomber, he was going to wait until the canteen was jampacked full of infidels before he'd detonate. Satisfied with his deduction, he returned his attention to his paper and resumed where he left off.

Freddy Boom-boom slid a faux wooden tray along the three parallel, stainless-steel tubes that were attached to the glass display unit with angle brackets at waist height. The heat lamps provided life support for the remnants of breakfast that were still on display. Boom-boom opted for a cup of coffee and a blueberry muffin. Dandelion showed no interest in anything on offer until Boom-boom insisted it was his treat. Without missing a beat, he ordered a full breakfast with coffee and toast. They carried their trays over to a side table and sat opposite each other by a lace-curtained window that peeped into a drab, dimly lit corridor.

When Dandelion was pre-occupied buttering toast, Boom-boom reached into the chest pocket of his overalls to covertly activate the record button on his Bose tape recorder, an old birthday present he had no use for until then. He retrieved a tissue from that same pocket to mask his action. His plan - like the reels on his recorder - was now in motion. His intention was to counter Dandelion's extortion attempt with one of his own. He loved spy movies and to be acting as one in real life instead of driving that fucking school bus was the ultimate joy for him.

'Let's cut to the chase,' Dandelion said as he crunched into a mouthful of toast. 'I have a proposition for you. No wait... hold on.' He poked the space in front of him with his fork, as if to oust the word he was looking for and have it drop onto the table. 'It's more an arrangement between the County Council and myself.'

'An arrangement,' Boom-boom repeated.

'Yes, an arrangement, that's correct.' Dandelion nodded, satisfied that he had chosen the right word to enable him to sidestep the full glare of extortion. He jammed a loaded fork into his full mouth. He ate with his mouth open like a garbage truck, mashing and mincing debris.

'Will this arrangement benefit the County Council?' Boom-boom inquired, getting a little irate at having to *pull teeth* at that hour of the morning, not to mention the slow poke pace of the conversation which made a mockery of... cutting to the chase.

'Yes,' Dandelion agreed. 'The County Council will benefit greatly from this arrangement. However, everything comes with a price.'

'Please,' Boom-boom made a praying gesture with his hands, 'continue.'

'Recently you guys have been getting a lot of bad rap in the papers. I'm sure you don't want the public to know about your latest little fuck-up.'

'I really have no idea what you're talking about.'

'You were on my property last Saturday retrieving that probe thing that some idiot sent astray with his joy stick. That looked like an expensive piece of equipment that one of your boys from the County Council nearly lost by mistake. If the people of Ballydecuddle get to read about another County Council fuck-up - especially since the ink isn't even dry yet on the last one - I think heads will roll like bowling balls at nine-pin alley on league night. 5,000 euros will obliterate from my mind any memory of that unfortunate incident, if you get my drift.'

'Correct me if I'm wrong.' Boom-boom straightened up in his chair, and leaning forward, he directed his chest pocket to align the tape recorder with Dandelion's mouth. 'You want to blackmail the Town Hall!'

'Woe Nelly, woe,' Dandelion urged. 'Blackmail is a little harsh, don't you think? It's got kind of an ugly ring to it. Personally, I'd prefer business proposition. It doesn't leave a nasty taste in your mouth.'

'Semantics,' Boom-boom retorted. 'You can't call a spade a shoehorn.'

He needed Dandelion to explicitly vocalize his demands so that when he hit the *play* button in the police station, his intent to blackmail would be in no doubt.

'Okay, let me spell it out for you. I want five thousand euros for my amnesia.'

'Spells like B-l-a-c-k-m-a-i-l to me.'

'I think you are hung up on that word.'

'What word?' Boom-boom groaned like he was making repeated attempts to reverse a big rig into a tight-fitting loading dock with busted mirrors.

'Blackmail,' Dandelion replied, raising his voice in frustration.

Freddy Boom-boom's heart skipped a beat. He got him to say the word, but the word alone was useless. He was like a sheep dog trying to coax that one obstinate sheep into the pen. He was also concerned with all the pussy-footing around that his tape might run out.

'Tell you what,' he compromised. 'I'll say what your intentions are and you just qualify my statement. How about that?'

'Sounds good.'

'I want to extort money from the County Council,' Boom-boom spoke loud and clear.

'Hold on a minute,' Dandelion objected. 'I thought we agreed on blackmail. Extortion sounds even worse.'

'Well, why don't you tell me exactly what you want to do, in a clear and distinct manner.'

'I want to blackmail the County Council for my story, which I believe is worth five thousand euros.'

'At last, I understand the purpose of your visit.' Boom-boom spoke into the top pocket of his overalls.

Dandelion stopped eating for a moment. Somehow, he needed to regain control of the proceedings. He was the one supposed to be making all the demands and not the fat-ass 'elocution' teacher who kept leaning across the table, violating his personal space.

'*How many blackmailers have to spell out their shit?*' he asked himself, vexed by the whole carry-on.

Freddy Boom-boom - on the other hand - was chuffed. At last, he hooked the sentence that would bring in the big bucks. 'Sometimes, instead of a minnow on the line,' he heard himself say, 'there's a yellow finned tuna.' Suddenly, he pounded the table twice in quick succession. 'Boom, boom,' he cried.

Dandelion was startled by the antics of the big man across from him. His fork miscued on a chunk of sausage when his plate jumped about the table from the sudden heavy blows. The old man peered cautiously over his newspaper. He looked like he was expecting to be met with a blast of shrapnel. Relieved to be still alive, he immersed himself, like a swamp gator, back into his paper.

'I'll tell you right now,' Boom-boom insisted. 'Five thousand euro is not-going-to-fly with the Council.' His sudden shift to defiance surprised Dandelion.

'Four thousand euro or The Daily Mail gets the story,' Dandelion countered.

'Two thousand euro. That's my final offer.'

Both men stared each other down for a prolonged period of time. It was like a Mexican stand-off, without a poncho, a sombrero or a burrito in sight. Boom-boom needed to be a convincing County Council representative, so he decided - out of the blue - to start crying. He didn't know why. It seemed like the right thing to do.

'Fucking fags,' one of the teenagers commented as the pair left the canteen.

'Okay, okay, two-thousand it is,' Dandelion relented. 'Take it easy man, it's not your money.'

Freddy Boom-boom was smiling behind the crocodile tears. His plan was to get two-thousand euros from Maxi to pay Dandelion the so-called extortion money, except he had no intention of handing it over. He could have upped the ante, but he wasn't greedy. He needed to negotiate to get the price down to sound convincing. Dandelion didn't know it yet, but he was the one going to be blackmailed when Boom-boom played the tape for him. He'd have no option but to pay up or go to jail.

'Looks like you've bought yourself a piece of my mind.' Dandelion nodded as he reached across the table to shake Boom-booms' hand.

'Well for my peace of mind, if you follow my drift, I'm going to need the surveillance footage for last Saturday. We wouldn't want this little incident... popping up again in the future.'

'Of course, that goes without saying,' Dandelion assured. 'When do you think you'll have the money?'

'I have to confer with the finance officer, a man by the name of Levi Molasses. Do you know him?'

'No,' Dandelion declared.

'He's the financial big-wig for this locality. I'll have to run it by him. I expect the money won't be a problem. It just takes a little time to, well, you know yourself, red tape and all.'

'Yeah, yeah, I get it,' Dandelion interrupted, eager to wrap things up. 'So, ballpark, when do you think?'

'I'd say we could amicably conclude our business by... end of day Thursday.'

'Will your office be finished by then?'

'What?' Boom-boom momentarily forgetting about the paint job in 'his' office. 'Oh yeah... I mean, no. It will be painted but I'm getting a new carpet installed on Thursday. Tell you what, I'll bring the money to your yard and we'll do the exchange there.'

Dandelion left the canteen. He seemed content with the outcome. The old man also vacated the premises. Boom-boom remained seated at the table. He retrieved the recorder from his pocket and hit the rewind button. Ensuring that nobody was within earshot, he hit the 'play'. Dandelion's raised voice broadcasting his intention to blackmail the Town Hall put a big smile on his face.

Ella instinctively braced herself when she saw Boom-boom exit the building. The minivan dipped once again and rocked violently as he struggled to get in. He bounced around on the seat to find the sweet spot. At last, he was still. There was no point in reaching for the seat belt. He was so tightly packed in, he didn't need one.

'Well, how did it go?' Ella asked, trying to disguise her disgust as his big flabby body mashed her against the glass in the driver's door. His sweat permeated through her cotton cardigan and she could feel it seep into her under garments as she fought off the urge to gag.

'It went better than expected,' he puffed. 'I was able to get behind the counter, no problem. That IT idea of yours was brilliant.' He paused to catch his breath. 'When Dandelion came in and saw me dealing with an old lady behind the counter, that was the proof in the pudding. Plain sailing after that.'

'So how much to shut him up?' Ella inquired abruptly; she was in no humour to chew the fat.

'He wanted five thousand euros, but I worked my magic and got him down to two.'

'Well done,' Ella commended. 'That's around the number we were expecting. You told him we wanted those surveillance tapes, right?'

'Yes boss,' he retorted, raising his flabby arm in a half-hearted salute. '*We* have until

Thursday to come up with the money.'

Ella was a little confounded by his choice of words. '*Since when were 'we' an item?*' she wondered. Also, sarcastically calling her *boss* wasn't going to win him any awards. His ceaseless fondling of his big belly annoyed her from day one, and now his cocky attitude was getting on her nerves.

'Dandelion wanted to meet up again in my office in the Town Hall but as you well know, I don't have an office,' he said. He needed Ella to know the lengths he had to go to, to successfully complete his mission. 'I made up some lame excuse that I was having it renovated. I suggested that I do the *drop* at his yard instead.'

'Well done,' Ella said, faking a smile.

She was genuinely impressed with this man's aptitude to deceive. '*It must be encoded in his DNA,*' she thought. She had a queasy feeling in the pit of her stomach, not just the coffee stains and sweat. Her intuition was gnawing at her insides. It was telling her something wasn't right about this man.

Ella had to suffer Boom-boom's recanting his ordeal with Dandelion on the drive home. She pulled over where she picked him up and handed him an envelope with 250 euros. Once again, the minivan rocked violently as he made his exit. She felt it was a little odd to only have cross-streets on that slip of paper and not a proper address. She made up all sorts of excuses for him. Maybe finding parking outside his house was a problem. It may have been inaccessible due to road works or construction. Who knows, maybe the street he lived on was always congested? She studied him as he waddled away up the road. Normally, fat people are carefree and jolly. They don't have the where-with-all to mastermind a plan to rule the world. But somehow this guy was different.

When she arrived home, she parked the minivan on the road outside her house. There was no need to go through all the shapes of parking in the driveway when she was heading off again after her shower. As soon as she walked through the door, Jasper started barking at her, along with the pack of dogs.

'Where's me fucking dinner?'

All she wanted to do was get out of her stinking clothes and have a scalding hot shower. For a moment, she contemplated burning her clothes.

'Don't be daft,' she said as she ruffled each of the dog's heads on her way into the living room. 'It's only eleven o'clock in the morning.'

'I don't give a fuck. I want me dinner, now,' Jasper barked along with the dogs.

'Why now?' Ella moaned.

'Because I've been up since four o'clock and I'm fucking starving.'

'Well, you're just going to have to wait.' Ella replied. 'I'll fix you something to eat after I shower,' she vowed.

'I want my dinner now,' Jasper persisted.

He was in his temper tantrum mode, and Ella knew there was no abating those outbursts. He would rant and rave for the next half hour or so and eventually fizzle out like the last of the bubbles in a bottle of champers. Even the dogs knew the drill. They all scampered up the stairs the minute he started. Prudence, making a stand on his perch, was the only one to challenge him in that state.

'Shut de fuck up,' Prudence squawked as he thrashed about on his perch, losing a few feathers in the process.

'Shut your fucking beak,' Jasper screamed. 'I want my dinner now.'

Ella went upstairs amid the ruckus and took a long, hot shower. As she was getting dressed, her phone rang. It was Petra with a phone sex client. She declined the call even though she needed the money, badly. All her credit cards were maxed and her car insurance was due. She hoped and prayed that when she got back from Buca Brannigan's depot, she'd have Maxi's backpack with her and all her problems would be solved. As she came down the stairs, she imagined bales of bank notes scattered all around the living room floor, impeding her way to the kitchen. Jasper kept screaming and shouting, but she didn't hear. Eventually his outburst began to peter out, his shouts and shrieks reduced to groans and moans. Prudence had already given up the fight.

Ella stood by the deep-fat-fryer waiting patiently for the oil to come to a boil. Jasper was under strict orders from his G.P. not to eat any 'fatty' foods, cakes or confectionaries and to steer clear of sugar, salt, butter and alcohol. Ella imagined the headlines in the newspaper as she loaded - *Exhibit A* - the deep-fat fryer, with battered sausages, onion rings and chips and - *Exhibit B* – the frying pan, with a full packet of stringy bacon:

'Wife murders husband with buttery bullets and greasy bombs.'

She had to give Jasper credit for taking care of his end of the bargain, drinking alcohol from dawn to dusk. With both of them on board - collaborating in his demise - his days were surely numbered.

Ella presented Jasper with her *coronary* delights and he hogged into the food like the pig he had become.

'Bon appetite,' she said. *'Hopefully,* she mused, *'bon voyage?'.*

Feeling refreshed after her shower, she was ready for her next mission. She jumped in the minivan, but before she turned the ignition, she called Maxi. Omitting to tell him how suspicious she felt about Boom-boom, she relayed the gist of the meeting between the two men in the Town Hall.

'Wow, this guy's some operator,' Maxi surmised. 'How much is he charging us for doing the *drop*?'

'You know what,' Ella paused for a moment. 'We never discussed his fee.'

'That's unusual.'

'Yeah, you're right,' Ella agreed, feeling shameful that her abruptness with Boom-boom might have been the reason she didn't have a number.

'It is what it is,' Maxi confirmed. 'We still have a few days before Thursday to find the treasure. Let's focus on one thing at a time. You're going to Buca Brannigan's depot now?'

'I'm on my way as we speak,' Ella confirmed.

'Make sure you get a good look in the van. Soak up all the information you can when you're in the office. Be careful, there's a lot of shady characters in the haulage business.'

'Relax, will ye?' she assured him. 'I'm a big girl and well able to look after myself, thank you very much.'

'Just saying...'

Ella hung up and drove to Beat Street.

Chapter 19.

It took Ella about thirty-five minutes to reach Brannigan's recovery on Beat Street. She had no difficulty finding the depot; it was the epitome of tastelessness. The workshop and adjoining office were smothered in bright yellow paint and with the trim, a clashing purple hue, the whole structure screamed... loud. Ella parked her minivan in a vacant spot directly in front of the workshop, the coffee stained seats gnawing away at her like an itch she couldn't scratch. She sat quietly for a moment to revisit some fond memories she had in those cotton beige pants. Just then she realised she forgot to convey her annoyance to Maxi on the phone. He was going to get an earful later for sure.

She fixed her hair, as she always did in the rear-view mirror, before getting out and heading over to the office. She climbed the three steps to the shipping container whose seafaring days were over and now sat on cavity blocks, repurposed to spend its golden years as an office. She delivered the obligatory double-tap on the metal door, and without waiting for a response, reached for the knob to let herself in. Finding no knob, her shoulder collided abruptly with the door and she was left, still standing outside the office. After fumbling about the area where the doorknob was supposed to be, she was surprised she had to bend down to grab the knob. She guessed it had to be at least eighteen inches below the norm. She opened the door, recovered her posture and stepped into the office.

Sammy Brannigan, aka Buca, was seated behind his little desk, dictating numbers to someone on the phone from an open ledger in front of him. He acknowledged her presence with a barely discernible nod and invited her to sit, waving his pen like a wand at the seat directly opposite him. He continued talking and writing numbers. All she heard were his affirmations, negations and numbers. He made no other intrusion into the English language, or any other language for that matter.

Ella lowered herself into the chair, and as she sunk below the medium height of a regular chair, she got concerned. Once she passed the point of no-return, she had to trust gravity to take its course and hope that the seat would interrupt her descent - soon. She regretted wearing a skirt. Relief at last, as the possibility of her splaying all over the floor was averted when she finally docked with the seat. She sat, trying to look dignified with her knees propping up her boobs, like she was taking a dump in a Chinese latrine.

'Is this a joke?' she wondered.

Buca ended his call with one final sequence of numbers. He folded the ledger and stood up to return it to its designated spot in a filing cabinet by the wall to the right of the office door. Ella was dumbfounded by the size of the little man. He couldn't have been more than 3 feet tall. Suddenly, the realization that she had entered into the land of the Lilliputians substantiated the positioning of the doorknob and the properties of the little chair. She was indeed grateful not to have been tethered to the hard wood floor, like Gulliver was. She was now a part of his little world. She immediately appreciated the dichotomy whereby no quarter was given in her world for the likes of him, so why should there be any in his for the likes of her?

Buca returned to Ella's side of the desk. He reached out to shake her hand and introduced himself. Ella made a feeble attempt to stand up, but the energy required to achieve such a feat didn't match the reward. She shook while she sat.

'To whom do I owe the pleasure of a visit from such a beautiful lady as yourself?' he inquired as he sat, side-saddle, on the desktop with one little leg dangling in the breeze. His confidence did much to ameliorate his diminutive stature. He was so cute, she wanted to cuddle him like a teddy bear.

'Ella is my name,' she heard herself say, '...and the pleasure is all mine.' She was still in outer body mode with the shock. She should have said Lucy... Lucy Windsor, but she forgot.

'You know, you have given me an impossible task!' He presented a puzzled expression on his face for her to decode. 'How can I possibly attempt to make your day,' he insisted, 'any brighter than you have already made mine?' His puzzle in his little mind was a Gordian knot for, what his first impression led him to believe, a bimbo. The teddy bear misread Ella. Just because a woman is beautiful doesn't mean she's braindead.

'Oh, you are so kind.' she chirped. She opted to play into his hands and pertain to be a bimbo. 'The reason I'm here is to check to see if my brother's backpack is in the van that you guys towed here, after his unfortunate crash on Saturday evening.'

'Why send his lovely sister to do a man's job?'

'Because I'm afraid my brother is incapacitated in hospital,' Ella said.

'Oh, I'm sorry to hear that. I wish him a speedy recovery.'

'Thanks.'

Ella had mixed feelings for this man. She felt sad. Or was it pity? She wasn't sure. His head was disproportionately larger in comparison to the rest of his little body. However, she thought if it was transplanted – Frankenstein style – onto a *normal* sized body, that creation would be revered in society as an incredibly handsome man. His square jaw and high cheek bones, his dimples, his *come-to-bed* ice-blue eyes, his full lips and immaculate teeth, with a picture-perfect nose, a crop of jet-black hair, his clefted chin, key features that all women and some men found irresistible about the globe. If he were to post his mugshot, Ella thought, on any of those dating sites, he would be inundated with *likes*. However, if he relied on his mugshot alone, things might go a little askew on the first date!

'Yes, my guys towed your brother's van here early yesterday morning. In fact, it's still strapped to the flat bed of the tow truck.' His little finger pointed towards the carpark.

'Yes, I know,' she nodded. 'I saw it out there on my way in.'

'Do you know why it's still up on the flat bed?'

'I really don't have a clue,' Ella responded.

'There is the little matter of payment.'

'Oh,' Ella exclaimed. 'I thought my brother's auto insurance would take care of all that.'

'You say your brother is in the hospital,' he said, looking for clarification.

'He's in a coma... in the hospital,' Ella shot back from her little chair.

'Well then,' he replied, looking a little unnerved by her rapid retort. 'That would explain why we haven't heard from his insurance provider.'

'I'll notify them when I get John's information,' she assured as she put her *beast* back in its cage.

'That would be great.' He clapped his little hands together and he took a little deep breath.

'As regards the personal property of the crash victims, my crew collects up any valuables that are in the vehicles or strewn about the crash site. These items are then handed over to the police.'

'Yes, I'm aware of all that,' she replied. 'You see, I've already been to the police station and they don't have his backpack. If you don't mind, I would like to check the van, just in case it may have been overlooked.'

'A backpack, you say,' he said, sounding once again like he needed clarification.

'Yes, my brother's backpack.'

'A backpack is hardly something my guys would,' he said, pausing for effect. 'Overlook! I think for you to go through all that trouble would be such a waste of time and effort,' he assured as he arsed his way along the desk to sit directly opposite his captive in the little chair. 'You do realise that there's an accusation of sorts hidden in your request.'

'I don't know what you mean,' Ella meekly replied as she sensed the change in tone. She slammed her legs tighter together when she saw how the little-un had positioned himself for the perfect up-skirt action.

'Oh, come now, you don't believe me when I tell you that *all* the victim's property is handed over to the police. You need to see for yourself. How do you think that makes me feel?' He brought his little hands together in prayer to indorse his innocence while he waited patiently for an apology. An awkward silence ensued.

Instead of spending that interlude in repentance for her ghastly allegation, Ella scooped the office for intel. There was no doubt in her mind, even though he nailed the altar-boy impersonation, that same defensive strategy had been rattled off many times in the past to combat irate victims over '*missing*' crash site items. It was the classic '*rat in the corner*' scenario. Attack.

All the while, she could feel his stare raking over her body. She squirmed as a wave of nausea engulfed her. Tugging at the hem of her skirt with both hands, she willed the material to stretch and cover her bare legs from the prying eyes of the leering teddy bear.

There were only three pictures on the wall in front of her, and each hung at the same low altitude for his viewing pleasure. Everyone else would have to squat to appreciate the gallery. The other walls were bare except for a busy looking key-rack on one and a Playboy calendar on the other with some centrefold hussy straining to support, in her cradling arms, the biggest pair of artificial boobs Ella had ever seen. She found herself momentarily reciting the alphabet in a futile search for a bra size to fit them puppies. She could hear that song in her head: '*Who let the dogs out?*'

The next frame looked like it housed a diploma or certification of sorts with his name, Samuel Brannigan, scribbled across the middle portion while the right-hand bottom corner was festooned with a waxed seal that provided the parchment with some degree of sophistication. She squinted to determine the nature of the award. It could have been a degree in Neuro-physics or a licence to practice Voodoo… she couldn't tell without her glasses. Reaching into her bag for them at that solemn moment was not an option. Next to that, a framed photo of the little bare-chested man himself with his arm around some tall blonde woman in a bikini, both sipping colourful cocktails as they lounged on a beach somewhere in a sunny kabana by the sea.

'Strike tall,' Ella decided. *'Tall is redundant in his little world. Was she the wife, a girlfriend or a prostitute?'* she wondered.

The third picture showed him with his head sticking out the window of a tricked-out, neon green pickup truck with the extra-large wheels, the chromed rims, the gazillion lights, and all the bells and whistles deemed necessary to join the *'lame brains with limp dicks'* fraternity. The owners of such Megatron trucks should be commended, she mused, for their show of gaudy accessories, which unbeknownst to them act as a warning to the public at large that a small dick with a big chip on his shoulder is behind the wheel. This was taking the Napoleon complex to a whole new plateau. Ella predicted, if this little man had his choice of all the animals on earth to have as a pet, he'd choose a fucking giraffe.

Since no apology was forthcoming, Buca decided to turn on the charm.

'I don't see a ring,' he blurted out of the blue. 'Don't tell me a beautiful woman like you is single?'

'I'm married,' Ella snapped. 'Sometimes I forget to wear it.'

'I understand.' He winked and nudged his little elbow to signal. 'Mom's the word,' he said, and he winked at her.

'No, no, no, you don't understand,' Ella contested. 'It's not at all like that.'

'Oh, come now, a beautiful woman like you must have needs,' he insisted as he jumped down from the desk to invite her in to his open arms.

'I'll tell you what I need,' Ella screamed. 'I need to see inside that fucking van and I need to do it right this fucking minute.'

She struggled to break free from the little chair and at last, reclaiming her full height at five foot nine inches tall plus three inches for her heels, she towered over the little pervert.

'Right this way.' The little man cowered, making himself smaller still. He was blindsided by her rebuttal.

She was raging as she followed him over to the tow truck which had the crashed van stacked on top of its flat bed. Again, she regretted wearing a skirt. This was another repercussion of the coffee spill that morning. Not only did she lose her favourite beige pants which resulted in her wearing a skirt, she was obliged to climb up on the flat bed in order to search the van and in the process, put on a peep show for this fucking midget, who's diminutive height on that particular occasion afforded him the best seat in the house. It was a *grin and bear* moment. Buca Brannigan got an eye full and Ella got to check the van. Mission accomplished. No backpack. Maxi Dillon was going to get more than an ear full when she got home.

Chapter 20.

Ella's minivan skidded out from Branigan's depot and onto Beat Street, her screeching tyres articulating her urgency to vamoose. She gunned it down the road until she had put some serious distance between herself and that disgusting little man. Once she was well enough away, she pulled into some shopping centre and parked away from all other cars. Her whole body trembled in the after-burn of fury. She grabbed at her bag and rummaged about to find her Marlboro box. She was so shaken up from her ordeal, she had difficulty picking a cigarette from the pack. At last, she brought a shaky cigarette to her lips and lit it with a quivering flame from her Zippo lighter. She took a long, slow drag allowing the smoke to invade her lungs and smother the very essence of her being. She needed to soak... in smoke. Half way down her cigarette, she called Maxi to vent.

'Hi Maxi, it's me.'

'You seem upset. What's wrong?' Maxi asked.

'Is it that obvious?'

'Afraid so,' he confirmed. 'Tell me what happened.'

'Well, he's a midget,' Ella announced. 'Did you know that?'

'Who's a midget?' Maxi asked. 'What are you talking about?'

'That fucking pervert who owns the recovery depot, Buca - fucking - Brannigan, that's who.'

'Sounds like you and Buca didn't exactly hit it off.'

'Hit it off,' she snarled. 'All that little fucker wanted to do was hit on me.'

'Well Ella, can't say I blame him,' Maxi blurted... immediately regretting what he said.

'Don't go there,' she growled.

'Sorry, Ella, forgive me,' he pleaded. 'That was uncalled for.'

'Don't sweat it,' she said. She took a deep breath. 'I know you think I'm overreacting, but that little fucker's arrogance really pissed me off. He plays the midget card to bag his prey, but I tell ye he got some shock when I let him have it.'

'I bet,' he said, spurring her on.

'Anyway, that's neither here nor there. Bottom line, the despicable little prick claims he knows nothing about a backpack.'

'Did you happen to get a look in the van?' Maxi took a gamble that Ella was done with her dirty laundry.

'Yes, I did,' she proudly replied. She had to compose herself as Buca's cheap thrill vividly flashed before her eyes. 'Nothing,' she verified.

'Can't say I'm surprised.'

'Oh, by the way, you owe me a new pair of beige linen pants.'

'How come?' he asked, happy to be done with the perverted midget.

'Freddy Boom-boom attacked my minivan first thing this morning and made me spill coffee all over myself. They were my favourite fucking pants,' she exploded, and the stress hissed from her body like the expelled air from the brakes of a big rig.

'Shit,' he blurted. 'I meant to warn you about him. I'll buy you a palace when we find this treasure,' he promised. 'How about that?'

'That's fine as long as there's a closet in the master bedroom full of beige linen pants.'

'Deal.'

'So, how did it go with Nora and all her appointments?' Ella inquired, feeling a lot better after sharing her ordeal with Maxi.

'As well as can be expected, I suppose,' he replied with a hint of intrigue in his tone. 'Nora made it quite clear to everyone in the doctor's waiting room she shouldn't have to wait in line behind a foreigner.'

'Oh uh,' she moaned. 'Awkward.'

'Oh my God,' he continued. 'I felt so bad for that poor Polish woman and her child. I'm putting a muzzle on Nora in the future.'

Ella burst out laughing. The coffee spill first thing that morning set the tone for the day and it just got worse as the day wore on. It felt good to laugh, even if it was at Maxi's expense.

'Then the hairdressers,' he groaned. 'One nightmare after another. I spent nearly half a day listening to a bunch of old crockpots with pink and blue hair swap recipes for Shepheard's pie, debate over the best potions and lotions for sciatica and lumbago, not to mention other savoury topics like flatulence and incontinence. It takes me ten minutes to get a haircut.'

'The things we women do for our men?' Ella proclaimed.

'That's something ye women should do alone,' he remarked. 'No man should ever have to suffer so.'

'Boohoo.'

'Anyway, looks like we both had a shitty day,' he insisted. 'I think you should go home and have a nice glass of wine for yourself,' he suggested. 'I'm going to go and check the crash site just to make sure my backpack wasn't overlooked. If it's not there, then we know for sure, Buca Brannigan or his crew have it.'

'It's not wine-time yet,' Ella replied. 'But you know what?' she decreed. 'Today the clocks go back in Ella-World. Knock yourself out at the crash site. I really think it's a waste of time, but you won't be said or led so...'

'I'll call you later with the news.'

'Later.'

Maxi peeped into the living room to check on Nora. The four o'clock debate was reconvening after the mid-interval snack. He noticed the attractive Slavic woman Pia Katovich - he learned her name in the meantime - had returned with her pussy whipped husband. *'Lucky bastard,'* he mumbled to himself as he made his way from the back of the room, around the two rows of seats and up to the front where the all-informative 'white board' was positioned. He stood in his usual spot by the left of the board, drawing attention with his pointer to the question written in block letters: What is Knowledge?

Once the group had settled into their seats, he began his monologue.

'For the last hour or so, you ladies and gentlemen have been discussing knowledge and how it is acquired. I must commend you all on your astuteness. This is a "heavy" topic. Even some of the great philosophers had difficulty trying to get their heads around, what it means to be knowledgeable. Seems to me, we all agree,' he wrote on the board as he spoke. 'The sum of what is known is the body of truth, information and principles acquired by humankind.'

'I learn something new every day,' Daphne Dooley piped up from the second row with the same gusto as if she was the first to discover fire.

She certainly got the room's unbridled attention, especially since it was her first utterance all afternoon. Maxi felt how ironic it was for a simpleton to poke a stick in the eye of sagacity. He hoped for her sake he was mistaken, but when it looks like dog shit and it smells like dog shit... it's hardly going to taste like caviar.

'Problem is,' she continued. 'Unless I rehearse the new stuff over and over in my head, it just goes in one ear and out the other,' she confided. 'Knowledge is hard work.'

'Daphne,' Niamh Conway responded. 'Just because you recite something over and over in your head and you learn it off by heart, that doesn't make you knowledgeable.'

'Hear, hear.' The unanimous chant from the group.

'You are nothing more than a recorder,' Niamh continued, spurred on by the group's approval. 'If I press your play button, all I get back is what I put in. Knowledge is much more than that. It is the accumulation of facts and information acquired through education and experience which leads to ideas and axioms evolving through deductions and deliberations, sourced from this well of wisdom.'

Maxi gave Niamh Conway full marks for her confutation.

'What do *you* know?' Daphne Dooley growled at Niamh Conway, jealous of her low handicap and uppity address.

'Now, now, ladies,' Maxi interjected. 'There's no need to get your bloomers in a twist.' He wondered, was he politically correct with that word or should he have said 'knickers'? If his remark was directed at the Slavic bombshell, his predicament would have been identical, except his choice of undergarment would have to be either 'panties' or 'G-string'. He couldn't, in his mind's eye, see the beautiful Pia Katovich hauling up a pair of bloomers over those lovely shapely legs of hers, no matter what age she was.

'Daphne,' Maxi addressed the imbecile. 'We're trying to define what knowledge is and how it is acquired. Bickering is not going to get us anywhere. So, either contribute or be quiet.'

Daphne Dooley was speechless. She knew she was way out of her depth and chose to sulk for the remainder of the debate.

'Knowledge is the accumulation of facts,' Maxi announced. 'Do we all agree with this remark?'

He got a unanimous affirmation from the group.

'Good. Now let me ask you, what filters do we have in place to help us differentiate between fact and fiction?' He wrote fact and fiction on the board. 'Before you answer, remember fiction or a falsehood can be dressed up to look like a fact, so how can we tell them apart?'

'That's when we rely upon common sense to help us wade through all the do-do,' Archibald Townsend reasoned. He was the Slavic bombshell's partner, and he spoke with an irritating aristocratic English accent.

'Very good point, Archibald,' Maxi responded, barely succeeding in hiding his contempt for a name that was synonymous with

English gentry and the hundreds of years of oppression and subjugation meted out to the peoples of Ireland by the ancestors of this proper twat.

'*I bet my left nut,*' Maxi thought to himself, '*Archibald Townsend never got a blister on those lily-white hands of his. The only physical pain he ever suffered was stubbing his toe in the dark, and of course he managed to snare the most beautiful woman in the civilized world.*' He had to admit to himself that he was a little jealous of Archibald.

'Common sense,' Maxi wrote on the board and circled the result.

'What is common sense?' Maxi knew instantly he had struck a nerve by the eager reaction of his audience. As he back stepped away from the board and made his way out through the living room door, he heard a response over his shoulder.

'Knowledge is the father,' Nora announced. 'Common sense, the off-spring.'

She directed her comment at Masie Molloy, who beat her a decade ago in the Captain's prize with a twenty-four handicap. Nora was playing off two at the time and was still seething over her one stroke loss to Masie. A fortunate ricochet off an oak tree on the 18th fairway re-directed Masie's - otherwise lost ball - to within inches of the pin. Game over.

Maxi smiled to himself in the knowledge that his mother was loving these debates and that her will to live had been rejuvenated as a result. These two little words '*common sense*' would buy him enough time to search the crash site and return before the debate concluded.

It took him less than fifteen minutes to reach the crash site over by Cello Falls. He parked the car in off the dirt road with the passenger side wheels riding up on a mound of tall grass that flanked that side of the road. He got out and immediately began to search for clues. His eye was drawn to a disturbance on the mound where the tall grass had been trampled. A slow recovery of the flattened vegetation was already in progress, with some blades of tall grass already up and at it. He climbed to the top of the incline and looked down into the meadow below. Judging by the initial patch of unspoiled terrain immediately beyond the crest of the hill, it seemed the van must have been airborne for a spell before nosediving into the undergrowth. A large furrow was ploughed into the ground just before a clump of pine trees whose broken branches and scarred trunks confirmed their involvement in the crash.

He picked his way carefully down the slope through the long grass, stepping over some small bushes and brambles as he went. After ten minutes or so combing through the rough terrain, he was surprised to discover another backpack besides his own, concealed under a bush quite some distance from the van's trajectory. He knew instantly *his* was swapped out for this one. He searched the main compartment and the side pouches. The bag was empty except for a business card that got trapped within the lining of one of the side pockets. Printed on the card were the contact details of the '*Cockpit*' bar in Drago Dunes.

'Now, we're getting places,' he said aloud as he placed the card inside his wallet.

Just then, he heard rock music in the distance. He crouched down and made his way up the embankment to peep over the crest of the hill. He saw a gaudy green pickup truck with a roof rack of headlights, twin stainless-steel exhaust tubes running up on both sides of the truck and barrelling along on huge oversized tyres with polished rims. It was away in the distance yet Maxi could hear '*Highway to Hell*' by ACDC and he was half deaf! The closer the monster truck got, the louder the music.

He threw the backpack over his shoulder and raced back to his car. He jumped in and drove down the lane to a clearing in the hedge-grove. He hid the car in that vestibule of foliage and snuck back along the road to the crash site. The music sounded louder and louder. He ducked behind a felled tree and spied as the tricked-out truck came to a halt. Suddenly the music died, the door was flung open and a midget climbed down the steps onto the dirt road. There was no doubt this was Buca Brannigan in the flesh and his presence at the crash site proved he sure as hell didn't have the backpack either.

Chapter 21.

D rago Dunes was the brain child of Ziggy Antwon, a media mogul from San Francisco's Bay Area, who made his 'pink' fortune catering to the needs of the gay community in California. He ended up on Piper Island purely by accident. A business lunch he was hosting to promote the launch of his new magazine, '*Band of Sisters*', let out early due to one of his copy editors throwing a hissy-fit over the excessive caramelized burn on his Crème brulee. The thin crust of brown sugar congealed into an impenetrable lid, hindering his access to the rum and custard beneath.

'Somebody give me a fucking lump hammer so I can break into my dessert,' he screamed.

As a consequence, Ziggy arrived home unexpectedly to his luxury apartment on Nob Hill only to find his live-in boyfriend, Zanzibar Fettucine, on the business end of another man's cock. He was devastated. He immediately took a leave of absence from his media empire and somehow ended up vacationing on Piper Island off the west coast of Ireland, where he spent several weeks licking his wounds. It was there he realised there was no safe haven in Ireland for gay and androgynous people like himself to let their hair down. So, right then and there, Drago Dunes - the Disneyland for transgenders - was conceived.

Fuelled by Zanzibar's indiscretion, Ziggy returned to California and packed up all his stuff, sold his business and his luxury apartment for tens of millions of dollars and flew back across the Atlantic in his private jet to turn his vision into a reality. He descended on Piper Island and ruthlessly set about buying up as much land and real estate as possible. Above market pricing ensured an abundance of swift sales. Of course, as in any venture capital project, there were always the indomitable few who wouldn't be swayed. Little did they know, but their beloved island was not only

226

going to get a name change but a complete makeover with lipstick and mascara embedded in the very foundations to amplify the exclusive nature of that locality to the outside world. Ziggy Antwon's endless cashflow transformed Piper Island from being a remote rural entity to a modern-day enclave specifically engineered to accommodate the needs of the gay community. Shepherds and their sheep got their marching orders while pink poodles, snippets and pudges got to make Drago Dunes their new stomping ground.

Soon it would boast a supermarket, a gymnasium, an indoor swimming pool, saunas, steam rooms, a beauty salon, massage parlours, trendy shops, bars and restaurants and a whole slew of ocean front, luxury apartments. It had several helicopter pads dotted about the island and it even had its own landing strip for small aircraft. Sales of homes were snapped up from the drawings and the construction work began in earnest. Two years later the finishing touches were being applied to the network of boardwalks that connected the facilities to the homes while the new landlords and their tenants were being ferried in from the mainland to live their lives... at last among their own kind and free from persecution and prejudice.

The '*Cockpit*' bar and restaurant was Ziggy's pet project. No expense was spared fitting out the opulent dining area with several enormous crystal chandeliers hanging from the high ceiling, a Venetian plaster finish on all the curved walls to eliminate any sharp edges while the Atlantic Ocean - doing its thing - could be appreciated in any one of the many floor-to-ceiling windows that were installed all along its perimeter.

The bar part was more '*get down and party*'. It was a horse-shoe shaped bar with incandescent mood lighting embedded in the epoxy resin counter top. The numerous ceiling mounted laser lights were synchronized to the beat of the music playing on the high-tech surround-sound system that could perforate an eardrum if the dial went beyond two. Adult sized bird cages clung to the exposed rafters for performers to inspire patrons to dance. Big disco, mirrored balls were dotted about the ceiling to play havoc with the laser lights and have them ricochet and refract like innocuous fireworks. Upon completion, the 'Cockpit' bar/restaurant proved to be the most lucrative investment on the whole island. It had a steady flow of patrons during the day and it was always mobbed at night.

Mandy worked as one of the day time bartenders. She preferred to keep her nights free to plunder. She rented an apartment above the 'Cockpit' bar where she savoured the sights and sounds of the ocean. Of course, her operation - once she saved up enough money - would be the icing on the cake. She had to pinch herself from time to time with the luck she was having of late. Finding that American made backpack was an example of how the 'little things' impacted her day. Not only was it stylish and comfortable to wear, its contents - the metal box - solved a niggling problem she was having ever since moving into that apartment. After cleaning the dirt off the box, she was able to examine it carefully. Since it felt empty and it had no apparent lid, she deemed it worthless. However, it proved to be a God send when placed under her bedside lamp. It elevated the lamp just high enough so she could read comfortably in bed. Now she could keep abreast with all the latest medical advances and procedures regarding sex-change operations around the world.

She was in the midst of preparing dinner - cooking was something she truly loved to do - when Larry and Joe arrived in the apartment, each carrying an overnight bag, a case of beer and several bottles of booze. Mandy was already half way down her bottle of red wine. She stepped away from the frying pan, allowing the meat to brown while she released two beers from the case before stashing the rest into a plastic cooler that already contained a bag of ice. This was the drill on 'divvy-up' night. She handed a beer to each of the men and returned her attention to the sizzling hot pan.

'How did we do last night?' Larry shouted – his only speaking option – as he made himself comfortable on one of the high stools by the peninsula that jutted out into the open plan kitchen. He was eager to know how much his 'take' from the crash site was. He sipped his beer in anticipation. Joe sat next to him, his beer bottle disappearing in and out of his smoky halo as he, too, anxiously awaited a response.

'We did very well,' she replied. 'You'll see,' with her back turned to the two men, 'but only after we eat dinner.' There was a stern undertone imbued in her remark, which from experience, both men knew not to challenge.

'What's for dinner?' Joe puffed out his inquiry.

'Beef Wellington,' she replied, shaking her head in disbelief. *'What difference does it make?'* she thought, *'It all has to go in the fucking blender for gummy Joe.'*

After a satisfying meal, they all retired to the living room where the two men had graduated to the whiskey while Mandy stuck with the wine. She had a triathlon competition in a couple of days and didn't want to get wasted. It was time to divvy up the spoils. Mandy laid out the loot on the coffee table in an orderly fashion for the men's appraisal. There was a leather wallet with 30 euros inside, next to that a pair of binoculars, an envelope with 480 euros (40%'s wages), a gold cross and chain, a wristwatch and a few other miscellaneous items. The nylons were a 'no-show' as was the backpack.

Each of them sat back in their seats, and raising their glasses in celebration, they toasted their spoils. They drank into the early morning, recanting old tales of plunder and some 'close-call' episodes that nearly got them pinched. The more inebriated they got, the more embellished their stories became so that with numerous drunken recitations over the years, their tales became so far-fetched that they assumed an almost mythical status.

'Artemis, the Goddess of the hunt on her push bike, combed the darkness in search of prey. Indra, the God of thunder, barked orders at Vulcan, the God of fire, as they robbed the stars from the Heavens to fence to Ra, the ancient God of the Sun, for a song and a prayer.'

Larry slept in the guest room, Joe, on the couch. They had to wrap him up each night in a sheet, like an Egyptian mummy to prevent him from smoking while they slept. The siblings had good reason to be concerned. Not so long ago on one such *'divvy up'* night, they woke to a smoke-filled apartment with Joe's arm inside the armrest of the sofa, the guts of the padding burnt away by the smouldering embers, sparked by his cigarette. It was a miracle the apartment didn't go up in flames and all of them with it.

The following morning, two empty whiskey bottles lay on their backs, next to each other on the living room floor, surrounded by a slew of crumpled-up beer cans. A very full ashtray like an overcrowded life-boat seemed to sail a course across the coffee table, leaving many stragglers to fend for themselves. A pile of dirty dishes crowded the sink while the lid of the garbage can gave-up trying to conceal the overflow of trash in the can that everyone in the apartment deemed bottomless.

Larry and Joe had return tickets that evening for the five o'clock ferry. With the whole afternoon to kill before departure, Joe headed off down to the pier with his fishing-rod. Mandy devoted one large closet to nautical paraphernalia such as surf boards, wet-suits, life jackets, fishing-rods, nets and the like. She loved living by the sea. Such close proximity to sand and waves lent credence to her deep-rooted belief of herself as a walking, talking, tranny buccaneer. 'Har-har, me hearties.'

Larry went downstairs to the bar to have a few beers with his 'brother,' who was working the day shift. It was too early for the loud music and the laser light show, so the bar was practically empty except for a few people here and there. Give it a few hours and the place would be heaving. Larry was settling in for his second beer when his phone rang. He checked the caller ID. It was Buca Brannigan. He grabbed his beer and headed out onto the back deck to take the call.

'I just had a woman in here looking for a backpack,' Buca remarked. 'She says it was in the Ford van you morons recovered on Saturday night.'

'Oh yeah,' Larry replied. He had no idea what Buca was on about, plus it didn't help he was nursing a splitting hangover.

'Yeah, so where the fuck is it?'

'Where the fuck is what?' Larry asked, swapping his phone from one ear to the other as he began to get agitated.

'The fucking backpack,' Buca growled. 'You fucking nitwit.'

'I know nothing about a backpack.'

'You know nothing all right,' Buca agreed. 'Now tell me, where the fuck is it?'

'Listen boss, I swear I...'

'What about that other mutt?' Buca interrupted. 'What's his name? Would he have the balls to steal the fucking thing?'

'No. No way,' Larry contested. 'He travels in the truck with me so he'd have to hide it either in the cab or on the flat bed. There's no place to hide anything, especially something as big as a backpack.'

'Did you search the crash site?' Buca asked.

'Yeah, we always do. I'm telling you, boss, there was no backpack,' Larry confirmed.

'Where exactly was the crash?' Buca asked politely. He decided to change his tone so he could, at least, pull something out of the fire.

'There's a dirt road about ten minutes north of Cello Falls and if...'

'Yeah, yeah,' Buca broke in. 'I know it. I'm going over there myself to search for the fucking thing.'

Larry reckoned his younger sister must have taken the backpack. He couldn't believe that she would do such a thing. For years, when they divvied up the loot, each man always getting an equal share no matter what. Now he wondered what happened to sour that arrangement? Good thing Joe was down at the pier. Larry didn't want to include him in the conversation he was about to have with his sister. He felt it would be embarrassing to accuse his own flesh and blood of stealing from them. No. The real reason why he wanted a one-on-one with Mandy was because the whereabouts of this mysterious backpack seemed to concern not only the driver's sister but Buca himself. He equated that concern with a monetary value, which was right up there with the '*motherload*' herself.

'*What self-respecting thief worth his salt,*' Larry asked himself, '*is going to do a three-way split with the 'motherload' when a two-way chop is staring him in the face?*'

The torch he carried so ardently only moments earlier to herald his allegiance to his fellow henchmen was quickly doused by his own prodigious greed. He returned to the bar, his disappointment and excitement fused together into one alien emotion that he wasn't at all sure how to express. Mandy slipped him another beer while Larry, with his head bowed in deep thought, fumbled to light two cigarettes. He passed one over the counter to his sister.

'That was Buca on the phone,' he said as he took a long drag from his cigarette. 'Listen, I'm just going to come right out and say it and all I want to hear from you is the truth.'

'Say what?' Mandy inquired as she noticed the severity in her brother's tone.

'Where's the fucking backpack from Saturday night's crash?'

'What backpack?'

'Don't bullshit me,' Larry hollered, which drew the attention of a few heads at the end of the bar. 'What are you fucking looking at?' he shouted down the bar and suddenly the curious couple wasn't curious anymore. He refocused his attention on his sister. 'You took a backpack from the crash site and I want to know where the fuck it is.'

'Yeah, yeah, okay,' Mandy relented. 'Now I think I know what you're on about.' When her brother was that adamant about something, she knew it was best to come clean. 'Yes, I found a backpack in the bushes that night,' she admitted. 'It's much better quality than my old one, so I swapped bags. Big fucking deal.'

'It is a big fucking deal,' Larry replied. He felt a jab in his heart. His sister's betrayal hurt him. He had to clear his throat before continuing. 'We always split the loot. Why didn't you tell me about the backpack?'

'Look, I didn't think you'd give a shit about a backpack,' she confessed. 'I never saw you wear one. Look at me, I wear one all the time.'

'Let's not get into what you wear,' Larry pleaded. 'You know that shit still bothers me. Okay, forget the backpack for a minute. What was in it?'

'A rusty old metal box,' she answered.

'What was in the box?'

'I don't know,' she said. 'I couldn't open it.'

'You couldn't open it so, that's it, you left it?'

'Yep,' she replied.

'Where is it now?' Larry asked, raising his voice once more.

'It's upstairs in the apartment under my bed-side lamp,' she said. 'The backpack is in the closet.'

'Keep the fucking backpack. I want to take a look at that box. It must be worth something if Buca wants it back. I'll get it open, don't you worry.'

'Good luck with that,' she sneered. 'Fucking thing doesn't even have a lid.'

'I *will* open that fucking box,' Larry spat his pledge over the counter at his sister with a supercilious leer on his face.

'You go, bro,' Mandy encouraged.

'Fuck you, you'll see.' As he got off the stool to leave, he turned back. 'By the way, not a word to Joe. This is between us.'

'How's *he* not going to find out? He lives with you in that shitty basement apartment for fuck sake.'

'Believe me, he won't find out,' he said, stabbing his index finger in the direction of the ocean. 'Not a fucking word... okay.'

Larry raced out of the bar, up the stairs and into the bedroom of the apartment. He found the metal box under the lamp on the bedside table and started to examine it with the same attention to detail as a lab tech, a petri dish. Eventually, he resorted to shaking it vigorously in both hands. He listened carefully for any muted sounds exuding from the box. Nothing. It seemed to be empty. The lid, if it even had one, was not evident. There were no hinges. There was no apparent linear break in the metal that would suggest a lid. He growled to himself, realizing his sister was right, again.

'That fucker is always right,' he moaned, and he punched one of the pillows.

For the next few moments, he sat on the bed and just stared at the box. He was completely baffled by it. Suddenly it registered that the box might be like a shoe box, where one portion fits snuggly over the other. He studied it again with renewed vigour. No matter how he tried, he couldn't open the box. He decided he'd have to return the following night with an assortment of power tools. Just as he was about to replace the box under the lamp, Joe appeared in the doorframe. He still carried his fishing rod and tackle.

'Catch anything, Joe?' Larry asked, a little startled by his sudden presence.

'Only the handle of the rod.' Joe chuckled to himself. He really didn't care much for fishing. He liked listening to the sounds of the ocean, is all.

'Unlucky,' Larry replied.

'What's with the box?' Joe inquired.

'What? This?' Larry held up the metal box. 'Ah it's nothing. It's just an old metal box, that's all.'

'It's just... I never noticed it before,' Joe insisted.

'Well... it's just an old metal box.'

'I see that, but what's with it?' Joe persisted.

'There's nothing *with it*. It's just a metal box, and that's all there is to it.' Larry raised his voice to a holler. He made it clear he was done with the interrogation. 'We have a ferry to catch. Put away your shit and let's get the fuck out of here.'

Joe may not have caught any fish, but he sure could smell one in that bedroom. He did as he was told and replaced his fishing gear in the closet. He took the few remaining beers from the cooler and stuffed them inside his overnight bag, something to drink on the ferry. They both stepped out onto the balcony, and Larry locked the door behind him.

'Why don't you go on ahead, Joe?' Larry suggested. 'I'll catch up with ye at the pier. I want to have a word with my brother.'

Joe headed off down the boardwalk, leaving a trail of smoke behind him like he was powered by a steam engine. Larry dipped into the bar and beckoned his sister's attention.

'I couldn't open the fucking thing,' he confessed.

'Yeah, and you were looking at me like I was a wingnut,' Mandy replied with her arms folded defiantly.

'I'm sorry, all right,' Larry offered his apology. 'I'll be back tomorrow night. I'm bringing *tools*,' he said, looking up at the ceiling. 'I'll open you up,' he said, still staring at the ceiling.

'I'm sure you will,' his sister butted in. The way Larry was threating her ceiling was getting a little scary. 'Do you still think it's the motherload?'

'We'll soon find out,' Larry replied. He took one last pull of his cigarette and swigged down the rest of his beer. 'See ye tomorrow night.'

'What about Joe?'

'What about him?'

'How are you going to come back here tomorrow evening without him?'

'I'll think of something.'

Chapter 22.

With 40% out of action and the treasure AWOL, Maxi had no choice but to return to work in Eden that Tuesday morning. Being Dandelion's only target, he knew he'd have to endure an endless barrage of insults and abuse. However, he was confident Dandelion's preoccupation with the extorsion money, which was due to be dropped down to the yard on Thursday, would alleviate some of the strain.

Once all the gates were unlocked and the yard unleashed to the public, Maxi had to man the phones and deal with '*walk-ins*' until the Almighty arrived. All incoming calls, without exception, had to have their own slip of paper with a pertinent explanation for the call and the contact details of the caller. Even though the phone did all that, Dandelion was reluctant to step foot into the twenty-first century. When it came to running his business, he preferred prehistoric record-keeping practices. Maxi was grateful for small mercies. At least he didn't have to chisel names and phone numbers onto a slab of stone!

Some contractor inquired about load-bearing beams, a school teacher wondered about portable chalk-boards and a woman described a water feature that her daughter noticed earlier in the week and wondered, was there any 'wiggle' room with the price? Maxi burst out laughing. '*The only wiggling that price was going to do was up, up and away.*'

A distraught woman called, looking for help. Maxi had to inform her - amid her sobs and tears - she had called the wrong number. Admittedly, there was an understandable inclination to misinterpret the words 'salvage' and 'salvation' when paired next to each other in the phone book. He wrote '*wrong number*' on a slip of paper to describe that call. Since Dandelion followed up on every lead, he knew he would not accept his *synopsis* and invariably return her call.

He couldn't help but wonder about the fate of that suicidal woman and how the return call from Dandelion might very well be the catalyst to send her over the edge.

As he busied himself organizing the slips of paper, he got startled by a customer who appeared suddenly in the office window, beckoning him out into the yard.

'Hi there,' Maxi greeted the man. 'Is there anything I can help you with?'

'I'm looking for a ridge tile to match the one that blew off my roof in that terrible storm, way back in '77.'

'Right this way,' Maxi encouraged. *'Wow, that's over thirty years ago,'* he thought, *'this guy's all about getting things done.'*

He escorted the customer over to the section in the yard, which was devoted entirely to roofing materials. The man rummaged about for a while until he found the one, he was looking for. After a thorough examination, inside and out to detect the slightest imperfection, he seemed satisfied.

'How much?'

'Wait a minute,' Maxi stalled. 'I have to find out.' He held up his phone and waved it about for the customer's sanction.

'Okeydokey.' His customer nodded.

Not thinking, Maxi called the office, instead of Dandelion's cell and what's more, he used his own cell-phone to make the call. The portable office phone rang in his pocket to remind him of his blunder. All he got was the office answering machine instructing him to leave a message. Already his mind was preoccupied trying to invent a reason for his absent-minded call to the office. Whatever about one wrong number, two wrong numbers in quick succession would certainly not fly when it came to the little slips of paper. No doubt, he too was going to get a return call before lunch. He punched Dandelion's cell-phone numbers into the keypad on the portable office phone and tapped his foot in anticipation. Maxi's juggling of phones went unnoticed by the preoccupied customer, who was still fondling his find.

'Ballydecuddle Salvage, my name is Daniel, how may I...'

'Daniel, it's me,' Maxi interrupted. 'I have a client here who wants to buy a ridge tile. How much are they?'

'Fifteen euros,' he replied and hung up.

Maxi turned to the customer who was waving a five euro note in the air... his own estimation of the ridge tile's worth.

'Fifteen euros,' Maxi informed the man who embraced the ridge tile.

The customer's facial expression was identical to the one he would deploy if his G.P. sentenced him to death... with terminal cancer. 'What?' he gasped, like he'd been kicked in the bollicks.

Maxi knew not to repeat himself. It wasn't that kind of *what*. The customer stood perfectly still cradling the ridge tile in both arms while he agonized over the exorbitant price. Maxi kicked a small stone around in a circle, just out of range of the customer's pain. At last he reached into his pocket and retrieved a ten euro note to accompany the one he had in his hand. He threw the money on the ground and stormed off, muttering obscenities.

'You're welcome,' Maxi offered in his wake. 'See ye... in thirty years.'

At 9:30 on the dot, Dandelion's van appeared on top of the hill. Maxi jumped from the luxury chair, and positioning it exactly the way he found it, he started to pace the office floor, his thumping heart dictating the tempo of his stride. He felt like he had transmuted into 40% but with no mirror in the small office to consult, he had no means of clarification. He went out to the carpark to meet Dandelion by his van. It was pack-ass time. Dandelion begrudgingly offered him a slight twinge of recognition, and without a word, started to load him up with trash he had accumulated over the weekend. Maxi humped the stash of trash into the office where executive decisions, as to the alter-egos of those discarded items, would soon be determined by the Almighty Himself.

'See this old milkcrate,' Dandelion held it up in front of Maxi, 'with a lick of grey paint it becomes a filing cabinet. See that lockset over there,' he pointed at the floor, 'a coat hanger, and so on and so forth. You find a new purpose for something. You give it new life, and it doesn't hurt to pick up a few quid along the way.'

'How's 40% doing?' Maxi inquired in a desperate bid to topple the pompous podium that Dandelion was spewing horseshit from.

'No idea,' he replied. 'It's about time we got some work done around here. I want you to go down and continue relocating all those pallets that 40% was working on last week.'

'Right-e-ow,' Maxi responded as he tried to appear somewhat enthusiastic. He knew that there was a fine line between 'meek' and 'fanatical' and he needed to stay between the two if he was to avoid arousing suspicion. He left the office and went down the lane to the spot in the yard where 40% had left off. It sickened him to know that those pallets could be moved so easily with the forklift truck that Dandelion played about in, all day, every day. With no particular purpose, just senseless toil, Maxi witnessed the clock - unwilling to relinquish its hold on the day - defiantly drag its lazy ass around in circles.

His cell phone rang. Who else but Dandelion?

'Ballydecuddle salvage, returning your call. My name is Daniel, how may I be of assistance?'

'It's only me,' Maxi replied. 'I'm one of the wrong numbers.'

'I see that,' he said, recognizing his voice.

Maxi's curiosity got the better of him. 'Did you happen to call the other wrong number?'

'Yeah,' he proudly replied, 'I sold that hysterical woman a whole set of patio furniture, even though she doesn't have a patio. I told her to make sure that her next house had enough space for her new furniture. Because of me, that woman now has a reason to live. What did I tell you? It pays to follow up on every lead.'

The rest of the day was uneventful. It was a little after six o'clock when Maxi spotted Dandelion's van driving up the hill. That was his cue to begin the lockdown. He had to delve through the numbness in his mind to plug his brain back in. It took him a moment to shed the monotony of imbecilic work and acclimate to a meaningful task with a purposeful result. Locking the gates was exhilarating that evening.

He arrived home around seven pm and Juanita once again presented him with a dinner plate, for which he was truly grateful. Nora was watered and fed and snoozing by the fire.

'I go now, signor,' Juanita said as she grabbed her coat.

'Of course,' Maxi replied. 'Thanks again for dinner. Let me see you out.'

He jumped up out of his chair and passed Juanita in the corridor so he could open the front door for her. He could tell by her reaction she wasn't used to gallantry. He figured not many Latinos, when she was growing up in war-torn El Salvador, had occasion to attend classes in etiquette. He returned to his dinner, and while he contemplated how horrible her childhood had to have been, his phone rang. This time it was Debbie calling from work.

'Hi Maxi, Debb here,' Debbie sounded a little concerned.

'Yes Debbie, what's up?'

'I just started my shift in the ER and it seems like 40% is showing signs of coming out of his coma.'

'Showing signs?'

'Yeah, he's beginning to twitch his eyes and pinch his fingers. Oh, every now and then, he mumbles gibberish.'

'So how long before he's coherent?' Maxi inquired.

'Hard to tell. He could sit up suddenly and start a conversation or lie there twitching for months.'

'What kind of gibberish are we talking about here? Is he muttering words or just mumbo jumbo?'

'He started ranting on about a big black snake with shiny black eyes crawling all over him in the dark.'

'A big black snake with shiny black eyes,' Maxi replied.

'It's normal for patients to vocalize their hallucinations,' Debbie insisted. 'Especially with the regimen of drugs he's taking. I wouldn't be a bit surprised if Little Red Riding Hood herself showed up in one of his episodes to beat the shit out of the big black snake with her picnic basket.'

'So, there's no connection to reality?' he replied, sounding doubtful.

'Well, that's not necessarily true in all cases. Post-traumatic stress often paints a disturbing experience with a colourful brush to disguise its latent torment.'

'There's nothing colourful about a big black snake with shiny black eyes.'

The line went silent for a moment so they could both witness Debbie's hypothesis being blown to bits by Maxi's rebuttal. After that little hiccup, their conversation resumed, but with an air of formality that was directed at Debbie to impress her with the serious nature of their exchange.

'Do you know if his sister, Lucy, is still around?' Maxi inquired.

'Yes. She took a leave of absence from her job,' she confirmed. 'One of the day staff told me that she was here this morning. Visiting hours are over now so she won't be back, unless you want me to call her.'

'No, no, don't do that. Just keep a close eye on our man and let me know if there's any improvement.'

'Oh, I nearly forgot to tell ye,' Debbie interjected. 'Ida came up with the 2,000 euro we need for Dandelion's extortion money.' She was happy to have something tangible to distract from her earlier faux pas.

'That's great news. We still have a couple of days before the *drop*. Let's pull out all the stops to find the treasure before then.'

'I hear that,' Debbie agreed. 'Is there anything I can do to help in the meantime?'

'You just sit on 40% and keep an eye on his sister. By the way, did Dandelion pay our man a visit?'

'Yes, he was over here on Monday afternoon. He didn't stay long. With 40% out for the count, he had no one to berate.'

'Right, Deb, keep an eye on everything over there. Talk soon.'

Maxi finished eating his dinner. He cleaned his plate except for the 'fried banana' look-a-like. He noticed Nora's 'fried banana' was also left intact on her otherwise empty dinner plate. No surprise there; if it didn't '*moo*', '*oink*' or '*cluck*' she wasn't having it. He made two mugs of tea and brought a small plate of biscuits with him into the living room. He sat next to Nora on the couch. By that time, she was riveted to the TV and barely acknowledged his presence. She was watching a documentary on the American civil war with the battle of Gettysburg raging on the screen. She had a folder on her lap and with pen in hand; she was busy taking notes like she was prepping for an exam. Only then did it dawn on Maxi that she was burning the 'midnight oil' to stock pile her arsenal for the '*Freedom*' debate the following afternoon.

'I take it,' Maxi jabbed, 'Masie Molloy will be along for the debate tomorrow.'

'I have no idea who's coming or going,' Nora lied.

'The fight against slavery and the origin of the Constitution,' Maxi said as he pointed at the screen. 'First amendment, freedom of speech and all that good stuff.'

'Well, isn't that a coincidence.' Nora wiggled in her seat as if to shake off her guilt.

'I guess,' Maxi agreed.

They both smiled at each other. The documentary ended with the two bearded generals, Grant and Lee staring each other down as the lines of credits scrolled across the screen in military like formation. Maxi put Nora to bed at nine o'clock, and as usual, poured himself a vodka with plenty of ice. He called Ida.

'Yeah Ida, it's me.'

'Hello Maxi,' Ida chirped. 'What's up?' She was the quintessential bubbly blonde bimbo and she used it to her advantage.

'I want to thank you for coming up with the extortion money, especially with such short notice.'

'No problem,' she giggled. 'Glad to help out.'

'Funny you should say that; I'm going to need more of your help.'

'Let's hear it,' Ida asked with genuine inquisitiveness.

'Are you and Sebastian still an item?' Maxi asked.

'Well, let's just say, we still go on dates and stuff but unless he steps up from his dinky Cessna 150 to something jet powered in the very near future, I'm afraid his days with this eye-candy are numbered. A girl like me has wants and needs, you know. To be honest with ye, Maxi, I'm mortified getting in and out of that tin-can of his. Everywhere we fly, private jets litter the runway all around us. It's not like he can't afford one, you know.'

'Ida, nobody said it was going to be easy.'

'Thanks for caring,' Ida replied sarcastically. 'So, moving right along, I assume Sebastian has a role to play in our little treasure hunt?'

'Indeed, he does, and coincidentally, so does his humiliating, dinky Cessna 150.'

'I'm glad you included the plane because these days, him and his 'wings' are inseparable. It's gotten so bad, I'm sure if we were out of milk, he'd fly to the store for some.'

'Wow,' Maxi exclaimed. 'Then he'll be delighted to fly us to Drago Dunes tomorrow night for dinner.'

'Once again,' she said. 'Not much notice, but then again, Sebastian doesn't need any when it's coming from me.'

'There's one little snag.' Maxi tugged on the reins.

'Hit me.' Ida chomped at the bit.

'You will have to loan me Sebastian. I need a boyfriend for dinner.'

'Interesting.'

'But wait, there's more,' he insisted. 'Ella will be your date for the evening.'

'I see,' said Ida. 'You want us to blend in with the natives.'

'Exactly.'

'Sounds like we're in for some kinky action,' she said. 'The only problem I see is Sebastian might fall in love with you, Maxi. He's very impressionable, ye know, so don't encourage him. I need to spend a lot more of that man's money before I cut him loose.'

'Don't worry,' Maxi assured. 'I'll be gentle with him.'

'Does Ella know the plan?'

'Not yet, but she will.'

'Well let me give my *gay* boyfriend a call and get this circus on the road.'

'Call me back with confirmation. Remember dinners at seven. Make it happen, Ida.'

'Will do.'

His plan was gathering momentum. All he needed was Ella on board. He checked his watch. It was a little after ten pm and since Ella didn't go to bed until all hours, he decided to pay her a visit. He grabbed the half empty bottle of vodka, tippy-toed out through

the front door and quietly into his car. He didn't want to wake
Nora. With the medication she was on, it's doubtful she'd wake up if
'*Megadeath*' showed up to do a gig in her bedroom. He arrived over
at Ella's house and let himself in. He was pleasantly surprised not to
have been accosted by the pack of dogs. Seemingly it was past their
bedtime. Guard dogs with a curfew, who knew?

Jasper was out for the count like Nora - same meds. Prudence was
asleep on his perch in the living room. Ella beckoned him into the
kitchen with her index finger to her lips. Prudence was a light sleeper.
Maxi closed the double doors gently behind him and sat opposite her
by the kitchen table. He produced the vodka from his jacket pocket
and got a favourable smile from her. She was fresh out of the shower
with a towel wrapped around her head, turban style, and she wore a
fluffy polka-dot bathrobe with Daffy Duck slippers.

The fragrance from her soaps and oils pervaded the air. He felt
like he had fallen head-first into a lush garden of marigolds, lilacs
and roses. He could only savour the scent through one functioning
nostril, the other he lost to blow. Once again, he had to push his
willpower to its limits to stave off a throbbing hard-on. It didn't help
his situation any, knowing she was naked underneath that robe. She
fished out two glasses from one of the cabinets and got some ice from
the freezer. She was well aware of Maxi's pet peeves, having been his
friend for so long. She filled his glass with ice and popped a solitary
cube into her own. Maxi poured a measure of vodka into each glass
and lit two cigarettes. He filled her in about the shit day he had at
work. He told her what Debbie said about 40%'s big black snake
with the shiny black eyes and how Ida came up with the extortion
money. He told her about his plan to fly to Drago Dunes for dinner
in Sebastian's plane as two homosexual couples.

'Wow, this is what you come up with when you're left alone for a
day. I'm impressed.'

'Will you be able to come along tomorrow night?'

'Wild horses on crystal meth wouldn't keep me away,' she confirmed. 'I've got to see this.'

'Cheers.' He lifted his glass and clunked hers.

'I'm curious. Why the plane? I thought you hated flying.'

'I do, but since Drago Dunes is only twenty minutes away in the sky, I'll manage. Anyway, it beats having to take the ferry.'

'Fair enough.'

'There's another reason.'

'Go on,' Ella encouraged with her big, bright smile.

'When I found the business card in that backpack with the address of the 'Cockpit' bar... I started thinking. What if I got some flyers made up, with a description of the missing box, like you would if you lost your dog or cat?'

'I'm listening,' she said as she took a sip of her drink.

'We get the ferry to Drago Dunes and staple a whole load of flyers to every lamppost and tree on the island. Then when I was talking to Ida, Sebastian's plane flashed before my eyes and I could visualize these flyers floating down from the sky like propaganda pamphlets from WW11.'

'Wow,' Ella exclaimed, 'you're going to blanket bomb the island with your flyers.'

'Correct,' Maxi agreed. He retrieved a printed sheet of paper from his inside pocket and handed it to Ella. 'Here's a sample. What do you think?'

'I like it. It's got the description of the box, your contact number and a five-hundred-euro reward. More mad-money I see.'

'Yeah I know. I've ordered a thousand of them from that print shop over by Song Bird road. That's another hundred euro gone for a shit. I'm going to pick them up on my way home from work tomorrow.'

'Do you think this flyer has wings?' Ella held up his sample and smiled.

'Nice one, Ella.' Maxi laughed. 'I hope so. I only had a quick look at that box, but I couldn't see how to open it. I'm hoping whoever stole it won't be able to open it either. It's a long shot, but ye never know.'

'You think a thief is going to come forward and hand over the box for the five-hundred-euro reward?' Ella said, blowing her smoke in his face.

'Remember, the thief doesn't know the box is a buried treasure,' he replied, blowing his smoke into her face.

They both laughed out loud.

'Just because the box was buried doesn't automatically make it a treasure.' Ella sighed, realizing for the first time the disconsolate truth of her own remark.

'I know,' Maxi moaned, 'but we're so far invested we...'

'Of course,' she rallied. 'We have to do whatever it takes to see this thing through.'

Chapter 23.

Maxi's workday in the yard on Wednesday was almost a carbon copy of the previous day except for a few edits here and there. A light rain persisted throughout the morning, promising to add another layer of woe to an already woefully packed day. He continued relocating pallets, item by item from one to the other while being taunted by the same 'drag-ass' clock whose ticks and tocks had their own agenda. However, on the bright side of that wretchedness, his plan to bail out early worked like a charm.

Around 4 pm., he dropped everything and ran towards the fork-lift truck, waving his arms about to get Dandelion's attention, but deliberately rendering a bastardized version of the way he had been tutored. Dandelion was sitting in the cab of his JCB, doing the same as Maxi – moving shit from A to B – but on a much larger scale and in his own little world, where ironically, there wasn't enough time in the day. He saw Maxi approaching, and it annoyed him to witness all his training go out the window.

'Daniel, I have an emergency,' Maxi shouted over the din of the diesel engine. 'My mother fell and hurt herself. I have to take her to the hospital right away.'

'Oh, I suppose, you got to do what you got to do,' Dandelion grumbled as he studied his watch to do a quick calculation. 'You'll be docked two hours from your pay.'

That was Dandelion's lethargic response to a calamity, albeit contrived, while in the same breath he managed to put a monetary value on it. Maxi wasn't surprised by his indifference. In fact, in that instant, he had apodictic evidence that such an animal as a universal generalisation with no exceptions to the rule did exist, at least in Dandelion's little world:

'Everything, no matter what, from the seven deadly sins to the very air we breathe, came with a price tag.'

Dinner was at seven, so Maxi needed to hustle. He had to pick up the flyers from the print shop, cook Nora's dinner, have a shower, change into some cool duds and collect Ella at her house before driving over to the Wilmington Stud on Soprano Drive. There they would hook up with Sebastian, Ida and the 'despised' Cessna 150 which was parked on the runway behind the house. It was almost six o'clock by the time Maxi and Ella drove up the long avenue that led to the stately mansion. Weeping willow trees flanked the approach, and like ladies in hooped dresses, their hems and frills were tossed about by a gentle breeze. A manicured carpet of fine green verdure covered the fields as battalions of wild flowers staked their claim to the property. The car tyres made a clapping sound as they passed over the cobbles. Suddenly, two young stallions appeared out of the twilight, and racing along by the wooden fence, they seemed intent on overtaking the car. Maxi stood on the accelerator, his competitiveness urging him on.

'What are ye doing?' Ella asked.

'I'm not letting those two fucking nags win,' Maxi assured her as he leaned forward in his seat like a runner in a sprint, intent on gaining maximum advantage over the competition.

'Really?' Ella sniggered as the horses sped past. 'That's their job, they're racehorses.'

Once the pair of stallions put some distance between them and the car, they pulled away into the pasture to celebrate their triumph by leaping up on their hind legs, body-slamming one another and high-fiving hooves. George Orwell's 'Animal Farm' sprung to mind, and it sent a shiver up Maxi's spine to think that these horses were mocking him. He made a promise to himself that if he ever came back this way again, he'd drive a car with some attitude under the hood - not his mother's car with the torn fan belt and leaky rad. He'd make those smart alecks eat his dust.

They were greeted at the huge front door of the twenty-two-bedroom stately manor by Alfonse, the imported English butler who was as old as Methuselah and had, by that stage, four generations of Wilmington 'ass-licking' under his belt. He directed the couple into the lavish living room where Ida was sunk like quicksand into a soft comfy looking recliner by the open fire. She lifted her glass of bubbly in salutation, but being so embedded in the chair, she didn't bother to get up. Ella and Maxi sat together on the velvet couch while Alfonse dutifully poured two flutes of bubbly. He presented the drinks to them on a small silver tray that he carried in white-gloved hands. He bowed his head and began to reverse from the room, in a manner that imprecisely mimicked Michael Jackson's *moonwalk*. The joints in his bygone knees and the discs in his ancient back could clearly be heard to creak and crack like bone-dry twigs being stepped on in the forest. It was cringeworthy for all concerned to witness the ramifications of a lifetime of servitude. This poor man having been stripped of all honour and integrity and left with nothing else to call his own, other than his pulse. Three prepositions encapsulated that man's entity. Alfonse was pleading from the *inside* for someone on the *outside* to come along and put him *down*.

Maxi marvelled at how beautiful the two girls looked that evening, especially in the glow from the flames of the fire. Ida wore a tight yellow leather skirt, matching knee-high leather boots and a cream blouse open at the neck to display a peacock blue silk scarf that picked up the icy blues in her fluffy Afghan jacket. Her bleached blond hair was woven in a tight, intricate pattern on the left side of her head while the rest of her long hair fell freely onto her shoulder. Big silver rings adorned her ears. Her manicured nails, each one with its own meticulously detailed painting, deserved to be on exhibit in some miniature art gallery. Her teal coloured Louis Vuitton tote with rose petal applique clung by a silver chain to her shoulder. She wore a matching teal coloured eyepatch, and with the sparkles from the crystal studs embedded in the fabric, the presence of her injured eye went unnoticed. She looked absolutely stunning.

Ella was by no means outclassed by Ida, even though she opted for a more casual look. She chose to tie back her long jet-black hair in a loose pony tail and secure it with a blood red ribbon, which she tied in a bow, at the back. She wore a black 'musketeer' leather jacket over tight fitting blush jeans and an apricot t-shirt with the word 'REVOLT' daubed on it in navy blue paint by some epileptic artist who must have been in the throes of a fit. Around her neck, a multicoloured beaded necklace and a pair of black, whittled 'sharks' about three inches long, clung to hooks on each earlobe. Her green belt was made of faux alligator skin with an optical illusion of sorts going on inside the buckle. To complete this ensemble, she wore black studded combat boots stitched together with red thread and tied up with bright red laces. All her nails were painted black and every other finger wore a ring, a skull on one finger, an asp on another. There was clearly a 'Goth' influence in her dress sense, but because of her subtle make-up and poise, she infused that 'look' with eloquence and sophistication, making it her own. Ella could never kick her 'tomboy' persona to the curb. That's what gave her, her mystique. She was the consummate cat among the pigeons. Because of that, any engagement with her was bound to be garnished with equal measures of excitement and intrigue.

The two women sat by the fire sipping their drinks and nattering on about the likelihood of them being filthy rich in the not too distant future. Ida's take on the whole treasure thing may not have been as perfervid as Ella's – hers being somewhat diluted by Sebastian's opulent wealth - but she was keeping her irons in the fire just in case. '*Tinseltown*' was her temporary address, but with financial independence it would become her primary residence.

Meanwhile Maxi wandered about the foyer, awed by the craftmanship of the artisans who put that house together. The hand-carved detail in the mahogany staircase blew him away. A pride of lions was depicted lounging about in the shadow of a large Acacia tree in one panel, a monkey in flight watched by others clinging to vines in another, several giraffe grazing in tall trees, a water buffalo wallowing in the mud and a number of other scenes with wild animals in their natural habitat all painstakingly chiselled into the wood in exquisite detail. It was only when his eye reached the landing that the whole serenity of the exhibition took a drastic turn. Humans wearing 'pith' helmets appeared in the next panel, riding in a wicker basket atop an elephant's back. Even though it was an innocent scene, Maxi felt a little queasy. His uneasiness was justified in the next panel where a magnificent tiger lay sprawled out dead in a clearing in the jungle – the etch of the hunter's rifle – the cause of its demise.

Why the British colonials felt the need to butcher African wild life was beyond his comprehension? Where did they get the time? Weren't they already swamped committing atrocities against the natives? All he could think of was that when a country was conquered, everything within its four walls was fair game to the victor. However, since you couldn't mount the head of an African chief or a Zulu warrior on the wall above the fireplace without making the room feel a little tense during afternoon tea, it was deemed appropriate to have the severed head of Leo the lion leering at you instead.

Maxi did a quick calculation in his head, and the estimated cost of the staircase alone was astronomical. He wondered how much blood had to be spilt to achieve such wealth. Immersed in all that opulence, he tended to agree with Ida that Sebastian - the cheap bastard - should spring for a private jet and save them all the embarrassment of being seen in the tin-can Cessna... the very same one he hadn't even seen yet.

Sebastian was outside on the runway '*tinkering*' with his plane. Not exactly a word that would instil a boat load of confidence when it came to defying gravity. Maxi didn't care to fly at the best of times, but when it came to a small twin-engine plane, he was petrified. In his mind, that little plane was nothing more than a glorified lawnmower with wings.

'*What if,*' he wondered, '*you leave the choke out too long and you flood the engine? With the lawnmower, it can be frustrating you have to wait a little while before you get to cut the grass. However, a plane cruising at 10,000 ft and that shit happens, it's curtains. Everybody dies!*'

The horror of his deduction overtook him. To perish the thought, he waved his hands furtively about his head, like a mad-man warding off angry bees. Just then, Sebastian entered the room wearing overalls and a startled look on his face.

'Hey Sebastian,' Maxi greeted him. 'Just getting some blood to the head before dinner.'

'Good idea,' Sebastian replied. 'However, I find you get better results like this.'

He threw the rag he was wiping his hands with onto the marble floor for Alfonse to retrieve, and went over to the wall by the side of the stairs to execute a head-stand. Maxi's excuse for his maniacal behaviour backfired. He had no choice but to follow suit. Both men stood on their heads next to one another on the hard marble floor. Barely a moment into their acrobatics, and each one was offering the other assurances that they were already feeling the benefits from their joint venture. They each willed the other to abort before one of them had an aneurism.

'Well, well, well, what have we here?' Ella smirked as she rounded the corner in search of the restroom.

'Just boys being boys,' Sebastian moaned, his ruddy face assuming the colour of Ella's crimson laces, which were right up in his face by that stage. He behaved like a short-sighted chameleon that required a close-up of the subject matter for him to correctly copy the hue. Sebastian was first to flip onto his feet and stand up. He was a little disoriented at first. Maxi did the same. They stood with their backs to the wall and their heads bowed like disobedient children.

'Where's the restroom?' Ella asked, skipping over the incident.

'Right behind the stairs,' Sebastian replied, pointing without looking, his head still bowed.

Ella followed his directive and disappeared behind the stairs.

'Well, I better freshen up,' Sebastian said. 'I'm dressed already,' he ventured, undoing several buttons of his overalls to shed them like the skin of a snake onto the marble floor, once more for Alfonse to gather up.

'*So, this is how a filthy rich playboy dresses for dinner at a gay restaurant,*' Maxi mused as he studied Sebastian from head to toe. He wore a brilliant white shirt with a chequered, white and navy-blue dicky bow. His teal coloured waistcoat was buttoned up all the way and the gold chain from his pocket-watch glinted along with the gold buttons on his Luigi Borrelli, banana-coloured velvet jacket. Tucked inside the breast pocket, a chequered handkerchief to match his bow tie. He wore tight fitting salmon coloured pants that were deliberately cut at half-mast to showcase his pinstriped white and navy-blue socks. On his feet, a pair of white Bruno Magli leather shoes with yellow laces. The cherry on top, his white straw hat, by Massimo Dutti.

'I just need to wash my hands and then we're off,' Sebastian decreed.

'Take your time, sweetheart,' Maxi replied with his hand on his hip and his shoulder elevated in a girly manner.

'Let's hold off until we get there,' Sebastian requested. 'Don't worry, Ida filled me in. I'll get into *character* in the sky.'

The two couples boarded the little plane and spent a few moments buckling their seatbelts and adjusting their headsets. Sebastian flipped an array of switches and turned several dials. The cockpit lit up and the single propeller engine came to life. Maxi was shocked to see only one propeller. His mind started to scatter seeds of dread all over the runway.

'How the fuck is that little propeller going to get the four of us up into the sky?'

'Joy-stick! What comedian came up with that name?'

'I'm so squashed into this seat, I may as well be wearing the fucking plane.'

While Maxi's mind tormented him, he was unaware that they were already airborne and cruising at an altitude of fifteen-hundred feet. Ten minutes later and Drago Dunes appeared to rise up from the sea. Maxi moved for the first time since take-off. He reached into his satchel and retrieved two bundles of flyers. He left some in the bag to be pinned to pillars and posts once they landed. He handed one bundle to Ella, who sat next to him in the back seat.

'Sebastian, will you do a wide sweep around the island so we can drop these flyers?' Maxi spoke into the mouthpiece on his headset, but by the reaction he got from the receiving end - a little too loud.

'Sure thing, darling,' Sebastian replied as he adjusted the volume control. He was eager to show off his aviation skills. Maxi directed his attention to Ella. 'As soon as we get low enough, pop your window and let 'em rip.'

'Roger that.'

Sebastian pushed the joystick forward and the nose of the plane dipped considerably. Maxi let out a loud 'yelp'. He wasn't expecting the plane to go into a dive. The engine roared, and the fuselage began to shake and wobble. He dug his nails into the back of the seat in front of him and he began to make his peace with the Lord. He noticed the two girls in his peripheral vision and they were not at all bothered. Their indifference didn't do him any good. At last the plane levelled out and it was Ella who had to poke Maxi in the ribs to bring him back from the hereafter or where ever he had gone.

'Bombs away,' she shouted.

They dispatched the flyers through the open windows, one fistful after another. Sebastian banked the plane to the right and completed a full circle around the island, all the while feeding the flyers into the night sky. As he lined up for the landing strip, Maxi's attention was drawn to a mini-fireworks display, happening on the roof of one of the buildings.

'There, there it is,' Maxi pointed at the neon sign for the '*Cockpit Bar'* directly below the light show.

• • • •

LARRY RETURNED TO DRAGO Dunes on Wednesday evening with his safe cracking tools in his shoulder bag. Mandy wouldn't allow him to work on the metal box inside the apartment, so he set up shop on the outside deck. Using every tool at his disposal, all he got for his trouble was a bunch of red-hot toothless blades. Finally, he resorted to the grinder. Needles of fire shot into the darkness and hordes of sparks be-speckled the work area. Thick black smoke curled into the night air. Again, no progress, only worn-out grinding disks and little or no impression on the box. It had several insignificant scars from the grinder and a dink and a dent here and there, from all the hammering. Such super strong material, he had never encountered before.

Larry was unaware that his work was being appraised from on high. He never saw the plane fly over, but he couldn't miss the flyers that began to fall from the sky like autumn leaves. Several fell on the deck, with others landing on the stairs. He picked one up and studied it carefully. According to the description, there was no doubt, but the box he was tampering with was the one this Maxi

Dillon fellow was looking for. Instantly, a whole barrage of questions jostled one another in his head, all demanding answers.

'*What's in this box?*'

'*Will I just take the reward and be done with it?*'

'*Is this really the motherload?*'

'*Who's Maxi Dillon?*'

'*How did he know to drop the flyers here?*'

Unable to answer any one of the questions, Larry gathered up all his tools and put them back in his bag. He took the metal box inside and replaced it under the lamp in the bedroom. He couldn't risk bringing it home with him in case Joe got wind of it. The five-hundred euro reward certainly grabbed his attention. However, when he began to appreciate all the trouble this Maxi Dillon fellow had gone through to recover the box, not to mention his substantial investment, what with the expense of hiring a plane, the cost of the flyers, the reward money, his belief that he had the 'motherload' in his possession was further substantiated. He was determined more than ever to find out what was in that box.

The only thing he could think of that offered any chance of success was to burn his way in. Fortunately, he had the means to do so in his basement apartment, but to get that acetylene blow torch with its tanks and hoses over to Drago Dunes – without arousing suspicion – would be no mean feat. He already had a tough time earlier that evening, trying to explain to Joe why he needed his shoulder bag full of tools to go visit his sister. He convinced him that she needed a vent cut into the wall for her washer/dryer combo. He would have to dig deep down into his cache of lies to come up with something extraordinary to explain away the blow torch.

Mandy finished her shift in the 'Cockpit' and joined her brother in the upstairs apartment. She entered, waving a flyer that she picked up en route.

'Yeah I know,' Larry replied, nodding to the flyer on the bedspread. 'I have one too.'

Larry explained to her that no matter what he did with the assortment of tools at his disposal, he couldn't open the box. They debated whether or not to accept the reward, but opted to have one more go the following night. If that last attempt failed, they agreed to accept the reward. It was almost time to catch the ferry. Mandy was dressed in no time in her black spandex leotard with her aerodynamic helmet and skin-tight gloves. She was quite a magnificent specimen, regardless of her conglomerate of mismatched features. She grabbed her bike and headed down the steps to the boardwalk with her brother. They walked at a brisk pace, side by side along the boardwalk towards the ferry, until they were obliged to form a single line in order to allow two couples who were headed for the restaurant to pass.

Maxi, who was last in line, had to squeeze by the tall transgender with the bicycle and for some reason he was reminded of 40%'s big black snake with the shiny black eyes. Larry and his 'brother' made it to the ferry with two minutes to spare. Mandy stowed her bike away in the cargo area and joined her brother on the upper deck. They always enjoyed a cigarette with a beer on the short trip to the mainland. Their whole conversation was devoted to the metal box and its probable contents. They disembarked and walked to the carpark. Larry threw his tool bag into the back of his pick-up truck while Mandy loaded up her bike. They set off for the recovery depot over on Beat Street, about thirty minutes away.

Joe was there waiting for them when they arrived. He had the usual inventory for a stake-out; the police monitor, two cardboard boxes, one for loot, the other for the police and a flask of tea and sandwiches. As the men prepared the recovery truck for the night's work, Larry paused by the murky work shop window to study the white Ford van. It was up on the hydraulic lift, under repair, with bits and pieces of its engine strewn about the garage floor.

'What's in that fucking box?' he snarled, smacking the corrugated door with his fist. He stood there for a moment, as if to allow the van time to telepathically transmit the answer to him. Still none the wiser, he turned away and headed over to the recovery truck.

Mandy strapped her bike to the flatbed of the truck and the three men headed off into the night. It wasn't long before the police radio clued them in on the location of a car crash at Quartet Quay about fifteen minutes away. Larry flipped the switch for the flashing lights and stepped on the accelerator. Even though motorists were not obliged to give way to a recovery truck as they would an ambulance or a police car, they were conditioned by the flashing lights to do so. Two minutes out from the crash, Mandy was dropped by the roadside with her bike. As usual, she'd follow behind and hide at the crash site to await the signal to plunder.

It was a two-car collision, but unfortunately the two men drivers were up and about, a little shaken by their ordeal but otherwise unscathed. Plunder had to take a rain check that evening. Larry gave Mandy the nod to split. He got busy attaching the steel cable to one of the cars while Joe grabbed his shovel and broom to sweep up the debris from the road. He popped a cigarette in his mouth and searched frantically in all his pockets for his lighter. Figuring he must have dropped it in the cab of the truck, he went back to look. As he patted the floor under the driver's seat of the truck, he came across a crumpled-up piece of paper. He straightened out the creases and read what was printed in bold type. It was one of the flyers from the night before. It must have got stuck to Larry's boot or maybe it hitched a ride in the hood of his jacket, who knows?

Joe was now up to speed with the 'fishy' metal box that tweaked his interest in the bedroom the day before. He shoved the flyer in his pocket and in that same pocket, he found his lighter.

'Just a metal box, huh,' he hissed, discharging spittle and smoke as he returned to his shovel. He was so disgusted he couldn't even look at Larry. He carried on working as usual. Initially, he felt betrayed, but it wasn't long before rage took over and the screams from inside his head made his whole-body tremble.

'Fuck you and your freak brother,' Joe cursed the ground he was sweeping. His expletives were muted by the loud motor driving the cable winch on the recovery truck. 'Five-hundred euros will get me a nice chunk of high, motherfuckers.'

Chapter 24.

'Dillon, party of four.'

The maître d' in a bright pink monkey suit ran his manicured index finger down along the names on the reservation list and arriving at 'Dillon' he raised his head triumphantly. With a big fake smile plastered across his face, he welcomed them, one and all, to the '*Cockpit*' bar and restaurant.

'Right this way.'

The group was forced to follow, almost in double-step, through the bustling tables to keep up with the pink suit who was either hyperactive or bursting for a piss. They were non-ceremoniously deposited at a table that was snuggled neatly into a niche by a bay window with floor to ceiling glass that offered itself entirely to showcasing the spectacular seascape, in all its tumultuous glory. The breath-taking view alone was worth the trip. Once seated, they were handed their menus, and the maître d' recited the evening's specials in a bored monotone that left everyone at the table in no doubt that he truly hated his job.

Soon after, Fredrik, their waiter, came by to take their orders. From the moment he arrived, he spent every second at the table, gaping at the two hunks. The two beautiful women could have been on fire and he wouldn't have noticed. The bulge in his pants, which he made no effort to hide, signified his profound desire to bang these two studs right there and then. Maxi was obliged to defend his virtue by ostentatiously wooing Sebastian. Ida, relishing all the sexual tension at the table, began to flirt with Ella, who played along willingly. However, when it came her turn to order, she glared at Fredrick. It was fairly apparent to all at the table, Ella didn't care too much for her waiter's salacious behaviour and especially so when her Maxi was his crosshairs.

Once Fredrick reluctantly left the table with their dinner orders, Maxi excused himself and went over to the bulletin board by the main entranceway. He relocated a number of notices to other spots on the board so he could pin up one of his own flyers, smack dab in the middle. As he perused his flyer, he realised it was his first public address in ink to the masses - his very first *publication*. Brimming with pride, he returned to his seat at the dinner table. They ate a very satisfying meal with empty plates all round. Just as dessert was being served by Fredrick and his erection, Maxi's phone rang.

'Hi Maxi Dillon, my name is Pierre and I have a metal box just like the one you describe on your flyer which only moments ago I had to retrieve from the top branch of my Tasmanian Snow Gum tree. Lucky for you - it hasn't fully matured yet - or you'd be up a tall ladder right now, picking up your litter.'

'Oh yeah, that's great,' Maxi replied, a little unnerved by the rapid response generated by his flyer and a little confused by the information overload. 'Where exactly did you come by this metal box?' He activated the speaker mode on his phone to involve everyone at the table while his whole body visibly tensed in anticipation.

'I don't know. It's my father's toolbox. I inherited it when he passed.' The caller's tone changed as if he needed to elevate himself above blue collar status. 'Believe me,' he confessed. 'That toolbox was never opened by me. I have never handled a hammer in my life and have no intention of ever doing so. So, when can we meet to do the exchange?'

'Sorry,' Maxi replied, noticeably disappointed. 'That's not the box I'm looking for. Good bye.'

Ella shrugged her shoulders and lightly punched Maxi on his upper arm. 'The police get crackpot callers all the time,' she assured him. 'They clog up those helpline numbers with their bullshit and the police are forced to take the call in the off chance that it might be legit. I guess your flyer is no different.'

'Yeah, I expect you're right,' Maxi smiled at Ella. 'At least we know the flyers are doing their job.'

'No kidding, they hit the ground running,' Ida joked. Everyone laughed.

Once they finished their dessert, Maxi called for the check. The waiter informed him that it had already been taken care off. Thank God, Sebastian beat him to it. It was an expensive dinner. Even though he was off the hook, to save face, he was obliged to lambaste Sebastian for not giving him the opportunity to squander nearly all of what was left of his life savings on a meal.

'Don't be silly Maxi,' Ida interrupted. 'It's going to take a lot of determined people, working diligently around the clock - year in, year out - to even make a dent in Sebastian's ever-growing stash of cash. He's making thousands as we speak. Isn't that right, dear?'

'Absolutely,' Sebastian shamefully replied, his eyes averted as the magnitude of his wealth strutted among the empty bowls and condiments on the dinner table for all to appreciate.

'Let's get out of here,' Maxi remarked as he leaned in towards Sebastian with pouted lips. He air-kissed his boyfriend and held his hand as they stood up to leave. Ella felt a sudden urge to drag Sebastian out of the way and plant her own big, juicy kiss on Maxi's lips. Fredrick, their waiter, looked like he was beside himself with lust. His whole body shook violently when they passed, leaving Ella to wonder... had he just bust a nut?

They left the restaurant and made their way down the boardwalk, pinning the remaining flyers that were stashed in Maxi's shoulder bag to trees and lampposts along the way. They took a detour down to the dock and pinned some flyers on the notice board by the ticket office for the ferry. Once they got rid of all the flyers, they made their way back towards the airstrip.

'Oh, while I think of it.' Ida turned to Maxi before they got on the plane and handed him an envelope. 'Here's the blackmail money. The plate number of the pickup truck that was parked at the depot last night is in there as well.'

'Well done,' Maxi complimented. 'I'll call my police buddy in the morning and have him *run* the plate.

'Police buddy?' Ella teased.

'Yeah, my police buddy,' Maxi confirmed, a little annoyed at Ella's jab. 'Am I allowed to have a police buddy?'

'Easy,' she cautioned. 'You're allowed.'

'Thank you very much,' Maxi replied, white in the face with fear.

Ella knew his mood swing was directly related to their return flight. It was obvious he was terrified. She knew once the flight was over, he'd be back to normal. They boarded the plane and flew back to the Wilmington Mansion. Mission accomplished. All they could do now was wait.

Chapter 25.

Maxi was awakened early on Thursday morning by yet another hopeful caller who was convinced his metal box was the one Maxi Dillon was looking for. That call was the third call already to have been prompted by one of the flyers from the blitz over Drago Dunes the night before. Like the previous calls, this caller's box had no association with Cello Falls - the crash site - so it was instantly dismissed.

He was aware the information on the flyer was vague, but that was deliberate. He knew he was grasping at straws by deploying those flyers into the night sky. He was hoping somebody on Drago Dunes heard something or saw something relating to the metal box and that they would be encouraged by the reward money to make the call. At the very least, he wanted to unnerve the thief and infuse a little paranoia into the mix, by letting the perpetrator know that he was hot on his trail. While Buca Brannigan proved he had no knowledge of the missing backpack, Maxi's focus shifted to the crew that recovered the van on the evening of the crash. He preferred not to have any further dealings with Buca, who was obviously interested in recovering the backpack for himself. That's why he sent Ida over to Beat Street to record the licence plate numbers in the depot carpark. One beat up pickup truck was all that was parked there and since Buca had only one recovery truck on the road, he was fairly confident whoever was registered to that pickup was the man who stole the treasure.

Just as Maxi finished his breakfast, Juanita arrived in the kitchen with the newspaper and an assortment of doughnuts for Nora's sweet *dentures*. As much as he was delighted to see her, she was another hundred euros a day that he could ill afford.

'Good morning, Signor Dillon.'

'Bonus dies, Juanita,' Maxi replied, and she giggled at his pidgin Spanish.

He arrived down to the salvage yard, and after unlocking all the gates and steel doors, he entered the office and made himself comfortable in Dandelion's 'forbidden' leather chair. He cranked up the vibrators in the backrest and settled in for a vigorous spinal massage. He dutifully answered the incoming calls and transcribed the details of each call onto separate slips of paper. About twenty minutes later, he was rendered unconscious, the oscillating chair having lulled him to sleep.

Dandelion arrived down the hill at 9.20. He was ten minutes early. The image of the grey van on the security monitor somehow woke Maxi. He jumped up from the chair in a panic and hit the off-button on the control panel embedded in the armrest. As he realigned the chair to its original position, he stood transfixed in horror while the chair continued, defiantly to vibrate. He dropped to his knees and yanked the plug from the wall socket to sever its life-support. The chair persisted.

He swore at the chair. 'Don't rat me out, you Ginny bastard.'

He was obliged to meet Dandelion in the yard, so he had no option but to race out to greet him. As he went, he conjured up all sorts of delay tactics that might afford the chair a chance to reconsider. That morning Dandelion was travelling light. Even though he only handed Maxi two items of trash from the back of the van, he seemed quite jovial in his comportment. Of course, today was *Extortion day* for Dandelion, so he was humoured with pleasant thoughts of a free Caribbean cruise, not to mention all that free booze.

To buy some time, Maxi dropped both items on the ground and 'accidently' kicked the lamp shade under the van. He made a big deal of retrieving it. Once back up on his feet, he led the way back into the office, willing the chair with every step to cease and desist. What a relief to see the Italian import had thrown in the towel.

Dandelion placed his laptop on the 'antique' desk along with his lunchbox and the newspaper. He then sat in his throne with his hands interlocked behind his head and his legs stretched out in front of him. Suddenly he sprung upright in the chair, and raising one leg off the ground, he propelled himself with the other. He began to spin round and round in an anti-clockwise direction. He achieved several complete rotations before running out of steam. It was a smooth ride – the chair spinning effortlessly on its ball bearings - a testament to its precise Italian engineering. Maxi noticed him on several occasions during the week, preforming much the same feat in his JCB digger – the hydraulic bucket bent like an elbow as the metal beast performed pirouette after pirouette before an audience of stacked pallets in a type of salvage yard ballet. Maxi deduced it must have been his way of expressing his joy. He certainly never saw him smile.

It was time for him to stand like a schoolboy in front of the 'spinning' headmaster and deliver an oration on the morning's proceedings, which, as usual, had to be endorsed with cogent paperwork. He concluded his brief and presented Dandelion with the small stack of notes. There were only four inquiries that morning, but each query was handled by Dandelion as meticulously as a goldminer sieving through his pan for the tiniest, twinkling speck. While he played the phone messages and prioritized the corresponding slips of paper according to their monetary value, he was interrupted by '*You're so vain*', his personalized ringtone on his cell phone. He allowed the song to play while he bopped his head from side to side. Maxi noted how exceptional his mood was in that moment.

'Hello?' There was a slight pause. 'Oh yes, Lucy Windsor, John's sister,' Dandelion confirmed.

Maxi nearly threw up on the spot, that very same spot he froze in, barely thirty minutes earlier, when the defiant chair refused to comply. He listened intently to the phone conversation, but was only privy to this end of the call. It didn't take a genius to know that 40% was coming out of his coma and probably singing like a canary - his lyrics having nothing to do with the working conditions in the coalmine!

'I'm delighted to hear he's doing so well,' Dandelion cheerfully replied. 'Sounds like he'll be up and about in no time.' He stole another quick revolution in his chair. While in transit, he realised that Maxi was still in the office - frozen like a stalagmite to the concrete floor. He placed one hand over the mouthpiece and with the other he delivered his customary, 'piss-boy shoo'.

Maxi was dizzy leaving the office. You'd think he was the one doing all the spinning. He heard enough to know that 40% was on the mend. As soon as he got back to where he was working, he hid down behind a stack of pallets and called Debbie. She knew immediately the reason for the call.

'I'm only after finding out myself,' Debbie argued in her defence. 'One of the nurses called me a few minutes ago to let me know.'

'Are you working today?'

'I'm driving over to the hospital as we speak,' she confirmed, even though it was her day off. She knew the gravity of the situation, so she decided to bite the bullet and go to work. She'd forego the 'pat-on-the-back' until later.

'That's great,' Maxi's sighed, not caring to disguise his apparent relief. 'Lucy Windsor just called Dandelion to fill him in on 40%'s recovery. I was ejected from the office during the call, so I have no idea what's going on.'

'Susy - that's the nurse who's caring for 40% right now - told me that even though he's responsive to his environment, he's still going on about black snakes with shiny black eyes crawling about in the dark. He's scheduled for a brain scan sometime this afternoon.' Debbie took a breath. 'I don't think you need to worry that he'll spill the beans about the treasure. Even if he did, no one would believe him in his present state.'

'That's all very well. Deb, I'd still like you to keep these two mutts apart if Dandelion shows up at the hospital.'

'You can rely on me on that front,' she vowed. 'But what's to stop these mutts - as you call them - talking on the phone?'

'40% will never put a cell phone to his ear. He's convinced he'd croak from toxic radiation. He always stands clear of anyone using a cell phone. As far as he's concerned, they may as well be talking to a live grenade. The land-line is a different matter. To him, that's a slow and lingering death. He'll answer the phone, only if he has to, but he'll never initiate a call.'

'Very strange,' Debbie responded.

'Indeed. So, you see, a phone call is very unlikely.'

'If you say so. Right, I'm driving. Let me go. I'll keep you posted.'

Lunchtime eventually pulled into the station in Eden on the *Sloth express*. By then, Maxi had lost all respect for the way time behaved in that yard. It seemed like every occasion he checked his watch; his guesstimates of the time were way off. He vowed never to look at his watch again. He sat among the pallets to eat his lunch, preferring their company over Dandelion's. Just as he finished his sandwich, his cell phone rang.

'Hi Maxi, Freddy Boom-Boom here.'

'What's up?'

'Today's the day we pay Daniel the extortion money, remember?'

'Yeah, I know,' Maxi replied. 'I didn't forget. I have the money in an envelope for you down here in the yard. Come here around 5 o'clock and I'll pass it to ye through the car window.' He wanted to buy as much time as possible in the off-chance that his flyer would do its magic and save them all two-thousand euros in the process.

'Sounds good,' Boom-boom replied excitedly. 'See ye then.'

Once again, Maxi was surprised that there wasn't a pip out of him regarding his fee. He never mentioned a number to Ella either after the meeting in the Town Hall. Normally, before he'd lift a finger, he would drag Maxi over the coals to top up whatever money was offered, fortifying his objection with his war cry: *Drama's not cheap.* Even though this irregularity took up residence in the forefront of Maxi's mind, he brushed it off as an oversight on Boom-boom's behalf and got right back to work.

Approximately twenty miles southeast of the salvage yard, as the crow flies, Larry sat opposite Joe at the kitchen table in their dimly lit basement apartment, both men quietly eating their breakfast. Since they worked nights, rise-and-shine time for them was always between two and three o'clock in the afternoon. Larry was unaware that his roommate had discovered one of the flyers from Drago Dunes, right under his seat in the recovery truck, of all places. Joe didn't let on. He was furious that his so-called friend would flat-out lie to him when he inquired about the strange metal box in Mandy's bedroom.

'Yeah, it's just a box,' Joe repeated to himself, over and over, each time getting more and more incensed. 'A fucking box that happens to be worth five-hundred euros.'

The two men didn't really talk much at the best of times, so it didn't seem odd that there was little or no conversation that afternoon. They sat like poker players across from each other at the table, both of them trying not to give off any 'tells' about the plans they were both contriving in their conniving heads.

'Yoh,' Joe announced. 'I'm off to get me some blow.'

He got up from the table and as he closed the basement door behind him, all he heard was a grunt from Larry who regarded his quest for drugs as standard operating procedure. However, his early departure that afternoon, instead of arousing suspicion, was welcomed with open arms. Now he could load up his pickup truck with the acetylene torch and the gas tanks without fear of cross-examination. Once Joe was under the awning to the side of the building that topped the basement apartment, he patted his ass pocket to ensure he could feel the flyer before jumping on his dirt-bike and racing off down the road to catch the three o'clock ferry to Drago Dunes.

When he arrived at the ferry, he hid his bike behind a dumpster in the far corner of the carpark. He masked his identity by pulling his cap down over his eyes and covering his mouth with his scarf. He needn't have bothered. No one knew what he looked like and cared less to find out. He purchased a return ticket at the ticket desk and made the crossing to Drago Dunes. He hustled his way to the front of the line on the ferry so he'd be one of the first to disembark at the dock. He walked at a brisk pace along the boardwalk until he reached the 'Cockpit' bar.

He knew that Mandy was working the day-shift, so he had to be careful not to be seen. He ducked down below the side window of the bar and crept along the deck on his hands and knees until he reached the steps to the apartment above. The milling rain ensured the deck was deserted. He raced up the steps to the apartment and retrieved the key from under the potted plant to the left of the door. Battling momentarily with the stubborn lock, he let himself in. The two siblings had stripped him so bare of all responsibilities they never even gave him his own key. He went straight to the bedroom and grabbed the metal box from under the bedside lamp. After a brief examination, he couldn't, for the life of him, understand how that rusty old box could merit such a hefty reward. He denounced his own appraisal in lieu of the cash and stashed the box in his duffle bag. He locked the door behind him and replaced the key under the pot. He could have staged a robbery, to shift the blame, but by using the key, he made it quite apparent that he was the culprit and his inherent message to the two brothers was quite clear. *Fuck you.*

He returned back along the boardwalk towards the ferry, trying his best to look cool. This was his first 'hands-on' burglary; usually he was the accomplice. Even though he stood out like a foreskin in a Jewish sauna, nobody paid him any heed. When he reached the loading dock, he was stopped dead in his tracks by the sight of Larry on the gangplank. Luckily, the man's back was turned as he struggled to haul the trolley with the tanks and hoses onto the boardwalk. Joe ducked in behind the ticket booth and immediately lit himself a cigarette. He got a little dizzy on his first inhale. He realised he had never before deprived himself for so long without a smoke. Of course, never before had he been so energetic in his pursuit of a 'high'. With the reward money, he could afford a higher 'high' than the fucking sky. Regardless, he promised himself he'd never again suffer such withdrawal symptoms, no matter the cost. He finished that cigarette and instantly lit another.

Once the coast was clear, he climbed the steps to the upper deck on the boat and sat down on a seat in an empty row all the way to the back of the ferry. The inclement weather discouraged most of the passengers from going topside, but as always, a few undeterred fanatics braved the elements. From his vantage point, he watched Larry bully his way onto the boardwalk with his cargo in tow, shouting scabrous directives as he went. He could still hear his abusive bellows over the noise of the turbine engines even as the ferry pulled clear of the pier.

Imagining Larry when he realised the box was gone sent Joe into a fit of giggles. His laughter was so contagious it infected the nearest passenger, two rows away, who accompanied him in uncontrollable titters. As Joe's giggles morphed to guffaw's, his newfound chuckling cohort joined him with reckless abandon. Tears flowed down the cheeks of both men as they buckled over in painful laughter. Joe regained his composure, leaving his chuckling buddy to giggle away on his own. Several passengers within earshot grew concerned and left their seats to put some distance between them and what they believed to be a mental patient.

Joe was indifferent to the passengers swapping their seats. He was too busy complementing himself on his first *solo* successful robbery even though his re-enactment of events did down-play the fact he had a key. This was deliberate. He needed all the encouragement he could muster to embark on a solo career. So, what if the facts had to be altered for him to feel more adept in his chosen profession? Thieves need reassurance just like the next man. There was a whole big world out there, and Joe had big plans to pick it clean.

He knew Larry was held captive on the island at least until five o'clock, the time of the next ferry. He figured with that two-hour window, he'd surely be able to make the call, do the swap and collect the reward. Once he got the money, he decided he was done with Larry and his freak sister forever. As soon as the ferry docked on the mainland, he was the first one down the gangplank and off into the carpark to retrieve his dirt-bike. He whipped out the flyer from his back pocket and keyed in the contact number on his cell.

Maxi answered. 'Hello'.

'You looking for a box?'

'Who's this?' Maxi inquired.

'I got the box,' Joe confirmed. 'You got the money?'

'Hold on a minute,' Maxi instructed. 'Where did you get the box?' he asked.

'I found it in a field.'

'In a field. Where?' Maxi raised his voice; he was starting to get excited.

'Cello Falls,' Joe replied, coughing and gagging into the phone.

'Okay. Now you got my attention,' Maxi said as he tried to remain calm. 'How do you want to do this?' He allowed the caller to call the shots.

'Where are you?' Joe inquired.

'I'm at the Aechmea salvage yard in Ballydecuddle,' Maxi replied. 'Do you know it?'

'Yeah. Do you have the money on you?'

'I do.'

'I'm less than an hour away.'

'Wow, that's great,' Maxi cheered into the phone, but the line was dead.

His whole body tingled with excitement. If this guy panned out and there was no reason why he wouldn't, his one-way ticket to 'El Dorado' was assured. The next forty-five minutes flew by... a first in the slow-poke land of Eden. Then right on cue, a biker riding a dirt-bike came barrelling down the hill. Maxi raced over to greet him in the usual manner, with his arms flapping about like a kingfisher with one long leg dipped in lava.

'You the guy with the box?' Maxi asked the helmet with the blackened visor.

The helmet nodded.

Maxi directed the biker to steer his bike to a predetermined blind spot in the carpark where their transaction could occur in secret. That was the only location on the whole property where the multitude of security cameras drew a blank. Joe opened his duffle bag to exhibit the contents while still seated on his bike. Maxi nodded his approval, took the box and handed over five-hundred euros, no questions asked. Joe stashed the money in the inside pocket of his leather jacket, turned the bike around and high-tailed it up the hill.

Maxi felt sensational as he stared at the metal box. Then he began to tremble uncontrollably. He took a few deep breaths to regain his composure. He willed himself to focus. He still needed to hide the box in his mother's car and get it out of there without alerting Dandelion. He wrapped his hoodie around the box, and hugging the building to avoid the cameras, he slinked his way along until he came to the gable end of the building. Stealing a peek around the corner, he checked to see if the coast was clear. He never thought in his wildest dreams, the sight of a JCB digger, spinning in circles, round and round, would bring tears to his eyes.

He turned his attention to the happy head on Dandelion as he spun round and round in the cab of the digger. Knowing his location was a plus, but the man was revolving in a giant periscope in plain view of Nora's car. To get to the car, unnoticed, he would have to solve a real-life mathematical equation. He needed to calculate the time it took the digger to do a complete revolution, minus the increment of time the big happy head had the car in its sights, the distance to the car from a standing position and the velocity required to race to the car within that timeframe. He racked his brain to see, could he unearth some mathematical formula from his school days that might assist him in his endeavour. Unfortunately, the pickings were slim - he didn't care too much for math back then. However, what did spring to mind from his mathematical archive was the quandary with the two trains travelling at different speeds in opposite directions between two stations and the probability of both trains arriving on time. And still, nobody knows the fucking answer.

He decided to wing it. He waited for the happy head on Dandelion to orbit and then bolt into action. He managed to sprint to the car, open the passenger door and dive head-first into the front seat before the big, happy head returned. He hid the metal box under the driver's seat. Then he cracked the door open just enough to slip out and crouch down by the headlamp on the driver's side. He made another mad burst across the gravel. He felt like a grunt on the battle-field trying to outrun the turret of a tank. He made it back to the cover of the building with a nanosecond to spare.

There was a spring in his step as he returned down the lane to the stack of pallets he was working on. The relief he felt was euphoric, but he couldn't allow himself to relax just yet. He still had to get the treasure out of the yard, undetected. While he was trying to calm his nerves, his heart suddenly skipped a beat when he spotted the 1992 navy blue Subaru on the crest of the hill. With all the hoopla, he forgot about Boom-boom.

'No biggie,' he thought. 'A hundred euros should see him on his way.'

Maxi ran towards the car and resumed flapping his arms, hoping that this would be the last time he'd ever have to act the eejit again. He waved the car to a stop and engaged with Boom-boom.

'Right, give me the money,' Boom-boom demanded. 'Let's get this thing done and dusted.'

'I'm afraid there's been a slight change of plan,' Maxi replied, a little taken aback by the fat man's eagerness. 'I just got a call from the County Council guy, the man who is paying for all this cloak and dagger carry-on and he's not willing to pay Dandelion for his silence.'

'What?' Boom-boom barked, refusing categorically to believe his ears.

'The top brass in the County Council,' Maxi insisted. 'They don't care if Dandelion takes the story to the papers or not.'

'No... no, we have to pay him the money,' Boom-boom shrieked. 'There's no other way,' he bellowed.

'What are you talking about?' Maxi retorted. 'It's curtains, man. The show's over.' He cut his throat with his ridged index finger, mimicking a knife.

'What about our reputation?' Boom-boom wailed. 'It'll be in tatters if this story gets out.'

'Our reputation?' Maxi repeated. 'What the fuck are you talking about? You're an actor, for fuck sake. You're not a County Council worker.'

The two speechless men stared at each other in total disbelief. The only sound was the rhythmic chug-a-chug of the engine percolating through the broken muffler on the 1992 navy blue Subaru.

'What's all the shouting about?' Dandelion inquired as he materialized, as usual, out of thin air.

'Fucking hell,' Maxi's reaction.

'Boohoo! Did I scare ye?' Dandelion asked, making a half-hearted attempt at a scary face.

'If only you knew,' Maxi thought as he searched for clues in Dandelion's behaviour to determine if he heard anything that would jeopardize his current standing. No reaction, everything seemed to be copacetic.

Without waiting for a reply, Dandelion directed his attention to Boom-boom.

'I keep telling this man he should get himself a pair of hearing aids. Would do us all a favour, don't ye think?' He nodded his head in self appraisal at his own astuteness. 'You two can play catch-up on your own time. Now if ye don't mind,' he glared at Maxi. 'We have a little business to conduct.'

'By all means,' Maxi replied as he gladly swapped places with Dandelion by the open car window.

Freddy Boom-boom parked the car as directed and a moment later, his chaotic extraction from the sedan began. Dandelion stood by the car to accompany his money to the office, but when the door flung open and the violent rocking started, he stepped back - agog. Maxi, having seen that horror show before, stood still to watch Dandelion squirm as the big man attempted to exit his car. He could see Dandelion willing him on, to survive his ordeal... at least long enough for him to get his hands on the money. He decided to leave both men up to their own devices and go back to sorting pallets.

Maxi was anxious to know why the meeting between the two men was still going ahead. No money was exchanged, so there couldn't be any '*drop*'. One thing for sure, Dandelion wouldn't get to hear the captain of the Caribbean cruise liner shouting: *All Aboard*. Not only would he miss the boat, it was a safe bet the 'Ginny' chair along with the digger wouldn't be doing any *spinning* in the immediate future!

Maxi replayed his conversation with Boom-boom in his head and his initial reaction was that the man had lost his marbles. However, on closer scrutiny, when denied the money, Boom-boom went completely off the rails, giving him the impression that maybe he had an ulterior motive. No mention of a fee further corroborated his suspicions. He came to the conclusion that Boom-boom had no intention of ever handing over the money to Dandelion. His plan from the get-go was to keep it for himself. His betrayal was a little annoying, but what Maxi couldn't understand was why on earth would he want to continue with the meeting? He had to have had some other trick up his sleeve and whatever that trick was - knowing him – money had to be involved. He dismissed the notion that he might '*pull the rug*' on the whole operation and confess to being a paid impersonator. There was nothing to be gained financially from such contrition, especially with Dandelion already two-thousand euros out of pocket. With no definitive answers, Maxi's original deduction of the fat man '*losing his marbles*' was back on the table.

While the mysterious powwow between the two men got under way, Maxi called Ella on his cell.

'Guess what?'

'No,' Ella screamed. The timbre in his voice gave away his surprise.

'I've got it.' Maxi matched her scream.

'No way,' she contested. 'Tell me it's true.'

'Believe me,' he yelled. 'We're going to be rich.'

'How? Where? When?' Her rapid volley of queries afforded Maxi no chance to respond.

'The flyer,' he managed to squeeze in edgeways. 'Can you believe it? The actual thief picked up one of the flyers, called the number, we arranged to meet, he handed over the box, I gave him the money and that was that.'

'Wow, that's unbelievable.' Ella had to pause to catch her breath. Her body trembled with the excitement. 'I didn't want to say anything but those flyers - honestly - I thought they were a pure waste of time and money.'

'A longshot for sure,' he agreed.

'So, what's in the box?'

'I don't know yet,' Maxi whined. 'I couldn't open the fucking thing.'

'That's not good.'

'I know, but let's not panic. It's early days,' he replied, 'I'll get it open, don't you worry.' For the first time since the treasure hunt began, a shred of doubt tippy-toed in from the shadows to hog a spot in the forefront of his mind.

'If anyone can, you can.'

'Yeah, I know.'

'Oh wow,' Maxi gasped as he ducked down behind a stack of pallets.

'What's wrong?' Ella wondered as she prepared herself, once more, for further disappointment.

'Those clowns, Boom-boom and Dandelion are going at it in the yard,' Maxi moaned.

'Oh my God. What's he doing down there?' she asked.

'I forgot to call off the extortion bullshit. Oh yeah, we're up two-thousand euros by the way.'

'Wow, that's great,' she cheered. 'It's all good.'

'So far. Anyway, he freaked out when I wouldn't give him the money to pay Dandelion. I already had the treasure at that stage, so I told him the game was over. I'm sure he wanted the money for himself all along.'

'I always felt there was something off about that man,' Ella agreed. 'He's devious.'

'Hello,' he said in a taunting manner. 'Isn't that why we hired him? Listen Ella, I better get up there and break them two apart.'

'Yeah go. Later.'

'Come on guys, break it up,' Maxi pleaded with the two men who were slapping each other about the head like middle-aged women at a clearance sale.

'This fat fucker tried to blackmail me,' Dandelion yelled.

His shouts were muffled. He was trapped in a head-lock with his face buried under one of Boom-booms double-E tits. For the first time since they met, Maxi genuinely felt sorry for that man.

'He tried to blackmail me first,' Boom-boom retaliated, striking Dandelion about the body with a medley of harmless punches, his big belly cushioning every blow.

This is getting complicated, Maxi thought to himself. *'One blackmail attempt countered by another blackmail attempt. There's no keeping up with this guy.'*

'Can ye not work this out like men?' Maxi shouted above the grunts and groans of the combatants.

'What do you think we're doing?' Dandelion retorted, and freeing his head at last from a flaccid choke-hold, he managed to land a direct hit to Boom-booms navel. His whole fist disappeared briefly, like the sole of a boot in quicksand. He pried it free, but not without a struggle. Boom-boom resorted to 'bitch' fighting and began pulling the one solitary tuft of hair on Dandelion's head that stood between him and baldness. He wasn't to know that that was Dandelion's Thermopylae and that he would defend that tuft to the death. As

Dandelion battled to retain his self-regard, Maxi somehow, instead of separating the two men, got entangled in the scuffle. Suddenly, he became the recipient of all misdirected blows. After doddering around in circles for a spell, the threesome keeled over and hit the deck. They began to rock back and forth in unison, in the muck.

Freddy Boom-boom lay on his back with the two men straddling his big belly like suckling off-spring. Eventually Maxi broke free from the melee and the two men on the ground shuffled towards each other in the muck to fill the void. They locked onto each other like passionate lovers. While Maxi assessed the condition of his muddied clothes and dishevelled hair, he heard a wailing sound in the distance. Before his distracted brain could supply an answer, he saw a police car with all lights ablaze, screaming down the hill.

'Thistle Dick's on sentry duty,' he reckoned. 'Of course, he called the police. Who else?'

The police car concluded its dramatic entrance with a hand-brake turn by the front wall of the main building, hosing down the showroom door with grit and gravel. Maxi recognized the driver. It was none other than the 'chip junkie' from his earlier visit to the police station, his unmistakable red hair and ruddy complexion giving him the countenance of a fire hydrant. His buck teeth were first out of the car.

'What have we here?' he inquired, looking down on the ground at the two stubborn men who continued to brawl. By that stage, they were so exhausted that their respective blows had dwindled to mere twangs and twitches. He made no effort to separate them. Instead, he turned to Maxi, and cautioning him to remain put, he scrutinized the ground where he was standing and, after careful deliberation, took a step. He repeated this painstaking process with each step, over and over, until he stood next to Maxi. It was like he was trying to avoid detonating one of the many landmines he believed to be lurking below the surface. The red-head was acting like a homicide detective who wanted to preserve the crime scene and not a *stiff* in sight.

'Here, take this and play it,' Boom-boom begged the policeman, as he waved a cassette tape in his muddy hand. 'You'll soon see what this is all about.'

'I don't need to be distracted by audio tapes when a crime is being investigated,' the red headed policeman quoted verbatim from the policeman's log, it being the only book he ever read from cover to cover. He flipped open his own notepad and entered the date, time and location.

'It's evidence, you moron,' Boom-boom bellowed from behind Dandelion's shoulder.

'Verbally assaulting a police officer is also an offence,' the red-head replied, stomping his flat foot on the ground in the hope that the ensuing vibration would be felt by the feuding duo. After all, they did have the best seats in the house for any seismic activity. Maxi was impressed by Boom-booms effrontery. The man obviously taped Dandelion's blackmail attempt with the intention of throwing it right back in his face. He decided he'd have another go at separating the two men, but this time, no more Mr. Nice Guy. He bent down and grabbed Dandelion by the scruff of the neck and yanked him upright in one powerful motion. He, too, was covered from head to toe in muck. Maxi left him to teeter on the spot like a gelatinous version of one of those terracotta soldiers from the Qin Dynasty. Boom-boom was not a pretty sight either. Maxi reached down, took the cassette tape from him and put it in his pocket. He summoned the red-head to assist in lifting him off the ground. He reluctantly obliged. Their first few attempts failed miserably. It was only when they flipped Boom-boom onto his stomach were they able, with some meagre assistance from himself, to stand him upright.

'Play the tape,' he gasped.

'How?' the red-head asked. 'Who has a tape player these days?'

'I have one,' Boom-boom bragged, looking like a gollywog after he wiped the mud from his eyes. He reached into the breast pocket of his overalls only to realise that his recorder had been crushed in the altercation. Bits and pieces of the device fell to the ground.

'Well, that's that then,' Dandelion concluded as he started to make his way back to the office. 'I want to press charges.'

'Not so fast,' Boom-boom countered. 'There's a cassette player in my car.'

'Right then, let's go,' the red-head commanded.

He corralled the men together with his open arms and herded them over to the 1992 navy blue Subaru. Maxi gave the cassette back to Boom-boom who began the arduous ordeal of entering the car.

'Do you really need to get in?' Maxi pleaded with him. 'Can't you just hit the play button from there?'

'I have to,' Boom-boom puffed. 'The cassette player is temperamental. If I don't start the engine and keep my foot on the accelerator, it won't play.'

The three men crowded around the open car window with their ears cocked to discern whether or not any evidence of blackmail was caught on tape. Everybody was forced to inhale exhaust fumes as they listened intently. Boom-boom pressed the accelerator every now and then to spur on the reels in the cassette player, which made the recording sound high-pitched and somewhat distorted. The recording sounded like people who inhaled helium. One of the *chipmunks* on the tape was heard to say, loud and clear: 'I want to blackmail the County Council.'

Everybody swapped looks. There was no doubt about Dandelion's intentions. Then all eyes were on him with the same disdain like he was the one who farted in the elevator.

'How do you spell extortion?' the red-head inquired, pulling away from the car window, attentive once again to his notepad.

'Who said anything about extortion?' Dandelion retorted, obviously upset with the clarity of the tape.

The red-head repeated the word 'extortion' to himself, each time with a different emphasis on a different part of the word in an effort to aid him with his spelling. After burning up a full page of his notepad on a plethora of phonetic algorithms, he conceded defeat. He opted for 'blackmail' instead but still misspelled the word. Under the heading, *Complaint* he wrote;

Mr. Daniel Aechmea - (he knew Dandelion's name from all the previous visits he made to the salvage yard) – intended to *black male* the County Council. The big man in the 1992 Subaru intended to *black male* Mr. Aechmea.

'Blackmail is a very serious offence,' he said. 'I have to place you both under arrest.'

'Are you kidding me?' Dandelion objected, pointing at the cassette player. 'That doesn't even sound like me.' He pointed at Boom-boom. 'He's the blackmailer, not me.'

'Why am I being arrested?' Boom-boom contested. 'I'm the one who went through all the trouble of gathering evidence.'

'You tried to use that evidence to extort money from this man,' the red-head informed.

'Where's your proof?' Boom-boom demanded.

'I'm his proof,' Dandelion barked as he fended off the red-head's attempts to cuff him.

'Resisting arrest is another serious offence,' the red-head avowed and Dandelion surrendered immediately. He was too well versed in the law to know that multiple charges against the defendant didn't wear well with a judge.

'Don't make it any worse on yourself,' Maxi advised, trying to sound all regal while internally he was jumping for joy.

'Fuck you, whatever your name is,' Dandelion spat his reprisal as he was being placed in the back of the police car. 'You're fired. Now, get off my property.'

'Delighted to oblige,' Maxi chirped reaching immediately into his pocket to retrieve the big bunch of keys on the Eden key-ring. He threw them onto the back seat next to Dandelion in the police car.

Dandelion wailed, realizing he'd jumped the gun. 'Who's going to lock up the yard?'

'Beats me,' Maxi jeered. 'Maybe your girlfriend can come down and lock up. She's got no pressing engagements, especially now that she won't be setting sail on the high seas any time soon.'

Freddy Boom-boom was eventually crammed into the back seat next to Dandelion. Maxi was reminded of the A train or *African Queen* as it was affectionately known, the overcrowded subway train he used to take from Manhattan to the Bronx. He flapped his arms mockingly as the police car drove away. He doubted the joy he was feeling at that moment in time would ever be replicated in his lifetime.

• • • •

Chapter 26.

Every time Maxi drove out of that salvage yard, he felt a wave of relief wash over him, but that Thursday evening with Dandelion and Boom-boom under lock and key, it was tidal. At last, he had the treasure in his possession, and he planted it next to him on the passenger seat for the ride home. Now and then, he stole a peek at the metal box to bolster the endorphin *rapids* that pounded the inner walls of his pituitary gland, driving his opiate receptors berserk. He almost OD'd on pure bliss.

When he got home, he parked the car in the driveway, but before exiting, he looked all round to ensure that there were no prying eyes. Even still, he smuggled the metal box into the garage wrapped up in his hoodie like a pervert with his blow-up doll. He placed it on the work bench and entered the house through the back door. Nora and Juanita were seated together at the kitchen table, eating dinner.

'You're home early,' Nora remarked without lifting her head from her dinner plate. She was preoccupied sawing into a golden-brown piece of chicken Kiev, her favourite meal. She must have persuaded Juanita to steer clear of the plantains and focus on the parts of the planet where only flightless birds and fish 'n chips were acquainted with the deep-fat fryer.

'I no longer hold the keys to Eden,' Maxi proudly announced.

'Congratulations,' Nora cheered. 'How did you manage that?'

'Bravo senor,' Juanita applauded, even though she looked perplexed by the equivocation of the conversation.

'A walk in the park, you might say,' he humbly replied as he took an Edwardian bow before the two women.

'A fairly muddy park by the looks of things.' Nora chuckled.

'Oh yeah,' he replied as he toyed with his dirty t-shirt. 'That's another story.'

'How's that going to look on your CV, you walking off the job like that?' Nora teased as she nudged Juanita with her elbow to include her in their nuanced hodgepodge of idioms.

'Elementary, dear Watson,' Maxi replied. 'I never have to work again.'

'No trabajo, no dinero,' Juanita suggested.

'That's true most of the time,' he agreed with her. 'But sometimes, if you get lucky like me, you get to ride the gravy train for free.'

Now it was Nora's turn to look baffled.

'You get lucky, senor Maxi?' Nora imitated Juanita to flatter, not to mock. Juanita's laugh could be heard from the kitchen as she retrieved Maxi's dinner from the oven.

'I think so,' Maxi replied with a sly smirk on his face. 'Oh no, Juanita, not now,' he said when he saw her approach with the dinner plate. 'I'll eat later, if you don't mind. I have work to do.'

For someone who claimed he'd never work again, his eagerness to work was mind boggling. Juanita returned his dinner to the oven and Maxi beckoned her into the living room while Nora moved onto dessert.

'Sorry to spring this on you like this, but I won't be needing you to care for Nora anymore.' He paid her five-hundred euros even though she only worked four days.

'Muchas gracias, senor,' Juanita replied as she took the money and shoved it in the front pocket of her jeans.

'No, thank *you*; you were very good to Nora, so please, don't be a stranger.'

They shook hands and Juanita returned to the kitchen to say her goodbyes. Enough time wasted. Maxi raced into the garage to get busy on the box. He sat on a stool by the workbench, and after a meticulous examination under his work light, he failed to find any evidence of a lid or other means of access. Eventually, he reached the same conclusion as Larry. He figured he was dealing with a hat box where the whole outer surface of the container was the lid. He resorted to striking the seam around the bottom of the box with a hammer and chisel. He was gentle at first but evidently making no progress, his strikes intensified to full-blown, all out smarts. After bashing away tenaciously for almost forty minutes with the sweat stinging his eyes, his striking arm began to rebel, his enthusiasm started to wain and thoughts of failure began to pollute his mind.

He reassured himself that his circular saw would cut into the metal like a Samurai sword through a watermelon. He was wrong. All he managed to achieve was an abundance of sparks and a worn-out blade. He used his drill, his chipping gun, even his grinder, all to no avail. As a last resort, he placed the box on the ground and attacked it with a five-pound sledge hammer. Two hours later, with his whole inventory of tools strewn about the workbench and all over the garage floor, like casualties on the battlefield - some still smoking to timeline their involvement - he reluctantly conceded defeat.

By that stage, Nora had paid a number of visits to the garage to entice him to come and eat his dinner, but seeing how determined he was, she knew to leave him be. He sat on a stool by the work bench, dripping in sweat, staring intently at the box. He never let anything beat him before. He had exhausted all the ways he could think of to open that box... except maybe dynamite. A defeat like this was a hard pill to swallow.

He checked his phone. He had three missed calls, one from each of the girls. They were obviously curious about the treasure, but unfortunately, so was he. He decided to fess up and come clean. He called Ella on his cell and at that very moment he could hear her familiar ringtone - 'Reach out' by Shakespeare's Sister - over his shoulder. He turned to look and there she was standing in the doorway, her phone spoiling her surprise.

She saw the metal box for the very first time on the worktop, but instead of getting all excited, she got anxious. She deduced from her observations that Maxi was having trouble trying to open the box. She approached him from behind and began to massage his broad shoulders with her needy fingers. He groaned in response. She continued without saying a word, pinching and squeezing his shoulder muscles and gently caressing his neck until she could feel him wilt in her strong hands.

'So, this is it,' she said, slapping him inexpiably hard on the shoulder. 'The treasure that keeps on giving... nothing but fucking trouble.'

'Ouch.'

'Let me see,' Ella insisted as she leaned in to get a closer look at the metal box.

Maxi offered up his seat so she could examine the box just as he had done.

'I've seen a box like this before,' she exclaimed.

'No way,' Maxi yelped. 'Where?'

'Did I ever tell you about the time we all went to Italy on holiday?'

'No, I don't think so,' Maxi replied, a little surprised that *story-time* had taken precedence over the possibility of them becoming filthy rich.

'Charlie, my older brother, my mother and myself thought we'd have a great time dossing around Rome, checking out the sights, stuffing our gobs with pasta, drinking gallons of wine and me flirting with the Italian stallions. Instead, we spent the whole fucking week plodding around the Vatican after my father, who insisted we pay homage to the Almighty, on our hands and knees in the Basilica, the Sistine chapel and laid out prone on the ground before La Pieta. My father was a religious freak who had a hard-on for the Holy Land, Lourdes...'

Maxi interrupted, '...and the point of this story?'

'Sorry, got a little carried away,' she replied, clearing her throat to physically demonstrate that she was done with waffling. 'I saw a metal box similar to this on display in a glass case in one of the many shrines we visited in the Vatican. Its sole purpose, so I was told, is to transport religious relics from one place to another.'

'Wow,' he gasped. 'It must be made of supernatural armour plating.'

'It's not very big, huh,' Ella remarked as she turned the box upside down, though it was still unclear which side was up.

'I know.' Maxi sighed. 'I'm sure size doesn't matter.'

'Believe you me,' she vowed. 'Size matters and when it comes to treasure, it matters a lot.'

'Really?'

'Afraid so.'

'I hope you're wrong in this case.'

'Oh my God,' Ella gasped.

'What?' he implored as his heart slammed against his rib cage.

'Ah, it's just my phone vibrating in my pants.'

'Fuck sake, Ella,' he whined.

'It's one of the girls, better give 'em a call.'

'Let's wait until we see how you get on with the box.'

Unlike Maxi, Ella didn't require the use of any tools in her approach. Instead of brute-force, she relied on the sensitivity of her fingers and thumbs, pressing and kneading the entire surface area of the box in the hope of stumbling across a push-to-open catch of sorts, the type of closing mechanism common in many modern-day kitchen cabinets.

Maybe ten minutes or so later, she happened on the trigger that released the lid, and to their unanimous delight, the box sprung open.

'Holy shit, you did it,' Maxi exclaimed. 'Ye women are certainly wired different to us men,' he declared in an attempt to mask his ineptitude. His earlier joy at recovering the treasure was once again reinstated but unfortunately short lived.

Both of them stared, transfixed at the box and its contents. No gold coins, no emeralds or sapphires, no diamonds or pearls, just a sorry looking notebook with frayed edges, wrapped in thick plastic and imbedded in a cream-coloured epoxy type solution that consumed the interior of the box. Neither one could properly disguise their ardent dismay. Ella had a little difficulty removing the notebook from its tight confines. She had to use her nails as leverage to pry it free. 'Somebody went to a lot of trouble to safeguard this notebook,' Ella announced.

With that realization apparent to both, a glimmer of hope lingered about to challenge their growing despair. She handed it to Maxi. After all, he'd been through the preceding few weeks, she felt he was entitled to first dibs.

'Let's see what we got here.' He tried to appear enthusiastic, but by that stage he was at the end of his tether.

'I'm going to call the girls and have them meet up with us over here,' Ella suggested. 'Is that cool?'

'Hold off, will ye,' he retorted abruptly. 'Let's wait and see if we have anything of value,' he hissed. 'I don't want the girls getting all excited over nothing.'

'Take a chill pill for fuck sake.' She groaned.

'Sorry Ella, I'm just ...'

'It's okay,' she assured. 'I understand. We're all a little edgy.'

Maxi peeled away the plastic and opened the notebook. He studied it intently for several moments with Ella, all the while staring him down to read from his expression the value of the content, if any. He appreciated the elegant handwriting with swirling tails on the 'y's' and 'g's' and the bold strokes, like shooting arrows across the 't's'. Alas, a remarkable skill, he thought, made redundant by high-tech gadgets and laziness. Without saying a word, he turned over to the next page and the next and the next one after that. Ella got impatient with his poker face.

'Well?'

'So far, it reads like a confession by some married guy. Seems he had an affair and got some woman pregnant.'

'Is this a confession to a priest or just some guy unloading his guilt on paper?'

'Here, take a look,' he said, inviting her into the notebook. 'It's like this priest,' he flicked back to the beginning to retrieve the name. 'Fr. Armando Cruz has transcribed this man's confession verbatim.'

'Sounds Spanish.'

'You're right,' Maxi agreed. 'He's from Barcelona.'

'I thought confessions were supposed to be confidential.'

'They are and this one would be confidential too, only we came along and dug it up.'

'Looks like blackmail, and this box can't get away from each another.'

'I got that feeling as well,' he concurred. 'But now that the handwriting has changed, it's reading like an explanation.'

'Do we know who's making the confession,' she inquired, staring intently at Maxi.

Maxi flicked through the pages in search of the confessor and as he did so, a white envelope that was trapped between the pages slipped out and landed on the workbench. This further development distracted him momentarily as he witnessed Ella pounce on the envelope like a praying mantis on a tasty grasshopper. He weighed up the options in his mind whether or not it would be worth being gobbled up by her after they made love. *Fuck yeah.*

She held the envelope in her hand, content to wait for the confessor's name. A moment later, Maxi withdrew from the notebook with a stupefied look on his face that Ella found impossible to decode. He looked like he was dumbfounded, times ten!

'Brace yourself, Ella,' he cautioned. 'It's Ramone Aechmea.'

'So...' Ella replied with a bewildered look on her face.

'So, don't you get it?' Maxi taunted her. 'He's Dandelion's father.'

'No way,' she replied with her mouth dropped open in shock.

'Wait, there's more,' he encouraged as he reached out to hold her hand. He needed to comfort her with the next bombshell. 'The woman that Ramone Aechmea had the affair with died giving birth to her son. The boy was placed in an orphanage and when he was around ten-years old he was adopted by the Hickey family.'

'Wow,' Ella exclaimed. 'Same name as me. What a coincidence?' She threw her arms up into the air. 'Seriously, like... what are the odds?'

Maxi said nothing. He looked deep into her green eyes in order to nudge her in the right direction, to make the connection. Initially, she was bewildered, and then the smoke began to clear.

'Hickey,' she said, and Maxi nodded. 'Hickey, as in *my* Jasper Hickey.' He nodded some more.

'No,' she moaned. 'You can't be serious.'

While Ella came to terms with the shocking revelation, Maxi fished out two cigarettes and lit them both. He handed one to Ella and regained his grip on her hand. She took a deep draw, filling her lungs to the brim and after a slight delay blew her smoke at the notebook. It was like she was performing a magic trick and she wanted that notebook to disappear.

'Jasper was an orphan, that's true.' She sighed. 'His mother died giving birth, and he never knew his father,' Ella said, reeling off the facts. 'But this is ridiculous. Are you sure? You're not making this shit up... are ye?'

Maxi's silence was proof enough that he wasn't bullshitting.

'If that's the case then, Dandelion and Thistle Dick are Jasper's brothers.'

'Correct,' he replied. 'Brothers by different mothers.' Maxi squeezed her hand.

Ella took the notebook from him and read the content from start to finish. Ramone Aechmea's confession took up the first couple of pages and concluded with Fr. Armando Cruz, absolving him of his sins - the bread and butter carry-on of the clergy. Then the handwriting changed to a more refined and somewhat condensed style. That section was aimed directly at Jasper in an attempt by Ramone Aechmea to explain to his son the reasons why he had abandoned him:

I know it must have been hard for you to grow up all alone, without a father or mother in that hell hole of an orphanage. I led you to believe I was dead. I was too cowardly to step up and do the right thing. Selfishly, I didn't want to run the risk of ruining my marriage. I'm very sorry for all the pain and suffering I have caused you. I want to make amends. Will you ever find it in your heart to forgive me? I want you, my son Jasper Aechmea, to be compensated, yada... yada... yada.

His explanation and pleas for forgiveness continued on for the next number of pages. A brief biography of his mother was also included, more of an afterthought than anything else. In the last section of the notebook, the handwriting reverted back to Fr. Armando's style:

Your father asked me to personally present this notebook to you upon his demise. I am unable to comply with his wishes. Unfortunately, soon after Ramone entrusted me with this notebook, he had a horrific accident at the sawmill. A fork-lift tipped over, pinning him down with its cargo. His injuries were extensive, and he suffered serious head trauma.

It was a miracle he survived, but alas, he was pronounced brain-dead. To compound matters worse, I have been assigned a new post as a missionary in the Far East. I leave Ireland at the end of the week. With your father still alive and me on the move, I had to think of a way that somehow, someday, you would end up with this notebook in your possession.

I did some research on you. Fr. Boyle, the chaplain of the orphanage, told me you were a die-hard Manchester United fan and that Georgie Best was your idol. I managed to get an autographed photo of Georgie Best which I gave to Fr. Boyle before I left the country. He was to give it to you on your tenth birthday. I knew this poster would be something you would cherish and take with you everywhere you went.

So, if you are reading this, my plan was a success. Hopefully, this notebook will provide you with some closure. God Bless, Fr Armando Cruz.

'Wow, that's a lot to take onboard,' Ella gasped.

'I'll say,' Maxi agreed. 'How do you think Jasper will react?'

'I don't know. Should we tell him?'

'We have to tell him.'

'I suppose,' Ella mused as she juggled these revelations like hot rivets about in her head.

'Right,' Maxi proposed. 'Let's check out what's in that envelope?'

Ella tore open the seal on the envelope to reveal two neatly folded documents within. When she spotted the embossed seals on both documents, giving them that air of authority, she immediately handed them off to Maxi. Being a rebel, she despised bureaucracy and all its hyperbolic gobbledygook. It was her turn to light two cigarettes, and as she placed one between Maxi's lips, he could feel the tips of her fingers gently caress his mouth. Even that simple act managed to stir up the bubbles in that pot of erotica that was always simmering on the back burner whenever they were together. It felt like every one of his nerve endings was on high alert and that unmistakable hum normally associated with high voltage electricity was omnipresent.

Maxi studied both documents. The header on one document spelled out Deed in bold black lettering while the other was entitled, Last Will and Testament. As he trudged through the legal jargon, Nora suddenly stuck her head into the garage in a last-ditch attempt to entice her son to eat. She was surprised to see Ella sitting on the stool.

'Hi Mrs. Dillon,' Ella greeted.

'Please Ella, I insist you call me Nora.'

Ella was concerned that Nora's insistence was some sort of trap. Everybody she knew addressed Nora Dillon as Mrs. Dillon. Why on earth would this 'snob' encourage a pion like herself to call her by her first name? It didn't make any sense. She decided to play it safe and avoid names altogether.

'At last, you got it open,' Nora said, diverting her attention to the box. She stepped into the garage to get a closer look. 'So, where's all the money?'

'Looks like Ella's husband, Jasper,' Maxi proudly announced, 'has inherited a saw-mill and some forty acres of land.' He presented the deed to Ella.

'Holy shit,' Ella blurted. 'That's the Aechmea scrapyard.'

'It says here,' Maxi said, waving the Last Will and Testament. 'Mr. Ramone Aechmea, being of sound mind and body, bequeaths the saw-mill located at blah... blah... and the adjoining 43 acres of land to my eldest son, Jasper Aechmea. It looks all very official with his signature at the bottom of the page just above Fr. Cruz's signature, who is the witness to the proceedings before the solicitor, a guy named Johnathon Weatherspoon.'

'So, there's no money,' Nora confirmed.

'I wouldn't say that.' Maxi replied.

'What would you say?' Ella asked.

'I'd say Jasper is a rich man.' Maxi proclaimed.

'Fuck that,' Ella shrieked. 'Why is it Jasper always lands on his feet? After all the fucking shit we've been through...' Ella cried out, but realizing how offensive her language was, she relented. 'Sorry Mrs. Dillon, didn't mean any disrespect.'

'Ella, there's no need to apologise and please... call me Nora. As for that husband of yours,' Nora continued, 'he's made your life a living Hell.'

Ella was a little taken aback by Nora Dillon's show of support. It was obvious that knowledge of her unsavoury marriage wasn't confined to the four walls of her home, but she was surprised to learn that Nora, who was not in the loop, was very much up to speed with the whole carry on. It seemed her private life wasn't all that private. If rumours had a propensity to escape into the atmosphere to tarnish reputations, brutal facts could surely do the same, but in this instance, the finger pointed to Maxi as the messenger.

'What's Jasper doing in a will?' Nora whispered to Maxi.

'Long story,' he whispered back. 'Fill you in later.'

'He's certainly not going to do me any favours now,' Ella sighed. 'Forget about me! What did *he* ever do for anybody?'

'Not a damn thing,' Nora ventured, once again waving the flag in Ella's court.

It was obvious to Ella how Nora's agreeable comments were designed to win her favour, but she couldn't understand why. They barely knew each other, mere acquaintances, a generation apart with absolutely nothing in common... except Maxi. Now all of a sudden, they were bosom buddies.

'Hold on a minute, you two,' Maxi cautioned. 'Don't you think you're getting a little ahead of yourselves?' He held up the deed in his hand and directed the women's attention to it. 'The Aechmea brothers – who, by the way, are Titians when it comes to litigation - are not going to take this lying down? These wingnuts will fight like the *junkyard-dogs* they are to keep that property.'

'All the more reason not to bother with any of this,' Ella divulged.

'What are you saying?' Maxi snapped. 'We're talking two million plus here and you're not bothered.'

'May as well be a billion,' Ella retorted. 'Doesn't matter to me. It all goes to Jasper.'

'It's your money too,' Maxi confirmed, then he raised his voice. 'Hello... you're his wife.'

'Thanks for the reminder,' Ella snarled.

'I'm just saying...'

'I know what you're saying.'

'I'll leave you two at it,' Nora interrupted. 'I'm going in by the fire.'

'I won't be long,' Maxi pledged.

'Take your time. I'll be fine.'

As soon as Nora left them alone, Ella quizzed Maxi.

'How come Nora is so nice to me all of a sudden?'

'I don't know what you mean.'

'Did you hear her insisting that I call her Nora? Nobody calls your mother by her first name except Fr. Jim and her golfing friends.'

'So, she must like you.' Maxi held her by the shoulders and looked into her eyes.

'She doesn't even know me,' Ella stated.

'Maybe she likes you because,' he said, hesitating for a moment before admitting, 'I like you.'

'*You* like me?' Ella blushed.

'I do. I like *you* a lot.' Maxi blushed.

As both of them grappled with yet another incredible revelation, Ida surprised them both by showing up in the doorway.

'Please tell me,' she implored, 'we're the *nouveau riche* and I can cut Sebastian loose.'

'Afraid not,' Ella replied, somewhat relieved by the intrusion.

Maxi handed the notebook to Ida and explained the whole situation to her. Ella got on the phone to Debbie and did likewise.

'You know Ella,' Ida said, jabbing her with her fist. 'You have to keep Jasper *alive* until you get all this lot sorted.'

'This could take years,' Ella sighed. 'I'll be honest with ye. The only thing that gets me up in the morning is the hope that by the end of the day, that man is dead. God forgive me, but it's the truth. To keep him alive so he can claim his inheritance is a big fucking ask. I don't think I can do it.' She looked at Ida and then Maxi. 'I don't think I want to do it.'

'Ella, you'll get it all... when he dies,' Maxi assured. 'It's only a matter of time.'

'I think he stays alive just to spite me,' she moaned. 'Anyway, what am I going to do with a fucking scrapyard?'

'Sell the bitch and head off to Cambodia,' Ida urged. 'Like in your dream.'

'If it was left up to me, I'd burn this fucking deed and that stupid notebook, but since Jasper has a right to know who his father is, I'm morally obligated to do the right thing.'

'Whew. I'm glad to hear you say that,' Maxi cheered. 'Believe me, you won't regret it.'

'No more heart attacks on a plate for Jasper,' Ida suggested. 'Healthy garden salads from here on in.'

'Yeah, yeah, yeah, listen you guys, I'm out of here,' Ella said as she stood up to leave. 'My head is wrecked from all this bullshit. I'm leaving this stuff here.' She pointed at the notebook and the will. 'I'll get it another day if you don't mind. I need time to get my head around all this, whatever all this is.'

'Sure thing,' Maxi said. 'Take all the time you need.'

He embraced her and held her tight in his big, strong arms. Then he kissed her on the cheek with a lot more purpose than a mere goodbye. She tightened her grip on him, signalling her consent to escalate their friendship to the next level. He brushed her ear with his lips and whispered, 'It'll all work out... I promise.'

'Hope so,' she replied. 'Good night.' She broke free from his embrace and left.

In the meantime, Ida was pretending to be engrossed in the notebook when she noticed the sudden display of tenderness between the two lovebirds. She'd seen it before, but never up close and personal.

'I could have Sebastian take a look at these documents,' Ida offered. 'His crew of cronies will know whether or not they'll stand up in court.'

Maxi didn't respond immediately. He seemed preoccupied, making the return trip to terra firma after his brief deployment to the land of the smitten.

'Yeah, sure. That's a good idea,' he replied. There was no conviction behind his words. He sounded just like someone recovering from a general anaesthetic.

'I better be off as well,' Ida announced. She put the documents in her pocket book and waved at Maxi.

'Yeah, right. See ye.'

Chapter 27.

Later the following day, Maxi got a call from Ida. She told him that Sebastian had 'his people' authenticate the documents and validate the signatures. 'Not only will these documents stand up in court,' she assured him. 'They'll kick any opposing council in the teeth... or lower down the anatomy if necessary.'

'Wow, great news,' Maxi cheered. 'That was fast.'

'Money makes shit happen,' Ida confirmed. 'Lots of it makes it happen *faster*.'

'Ah, hah,' he grunted. 'Thanks Ida, you're the best.'

Maxi didn't want to bother Ella about the *will,* or anything else for that matter. He felt she needed some alone-time to process all the recent drama. Plus, he was petrified if he called her; he wouldn't be able to put two words together, now that they had relinquished their friendship in lieu of love. Ever since that half-assed kiss, his butterflies opted to wear hob-nailed boots and run around amuck in his stomach. His head was swimming in waves of trepidation with fornicating rip-tides tugging at his trunks. He had hot flashes and cold sweats, simultaneously. He tried to concentrate, but Ella bullied her way into his every thought. He felt so off he had to cancel the day's debates. Nora seemed happy enough to read her romance novel by the fire.

Ella was experiencing much the same symptoms and some. Not only did she have to contend with her queasiness after launching her love flair into the cosmos, she was trying her damn-best to recover from being *clotheslined* by Ramone Aechmea's notebook. Her attempts to focus on keeping her hateful husband alive were further thwarted by sightings of Maxi in the porridge bowl for breakfast and again in the garden salad for lunch. No matter what she did, she couldn't get him out of her mind.

She was surprised to see a full bowl of porridge, with blueberries, apples, hazelnuts and honey, licked clean by Jasper for breakfast with no complaints. Jasper didn't masticate his food, he inhaled it. He spooned whatever was in front of him, down the hatch, in a disgusting display that gave his pig parts a chance to shine. Maxi always timed his visits to that house, so he wouldn't have to witness Jasper in action.

Lunch was a different matter. When Ella plonked a plate of salad with mixed greens, cherry tomatoes and beetroot on the little side table next to Jasper, he looked up at her suspiciously. Ella did a double-take on the salad, thinking Jasper could also see Maxi hiding under a leaf of lettuce, staring back at both of them. Maxi was the furthest thing from Jasper's mind. He poked around with his fork, moving the cherry tomatoes and lifting the cucumber slices to peek under, to see if there was something *dead* on his plate to eat.

'Do I have to get my grass-skirt and spear and go out into the back garden to kill something for my fucking dinner?' Jasper roared.

'I thought a salad would be a refreshing change from all that greasy shit you normally eat.'

'Do I look like the fucking Easter Bunny to you?' Jasper snarled.

'How about a bit of fish?' Ella proposed.

'How about a double bacon cheeseburger, some onion rings and a basket of chips?'

'You must be confusing me with some fucking lackey who has fuck all to do all day except cater to you and your fat ass.'

Ella's ringtone interrupted their heated exchange. 'Thank God,' she gasped when she saw Petra's name on the caller ID. If it was Maxi, she didn't think she could physically take the call. Petra was calling to see was Ella available to take a phone-sex client. She headed upstairs to her bedroom to conduct the call in private. Twenty minutes later, she came back down to find Jasper asleep in his chair. She took his half-eaten plate of food into the kitchen. Disappointed by how little he ate, she began to jumble other healthy alternatives about in her head... healthy food that might be a better alternative to salad. As she busied herself washing the dishes, she heard one of her dogs, Caesar, whining in a way she hadn't heard before. The rest of the pack was out in the back garden.

'Chill Caesar, chill,' she commanded from the kitchen sink.

The whining stopped immediately. However, a moment later, it started up again. Ella was annoyed and appeared in the double doors with her arms folded, as if she was expecting some sort of explanation from Caesar for his defiant behaviour. He sat on his haunches and looked at her with his big brown eyes, and then he looked at Jasper. She looked at Jasper and then back at Caesar. They both looked back at Jasper. She knew immediately something was wrong. She raced across the room and lifted Jasper's slumped head. That's when she saw his mouth jampacked full of cherry tomatoes. Ironically, the healthy salad had way more *clout* than any mixed grill. Jasper choked to death.

She screamed. 'How dare you die on me?'

She slapped him hard across the face with her open palm. Several cherry tomatoes took flight across the living room. Caesar chased one down, but like Jasper, he wasn't too keen with his find. She plonked herself down in the couch across from Jasper and stared at him in disbelief. Several minutes elapsed before she regained her presence of mind. She got up and went back into the kitchen to splash her face with cold water. She dried herself with a kitchen towel. She held it to her face, expecting to cry. Not a single tear, after twenty years of marriage. She found her cigarettes and lit one. The only person she could think to call was Maxi.

'Hi Ella,' he managed before he had to take a quick breath.

'Maxi, I need you over here right now.' She hung up.

He stared at his phone in total disbelief.

NOTHING TO SEE HERE

305

'Wow,' he thought, *'no messing around. We be getting down to business.'*

He brushed his teeth, combed his hair and slapped some cologne on his face. He opened the top two buttons of his jeans to squirt some cologne on his underwear. His dick twitched in anticipation. His heart was pounding so hard he thought he'd crack a rib. He had to hold on to the sink with both hands and take a number of deep breaths to contain his excitement. He lit a cigarette and pulled on it so hard, the tip glowed like the distress beacon on a life jacket. He raced down the stairs and mumbled some gibberish to Nora, who watched him almost fall over himself as he raced out the front door.

When he got to Ella's house, he had difficulty getting out of the car. His full-blown hard-on in his tight jeans caused him to double over in her driveway. He was only able to stand upright once he aligned his erection to point up at his chin. He waddled like a constipated penguin into the house and was shocked to see Ella and one of her dogs transfixed by Jasper's chair in the living room - both motionless and sharing the same vacant look. It was uncanny how that scene was so reminiscent of a still-life painting by Edgar Degas. Maxi took a step closer, yet still no reaction from Ella, Jasper or the dog. He found himself momentarily trapped in that same still-life painting. There was no movement, no sound, nothing... just dead air.

Eventually, Ella directed Maxi's eyes, with her own, to look at Jasper. It took a moment for the shock of Jasper's dead body to strike a chord with Maxi.

'He's dead,' Maxi blurted, hoping his observation would be disputed by Ella.

'No shit... Steve Hawkins,' Ella replied.

'Steve Hawkins?' Maxi scratched his head. 'Ella, Jasper is dead! What did you do?' he pleaded.

'What do you mean?' Ella snapped. 'You think I killed him?'

'Well...'

'He choked on that fucking *stay alive* salad,' Ella wailed.

'It's okay, it's okay,' Maxi whispered as he stepped cautiously towards her with his arms open wide. He knew he looked ridiculous, like he was trying to corner a chicken to cook for dinner. But in that moment, that's all he came up with. Growing up in his family, he was never exposed to any TLC tactics. Love was never mentioned in the house, so now he had to wing it. Ella allowed him to wrap his arms around her, like a make shift straight-jacket. He held her tight. 'Easy, babe,' he assured her. 'It's all right. I'm here for you.' He squeezed harder. 'Take deep breaths,' he encouraged her. 'That's it... take another one. Breathe.'

He could feel her chest rise and fall along with his own. Her heart was racing. So was his. 'Don't worry,' he said, rubbing the small of her back with the heel of his hand. 'We'll figure something out... together. Everything's going to be okay... you'll see,' he lied.

'No! Everything's not going to be okay,' she cried. 'He's dead and now there's no fucking money. After all the shit he put me through, I still took care of that bastard,' she sobbed. 'I could have fucked him out of my house years ago. But no... not me! Miss Florence fucking Nightingale here... oh no! My fucking conscience wouldn't let me, and this is what I get. He ups and fucking dies on me.'

She broke free from Maxi's embrace and went over to Jasper's chair. She slapped him so hard across the face, Maxi's deaf ear heard the smart. Caesar got up on the spot and slinked away. Maxi wanted to bail as well but somebody had to play the role of knight in shining armour for this damsel in distress, and since he was the only one who showed for the audition - he got the part.

'Did you know about the affair?' he asked, thinking what better time to clear the air.

'What affair?' she replied, staring intently at him.

'You didn't know Jasper had an affair with that slut, Linda Langton?' he replied.

Just as he said the slut's name, he heard another loud slap, striking Jasper across the face.

After a brief interlude, she calmly inquired, 'Do you know today's date?'

'I'm not sure,' he retorted. 'Is it the twenty-eight?' He ventured a guess. He was perturbed by her sudden shift in focus. *Has she flipped out?* he wondered. *Under the circumstances, can't say I blame her.*

'It's the thirtieth of May,' she proclaimed. 'Georgina, the butcher boy's sister, is expected home today. What do you think about them apples?' she asked, rolling her eyes up to the Heavens.

'Oh shit,' Maxi exclaimed. 'You might as well put me in the box with Jasper.'

Ella then asked nonchalantly, as if completely detached from her surroundings, 'What do you think we should do next?'

Maxi wanted to say, 'For starters, stop slapping Jasper.' Instead, he asked her, 'What can we do?'

'We can make love,' Ella suggested in the same detached tone.

'I can't see why not,' Maxi answered in a similar detached tone.

With that confirmation, they attacked one another and began ripping off each other's clothes. They pressed their lips together and unleashed their tongues to invade each other's mouths. They licked and slurped one another, like children often do with the remnants of cake mix left in a cooking bowl. Caesar cocked his ears to try and decrypt the moans and groans that were coming from the entwined couple. Since they didn't signal a violent attack, infer a walk in the near future or suggest any food or treats that he was aware of, he drew a blank. He decided to hook up with his buddies out back and let them have at it.

Ella brought Maxi down to his knees... on the hard wood floor. 'Ahaa,' he grimaced in agony. Ella misinterpreted his pain for delight. Already bare-chested, they focused on buckles and buttons to dispense with the rest of their clothes. Naked at last, Ella wrapped her arms and legs around Maxi while he nibbled on her neck and squeezed the cheeks of her bare ass.

'Stop,' Maxi moaned. 'I can't do this.'

He unravelled himself and pushed Ella away. His throbbing erection begged for relief while Ella's rock-hard nipples stung with desire. He reached out for his leather jacket on the floor next to him and stood up. Ella, flustered and confused, covered her bare breasts in shame. He went over to Jasper's chair and non-ceremoniously threw his jacket over the dead man's head.

'Right... where were we?'

Don't miss out!

Visit the website below and you can sign up to receive emails whenever Brendan Walsh publishes a new book. There's no charge and no obligation.

https://books2read.com/r/B-A-NZIT-ABBYB

BOOKS 2 READ

Connecting independent readers to independent writers.

About the Author

I was born in Ireland in 1957 and I hold an honors degree in Applied Psychology from University College Cork. I've worked at all sorts of jobs in my lifetime, but none remotely related to the mechanisms of the mind. I was a lifeguard in Ireland, a production line worker in Amsterdam, and a janitor in Denmark. I was a fisherman in the Holy Land and a drummer in a rock band called, *Bill's Board Stiff.* When I arrived in New York City, I got a job as a plasterer's mate on a building site on Long Island. The loose translation in layman's terms for a job like that... a human cement mixer. From there, I graduated to banging nails, and slowly, after weaving my way through ne'er-do-wells, mamelukes, biker bullies, the bloods and the crips, and all other indigenous reprobates specific to the construction industry, I arrived out the other end, not at all unlike a bowel movement... a sub-contractor. I worked in New York City for thirty-five years and enjoyed every minute of it.

I'm retired now and living in Ireland doing what I love best; painting and writing. I go back to New York from time to time. It will always be a part of me. It's my second home.